# THE LAST BEEKEEPER

## VESPLING BOOK 1

### JARED GULIAN

WaysOut Press

*To CJ*

# CONTENTS

"Whoever fights monsters should see to it that in the process he does not become a monster. And if you gaze long enough into an abyss, the abyss will gaze back into you."

**Friedrich Nietzsche**
*Beyond Good and Evil* (1886)

# PROLOGUE

EMMETT JONES DIDN'T KNOW where the noise was coming from, or exactly what it was, but he'd never heard anything like it before in the End Woods. The sound reverberated among the darkening trees that surrounded him—a low-pitched, constant hum punctuated with something that sounded like an intermittent clicking. This was not a gentle noise. It sounded almost, well, malicious.

At seventy-eight, Emmett knew his hearing wasn't what it used to be, but he also knew that this sound was just not right. He looked around the woods, trying to identify the source. The trees on either side of him were tinted with shadows. From this spot, the evening sky had been reduced to a single indigo line which cut through the canopy, mirroring the rugged track at his feet. He hadn't paid attention to the time, but it was now just past sunset. He had no flashlight. When the last of the light was gone, it would be impossible to see. His eyes were already struggling in the gloom.

His dog, Sandy, was up ahead—an energetic yellow Lab. He looked at her and felt some comfort to have her with him.

He picked up his pace.

Every evening he walked this track with Sandy, so they both knew it well. This was the old access that hunters used—just two ruts worn from years of tires passing through. Locals called it Miller's Track, for reasons nobody remembered now, not even Emmett. Grass grew between the tire ruts. It was the only thing remotely resembling a road out here.

Normally, Emmett's walk went like clockwork. He always left an hour before sunset and came home in twilight. But earlier this evening he'd stopped to watch the sky turn orange above the treetops, and he must have watched it a bit longer than he'd thought. It happened sometimes now. He'd lose entire mornings, and afternoons would occasionally disappear as though they'd evaporated. For Emmett, time had become a malleable, changeable thing.

The hum continued, rising and falling like a strange, long thunder. The clicks echoed against the trees. The sounds seemed to come from every direction at once. Could it be a machine? Was someone doing work out here? At this hour?

"Hello?" he called out hopefully, in spite of the fact that he rarely came across anyone in these woods. There weren't many people on the island, after all, and there weren't many people who came into these woods, especially at this time of day.

Up ahead, Sandy appeared as a pale spot among the shadows. He loved that dog. She was almost too much for him, really, with her endless need to be outside and moving, but he believed she kept him young, kept the fire in his belly. She needed him. It was important to be needed.

She'd been sniffing around for a bit, but now she stopped, looked off to the left, and growled.

"What's out there, girl?" he asked. His voice was strong but gravelly.

Everyone told Emmett he was a feisty old man, and he always took it as a compliment. He didn't ever want to be the kind to sit back and die. It was like the poem said, the one he'd copied out and pinned to his cork board at home. *Do not go gentle into that good night.* He kept busy. He still worked part-time at the hardware store because he liked to see people. He cared for his garden and fruit trees with a kind of obsessive joy, and he made jams and jellies from the bounty. He tinkered with old radios in the garage to pass the time. He'd never married, never had kids. He'd had a series of dogs, though, and had long ago come to the conclusion that good dogs like Sandy were all the companionship a man needed in this world.

When folks on Gull Island asked Emmett what kept him going, he always talked about these evening walks with Sandy. He'd seen other people his age become stuck in the house with bad knees and hips. For Emmett, that would be a fate worse than death. He always said, "When I'm too old to walk, I'm too old to live." And he meant it.

Now, as quickly as the noise had started, it stopped. The woods were deathly silent. There was no evening birdsong. There was no rustle of little critters in the brush.

He didn't waste any time. He began walking as fast as he could, almost running—or as close to running as his weary legs would allow. There were two possibilities in his mind. Either he was being a silly old man, or he wasn't. He didn't much care. Either way he wanted nothing more than to get home, to sit in his armchair with a good book before the rest of the darkness fell. There was something new and not entirely normal in these woods tonight, and for the first time in his life he felt uneasy out here.

"Come on, Sandy," he said, walking past her. "Let's go."

She didn't budge. She sniffed the air at the edge of the track. When Emmett looked back, she turned and looked at him as if to say: *Can I? Can I go into the woods?*

"Leave it," he said in his most commanding voice. "Come." He slapped the side of his leg firmly, and she followed. Right away she outpaced him, returning to her spot a few yards in front of him.

The End Woods held all sorts of wildlife. He used to hunt here, in his younger days. There were rabbits, grouse, and ducks, but also deer and beaver and the occasional fox or raccoon. It had always amazed him how well these woods hid the fact that you were on a small island in the middle of Lake Michigan. Here the shoreline felt far away.

Nevertheless, there was no animal out here that made a noise like that.

Up ahead, Sandy took a few steps off the track to the left, toward the trees.

"Hey," Emmett said sternly.

She stopped moving forward but stood and sniffed the air defiantly.

It could be a coyote, he supposed, as he paused alongside her. There were certainly plenty of coyotes out here. Many referred to Gull Island as "The Coyote Hunter's Paradise," with hunters coming from all over the Midwest. But Emmett had never heard a coyote make a noise like that. What he'd heard was not a growl, not a howl. It was definitely a hum and a deep, sinister clicking.

He squinted as he looked into the trees. There were no coyotes that he could see, but of course the light was dying. They must be out there. He hated those damn pests. They got into trash bins, bird feeders, and pet food. They took chickens, ducks, cats, and even small dogs. Back at his own property, just about two miles down the track now, he had fenced off a large area years ago to protect his garden and his fruit trees.

Sandy growled again, still staring into the dark quiet woods.

Somehow, the silence was now worse than the noise had been. He approached Sandy and patted her side. "Come," he said, continuing on. She followed.

He was starting to feel more than just uneasy. Maybe it was his mind playing tricks on him, but he was scared. Maybe this was how it started, when old folks' aged brains began to see everything as a threat, when simple things caused great confusion. He'd always dreaded losing his mind. Perhaps this was it. Maybe tomorrow he'd have trouble remembering the small things, like this walk tonight, like that god-awful noise.

As he hurried down the track, he thought of the coyotes. Of course, it was unlikely for a single coyote to go for Sandy. She was a good-sized dog, about sixty pounds. Coyotes were smaller, between twenty-five and forty-five pounds. If there were several coyotes out there, then sure, they might gang up on her. Or if a coyote were rabid. There had been some trouble with rabies on the island lately. Last summer a rabid coyote attacked a tourist on a hiking trail.

It was because of the coyotes that he never let Sandy run off alone into the woods. Yes, he thought now, trying to reassure himself, it must have been a coyote. Or more likely it was several. That's why the noise sounded strange, because it was a pack. Yes, that was it.

He hurried on.

Sandy walked further along the trail ahead of him, where she always liked to walk. It felt right to have her up there.

Everything was okay. They'd be home soon.

Suddenly, Sandy took off to the left, and he lost sight of her entirely as she disappeared among the trees.

"Sandy!" he shouted.

There was a rustle of undergrowth. He stepped to the edge of the track and stared into the woods, but he still couldn't see her.

"Sandy!" he yelled. "Sandy!"

Just a moment later, she came bounding out from the trees a few feet away, running directly toward him, tongue flapping. She stopped in front of him and looked up. Her tail was wagging cheerfully.

A person could not help but smile to see a dog that happy. She was beaming. He patted her and laughed with relief. "Good girl. You stay with me." He reached into his pocket for the leash, but she turned and ran forward along the track again. When she paused and looked back at him, checking impatiently to see if he was coming, he followed. They were only a mile from home when he heard it again.

*Hmmm. Hmmm. Cli-click.*

He wondered if it was following them.

Sandy stopped and looked off to the left. The entire woods seemed to fill up with that hum and click. Sandy began barking with more urgency, and she walked forward.

"Sandy, heel!" Emmett yelled. He pulled the leash from his pocket and got ready to attach it to her collar.

But she ran straight into the woods.

"Sandy! Sandy!"

He heard branches snapping as she ran deeper through the brush. He was already moving after her, without thinking, into the shadows. He stepped as carefully as he could. Here and there he held onto the trees to keep his balance. It wasn't easy to move quickly—it was like an obstacle course, really—but he went as fast as his legs would carry him.

Out here, in the thickness of the trees, what little light that was left made for a strange and murky blue world. Emmett's eyes struggled to adjust. It was the middle of August, and the trees were still thick with leaves. He could no longer make out the sky at all. It got darker the deeper he went. And that dreadful humming and clicking continued. It was louder now. He stopped and looked straight ahead, trying to spot Sandy's pale coat. There was nothing out here but the dark lines of tree trunks. He looked around. Which way had she gone?

Her bark came from somewhere up ahead to the right. It was a feral, angry bark. That wasn't like her, and it was troubling. He yelled out her name and began moving toward her.

The humming stopped, and there was another sound, like quick footsteps in dried leaves.

Something else was out there with them. Something running. And it was coming in their direction.

Sandy let out a high-pitched yelp, and everything went quiet again. There was no rustle in the undergrowth. There was no barking, no terrible humming. The woods were deadly still, without so much as a breeze in the trees.

"Sandy?" he called out, his voice faltering slightly. "Sandy? Come here, girl. Come here." He was aware of the change in his own voice. He sounded like a man who was pleading, rather than commanding.

The silence was terrifying. He slowly scanned the area to see if he could spot anything moving in the trees around him. He looked for coyotes. It must be coyotes, he told himself again, although it was getting harder and harder to make himself believe it. He bent down and picked up a stick, ready to throw it.

"Go away! Go away!" he shouted as he waved his arms.

He knew this was how you were supposed to scare coyotes away. Throw a stick. Make noise. Appear large. Don't turn your back. Don't run. He stomped his feet as he walked. He kept moving, looking for Sandy.

It seemed that there was something up ahead—an empty area with fewer trees. There was a slightly brighter, dusky light up there. He walked as quickly as he could now, to get away from these dense trees and out from under the heavy canopy. Anything could be hiding in the shadows.

He found himself in a clearing. In the dying light, he could make out a fallen tree in the middle of the open space, with low ferns and shrubs nearby. The woods made a dark circle around him. Even the trunks of the trees were barely visible among the shadows. He stood there for a moment, watching the darkness.

The sound of the hum and click began to grow slowly again. It was heavy and deep. This was no machine. This was no pack of coyotes. He couldn't tell himself stories anymore, just to make himself feel better. This was something much worse.

It was getting closer. Where was it coming from? He looked left, then right.

"Sandy?" he whispered.

There was no sign of the dog. Nothing showed through the dense canopy beyond the clearing, not even small fragments of the dusky light. The noise came even closer. Was it at the edge of the clearing? He turned around.

Something shifted in the undergrowth to his left. There was a loud crack, like a tree branch breaking. He turned to face whatever it was, holding his stick high. He would not be taken down by some dumb, hungry animal in these woods. He would beat the crap out of it if he had to.

His heart was beating fast. His breathing was shallow.

There was nothing to be seen in that direction but the blueblack shadows of the brush. The sound continued, as though it was coming from everywhere.

He scanned the trees again, and that was the moment he realized that he'd become disoriented. Which direction was Miller's Track? How would he find his way back?

"Sandy?" His voice was shaking. "Sandy?"

The fading light was starting to cast dark shapes in the gloom. Then he heard branches quickly breaking again.

Something was running. Whatever it was, it was heading in his direction. He gripped the stick tightly, trembling.

"Sandy!"

It hit him hard and fast, knocking him to the ground. It was on top of him, pinning him down. He fought fiercely, pounding it with his fists, the stick having fallen to his side. It was no coyote. There was no fur. It had arms. Its skin felt thick and tough. It was too strong. It was too big. It was smothering him. He couldn't even fill his lungs enough to scream.

# PART 1
# BURNING THE BEES

1

JIM PARKER LAY ALONE in his large double bed—barely awake, the phone pressed to his ear, struggling to make sense of the horrible news. It was 6 a.m. Someone had used gasoline to torch his beehives during the night. It made no sense. If ever there was a risk to beehives these days, it would be theft, not arson. Bees were simply too valuable to burn. Besides, things like this just didn't happen on Gull Island.

"I'm on my way," he said.

He fumbled to hang up the old landline, placing it back into its cradle on the nightstand. He hated phones. They were invasive and they never brought good news. He got up quickly and threw on shorts and a t-shirt, then headed toward the back door. He moved quietly past Ava's bedroom door. She was still sleeping. She kept teenager hours—staying up late every night, messaging her friends, watching videos, and sleeping late every morning. He didn't know what to do with her anymore.

At the back steps, he locked the door behind him, as he always did, for Ava. His most important job was to keep his daughter safe. He didn't leave her a note, but it didn't matter. He knew she wouldn't be worried even if she did wake before he got back home. It wasn't unusual for Jim to disappear into the woods in the early morning. It was like going to church for him.

The trees that surrounded the property rustled in the morning breeze. Sunrise wasn't for another half an hour, and the light was soft and blue as he walked from the house to the garage. The side door was unlocked, as always. He was never worried about theft here, only about protecting Ava.

Climbing into his black pickup truck, he grabbed the rear-view mirror. Lately he barely recognized the face of the middle-aged white guy who stared back at him. When did those flecks of gray appear in his otherwise brown beard? His face right now was puffy with sleep, and his hair was sticking up. At forty-five, he managed to keep fit and healthy not by visiting the gym but by being outside and working, by lifting and turning. Even so, he was deeply in touch with the fact that he was getting older.

He grabbed the black baseball cap he'd thrown on the passenger seat yesterday and put it on. On the front, yellow letters spelled the name of his company, Parker Pollination, next to three yellow hexagons, like honeycomb.

As he made his way down the long driveway, the headlights lit the woods on either side. Stones crunched under the tires as he pulled out onto the narrow, dirt surface of Reserve Road.

The entire span of the Gull Island Forest Reserve loomed tall on the northern side of the road, reaching out and touching the younger trees on the southern side, making an archway. The reserve—known locally as the End Woods—was a dense, old-growth forest, and it covered almost a third of the island. Jim's property was at the edge of these woods. His was one of the few areas of private land that was surrounded by the Forest Reserve on all sides.

It was no coincidence that he'd come to live on a dirt road in the most secluded part of a remote island. After everything that had happened back in Ann Arbor, moving to the middle of Lake

Michigan was his retreat from the world, his sanctuary for Ava. This was where he'd brought them both to heal.

Ava said she hated it here, but he knew Gull Island was good for her. Someday she'd thank him. Yet lately they'd been fighting even more than usual. He wished he knew how to change that.

Soon enough, he was standing alongside his truck, surrounded by rows of waist-high blueberry bushes. In front of him were several piles of scorched, black boards on the ground. They were still smoking, and there was the distinct smell of gasoline in the air. He could just make out the blackened planks of five elevated hive stands.

By this point in the summer, his colonies were large. He quickly did the math in his head. Each hive here would have been home to nearly fifty thousand bees. In one night, he'd lost a quarter of a million of them.

His head was a swirl of emotions. He was heartbroken at the loss of so many bees—now officially an endangered species, ever since the Global Bee Crisis had been finally declared five years ago—but he was also absolutely, insanely furious. Who on earth would do this? Who in their right mind would burn bees?

The stout frame of Connor Davies emerged from a gap in the blueberry bushes. He was wearing green grease-stained coveralls and his hair was slicked back with sweat. He was the owner of this blueberry farm. Jim noticed the bushes around him were laden with berries, a sign of the good pollination work Jim's bees had done back in spring.

"I called you as soon as I saw," Connor said. "I was out this morning doing harvest prep when I found it."

"It's disgusting," Jim said. "They're live animals. They're endangered. They're so hard to keep healthy these days. It just makes no sense. I'd be less upset if someone stole them."

Jim knew that out in California organized crime syndicates were behind an increase in orchestrated beehive heists. Thieves usually split the hives and sold them to desperate growers. But nobody burned them. Nobody.

He and Connor both fell silent as they stared at the smoking remains. A few dead bees lay nearby on the ground. Jim bent down and picked one up.

"Do you think any made it out?" Connor asked.

Jim studied the dead bee. "Smoke triggers a defense mechanism," he said. "They gorge themselves with honey and swarm the hive, if they can. But from the smell of this gasoline, they wouldn't have had time to get out. And even if they did, unless they got out with the queen, they wouldn't live long away from the hive. Bees are a superorganism."

"Huh?"

"They're not viable alone. They need each other to survive."

Connor nodded.

Jim looked closely at the dead bee between his fingers. Its wings had been singed to nothing. He tossed it onto the smoking wood.

"I'm sorry, Jim," Connor said. "The house is too far. I didn't hear a thing."

"It's okay. Thanks for calling me."

Connor looked at Jim and seemed to hesitate before he spoke. "Does this, ah, does this mean I don't get my security deposit back?"

Jim stared at him, amazed. "It's a little soon for that conversation, Connor."

"No, I just, I mean. Things are tight. I just need to know. My last Beelord was Chuck. He's a jerk. He screwed me over every chance he could."

Jim knew Chuck Norman. He had a history with the man, and it wasn't good.

"You're a much better Beelord than Chuck," Connor said. "For one, you can keep the bees alive. Unless you're up against this." He glanced over at the burnt remains.

"I'm not a Beelord," Jim said. "I'm an old-fashioned beekeeper. Pure and simple."

"You got a company." Connor gestured to Jim's truck, which had 'Parker Pollination' written on the door in yellow letters, along with the same triple-hexagon logo as his baseball hat. There was a commercial truck cap on the back. That was where Jim stored his beekeeping equipment—his veil, bee suit, and gloves, a smoker, a stack of extra frames, and a few hive tools to open the hives and scrape away any extra beeswax.

"I'm a guy with a pickup truck," Jim snapped. "I'm not big agritech."

They both fell silent for a moment.

"Anyway, I, ah, I just need to know if I can get my security deposit back," Connor stammered. "I know Chuck wouldn't have given it to me if this happened with his hives. But like I said, the man's a jerk."

Jim took a few steps away from Connor. He needed to think.

Although he had never provided professional pollination services before coming to Gull Island two years ago, Jim knew bees. He'd started with hobby hives when he was seventeen. As an academic researcher—he was a trained biologist, entomologist, and naturalist—bees had been his specialty, along with the wasps they'd evolved from.

As a result, he understood how to care for a beehive in spite of the modern cocktail of perils that threatened them: varroa mites, fungi, viruses, immunodeficiencies, plundering wasps, loss of natural habitat, not to mention the menace of corporate farming practices like heavy pesticide and antibiotic use, monoculture farming, and long-distance transportation of hives for pollination. In a world where the bees were dying, a man who could keep a hive alive was highly sought after, and Jim could just about name his price.

Unfortunately, in establishing his business on Gull Island, he'd unintentionally put the existing local pollinator, Chuck Norman, out of business. Nobody liked Chuck, and apparently Chuck didn't much like anyone either. He seemed like a man who held a grudge.

"So, ah, what do you say?" Connor asked, speaking out across the distance Jim had created between them. "About the deposit?"

Jim turned around. He knew Connor ran a family business. Connor was a good man and a good tenant.

"You know how it works," Jim said, wanting to be fair, but clearly needing to spell things out. "It's like renting an apartment from a landlord. You rent the hives, and I maintain them. You're the tenant, and I'm the Beelord, although I hate using that word. If a tenant damages a hive, the security deposit helps pay for it—"

"I didn't do this," Connor interrupted.

Jim nodded. "I know, Connor. No farmer would do this. It had to be kids, right? A little bit of vandalism for kicks."

"Ah, I'm not so sure."

"What?"

"It's not just a little bit," Connor said.

"What do you mean?"

Connor shook his head and looked down.

"What about my other hives?" Jim asked urgently, glancing around to see if they were visible. At commercial blueberry farms like Connor's, Jim typically stocked five hives per acre. Connor had twenty hives in addition to these five that had burnt, but from where Jim stood now they were all hidden by blueberry bushes. "Have you checked the others?"

Connor hesitated again, then finally said, "I just got back. They're all gone."

Jim felt like the ground had just shifted underneath him. "All of them?"

"All of them."

Jim sat down on the ground and put his head in his hands. He had other hives on other farms dotted across the island, but losing every hive here was a huge blow. "That's more than a million bees."

Connor spoke quietly. "Do you, ah, do you think you'll be able to get me enough bees in spring?"

Jim looked up in disbelief. "I'm really sorry if this is any inconvenience to you."

"It's just," Connor said. "I mean, it's my livelihood. I need pollination, and we both know there aren't enough wild pollinators left anymore. I need honeybees."

"It's my livelihood too, you know. These bees are my livestock. Imagine if a dairy farmer lost his herd overnight."

"But you have other hives, right? At other farms? And federal insurance?"

"Of course I do, but I'm still a small operation. And bees are hard to get, and expensive at that. The insurance doesn't cover everything."

He looked back at the burnt remains. He couldn't believe it. In just a few weeks' time, he would have been harvesting the honey crop from those hives—another good source of income, as honey was increasingly scarce. After that, he would have prepared the hives for winter. It wasn't easy to get a hive through a Gull Island winter, but now he didn't have to worry about that. Not for these hives.

Connor squatted down next to him. "I'm sorry, but I'm worried. If you can't get me enough bees for spring, then I'll need to get a migratory Beelord in. I'll need to start making calls to bee brokers immediately."

Jim shook his head. "Connor, my hives are still smoking for God's sake. I can't have this conversation now."

"Well, it's just, Beelords get booked up a year in advance…"

"Give me a moment," he snapped. "And don't go calling any of those goddamn corporations."

Connor stood up and stepped back.

Jim wasn't angry at Connor. He was angry because corporate

Beelords were part of the problem. They practiced migratory beekeeping on a massive scale, a practice that stressed bees, spread disease, and contributed to the decline of bee populations.

"I'm sorry, Connor," Jim said. "It would just kill me if I lost out to a migratory Beelord."

Connor rubbed his hands on the legs of his greasy coveralls. "I might not have much choice. If I don't have bees, my business is doomed. I've got a family to support."

Jim understood. Connor needed pollination, and if Jim couldn't provide it then he would have to go elsewhere. He was staring at the grass and dirt, considering the ramifications of this, when something caught his eye. There was a piece of charred, pale green foam near the burnt hives, like something from the inside of a pillow. He walked over to it. It was just a small piece, but somehow it had survived. He looked at the ground and realized there might be footprints.

"We need to keep this area clear," he said. "Any footprints might help Deputy Gabby figure out who did this."

They both took a few steps away from the hives. Jim stuffed the bit of foam in his pocket and scanned the ground carefully. He'd spent a lot of time tracking animals in his life. Now he was looking for human footprints.

"I don't think any locals are capable of this," Connor said. "It must have been mainlanders, right?"

"Maybe," Jim said, thinking.

This island was like a place lost in time. The locals still didn't lock their houses. People left their bicycles unattended in front of stores on Main Street with no fear of them being stolen. There was almost no crime, certainly no violent crime. He'd chosen this place as he wanted a safe haven for Ava to finish high school. He'd wanted to retreat and take care of his bees. But now there was this. Was the outside world finally coming to Gull Island?

His phone went off in his pocket. He didn't recognize the

number but was surprised to find that it was Deputy Gabby, the island's only year-round law enforcement officer.

"Your ears must have been ringing," Jim said. "I was just talking about you."

"Why's that?" Her voice was strong and confident, and right now it held some urgency.

"I'm standing in front of an arson site," he said. "It's still smoking."

"Where?"

"Connor Davies' farm. Someone torched all my hives."

"Then this is worse than I thought," she said.

"What do you mean?"

"I'm over at Bennett Orchards," Gabby said. "Someone burnt your hives here too."

2

GULL ISLAND WAS small and sparsely populated—just sixteen miles long and roughly five miles wide, with only 651 year-round residents. It was a green oval from north to south in the middle of the deep waters of Lake Michigan. Heavily wooded and somewhat isolated, the island was dotted with small farms and quaint B&Bs.

Its natural beauty was the main tourist draw. There were no malls, no movie theaters, and no buildings over two stories tall, unless you counted the two lighthouses—one on either end of the island. There was one little town, Saint Peter, but there wasn't much there. To get to the island, the quickest route was a thirty-minute, twin-engine flight from Au Bois, but most favored the two-hour ferry ride.

In spite of its remoteness, the tourists came every summer for the fine weather, the sandy beaches, and the relaxed pace of life. The population grew to five times its normal size from late June to early September.

Jim clutched the steering wheel as he sped toward Bennett Orchards, his black pickup being jarred and jolted down the potholed gravel road. Trees flashed by on either side.

Bennett Orchards, like Connor's blueberry farm, wasn't far from the End Woods. When Jim turned into the gate, he saw the large, red barn with the black roof. Rows of fruit-laden apple trees lined either side of the long driveway. He knew this crop was worth quite a bit, since apples were such an expensive rarity.

He spotted the deputy sheriff's SUV parked in front of the barn. The vehicle had "Keskkauko County Deputy Sheriff" painted on the side, along with a sheriff's badge and an outline of Michigan's upper and lower peninsulas. Deputy Gabby Martinez herself was not far away, standing at the edge of the orchard.

He parked his pickup and walked toward her.

"It's bad, Jim," she said.

Gabby's relatively small size didn't stop her from having an extremely commanding presence. She was a woman who was equally tough and attractive. She was in her early forties, with an authority strengthened by maturity. She wore the drab, brown uniform of the local police force—beige pants and a brown short-sleeved shirt with epaulets and flaps on the front pockets—and her silver Deputy Sheriff's badge caught the sun. Her long, black hair was pulled back in a practical ponytail, and though she seemed to be wearing no makeup, her olive skin and dark eyes were naturally striking. There was a handgun in a belt at her side. She looked like she meant business.

Jim didn't know Gabby well. He knew only that she was from out of state. He'd talked to her just once, really, when she'd made a point to stop by the house to introduce herself when he and Ava first moved to Gull Island. It had been a brief and polite welcome.

"How many hives did they get?" Jim asked her.

"I'm sorry, Jim," she said. "All of them."

He was shocked. "Are you sure? All throughout the entire farm?"

"I just went around with Vicki. She called me as soon as she found them. I'm afraid every single hive is gone."

He ran the numbers again. Vicki Bennett's farm covered about forty acres, and the orchard made up about thirty acres of that. On apple farms, Jim typically used three hives per acre to achieve good pollination, so he had ninety here—or rather, he *used to have* ninety hives. He began to feel sick to his stomach.

"I had roughly four-and-a-half million bees here," he said. "With Connor's place, I've lost almost six million overnight."

"I really am sorry." Gabby spoke gently. She lifted her hand as though she was about to touch his arm, but then pulled away. Her voice turned suddenly businesslike. "Let me show you the scene."

She led him down the rows until they arrived at a space in the trees where some of Jim's hives had stood. It looked just like the charred mess he'd seen at Connor's farm. Here, however, yellow tape that read "POLICE LINE DO NOT CROSS" was already strung up, blocking off the area.

"We found this," she said, pointing to a red, plastic jerry can on the ground. It was a square, five-gallon container. "It's empty."

"Jesus. They weren't messing around." As he spoke, he could feel Gabby watching him closely.

"We'll find who did it," she said. "I've already called in a preliminary report to Au Bois."

Jim noticed that, even though she wasn't local, she pronounced the name of the city like a Michigander: *Oh Boy*. Technically it should be pronounced "Oh Bwah," with its history tracing back to the 1700s when French colonial traders and fur traders left their mark on Northern Michigan. She must have learned that Michiganders looked sideways at anyone who pronounced the state's French names correctly.

"We had some rain last night, so the ground is soft," she continued. "We'll do forensic photography and see if we can't get any footprints or tire tracks."

"There might be footprints at Connor's place too."
Gabby nodded.
"Where's Vicki?" he asked.
"She's dealing with the harvest team. Her commercial harvest

starts this week, and she's trying to figure out how to do that while her farm is a crime scene. She's not taking any U-pick tourists today. We have to make this investigation quick, so she can get back to business. It'll be the same thing with Connor's farm. I'll head there next."

"They did it at night," Jim said. "When all the bees would be in the hive. They clearly wanted to make sure they killed them all, not just destroy the hive frames."

"Or they just didn't want to get caught," Gabby said, looking at him. "Can you think of anyone who would have a reason to do this?"

"I'd just be guessing."

Jim walked up to the police line surrounding the smoking embers. Among the burnt remains he saw a few pieces of pale green foam, burned around the edges. He pulled out the piece he'd collected from Connor's and reached out to hand it to Gabby.

"I found this over at Connor's place. It's like they put foam up in the hive entrance before they burned them, to trap the bees inside."

As Gabby took the foam, their fingers touched. "Is that what you would do? Block the entrance?"

"If I wanted to kill all the bees, sure."

"So, you've thought this through?"

He paused and looked at her firmly. "It's what you do with foulbrood."

"Foulbrood? What's that?"

"American foulbrood. It's a disease."

"What kind?"

It was a disease Jim hated, because it was incredibly contagious and the treatment was extreme. He'd had to deal with it only three times in his life, and each time it broke his heart.

"It's caused by spores of a bacteria that turn bee larvae into a nasty smelling slime," he said. "There's no cure for it. They used to use antibiotics to help control it, but now it's become resistant.

You have to burn your hives if they get infected. Some people cynically call it 'the fire cure,' but it doesn't really cure anything. It just stops the spread."

Gabby was listening carefully. "How do you do that? Burn the hives?"

"Well, first you have to kill the bees. So you block the entrance at night when the bees are inside." He gestured to the piece of foam Gabby held in her hand. "Foam like that would work well. Then you open up the top of the hive, pour gasoline inside, and let the fumes kill the bees. It's horrible. Like killing a city. When they're all dead, you burn the entire thing, bees, frames, honey, and all. The beeswax burns fast."

"Seems drastic."

He nodded. "Sometimes drastic measures are the only way to stop a terrible thing from spreading."

She looked at him closely. A breeze caught in the apple trees. Jim looked away and stared at the burnt remains.

"Did these hives have that disease?" she asked.

"Absolutely not. I checked them just the other day. They were perfectly healthy. In fact, right now there's no foulbrood on Gull Island at all."

"Because you're conscientious."

Jim said, "I try."

"And you have no idea who else would want to burn your hives?"

"No."

Gabby looked very serious. "Any possible leads will help the investigation. I really need you to think about who could have done this."

He turned to face her. "It would just be conjecture. Slinging mud at people. I don't like that. I stick to myself."

"That's why people like you, Jim. People say you're a good member of this community. A bit of a stubborn, solitary type, of course, but everyone says you're a good guy."

Jim looked down. Praise made him uneasy.

Gabby's posture changed. She leaned forward. "But are you, Jim? Do the people on this island have you wrong? You've only been here two years. What do we know? Do you have good insurance? For your bees?"

Her gaze was stern and accusatory. She was small but threatening.

"Excuse me?" he said.

"You will answer my question. Do you have good insurance?" There was an incredible well of confidence and command in her voice. She expected an answer.

"Of course I have insurance," he said. "I'm covered under the Federal Bee Crisis Insurance Act. That doesn't mean I did this."

She raised an eyebrow. "I didn't say you did."

3

AVA WAS LYING in bed with a terrible sense of regret. The noise from her dad's pickup truck had woken her, and now she couldn't get back to sleep. She'd made a bad call. She knew it. Now she was stuck with the consequences.

Her German Shepherd, Bailey, was curled up at her feet, fast asleep. She tried not to disturb him as she slipped out of bed. She turned on the black light that lit her fish tank and then opened the curtains on the big sash window that looked out across the front porch to the trees beyond. The sun was just coming up, and the wind was moving the branches of the pines. She wished she could open the window and let in the breeze, but unfortunately, it was nailed shut. Her dad was such an overprotective ogre.

As she climbed back into bed, Bailey settled down next to her and put his head on her leg.

This bedroom was the only personal space she had in the entire world. There was no privacy on a tiny island where everyone knew you were the beekeeper's daughter. She hated this place. Her final year of high school was starting in just two weeks, and while she was dreading it, at least after that she'd be able to go away to college. Anything to get out of here.

But she did love her bed. It was a single bed with a white headboard, pale purple sheets and blankets, and lots of neon-colored throw pillows. It was comfortable and soft, and it never told her what to do, never nagged her, and always encouraged her to sleep in. What was there not to love about it? Ava kept a gratitude list, updating it periodically to stop herself from slipping too far into despair. Currently her bed was at number four.

The walls of her bedroom were dark purple. Her dad had said the color was too dark, but he let her choose it anyway. A month ago she'd dyed her hair purple too—not as dark as the walls, but purple still. It was shoulder-length, and she liked how sometimes she caught glimpses of purple in the corner of her vision. Of course, her dad had been furious when he came home and saw what she'd done, but that was no surprise.

The light in her fish tank was filling the water with a purple glow. The tank was number three on her list, which meant she loved it more than her bed, and that was saying a lot. The sound of the gurgling bubbles soothed her, and she loved watching the Stardust Blue Tetras and Pulsar Purple Danios darting around. All of them were FluoroFish—gen-mods that had jellyfish and sea coral genes. Her dad hated them, of course, just like he hated everything she loved, but he'd given in when she'd said last year it was all she wanted for her birthday. With the purple walls and neon throw pillows, her entire room felt like a beautiful fish tank. She liked how when she was in here she blended in and disappeared.

Her regret surged to the surface again. There was no way she could tell her dad about what she'd done this time. If he'd been furious about her hair, he'd absolutely go through the roof over this. She could have told her mom about it. She would have been disappointed, of course, and would have given Ava a gentle lecture. But she wouldn't have made a big deal about it, not like she knew her dad would.

Ava's phone beeped. She sat up and quickly rolled over, grabbing the phone off the floor next to her bed. Bailey raised his head with a start.

For the past week, her heart jumped whenever she got a new message. Every time she wanted it to be Eddie. All she needed was one little message to let her know that he was okay, that everything was going to be fine. Not hearing from him was breaking her heart.

But the message wasn't from Eddie. This time, it was her best friend Claire, asking if she'd heard from him. Ava hadn't told anyone exactly what had happened between her and Eddie, but her friends all knew that he hadn't contacted her in a week. She ignored the message and dropped her phone back onto the floor.

She leaned her head back on a pile of pillows and rubbed her bare feet against Bailey's side. He blew air out of his wet nose in response. She loved this dog so much. He was her constant companion. He was, in fact, number two.

Looking over at the window, staring at the nails in the window frame, she thought about the day they'd moved in. On that very first day she had had a big fight with her dad about this room—and about this window in particular. He wanted her to take the larger bedroom because it was at the back of the house and the window was smaller. He didn't like the fact that someone could stand on the front porch and look into her room. He had gone on and on about it.

She had become furious. The larger bedroom was clearly the parent's bedroom. He was being weird and overprotective, and he just wouldn't drop it. She ended up yelling at him, saying how they were on a stupid island in the middle of nowhere and there were no creepy men staring in the bedroom windows of teenage girls. Things like that didn't happen here. Ever. Besides, creepy men could stare in the back window as easily as the front.

The front bedroom was better because the view into the trees was nicer than the fenced vegetable garden at the back. And anyway, it would have just been strange for her to have a bigger bedroom than her dad. None of her friends' parents would do that.

It took a long screaming match for him to finally give in. Even then, the agreement came with two rules. First, she couldn't sleep with the window open, because it opened onto the porch. Second, the curtains had to be drawn at night. Her dad was fixated on the idea that some psycho was going to climb in through her window. Whatever.

Once, on a hot night not too long after they'd settled in, her dad had wandered around to the front of the house to make sure her window was shut. She'd of course left it open that particular night, with the curtains pushed back to let in the breeze. She loved a night breeze. He immediately stormed inside and woke her up by shouting at her, shutting the window, and closing the curtains. The next day he actually nailed the window sash shut permanently.

She didn't speak to him for over a week. That was when she started referring to him in her journal as the "Window Cop." She took pleasure in thinking about him that way. It was like a silent revenge.

Looking out the window now, she watched the gentle breeze blowing the leaves on the trees beyond the clearing.

She supposed she did still love her dad, but he'd become something different than he used to be. Over the last two years on this island, she'd watched as he had slowly turned into a weird hermit. He was spending too much time alone, obsessing about his bees, seeing danger everywhere she went. At times it almost felt like he was even becoming a bit delusional, as though he still believed she was only eight years old. He was a man who wanted to live in the past—a past where she was still a little girl, where things were simpler. Where her mom was still around.

Ava wished her mom was still around too, of course. That was probably the one thing she and the Window Cop agreed on. In the three years since that horrible night in Ann Arbor, a painful darkness had taken up permanent residence inside of Ava. With every day that went by she missed her mom more. She looked down at the bracelet on her wrist, remembering the day her mom had given it to her. So much had changed since then.

Bailey sat up and let out a big yawn, his jaws opening wide, his pink tongue curling up at the end.

Ava turned in the bed and wrapped an arm around him.

"At least you haven't abandoned me," she said.

The big, adorable dog lay back down and let out a deep and satisfied sigh. Ava closed her eyes and slowly drifted back to sleep.

4

"YOU IMPLIED that I burnt my own hives," Jim said, turning away from Deputy Gabby.

He was angry. She was treating him like a suspect. He looked out at the apple trees that surrounded them. Geometric rows of trunks moved across the landscape. The thick, green branches were dotted with red apples everywhere.

Deputy Gabby walked over and stood between him and the trees, demanding his attention.

"Maybe you *did* burn your own hives for the insurance money," she said. "Maybe you want to get out of the business. It must be tiring work. It's hard keeping bees alive, isn't it?"

He was dumbfounded. "Are you serious?"

She looked at him critically, like she was assessing him. "I have to think of all the possibilities. I have a crime on my hands. And these things don't normally happen here. You've only been here a relatively short time." She went over to the yellow police tape, ducked under it, and started looking at the ground.

"I wouldn't kill my own bees," he said to her back. "I wouldn't kill *any* bees."

"You're a Beelord," she said almost absent-mindedly, still scanning the ground. She leaned down and picked up a piece of foam. "You Beelords are in it for the money, aren't you? You're all just taking advantage of the Global Bee Crisis to line your pockets, right?" It was as though, having regained his attention, she had full confidence that she was back in control.

"I'm not a Beelord," he said. "I'm a traditional beekeeper."

She stood up straight and turned around. The yellow tape divided them. "Tell me. What exactly is the difference?"

"Beelords are usually big corporates, for one. And they're migratory."

"And that means what, exactly?"

"They throw tarps over their hives at night, lift them with fork-lifts onto the back of huge trucks, and cart them across the country," Jim said, not certain if she was actually asking for an explanation. "They run massive operations, typically with something like 200,000 migratory hives. I have only 300 stationary hives."

"Are you on the national Beelord register?"

"I have to be. Otherwise I can't provide pollination services."

"Well, then you're a Beelord." She crossed back under the yellow tape and held the two pieces of foam in front of Jim's face —the one she'd just picked up and the one Jim had given her from Connor's place. "They're definitely the same."

"Are you talking about the foam or me and the Beelords?"

"Both."

"I'm not an agricultural megacorporation. I'm just a guy with bees."

"A guy who makes his living off of the fact that bees are dying."

Jim took a deep breath. It wasn't the first time someone had accused him of profiteering off the Global Bee Crisis, but it always upset him. He'd devoted his entire life to saving bees.

He thought of all the things he could say to explain his motivations and his history, but it would just sound like defensiveness or, even worse, boasting.

Before coming here, Jim's academic career had placed him among the world's leading experts. For over a decade, he'd been the Distinguished Randall Professor in Entomology at the University of Michigan in Ann Arbor. It was there that he'd established the Center for Pollinator Research when global decline in bee populations took another precipitous downward turn. His TED talk on why bees were disappearing had gone viral. It was only four years ago that he'd received his MacArthur Fellowship—commonly known as the "Genius Grant"—for his work studying colony collapse.

And now he was standing here with a small-town deputy who knew absolutely nothing about bees, and she had the gall to accuse him of being a money grubber who killed for the insurance money. Why didn't she trust him? What had he done? He wanted to scream.

Instead, he tried to speak calmly. "You have no idea how much I care about bees. I would never, ever intentionally harm them. They are my life. The only thing more important to me than my bees is my daughter, okay? I did not do this."

Gabby looked at him for a long time. It felt like she was trying to see through him. Finally, she said, "If you didn't do this, then you'll tell me who you think did."

He rubbed the back of his neck. "Well, Chuck Norman does come to mind."

"Why?"

"He hates my guts."

"Ah, then there's at least one person on this island who doesn't like you." Her face was stern. Her tone was unmistakably accusatory.

"Excuse me. I'm not sure why you're being such a prick."

As soon as the words came out of his mouth he knew he shouldn't have said it. Sometimes he lacked a filter. He didn't know how to be around people.

She looked incredulous. "Mr. Parker, I will remind you that I am the law here, and you need to treat me with respect."

"I think that goes both ways, *Deputy Martinez.*" He stressed the formality of using her surname. Most called her Deputy Gabby. "You're treating me like a criminal." He stepped back and shook his head in disbelief. "I'm sorry. This just isn't going the way I expected."

"What? You thought I'd give you a pat on the back? Right now you're my primary suspect. Who knows better how to kill a beehive than a professional Beelord? Block the entrance, you say."

"It wasn't me. You should think about Chuck."

"Just because he doesn't like you?"

"I took all his customers."

"Ah, so you pushed him out."

Jim held back. He didn't say what he knew to be true about Chuck, that the man didn't take care of his bees. They died. The crops Chuck was hired to pollinate simply didn't get pollinated. As soon as Jim arrived here and started his business, all the local farmers started coming to him. He actually reached out to Chuck and offered to teach him what he knew. After all, there was more than enough business for two beekeepers on the island. Chuck had refused the offer.

"Lately," Jim said, "I've been hearing that Chuck wants to use drones."

"Drones? You mean, what, male bees?"

"No. I mean, yes, male bees are called drones too, but that's not what I'm talking about. Chuck wants to use pollination drones. Little flying robots."

"Does that work?"

"Some people like to think so. There are a lot of people trying to solve the bee crisis in different ways. Some are trying pollination drones. Others are trying gen-mods."

"Gen-mods? Really? You mean people are making genetically modified bees?"

"Sure." Jim looked over at the charred ground. Ever since the Genetic Modification Experimentation Act had been passed a few years earlier, biotech companies had been racing to make a more resilient strain of honeybee. "But Chuck's not playing with gen-mods. He's buying drones."

"How do you know?" she asked. "Did he tell you?"

"It's a small island. People talk. He orders them online."

"And you don't think drones will work?"

"Maybe someday, when the field of microrobotics is more advanced. The problem is that the drones available today just aren't as good at pollination as actual bees are. Plus they break down. And if I know Chuck, they won't last long. He's a train wreck."

Jim had studied the trend extensively. The big corporates had been trying out drones for the Californian almond pollination for at least a decade. It was proving more costly than actual bees, and less effective.

"So you think Chuck's wasting his money?" Gabby asked.

"Look, I know bees. Bees and wasps, actually. It's what I do. Bees have been pollinating plants for over 120 million years. They evolved for it. The idea that you could build something as cost-effective and efficient as *Apis mellifera* in just a few years is delusional."

"*Apis melli-what?*"

"*Apis mellifera*. The western honeybee. The most common honeybee worldwide. It's not the only bee currently endangered—bumblebees and other wild species are suffering too—but the western honeybee is especially good for food production, and it's the one I have. Drones are just a band-aid. The bee crisis is happening because the planet's hurting. We need to fix that, not make tiny robots or gen-mod Frankenbees."

Gabby crossed her arms. "So, let me get this straight. You think Chuck Norman destroyed your hives so farmers on Gull Island would come to him for a robotic pollination business?"

"I didn't say that. But it's not out of the question."

"Thank you. I'll talk to Chuck." Suddenly her tone of voice changed, becoming accusatory again. "In the meantime, I don't want you leaving Gull Island, understand?"

"I have absolutely no plans to go anywhere, *Deputy Martinez*. This island is my home now." Jim couldn't stop the anger from showing in his voice.

He quickly turned and walked back to his truck. As he drove away, he looked back. Gabby was still standing there with her arms crossed, watching him. He felt as if he'd just been put on trial. She'd spent more time accusing him than helping him. There was no way he was going to stand back and leave this up to her. This was too important. Someone was destroying his bees and threatening his livelihood.

He was a scientist at heart, and the scientific method was nothing more than a system for accumulating data and eliminating false possibilities. It was about solving mysteries. He was going to have to start gathering evidence. He was going to have to catch this arsonist himself.

5

JIM WAS STILL FUMING as he drove south along the island's western edge, away from Bennett Orchards. At the same time, he was worried about his remaining hives. What if the arsonist came back tonight? He wanted to be ready.

His remaining beehives were dotted around the island, and they were vulnerable. There were 185 hives left in six locations, in the middle of farms and orchards. It was impossible to guard them all. His biggest concern was for his eight home hives. They were his queen rearing hives, and they were on his private property, at the edge of the woods behind his house. The right equipment would help him catch the arsonist. To get that equipment, he had to go see Bob.

He was heading toward Saint Peter, the tiny town nestled next to the harbor at the bottom of the island. As he drove, his thoughts kept returning to Deputy Gabby. He just couldn't get her unpleasantness out of his head. She was misguided and grasping at straws.

To his left, he could see the shoreline and Lake Michigan beyond. It was a massive lake—more like an inland sea than a lake. The water stretched to the horizon. As he neared the southern end of the island, more buildings appeared among the trees. He passed the Woodland Motel and some relaxed, weather-beaten cottages. Eventually he turned onto Main Street.

Saint Peter wasn't much of a town. On one side of the street, quaint wooden buildings stood in an orderly row. On the other side, the view opened directly to the harbor. There was a restaurant, a bakery, a gas and charging station, a grocery store, and a hardware store with a tourist shop tacked onto the side.

As Jim drove down Main Street, the town was almost empty. This was the quiet, slow pace he liked. A few pickups and 4x4s were parked on the side of the road. A handful of tourists strolled down the sidewalk, and some people lingered near the timber facade of the Harbor View Hotel, with its old-fashioned balcony and wooden columns.

He parked his truck in front of Gull Hardware. Some kids had left their bikes on the sidewalk nearby, unlocked as always. Over at the dock, the morning ferry to Au Bois was just leaving. People were waving to friends and family on the upper decks of the ferry as it pulled away. In the distance, the Harbor Lighthouse stood tall and white out on Odawa Point.

He loved this simple village. Gull Island felt like the best place in the world to keep Ava out of harm's way. He wanted it never to change.

With Ava on his mind, he decided to make a stop off at McClelland's Grocery, wanting to get something special for her. They were fighting too much lately. A peace offering might help.

Even after all these years, he'd never quite adjusted to how much grocery stores had changed since when he was a boy. He was met now by a small section of fresh, wind-pollinated produce —beets, swiss chard, sweet corn, and spinach. They were all still reasonably priced and readily available, but it was just a thin veneer of normalcy.

The Global Bee Crisis had brought the global food supply to the brink of collapse. Crops pollinated by bees everywhere had record low yields. Many farmers were converting their fields to productive, wind-pollinated wheat, and as a result diets had turned bland and boring. Looking around the grocery store now, Jim thought back fondly on the stores of his boyhood, where large aisles practically overflowed with fruits and vegetables, and long counters were jam-packed with fresh meat, all relatively afford-able. It wasn't like that anymore. The sense of abundance was gone.

A wall of canned fruits and vegetables stood nearby, all of which used to rely on honeybee pollination. There were cans of celery, cucumbers, broccoli, cauliflower, onions, carrots, and fruits like apples, apricot, and peaches. Most were imported from China, where hand pollination had taken over from honeybees. The technique was viable at a large scale there only because labor was so cheap.

He moved past all of this quickly and headed to the back of the store, where the luxury items were kept. He ignored the displays of the fresh, designer produce. Despite the fact that Ava was always eager to try the latest trademarked vegetable—often launched as part of some celebrity's lifestyle brand—Jim abso-lutely hated them. Those new, gen-mod foods were engineered to be wind pollinated, but they were still extremely expensive. As far as he was concerned, apples that tasted of cinnamon and pears that were bright purple inside were just ridiculous. Their branded markings were even worse—stripes and spirals and even company logos, all achieved through manipulating the genome.

No, thank you, he thought. He liked traditional things. He headed directly to the fresh, old-fashioned, bee-pollinated fruits and vegetables. They were displayed meticulously in a small glass case in the very back corner of the store. There were a few carrots, a couple heads of broccoli, a single avocado in a foam protector, a handful of limes, and a small cluster of oranges.

Today there was also cheese—two bricks of cheddar and three packages of swiss. It was his lucky day. Real beef and dairy were expensive and rare. Alfalfa was widely used as cattle feed, and the plant's preferred pollinator, the alfalfa leafcutter bee, was one of the bees now endangered. Given recent advances in synthetic proteins, many kids growing up these days had never tasted real meat or dairy.

Ever since Ava was a little girl, she'd loved Jim's breakfast tacos. He filled them with lots of real cheese, eggs, fresh salsa, and his special homemade guacamole. But as Ava had grown, several of these ingredients had become extravagances. Even though he was a beekeeper now, he was no millionaire. He didn't charge corporate Beelords rates, and he had only 300 hives.

He caught himself. Only 185 hives now.

The ingredients for the salsa—fresh tomatoes, onions, and cilantro—were all growing in his back garden. His home hives pollinated the onions and the cilantro, and he pollinated the tomatoes by hand, since honeybees didn't pollinate the tomato plant. Now he just needed to buy real cheese, a lime, and an avocado. Although his spending habits were normally austere, he would do this today, for Ava. They might even make breakfast together, like a father and daughter who actually enjoyed each other's company.

"Can I help you?"

A young man with white gloves and a tie was standing on the other side of the produce case. He looked like he could have worked in a jewelry shop.

Jim asked for a lime, one of the small bricks of cheddar, and the avocado. The avocado was the most expensive thing in the case, but it was a beauty. Ava had always loved his homemade guacamole, and while one avocado wouldn't make much, it would be delicious. The young man handed the goods over carefully and with great ceremony.

A woman standing nearby looked over at Jim and said, "Oh, an avocado. Special occasion?"

Everyone knew that honeybees were important pollinators for avocados, and with yields down their prices had skyrocketed.

Jim smiled back at the woman. "You might say that."

On his way to the scanner, he picked up a carton of free-range eggs and some flour tortillas. He couldn't wait to surprise Ava.

But first, he had to get what he'd come to Saint Peter for. He had to visit Bob and get the equipment that would help him gather the evidence he needed. He wanted to set a trap.

6

WALKING into Gull Hardware was like walking into chaos. The shelves were scattered with random odds and ends—everything from circuit breakers, outlet cover plates, and frying pans, to door hinges, automotive parts, and semiconductors. A doorway to the right led to the tourist shop, with disordered stacks of merchandise. Bob Morris, the enterprising owner of Gull Hardware, had built the extension years ago so he could start selling Gull Island t-shirts, mugs, key chains, and even shot glasses. Out back Bob had a small and equally shambolic lumber yard.

Jim saw Bob stocking a shelf with electronics parts near the front door. He had long, silver hair and a bushy, horseshoe-shaped mustache that looked like it belonged on a biker.

"Good morning," Jim called out. He spent a fair amount of time and money in Bob's shop, buying wood and nails and tools for various jobs around the property and for his beehives.

Bob looked up and greeted him warmly. "Morning, Jim. I just heard your hives got hit by an arsonist. Sorry to hear that. Terrible."

Gossip here travelled quickly, but this was fast even for Gull

Island. Jim had only received the call from Connor a few hours ago. Everyone must have been nervous about the lack of bees.

"That's right," Jim answered. "I just came from there."

Bob shook his head as he stacked the circuit boards on the shelf. "The world's going to pot. Even here on the island. Does Deputy Gabby know who it was?"

Jim rankled again at just hearing her name. "No. She's too busy accusing me."

"You? You're kidding."

"I wish I were. She did say that she'd follow up on some other leads at least. Listen, you don't have any security cameras, do you?"

"Oh, I tried stocking them," Bob said, frowning. "I was thinking rich folks with fancy weekend houses might want some. Didn't sell. Nobody sees the need here."

Jim was disappointed. If he couldn't get security cameras he'd have to think of another plan. He might have to head over to Au Bois for the equipment, but that meant taking the morning ferry and that would take him all day.

"So you have nothing?" he asked. "Really? I need to monitor my home hives."

"Hmmm." Bob thought for a moment. "Actually, let me check in back. I just might have one I haven't returned yet."

Jim followed Bob to the back of the store, where a big stack of long, cardboard boxes was partially blocking the aisle.

"Stocking up on coyote rollers?" Jim asked, gesturing to the boxes.

"Yes, indeed," Bob said. "That's one thing that sells like hotcakes. Can't keep enough of them in stock. Damn coyotes are getting worse, I'd say. Pestering everybody."

Jim nodded in agreement as they stepped around the stack.

"Sorry about the mess," Bob said. "Emmett was supposed to sort the stock out this morning, but he hasn't shown up. Hang on while I check the store room for that camera. Be right back."

Jim waited, staring at the boxes on the floor. He'd installed coyote rollers himself just a few months earlier, after he'd been surprised by the coyotes jumping the seven-foot-tall cyclone fence that surrounded his vegetable garden. The rollers were long, aluminum tubes designed to spin and stop hungry coyotes from getting the foothold they needed to get over a fence. It had done the trick, and Jim no longer had coyotes digging up his garden.

"Looky here," Bob said, coming back out through the doorway with a box in his hands. "You're lucky I'm lazy and disorganized. Still got this one. It's a wired security camera with CCTV for farm surveillance, where your wi-fi won't reach."

It was perfect. Jim needed surveillance at the back of the property where there wasn't any wi-fi. "What's it come with?" he asked.

Bob squinted to read the print on the box. "Okay, this farm unit has two CCTV security cameras, 100 feet of cable, connectors, and it has a phone app. Has hi-res night vision too."

"Good. I'll need extra cabling. Maybe 300 feet total."

"That I got." Bob led Jim back around the stack of coyote rollers to a rack of cables. "It must be hard enough being a Beelord without someone burning your hives," he said, handing Jim the box and extra cabling.

Jim was tired of telling people how he didn't consider himself a Beelord. He just said, "It's not easy."

Bob led him back to the sales counter to pay, and then Bob said, "Could I ask a favor? I'm a bit worried about Emmett."

"What's wrong?"

Bob's brow furrowed. "Well, it's just not like him to not show up for work. I've been calling his house, but there's no answer. He lives near you, doesn't he?"

"Just down the road a bit. You want me to check on him?"

"Would you mind? He's an older fellow. Lives alone. I'm sure it's no big deal, but it would be good to make sure. I won't get out of here until this evening."

"Sure. I'll stop by on the way home."

"Thanks. He was fine on Sunday when I saw him last. Left here to go walk his dog, like always. I'm sure he's okay, but thanks for checking on him."

Jim said goodbye and walked back to his truck. He didn't know Emmett well at all, but he was happy to stop by. It was the neighborly thing to do.

He started his truck and headed north.

LIKE MOST HOMES on the northern end of the island, Emmett Jones' house was a modest wooden home set back from the road and hidden by trees. Jim knocked on the front door, but there was no answer. Three attempts yielded no results.

"Emmett?" he called out. It was almost 9:30 a.m. Surely he'd be up by now. He walked around the back of the house and called out again.

"Emmett, you here?"

When there was no response, he started peeking in the windows. He saw nobody inside. The wind rustled the trees of the End Woods nearby. Behind the house was a large garden and several mature fruit trees, surrounded by coyote-proof fencing. Maybe Emmett was working in the garden? But there was no sign of him outside. Back at the front door, Jim tried the doorknob. It was unlocked. He pushed it open.

"Hello? Anybody home?"

He took a tentative step through the doorway. He'd never been in Emmett's house before, and it felt oddly intrusive to just walk in. But what if Emmett was sick? What if he'd fallen and hurt himself, or even worse, had a heart attack? Jim had learned some time ago that people on Gull Island looked after each other. He felt a responsibility to go in and check.

"Emmett?" he called out. He was met with silence.

The house was silent and strangely bare. There was nothing hanging on the walls, and there was minimal furniture. He called out as he walked quickly from room to room, checking the kitchen, the bathroom, and the bedroom. There was no sign of him anywhere. Emmett's car key fob was lying on the kitchen counter. Wherever he was, he clearly left planning to come back soon.

Then Jim noticed some dirt on the vinyl flooring in the kitchen, as though somebody had trailed a bit of mud in. There was a good-sized dog flap in the back door, and the dog bowls for food and water were both empty. Jim assumed the dirt was from Emmett's dog, Sandy, but it did surprise him as the house was generally very tidy and clean otherwise.

Had something else come in through the dog door? He started to feel uneasy. Had a person walked in? He checked the back door. It was also unlocked. Someone could be in the house right now, hiding somewhere. The hair stood up on the back of his neck.

He yelled out, "Hello?"

Silence.

He began walking through the rooms again, quietly this time. He paused and listened for any noise. He began looking everywhere—under the bed, in the closets, and even behind the shower curtain. It was a little silly, but he felt compelled to do it. He just couldn't shake the feeling that someone had been in the house, or still was. But there was nobody there.

Back outside, he circled around the house one more time, and then walked over to the garage. The side door was wide open. He stood just outside and peered into the darkness. Had someone come in from the woods?

"Emmett?" Jim shouted through the doorway. His voice was hesitant. "You in there?"

Again, no answer.

As he stepped forward into the gloom, his eyes slowly adjusted. A dusty car was parked in front of him, and beyond that there was a workbench with a couple of old radios in various states of disrepair. There was a large chest freezer against the far wall, and just beyond, a few boards had been stacked on top of old cement blocks, making a set of shelves that stood about waist high.

Jim walked around the car and was surprised to see that, on the floor in front of the shelves, glass jars lay broken and shattered. He picked one jar up. A sticky, red residue clung to the glass. Scratchy handwriting across a white label read, "Strawberry Jam." On closer inspection, the other jars contained traces of apple jelly, or apricot or blueberry jam. Every single one had been opened, the contents eaten, and the jar thrown aside. There were over thirty jars on the ground. Who would eat so much jam? Was it Emmett? Perhaps he'd had some sort of psychotic episode. Jim quickly checked inside the car and then underneath. There was no sign of Emmett, or anybody else for that matter, anywhere.

When Jim stepped back outside, he felt relieved to be in the open again, and he quickly shut the door behind him. Something wasn't right here. Emmett was missing, but someone or something had been here. Maybe an animal from the woods. His heart sank when he realized what he had to do next.

He was going to have to call Deputy Gabby—the very person who earlier that morning had treated him like a criminal—and explain what he'd found. He didn't know if she would believe him.

8

AT THAT VERY MOMENT, Deputy Gabby Martinez was pulling up in her SUV in front of the dilapidated house where Chuck Norman lived. The house stood in a small clearing surrounded by pines. Chuck's old, red pickup truck was parked directly in front, with "Norman Services" on the side in white letters. At the edge of the clearing, Gabby could see three rusted-out cars that had been abandoned. The ground beyond the clearing was covered with a blanket of dead pine needles that had faded into the reddish-brown color of dried blood.

Chuck's house had always been broken-down and shabby. She remembered that last time she was here he'd bragged about how he was going to fix up the place. He'd done nothing. The exterior was still covered in aging plywood. The metal roof was still rusty. There were two things she noticed that had changed about the house, but not for the better. The solar panels on the roof now had grass growing between them, and one of the windows on the side of the house was boarded up. She walked up the set of disintegrating wooden steps to the porch and knocked on the peeling paint of the front door. Then she waited, bracing herself.

She'd never liked Chuck. He had a reputation for being a bitter old man and a mean drunk. He yelled at kids he came across in the woods, and he was known for getting belligerent down at Coyote Kylie's. He was a braggart. When he was drunk he tended to start fist fights over foolish things like who was a better outdoorsman.

She didn't trust most people. It was her natural disposition. She didn't trust Jim Parker either, although with Jim she did feel a bit more conflicted. She hadn't had many dealings with him previously, so she didn't have a lot to go on. While on the surface he seemed nice enough, something about this bee arson was just not right, and you could never be sure about people. Admittedly, there was something very appealing about Jim's solitary, earthy ways. His good looks, nicely trimmed beard, and long, lean frame didn't hurt either. Regardless, she had a crime on her hands that just did not make sense, and it was entirely possible that Jim Parker was guilty. She had to be careful not to be biased, but she'd begun to wonder if perhaps she'd overcompensated this morning. Could her attraction to Jim have actually caused her to treat him more harshly than she would have otherwise?

Now she could just make out the sound of a radio from inside Chuck's house, but nobody answered the door. She stepped to the side and looked in the window. The glass was dirty, but she could see the small front room. There were two shabby armchairs and a coffee table. A large, braided rag rug covered the floor. There were stacks of hoarded newspapers in the corners, and opened boxes full of bubble wrap everywhere. It looked like he had had a recent delivery.

She turned to look out at the clearing. Maybe Chuck was out here somewhere. The rusted cars and the faded pine needles filled her with a strange sense of sadness.

Suddenly, she heard the radio turn off, and turned back to the house to find a face staring at her from the other side of the window. It was Chuck. The look in his eyes was unsettling—a cold, angry leer. And then he was gone, as quickly as he had appeared.

"Chuck?" she called out. "I need to talk to you."

There was no answer.

She knocked again. "Chuck?"

The front door cracked open. She could just make out one eye staring at her.

"What do you want?" Chuck said. His voice was gravelly and gruff.

"Open the door, Chuck." She said this firmly, with no pretense of politeness. This was the voice she used when she wanted to make people do something. She'd found it years ago, when trying to manage her own drunk father back in Chicago. She thought of it as her control voice.

The door opened fully, and she saw Chuck standing there, looking irritated. The thick, red hair on his head was as messy as his long, red beard. He was wearing a pair of stained work trousers and a grimy white tank top. On his right bicep, she noticed a tattoo of a horseshoe pointing up toward his shoulder. Underneath there was a scroll etched with the word *Lucky*.

"Hello," she said.

There had always been something odd about Chuck's face, at least the part which wasn't hidden by beard. His nose was slightly misshapen, so that the nostrils didn't exactly match. The left nostril was larger and angled out at an odd slant. It was subtle but noticeable.

"What do you want?" He was squinting at her.

Gabby was used to men like this. Gull Island seemed to grow them this way—independent, peculiar, angry, hiding in the woods.

"How are you doing?" she asked.

"I don't expect you came here to make small talk."

"Looks like you got some new packages." She gestured toward the front room behind him.

"I don't have to talk to you."

"Actually, you do. Because if you don't, I'll just arrest you and take you down to the county sheriff's office."

He paused. "I ordered some stuff online for my business. Came a few days ago. Nothing to do with you."

"Which business?" Gabby knew that the "Norman Services" emblazoned on the side of his truck was a catch-all for a variety of activities. In addition to running an unsuccessful pollination business, Chuck chopped and sold firewood. He was also a general handyman and mechanic, although you'd never know it to look at his own place. "Is it for your pollination business? Your firewood delivery? Or a new business?"

"I got some pollination drones. Robot bees. You know, that sorta thing."

"Can I see?"

"No."

"Why not?"

"You got a search warrant?"

"I don't need a search warrant."

"Huh?"

"You know that. Ever since the Safe Americans Act."

"Mmmm," Chuck said, and his eyes narrowed.

Gabby wondered for a moment if Chuck, drunk as he often was, had actually somehow forgotten. Five years earlier, in an effort to control the increasing organized violence related to food supply chain issues, Congress had enabled law enforcement officers to search property and people at will. There had been too many gangs stealing trucks full of groceries and selling them on the black market. Now enforcement officers wanting to search property no longer had to provide justification, obtain consent, or secure court permission—regardless of what they were looking for. The new law and Constitutional amendment entirely did away with the concept of unreasonable search and seizure.

It still made her uncomfortable to use the new powers. She always started out trying to get homeowner consent if she could.

But, since there was no longer any formal process for even applying for a judge-issued search warrant, she often had to force her way in without either court permission or homeowner consent. She didn't like doing it.

Chuck leaned back and crossed his arms. "This is my house, and it's private."

Sometimes Gabby found it effective to switch from control to kindness, and she did that now. While being firm was often how she got things done, she knew you had to occasionally break down barriers with talk.

"How long have I known you now?" she asked.

"Well," Chuck said. "You came to the island six years ago, right?"

"Yes, that's right."

"So six years. Obviously."

"I know all sorts of things about you, Chuck. I know about Elsie. I know about your businesses. I know you yell at kids in the woods. And I know that normally on a Monday night you drink at Coyote Kylie's, to take advantage of the two-for-one pitchers."

He gave her a slow, resentful stare.

Gabby wondered if the death of Chuck's wife, Elsie, was the reason he was so bitter. She'd died decades ago. There were no children.

She met Chuck's stare and said, "But I hear that last night you weren't at Coyote Kylie's. What were you up to?"

"I'm not there *every* Monday night."

"No, but usually. The regulars notice when you're not there. They miss you, it seems." She smiled.

"Well, I wasn't there last night."

"Where were you?"

"Here. At home. Drank here. Cheaper than Kylie's prices, even with her special. I stayed home and opened my drones. Lotsa boxes." He smiled. "Sorta like Christmas."

Gabby noted his smile. It was working. "Of course. That's exciting. How is your bee business going?"

"Not so good."

"Why not?"

"You know why. Everyone knows."

"It must be frustrating to have a business that's not going so well." Empathy, she thought. Empathy made people open up.

Chuck glanced at the room full of opened boxes behind him. "Bastard Jim Parker ruined my business. Came here and took it all."

"I heard your bees kept dying."

"Because Jim killed them." Chuck tipped his head back and looked at her down the length of his irregular nose. "He poisoned my hives to put me out of business. My bees were good before he came here. Good enough." He sounded spiteful and angry.

She looked at him closely, studying him, taking every aspect of him in. "If you're saying Jim Parker killed your bees, why have you never come to me with this complaint before? That's a serious accusation, especially in the middle of a Global Bee Crisis."

Chuck looked away. "Doesn't matter anymore. I got robot bees." He began shifting his feet and scratching his neck.

She could spot a liar from a mile away. It was a survival skill she'd learned long before becoming a cop. She'd learned it growing up. Right now she didn't believe Chuck as far as she could throw him. "So you don't want to lay any formal charges?"

"Nah. I'm moving on."

She looked back towards the table behind him. "Those robot bees must be expensive."

Chuck shrugged. "You done with me?"

"Where'd you get the money to buy pollination drones?"

"I got money. Don't go thinking I'm poor just 'cause my house ain't fancy."

She studied him carefully. There were rumors that he kept cash in his mattress.

"So last night," she said. "You were here at home?"

"That's what I said. Now I'm done with you." He began to shut the door.

"Wait a minute." She quickly shoved her foot in the door jamb and pushed her arm against the door. "I'm not done with you. Were you alone last night?"

He paused and glared at her. "What kinda question is that? I been alone since Elsie died."

"Well, you could have had friends over."

"I don't like people coming 'round here. I don't like people standing on my porch, looking at me, talking at me like they know me when they don't."

"Okay, so you *were* alone last night. I just wondered if there was someone who could confirm you were here. That's all. I'm trying to help you, Chuck."

Chuck sneered. "Oh yeah. Trying to help. I don't think so. You're trying to blame me for something, and I don't know what it is. I was home alone. Same as most nights. Unless I'm at Coyote Kylie's. Now, if you'll excuse me. I got some business to attend to."

He tried again to push the door closed.

"Stop," Gabby said, in her best control voice as she leaned into the door. It worked. Chuck stopped. She continued speaking as if it weren't at all unusual to have her foot and arm blocking his front door. "Last night someone torched Jim Parker's beehives over at Connor Davies' farm. Also at Vicki Bennett's orchard. Do you know anything about that?"

"So that's what you're trying to blame me for." He scowled at her.

"Answer the question. Do you know anything?"

"No, ma'am. I do not. I ain't a fool. I wouldn't do that, but I can't say I'm upset to hear it."

"I understand Connor and Vicki used to be your customers. Is that true?"

"Lots of folks used to be my customers."

"But those two were definitely your customers, weren't they?" Chuck nodded.

"And now they're Jim Parker's customers, aren't they?"

He looked indignant. "Yes, they are." He tilted his head and jutted out his chin. "What are you trying to say?"

"Just asking questions, Chuck. That's all."

"Excuse me, ma'am. I don't feel so well."

"No, Chuck. I'm coming in. I am going to search your property."

He didn't move. Instead, he squinted his eyes and gave her an angry, hateful stare. "Like hell you will."

9

JIM STOOD in front of Emmett's house and took his phone out of his pocket to call Gabby. He didn't have reception. Mobile phone coverage was often patchy on the northern tip of Gull Island, so he climbed back in his pickup and drove home to call Gabby from his landline.

His was a modest, single-story home, nestled next to a cluster of three enormous eastern white pines. The exterior was covered with dark brown wood siding, the tin roof was forest green, and it had a quaint, fieldstone chimney. Jim had chosen this house in part because it had all the nostalgic charm of an antiquated cabin —not to mention that it was as far from Saint Peter as you could get and still be on the island. This home was his haven and his retreat from the world.

A covered porch ran across the front of the house, sheltering the front door, the window to the living room, and the window to Ava's bedroom. He was still uncomfortable with the fact that anyone could stand on the front porch and look into her bedroom, but he'd done as much as he could by nailing the window closed. He did it because he loved her, because he didn't want anything to happen to her.

Behind the house there was a beat-up, free-standing garage, not dissimilar to Emmett's, and he parked his pickup truck there now. He carried the groceries and the video equipment around to the back door and paused for a moment to look out at what he and Ava called the "back acre."

This was more than just a backyard. It was a full acre of land bordered by the End Woods on three sides. There was the old wooden garden shed, the rusty beige swing set left behind by the previous owners, and the weather-beaten picnic table where he and Ava ate meals in the summer. His large vegetable garden stood in the middle of it all, surrounded by the seven-foot-tall cyclone fence which had the newly installed coyote rollers. In the far back corner of the property were his eight home hives. The dark trees of the End Woods surrounded the entire thing like a tall, defensive wall. He loved this place.

He stepped into the rustic, wood-paneled kitchen, where the floor was faded green linoleum and an ancient refrigerator stood next to a sink with cracks in the white ceramic glaze. Every old thing about this kitchen gave him comfort. He set his purchases on the kitchen table.

The cordless landline phone was on the counter, underneath the small chalkboard where he and Ava sometimes jotted down notes and phone numbers. Ava always made fun of that phone, saying it belonged in a museum. She'd never lived in a house with a landline before coming to Gull Island.

Jim decided to call Bob at the hardware store first, putting off the dreaded conversation with Deputy Gabby. When Bob answered, Jim quickly explained what he'd seen at Emmett's place.

"That's weird," Bob said.

"I'll call Deputy Gabby and let her know Emmett's missing," Jim said. "Remind me, when did you see him last?"

"Two nights ago. Sunday night, when he left work. Thank you, Jim. He's supposed to be at work again tomorrow. If I hear from him, I'll let you know."

Jim tried Deputy Gabby, but the call went straight to voice-mail. He left her a brief message, explaining what he'd found at Emmett's and asking her to call him back.

When he hung up, he paused. He felt uneasy. Things on Gull Island were supposed to tick along smoothly. People didn't disappear. He tried to shake off the feeling. Emmett was probably just off on a long walk somewhere. Some animal had come in from the woods and made a mess of his garage. That was all.

He took the avocado out of the grocery bag, removed its foam protector, and held it up to look at it. This was a dark green treasure, perfectly ripe and ready to eat. Ava would love it. He carried it in both hands as he walked down the short hallway toward her bedroom. She should be up by now. It was almost 10 a.m.

He knocked on her door. "Ava?"

There was no answer.

"Ava?"

A low groan came from the other side of the door.

"I have a present for you," he said.

Another groan, this one longer.

"Are you up?"

Finally, she spoke. "I'm sleeping." The words were a grumbling protest.

"The day's passing you by, Avey Bavey. You should be up."

"Oh my God, Dad. I'm not eight years old."

He knew her childhood nickname bothered her now, but old habits died hard. She was seventeen. That adorable nickname felt like a memento from another, better life, and he hated to let it go. She used to help him with his beehives. She used to smile brightly when he came home. He missed that little girl.

"I got you something," he said. "You want to see?"

"Seriously?" She sounded exasperated. "Now?"

"Can I come in?"

There was movement from the room, and her door swung open. She stood there with her purple hair tousled and puffy eyes.

She looked deeply annoyed. Behind her, the black light from her aquarium glowed. Unnaturally fluorescent fish glided and flicked their tiny fins.

What struck Jim most in that simple moment, standing at his daughter's bedroom door as she wiped the sleep from her eyes, was not how annoyed she appeared—lately she was always irritated about something—but rather how much she looked like her mother. The hair was still horrible. He was still angry that she'd dyed it without his permission. But there was something about the tilt of her head, the strong line of her jaw, the intense cheekbones. Momentarily, she appeared to be almost a carbon copy of Sarah.

In fact, he realized, it was the exact angle of her chin in that moment. It was just the same as in the photo of Sarah he carried in his wallet. It was unnerving, and wonderful.

He held up the avocado and beamed. "Look."

Ava raised her eyebrows. "An avocado? You woke me up to show me an avocado."

"I thought you'd be happy. I can't remember the last time we had avocado. These things are precious. Guess what I'm going to make."

She just stared at him.

"Breakfast tacos," he said.

Her voice dripped with sarcasm as she responded slowly. "Hooray. I was actually sleeping."

He couldn't help but feel crestfallen. It was a silly thing, he knew, but it hurt. He could try a million different ways to reach out to his daughter, to bridge the gulf between them. Yet no matter what he did, he seemed forever unable to get to where she stood. Was this how it was going to be forever?

Further inside Ava's room, Jim could hear Bailey jump down off her bed. He walked out into the hallway and greeted Jim with a wet nose and a wagging tail. At least the dog was happy to see him.

"Ava," Jim said, "It's not good for you to stay up all night watching movies on your laptop and messaging people."

"I don't stay up all night."

"You do. I see the internet usage."

She rolled her eyes, which had become a bit of a habit of hers lately. Then she said, "You're a goddamn spy."

"Hey! Watch it!" He was instantly angry. "Show some respect. You sound like a truck driver."

"Well, I see we're off to a good start today."

He took a deep breath. "Look, I'm going to make us breakfast tacos. I wanted to surprise you with a treat. It would be nice if we made them together. Like old times."

She stared at him. "Oh goody. After that maybe we can color together. Or make a fort."

He paused. In moments like these, he didn't much like his daughter. He felt guilty for the thought.

"I'll be in the kitchen making us breakfast, or rather, brunch at this point. Join me if you'd like."

He didn't even mention that he'd dealt with arson this morning. She wouldn't care. He turned and went back to the kitchen. Bailey was already there, waiting by the back door. Jim let him out.

As he stood at the back door and watched the dog sniffing around, he tried hard to shake off Ava's attitude. He didn't know why he let it get to him. Ever since they'd moved to Gull Island, she'd been increasingly difficult. He missed his little girl.

A memory came to him, a warm summer day when Ava was seven or eight. They had been in a park and Ava was crying out after having got stuck up in a tree. "Papa! Papa!" she yelled. She didn't call Sarah, who was also there. She had called him. Her pigtails flew wildly in the air as she landed in his arms.

Where was the one who adored him, who called him "Papa" and wanted him to catch her? She hadn't called him "Papa" in almost ten years. Lately, she barely even called him "Dad," and when she did, she spit it out as if it was a swear word.

In a few weeks she was going to start her senior year at Gull Island High, and already she looked like a grown woman. He was not ready for that.

He stepped outside and walked toward the vegetable garden. The tall cyclone gate swung easily in his hand. Within, surrounded by the tall fence, the garden was practically bursting. There were beans, cucumbers, beets, eggplant, and tomatoes. The wind-pollinated vegetables had their very own section—spinach, beets, and a few rows of tall corn.

The cilantro had nearly all gone to seed, but there was still some left. There were plenty of ripe, red tomatoes to choose from. He picked the best ones, and he resigned himself to making the breakfast tacos on his own.

10

GABBY CONTINUED to hold her foot in the door jamb and her arm against the peeling gray door. "Chuck, if you deny me access, I'll have no choice but to arrest you. Don't make me do that."

"You wouldn't arrest me." Chuck sneered at her. "Jim Parker is the criminal. Arrest him."

"Listen, Chuck. I don't like doing Safe Americans arrests, but I will. I can arrest you immediately. You need to know that denying access is an offence punishable by up to five years in prison."

"That ain't right."

While Gabby didn't disagree with Chuck's assessment, it didn't change the fact that she had no other options. "It's the law," she said. "And I'm here to enforce it."

"Goddamn it," he said, and stepped away from the door.

She watched him closely. He wasn't exactly welcoming her in with open arms, but at least he was complying. She felt her phone go off in her pocket. She ignored it and stepped inside, following Chuck into the living room.

"What are you looking for?" Chuck said.

"I'll know when I find it."

She glanced quickly around the room, which smelled like old

beer and stale cigarette smoke. The two armchairs were covered in a worn brown corduroy fabric, and old newspapers were piled everywhere. There were empty beer cans on the floor next to each chair. Someone had been drinking with Chuck here. On the coffee table, behind one of the opened cardboard boxes, was a cluster of small, metallic objects. They looked like long, thin silver matchsticks. She stepped past the boxes and bubble wrap for a closer look.

Each silver stick had a pair of clear plastic wings. There were four tiny legs that ended in soft tips, like microphone covers. They didn't exactly look like insects, as they had no heads, but she could see the resemblance. She picked one up. It was about two inches long, and the wingspan was maybe three inches.

"Careful," Chuck said behind her. "Those things are fragile."

"Are these your robot bees?"

"Yes."

"How many are there?"

"I got 200 total. Just to start."

"What are you going to do with them?"

"Put that Jim Parker out of business."

"Are these microphones on the legs?"

"No. Those are pollen distributors." He stepped closer. "See. These are the little tips the pollen sticks to."

She couldn't smell any alcohol on his breath. Surprisingly, he smelled like soap.

"These little guys move pollen from plant to plant, and also do buzz pollination," he said. He was like a man transformed, from one full of anger to one brimming with enthusiasm.

"Buzz pollination?"

"Bumblebees do it. They move their flight muscle real quick, without flapping their wings. Makes their body and the whole flower vibrate. Shakes loose pollen. Some plants do best with buzz pollination, like tomatoes. Honeybees don't do it. So, you see, these little drones are better than Jim Parker's old-fashioned bugs." He smiled triumphantly.

Gabby set down the tiny robot and took a step away from Chuck. He was several inches taller than her, and probably seventy pounds heavier.

"You really hate Jim Parker, don't you?"

Chuck seemed to consider the question, and as he did his anger returned. "I told you. That bastard killed my business."

"Some people say it was your own fault, because you couldn't keep your bees alive, and Jim could."

"Some people don't know what the hell they're talking about. Jim Parker is an arrogant prick. Thinks he knows things 'cause he's booksmart. I'd like to see him go down."

"What do you mean?"

His uneven nostrils flared. "Nothing."

Gabby nodded. "I'm just going to look around," she said, glancing past him toward what she presumed was the kitchen.

"You've seen enough." Chuck stepped in front of her and blocked her way.

She realized then that she shouldn't have mentioned Jim Parker again. People were like machines. If you pushed the wrong button, you got the wrong result. Now she gave Chuck the most compassionate look she possibly could and shook her head as a sympathetic warning. Her expression said: *You and I both know that we have to do this. Don't make it harder than it needs to be. You won't win.*

The big man stepped aside.

She walked through to the kitchen and opened a few cupboards and drawers. There was nothing unusual—just plates and bowls and silverware. In the fridge there were two large cases of beer. At the back of the kitchen, there was a laundry area that led to the back door.

Next, she searched his bedroom. He stood at the door and watched her. There were more newspapers stacked in the corners.

She opened each dresser drawer. In the nightstand she found an old M1911 pistol. Gabby knew her guns, and this one was pretty much an antique. It was a single-action, semi-automatic, magazine-fed, recoil-operated pistol.

"When was the last time you fired this?" she asked, pointing at the gun, taking care not to touch it.

"Long time. I keep it there for safety."

She was looking for something that would connect Chuck to the arson of Jim Parker's hives, and a gun was not that. She shut the drawer.

"Why do you save newspapers?" she asked.

"Seems like a waste to throw them away."

She walked over toward the double bed. It was unmade. She flipped up the edges of the sheets to get to the mattress and moved her hand along the side and underneath.

"What are you doing?" Chuck asked.

"Looking," Gabby said. She walked around to the other side and did the same there. She found three stacks of fifty-dollar bills lined up carefully between the box springs and the mattress, each with a paper currency strap on them marked "$5,000" in mustard-colored numbers.

"Chuck," she said. "That's 15,000 dollars. You should keep it in the bank. It's safer."

"None of your business where I keep my money. There's nothing illegal about keeping money at home."

"I've heard rumors you have money there."

"What? Under my mattress?"

"Yes."

"Who told you that?"

"Several people, actually. It's a bit of an open secret, it seems. Where did you get it?"

"It's my savings."

"Savings from what?"

"Working."

She considered this. It wasn't impossible that he'd been paid to torch Jim's hives.

"Well, if you won't put it in the bank, you should at least hide it somewhere better. People know you stash it there."

"A man's got no secrets on this island."

"Are you sure you didn't tell somebody about it, one night when you were drunk down at Coyote Kylie's?"

"I'd never tell that. Don't think so."

"Put it in the bank, Chuck."

She walked into the bathroom. Chuck followed her very close behind. When she turned around to look at him, he almost walked into her.

She automatically put her hand on her weapon, a 9mm Glock 17, as a reflex. "I need you to keep your distance."

"Why? Nervous?" He was goading her.

"Chuck, you will do what I say."

In other moments, when Gabby sat alone at home thinking about it, she figured that her control voice took its strength from something like a forceful yet charitable righteousness. She was right and she was powerful, and the other person was wrong and weak. The conviction in her voice made it so.

Even when she was sixteen, when dealing with her father, she could make her words come out with all the authority and command of an army sergeant. "Go to bed, now," she would tell him when he'd had too much to drink.

Her father was two men: overprotective when he was sober and deceitful when he was drunk. She knew, when she was being honest with herself, that it was probably her complicated relationship with that man that made her prone to distrust. She also knew that learning how to control her father had given her the upper hand in a lot of situations, especially with men like Chuck.

And it still worked. As her father had years before, Chuck listened to her now. He stepped back and put up his hands in a mock surrender.

She stepped into the bathroom. Here was the window she saw boarded up at the side of the house. She checked the medicine cabinet for any unusual drugs, but there was nothing but standard pain relievers and blood pressure medication.

"What's out back?" she asked.

"Nothing."

"Then you won't mind if I have a quick look," she said.

"Seems I couldn't stop you even if I tried."

"No, you can't."

She walked through the kitchen toward the back door and stopped when she saw a small mud room tucked away to the left of the door. There was a black metal gun safe standing in the corner. It was narrow and stood at about four feet tall.

"I'll need you to open that, please," she said.

"Nothing but my hunting gun."

She looked at him firmly.

He stepped into the small room and entered a combination on the number pad. The door swung open.

"Stand over there," she said, gesturing to the kitchen.

He did as he was told.

Inside the safe she found a Remington Model 1100.

"Deer gun," Chuck said from the kitchen. "12 gauge semi-automatic. It's got a rifled slug barrel. Quick point scope. Slug gun gives a cleaner kill."

"You've got only the one long gun?" she said.

"A man can only shoot one deer at a time."

"Thank you. Please shut it," she said, and she stepped out of the room.

A small clearing lay behind the cabin. The pines encircling it seemed to cluster closer behind the house, blocking out even more light. Chuck stepped out the back door behind her, but he was giving her space now, not trailing too closely behind.

To the left of the door there was a large, plastic water tank on a platform. It was connected to the roof to collect rainwater.

There was a big shed straight ahead. She walked over. It had double doors in front, secured shut with a padlock.

"What's in here?" she asked.

"Supplies."

She touched the lock. "Can you open it up, please?"

"You gonna open up my septic tank and look at my shit too?"

"I might. Now open this door."

Chuck pulled out some keys from his front pocket and unlocked the padlock. Then he pulled the doors open for her. "I suppose you want me to step away."

"Yes, thank you."

He took a few steps back.

Gabby walked forward into the shed. It was roughly nine by thirteen feet. Of course there were the usual things—a wheelbarrow, a chainsaw, a few shovels. But one entire half of the shed was full of plastic gas cans. They were red, square, five-gallon jerry containers, just like the one left behind at Bennett Orchards. There had to be twenty of them stacked on top of each other. She picked a few up, one at a time. They were full.

"That's a lot of gasoline," Gabby said. "What's it for?"

"Generator. I'm off-grid here. It's backup."

"It doesn't seem like you'd ever need this much gasoline," she said.

"Better safe than sorry."

Gabby looked around the shed. "Where's the generator?"

"Broken," Chuck said.

"But where is it?"

"Tom's." His eyes went shifty, looking everywhere but at her.

Tom's was the service station on the island.

"So, Tom is fixing it?" Gabby asked. She leaned into his view to get him to look at her.

He met her gaze. "Yes."

On the other side of the shed, there were ten or so more jerry cans, lying at odd angles on the floor.

"What did you use this gasoline for?" she asked, nodding towards the empty cans.

Chuck shrugged. "Generator."

"But your generator is broken."

Chuck paused. "A while back."

"What are these for?" she asked, gesturing toward a stack of green tarps. There must have been twenty of them.

"You know, covering firewood, dragging green waste, whatever. Always need a tarp for something."

"Was there anybody here last night with you, drinking that beer? There were cans by both armchairs."

"Nope."

She looked around the shed again. The equipment was here. She had probable cause.

The Safe Americans Act also terminated the need for an arrest warrant. In the past, she would have had to present the facts surrounding a case to a judge, who would determine if enough probable cause existed to issue an arrest warrant. Now law enforcement officers were able to make an immediate arrest—in public or in the home.

"Chuck Norman, I'm arresting you on suspicion of arson."

"Goddamn it," Chuck said. "The gasoline is for my generator. I didn't burn Jim's hives. I wouldn't do that."

She took out her handcuffs and cuffed him, searching for any concealed weapons or drugs, before leading him out front to her SUV. She was grateful that he didn't resist.

## 11

LESS THAN A MILE away from Chuck Norman's house, on the island's eastern shore—where luxury homes commanded expensive views of Lake Michigan—Lewis Wilson was listening to encrypted police radio communications through his home computer.

His rented house was a labyrinth of glass, steel, and concrete just above the steep precipice of Jason's Bluff. Waves crashed onto the rocks below. It was just a ten-minute drive to the Hadley Agritech Research Station from here. It was good to be close to work. Sometimes he needed to go into the lab at odd hours.

The first time Lewis saw this place, he thought it looked like something that, as a child, he never imagined himself being able to have. It looked like a place where rich white people lived. Yet he knew it was something he deserved. He signed the lease immediately.

This morning he was working from home, reviewing some recent research findings. His desk was positioned to look out the picture windows onto the blue expanse of Lake Michigan. There was not much else in the room. On the desk, to the right of the computer, there was a single photograph.

For most of the morning, nothing of any particular interest had come across the police radio. It was mostly just mainland Michigan activity. A traffic stop in Petoskey. Bored youths vandalizing a sign in Boyne City. But about an hour ago, something extremely compelling had come up. Deputy Gabby had signaled to dispatch that she was headed to Chuck Norman's. She went so far as to refer to him as a possible suspect in the arson of Jim Parker's beehives.

At various times in the past, Lewis had wondered if this decryption system had been worth it. On days like today, however, the illegal purchase clearly provided a significant return on investment. It had not been easy to secure.

The radio came to life again.

"Dispatch? Squad 48 here." It was Deputy Gabby.

"Go ahead," a young man from Central Dispatch responded.

"I've arrested Chuck Norman on suspicion of arson. Transporting suspect to the station."

"Roger that, Squad 48."

Lewis froze. He couldn't believe his ears. He felt conflicted—both relieved and guilty.

He looked at the photograph on his desk. It reminded him of why he did absolutely everything. In it his mother, a tired looking Black woman, was wrapping her arms around her two young boys. She was clearly exhausted as always, but she was never too tired for hugs. The boy on the left was his younger brother, Lamar. The one on the right was Lewis himself. His mother and brother were smiling—Lamar with his boyish grin and his mother with her chipped front tooth. Only Lewis was serious. He'd always been serious. Even then, at the age of eight.

Growing up, Lewis had watched with consternation the way his mother struggled to provide for her boys. Every year she found it harder and harder to feed them. The cost of fruits and vegetables went up all the time. Living in public housing in New York City, their cramped East Harlem kitchen never had any of the foods that relied on honeybee pollination—things like apples, carrots, or cucumbers. His mother could only provide what she could afford—breads, cereals, pasta, cakes, and donuts.

It was amazing, he thought, even now, that it all came down to the bees. Of course wheat, sugar cane, and sugar beet didn't need bees for pollination. Like many children whose families could not afford pollinated foods, Lewis and his brother had been raised on a diet of junk food. He still remembered the year that he and Lamar each got an orange for Christmas. He was twelve, and it had been like receiving a mythical treasure. Of course there were stories about children receiving a single orange as a Christmas gift back in the early twentieth century. Things were slipping backwards, it seemed.

The world, Lewis believed, had at some point turned cruel. Growing up in the middle of one of the wealthiest nations in the world, he and his brother had gone wanting. Did anybody try to help his mother when she struggled to feed her boys? Did anybody try to save his little family—or the countless others like them—from hunger and poverty and poor nutrition? No. They did not. As the world's food supply had become increasingly threatened due to the death of bees and other pollinators, it seemed to Lewis that humanity's natural selfishness had been exacerbated.

This was the motivation for his work. His intelligence had brought him here, along with the academic scholarships that opened up doors otherwise closed to a poor, Black kid in East Harlem. He'd worked hard to get where he was, and when he'd come to Gull Island to accept the role of Head of Pollination & Apiculture Research, he finally felt like he could make a difference.

Solving the Global Bee Crisis had long been his life's ambition. Doing so would not only secure the world's food supply, but it would help struggling single mothers like his own. She was gone now, although technically still alive. And while it was too late for her, he never wanted another mother to struggle with feeding her children.

Lately, however, he had become worried. The ultimate success of Project Defender, which had once seemed so close, now felt very far away. It was entirely possible that one stupid mistake from a junior member of staff could lead to his undoing. It seemed deeply unfair.

From now on, he would have to be even more vigilant.

12

"AVA, FOOD'S READY!" Jim called out from the kitchen for a second time. "Hurry or the eggs will get cold."

A faint response finally came from her bedroom. "Coming."

He went out the back door and walked over to the old picnic table, where he placed the tortillas in the center and sat down. He'd already laid out bowls with all the ingredients. He'd chopped up tomatoes, onions, and cilantro for the fresh salsa and squeezed in lime juice. He'd grated the cheddar, made the fresh guacamole with just the right amount of garlic and tabasco, warmed the tortillas in the oven, and carefully scrambled the eggs until they were light and creamy.

Now, as he waited for Ava, he made up two breakfast tacos—one for her and one for himself.

She came out a few minutes later wearing the shorts and tank top she often slept in. Bailey followed. She sat down in moody silence. As always, her phone was seemingly glued to her hand, and her purple hair was a mess. He wanted to say something about the fact that it was 10:30 in the morning and she wasn't even dressed yet, but he held his tongue. For this moment, now, over a meal she loved, he just wanted them to get along.

They sat facing each other like two strangers. Bailey sniffed the grass nearby. Ava barely managed to mumble a thank you.

He tried hard to make conversation. He finally told her about the arson that morning, but she'd already started checking her phone and was only half listening. She didn't seem to understand how serious it was.

Then he told her that he'd bought some surveillance cameras in town, for the home hives. "Do you want to help me install them after we eat?" he asked.

Her answer was short and sharp. "No."

He wasn't surprised. He tried mentioning how Emmett Jones was missing, trying to pique her attention. He told her how something had come in from the woods and made a mess of Emmett's garage.

Ava shook her head. "He's probably fine."

"Yeah. Probably. But I had a weird feeling. Like someone had been in his house. This is why I lock the doors when I leave you at home alone, Ava." He took a deep breath, thinking of how she was always forgetting to keep them locked. "This also is why I made the rules about your bedroom window."

She rolled her eyes. "Oh, right. I forgot. A boogeyman lurks around every corner."

"No, but the world *is* a dangerous place."

She sighed and went back to her phone.

"Ava, please put that phone away," he said. "I'm trying to have a conversation with you. You're being rude."

She moaned dramatically and shoved the phone down onto the bench at her side.

Ava seemed even more distracted and troubled than usual. It was as though there was something heavy on her mind that she wasn't sharing.

"Is anything wrong?" he asked. "Talk to me."

"I'm fine." She pulled open the taco he'd made for her and started picking at the salsa.

"How's everything with Eddie?"

Jim didn't much like Ava's choice of boyfriend, and he was secretly hoping they'd broken up. Sarah wouldn't have liked Eddie either, he was certain. Of course, he wanted Ava to find a good man someday, but not now. She was too young. She could settle down later, after college, and eventually have a family of her own. He looked forward to being a grandfather eventually. But all of that, fortunately, was very far away.

"I haven't heard from Eddie in a week," she said.

There it was, Jim thought. This was the reason she was so moody.

"I'm sorry, honey," he said. "But that's not really that long, is it?"

Ava rolled her eyes yet again. "Dad, we talk every single day. Multiple times. And we message each other constantly."

"Why didn't you say anything? Did you have an argument?"

"Sort of."

"What was it about?"

She shrugged. "Nothing. He said he was going hunting. His family has an old hunting cabin in the End Woods. Now it's been a week."

"I'm sure it's okay," Jim said. "He's hunting. That's all."

Why anyone would want to spend a week hunting was beyond Jim, and in his mind, this was somehow another strike against Eddie. Some might say Jim was a failed hunter. His father had tried to teach him everything he knew, but from a young age Jim had always been much more interested in studying animals than shooting them. His father had been horribly disappointed.

"Yeah, it's fine," Ava said, still picking at the salsa.

"Don't you like the salsa?" he said.

"Tastes like soap."

"Soap?"

"The cilantro," she said.

"You've always loved my breakfast tacos. They've always had cilantro."

She shrugged. "Just saying."

"Okay. Well, next time I'll leave the cilantro on the side."

Jim realized that he was trying too hard to make conversation, so he quit talking. If they sat in silence, maybe eventually his daughter would open up. For the next few minutes, as she continued to pick at her food, neither of them said a word.

It was during this silence that he noticed the bracelet she always wore on her wrist had been tampered with. He couldn't believe it. It wasn't just any bracelet. And now she'd ruined it.

"What did you do to your bracelet?" he asked.

"Took it apart and rewired the beads," she said, shrugging again. She was constantly shrugging, as though nothing mattered to her at all.

Her mother had given her that bracelet when she was eleven, on a family trip to California. The official reason for the trip was to visit Disneyland, but Jim had also wanted to see California's almond pollination. It was the largest managed pollination event on the planet. He'd read for years about the masses of bees trucked in from around the country.

Sarah had agreed to visit the almond farms only when he promised it would be a brief add-on at the end of the trip. He planned the vacation for mid-February, to line up with the almond pollination. After spending nearly a week at Disneyland, he dragged Sarah and Ava with him on his pilgrimage to California's Central Valley.

Ava hadn't wanted to leave Disneyland to go see a bunch of bees, and Sarah had promised her she'd buy her a present if she went and was good. He remembered how the three of them had stood in the middle of a huge almond farm on a sunny afternoon, absolutely astounded. Blossoming trees made pink rows for miles and miles. There were massive numbers of hives scattered throughout.

Much to Jim's surprise and happiness, Ava was as completely taken with the scene as he and Sarah were. She stood between them and looked out, flabbergasted, and said, "Papa, all the trees are pink. So many bees!" She reached up and took his hand on one side and Sarah's on the other. Sarah looked over to him and said, "Thank you for bringing us here. You're right. It's amazing. I love you for being such a bee nerd."

Later that afternoon they'd stopped at a tourist shop, and Sarah picked out the bracelet for Ava. It was made of black rawhide with silver alphabet beads that spelled out the word CALIFORNIA. "To remember our trip," Sarah had said. Ava wore it non-stop for a year after that. In the move to Gull Island, she'd come across it again in her keepsake box, and she'd been wearing it ever since.

But now, Jim saw, the bracelet was different. The black rawhide was gone, replaced by a thick, black wire. More surprisingly, Ava had rearranged the beaded letters and eliminated some. The silver beads now spelled out the words "CIAO LIAR" with a single black bead between the two words as a space.

"Why did you do that?" he asked, taken aback. "Why did you make it say that?"

"I wanted to."

"But your mother gave you that."

She reached over and began fiddling with the beads. "It's true."

"What do you mean?"

"Well, Mom's gone, isn't she?"

An incredible sadness overtook him. "Does it feel like Mom was a liar?"

"She used to say all the time that she'd always be here for me." Ava looked up at him with a cold, hard stare. "She's not."

"Ava, no."

"It's my bracelet. I can do whatever I want with it."

Jim felt like he'd been stabbed in the heart. "Your mother didn't abandon you."

"She was here and now she's not," Ava said, pulling her hand away from the bracelet and staring at her plate. "And she said she would be." She shrugged. "It's pretty simple."

"But it's not her fault."

She picked up her fork and began moving food around. Then suddenly she looked back up at him and said, "Dad, I want to ask you something. I really want to start running."

"What?" He couldn't believe she was saying this.

"These roads would be good for it." She gestured briefly toward the house and Reserve Road beyond.

His chest tightened. "Are you kidding? No. No way."

She didn't seem to register his response, just continued casually picking at bits of cilantro, as though she hadn't asked anything of any consequence.

"This place is safe," she said, as if responding to her own question. "I can go running here."

"You're not going running." He spoke more firmly this time. Why would Ava ask this now, especially just after talking about Sarah?

Ava locked eyes with him. "Dad, it's normal. I'm almost eighteen. I want to go running. That's all. No big deal."

"Do something else," he said. His chest was tightening. He felt like he was losing control. "A team sport. Join the girls' softball team, like I was trying to get you to do when we moved here. Do that finally. Or soccer. Anything. Not running. Not by yourself. Absolutely not." He could hear his voice becoming strained.

"You say I spend too much time in my room. Well, I'd like to do this. You should be happy I want to go outside."

Jim's mind was reeling. She was pushing hard. How could she think this was a good idea? That night in Ann Arbor remained lodged in his brain like a shard of glass. His last image of her. Sarah coming down the stairs.

Looking across the picnic table at Ava now, meeting her gaze head-on, he completely lost his temper. He wanted this moment and this conversation to stop. He began to shout. "I said no! No! That's the end of this conversation! No!"

Ava slammed her hands onto the table. She stood up, leaned forward, and screamed directly into his face. "Just because it happened to Mom doesn't mean it's going to happen to me! You can't lock me up like a fucking prisoner!"

"Watch your mouth!" he yelled back.

She paused then, and she sneered. He'd never seen her do it before, but she actually *sneered* at him. Then she looked down at her plate again, where her taco lay only half eaten, cilantro pushed to the side. With a powerful swing, she smacked the plate so hard that it went hurtling off toward the edge of the woods. Food flew through the air.

"Avaaaa!"

Her name came out sounding like the howl of a wild animal. Even as he screamed at her—at the one person in the world he loved more than anything—he knew that he shouldn't be doing it, that he should be responding like a wise parent instead of a raging madman. It felt almost as though he was above himself, watching it all unfold, as if he wasn't actually doing any of this himself. It was just happening. His memories were torturing him, pushing him in ways that he could not control.

Ava's face was full of tears. She turned and stormed into the house, leaving him alone at the table. He sat there stunned, feeling shaken, staring at the yellow eggs and red salsa strewn across the green, green grass.

13

JIM WALKED over to his beehives. He didn't even pick up Ava's plate off the ground. He just went to the far back corner of the property and stood in silence in front of his eight home hives. There were few things in the world that gave him the solace that watching bees did, and he needed that now.

The wooden bee boxes were painted in random colors—light green, pale blue, soft yellow. He'd placed them on the western boundary to catch the morning sun. Behind them, the white pines, red pines, and red maples of the End Woods loomed overhead.

The bees came and went. Everything was fine. He tried not to think of Sarah, of her coming down the stairs, of the last time he saw her. He tried not to think of that small room with the scratched white table. He stepped away from his feelings, from his memories, and he allowed himself to become lost in a state of observation.

He looked closely at the nearest hive.

Large numbers of bees were alighting on the landing board and crawling into the entrance gap at the base. Their pollen baskets, on the outside of their hind legs, were packed with big bulbs of yellow. Other bees, emerging from the darkness inside the hive, were stepping into the late morning sunlight before taking flight to forage. He watched their flight path. They were heading north, into the trees, deep into the End Woods.

It was the sacred order of the hive that soothed him most of all. They all had their part. The queen laid the eggs, and the worker bees, all female, were wonderfully productive—building honeycomb, foraging for nectar and pollen, and nursing the larvae. The male drones served their own singular purpose, which was to impregnate the queen. Together they made one miraculous and harmonious superorganism.

He felt his heart rate slowing. Even after so many years of studying and caring for honeybees, he still found magic in them. They were almost supernatural.

Then he saw something strange. There was a peculiar bee. It was just a flash, but it caught his attention. The color was off. The bees shifted, and it was gone. He stepped closer.

He didn't have his beekeeper's veil, but he was at ease. He wasn't here to open the hives. He was still wearing the shorts and t-shirt he'd thrown on earlier that morning, and periodically he felt bees bumping against his bare arms and legs. He stayed out of their direct flight path. He knew how to avoid making his bees feel threatened.

A long time ago, he'd learned that the most important skill he could possess as a beekeeper was the art of being calm and gentle. He wished he could do the same around his daughter.

Sarah had been wearing her running clothes, that evening when she came down the stairs. He remembered how the narrow back staircase came down directly into the kitchen. The house was a rambling, historic Queen Anne Victorian, on a safe and tree-lined avenue known as Professor's Row, just a few blocks from campus.

"I'm going for a run," she'd said.

He was at the kitchen counter preparing a marinade for the chicken. He turned to look just as she was coming down the last few steps. Her long, blonde hair was pulled back in a sloppy pony-tail. She was wearing the old white t-shirt she always ran in. Threads were coming loose around the neck. She smiled at him, and he admired the beauty in her disheveled, slightly disorganized look.

He didn't know that it was the last time he'd see her. If he'd known he would have paused, taken it in more, told her that he loved her. Instead he turned back to the counter and said, "But I'm starting dinner."

She came over and wrapped her arms around him, hugging him from behind. "Ooh, is that your good chicken?"

"Maybe, maybe not." He smiled, but he didn't turn around.

"You haven't even started marinating it yet," she said, poking his side. "I'll be back in forty-five minutes. I'm just running to the river and back."

And then he heard her head out the front door. He didn't even turn around. The screen door clacked behind her, and she was gone.

He pushed it away now, trying desperately to focus again on his hives. Even after all this time—three years now—it hurt too much to remember. He'd rather think about his bees.

A few of those bees landed on his arm now. He didn't mind. If the hive ever felt threatened by his presence, they would warn him. Their hum would change. Their flight would grow erratic. He'd have time to change his behavior, do something different, move away.

Wait. There was that strange bee, at the entrance to the nearest hive. He moved forward. It looked almost gray. Was it sick? Color could be a sign of disease. Sacbrood virus caused larvae to change color from pearly white to pale yellow. But shortly after he spotted it, another cluster of bees moved and the strange bee was gone again.

He could stand here for hours. There was so much he loved about bees—the way they worked together, the way they communicated. They used pheromones, like wasps did. He'd used his MacArthur Fellowship to study it. The pheromones were chemical signals that conveyed nearly all aspects of colony life. There were alarm pheromones, brood recognition pheromones, drone pheromones, and even egg-marking pheromones. The queen's mandibular gland produced a particularly important pheromone which helped regulate the entire hive.

They also used dance to communicate. It was how they shared information on best spots to find nectar and pollen. They could see polarized light, and that was how they oriented themselves. Then they used that information in a dance, called the waggle dance. They relied on the lines of the honeycomb to indicate the direction of the sun. So many tiny miracles were contained inside a beehive.

He looked closely at the hive entrance and the landing board there. Landing boards provided a bit of a landing pad for the bees, just in front of the hive entrance. These were Langstroth hives, the stacked bee boxes that contained vertically hung frames for brood and honey. The lowest box was for the queen to lay eggs in, and the top boxes were for storing honey. A queen excluder, which was a kind of grid placed between the boxes, stopped the larger queen from entering the top boxes and laying eggs among the honey.

And there it was again—on the landing board. The strange bee was lurking there. Or was it a second one? It was definitely gray. This wasn't normal. He moved forward to watch, but the bee moved and was quickly gone.

He was holding his breath without even thinking of it, as he looked for the gray bee. He turned away to breathe out—human breath stirred bees to attack—and then looked back.

At the entrance, guard bees were inspecting the foragers that had landed at the entrance, using their antennae to recognize nestmates and reject strangers. The hive was working as it should. Here was the order, the harmony that he loved and admired.

He stepped forward slowly, just a bit more, to get a better look. Yes. One of the bees was almost entirely gray. It had dark-to-light striations, but instead of multiple stripes encircling the abdomen, two black stripes ran lengthwise down either side of the body.

It didn't look sick. Perhaps it was an intruder. The guard bees didn't seem to care that it was there, which was odd if it was an intruder. He tried to think of a reasonable explanation for such a peculiar bee being accepted into the hive. Newly emerged bees could appear very light until their exoskeleton hardened, but this wasn't that. This looked like a different species altogether. He took out his phone and quickly took pictures of it.

He started to feel worried about the hive. What was happening here? He thought of other gray bees—*Andrena cineraria,* the ashy mining bee, or *Colletes compactus,* the cellophane bee. But those were both solitary, ground-nesting species. Neither would ever be accepted into a hive of *Apis mellifera.* And besides, the striations on this gray bee were all wrong for those species.

He was absolutely dumbfounded. What was going on?

## 14

THE LANDLINE RANG as Jim was doing the dishes. Ava had been sulking in her room ever since she'd stormed off. He'd wanted to reprimand her for throwing her plate, but his own behavior hadn't exactly been stellar either. Instead, he was giving her space.

When he picked up the phone, Minnie O'Donnell's voice came down the line, thin and feeble but very sweet.

"Well, hi there, Jim. I hope I'm not bothering you."

He hated taking phone calls, but he didn't mind hearing from Minnie. She reminded him of his own cookie-baking grandmother who had long since passed away. The ghosts of the dead surrounded Jim.

"You're not bothering me at all, Minnie. How are you?"

"Oh, I'm okay, I suppose," she said. "But I wonder if I could get your help. Something keeps getting into my garden. It comes at night, you see. It's going after my cantaloupes. I love those melons. Thank goodness I no longer have to hand pollinate them, since you have honeybee hives nearby. I won a prize for them one year, you know. When are you going to get some bumblebees? I'm tired of hand pollinating my tomatoes, Jim."

Jim smiled. "I'll get on that."

Although Minnie was becoming increasingly frail at eighty-four, Jim knew she refused to give up the things she loved—her bridge playing, her quilting, her Sunday mornings at church in Saint Peter, and most of all, her garden. The week he and Ava had moved in, Minnie had appeared on their porch with a basket of vegetables she'd grown herself. When Jim learned she was a widow and her children had moved away, he'd offered to help her out whenever she needed it.

"It's probably a coyote," he said to her now.

"No, no," Minnie responded. "I've seen it in the evening. It's bigger than a coyote. It climbs over the fence."

"Then you need coyote rollers. I've got them on my garden fence. They're good."

"But it's no coyote, Jim," she said, sounding very sure of herself. "It's bigger, but it's not a deer. I saw it, you see."

If an animal was getting into Minnie's garden, and it was getting over her fence, it was most likely a coyote.

"How dark was it," he asked, "when you saw it?"

"Dark."

"So, maybe you didn't see it very well?"

"Oh, I don't know. Possibly." Her confidence seemed to crumble. "Do you think coyotes could climb my fence?"

He remembered his own problems with coyotes. "Well, they were getting over my fence, and it's seven feet high. I'll come over and measure it up. I'm happy to install rollers for you."

"Well, maybe you could just come over and take a look, Jim. Thank you. You're very good to me."

When he reached Minnie's house, she came to the door smiling. Her flair for showy, hand-decorated sweatshirts always seemed at odds with her otherwise unassuming appearance. She kept her gray hair in a short, plain style, and she usually wore modest, khaki slacks. Today her bright, fuchsia sweatshirt was covered with butterflies, flowers, and purple sparkles spelling out the word *Blessed*.

"Oh, thank you for coming, Jim," she said. "You're my own private angel, with a tape measure."

He laughed and raised the large yellow tape measure in his hand.

"Just like Albert used to have," she said. "I was just going to make a pot of tea. Would you like to sit down with me?"

"I'm sorry, Minnie. I have to get back home and finish up a job this afternoon. Do you mind if we go straight to your garden?"

He felt a small pang of guilt for saying no, but Minnie nodded and smiled graciously.

"Oh, that would be fine," she said.

They walked past the dining table to a set of sliding doors at the back of the house. When she led Jim out onto the deck, she paused and raised her eyes to the trees. The sun was almost directly overhead now, and the canopy appeared bright green while the shadows below were thick.

Like the handful of other properties on the north side of Reserve Road, Minnie's property backed up against the End Woods. The trees seemed to encircle her house.

"You know, even after all these years I still love this view. *The woods are lovely, dark and deep*, the poet said."

Jim nodded. He knew that poem, and he'd always loved it. "Stopping by Woods on a Snowy Evening" by Robert Frost. The fact that Minnie was quoting it made him like her even more.

She looked over to him. "I'll tell you one thing, Jim Parker. I want to die on this property."

"Well, hopefully that won't be for some time."

"Whenever God decides to call me home to be with Albert. I know I've had a good life, in a beautiful place." She turned to Jim and gave him a grin. "My kids get so upset when I talk like that."

She quickly walked across the deck, down a few steps, and over to her large garden, which was surrounded by a cyclone fence slightly taller than Jim's.

"I've been keeping the gate locked to try and keep that darned animal out," she said, reaching for the key, which was on a chain around her neck. "I swear it opened up the gate itself one night, before I locked it up. Just look at those poor melons."

At the back corner, a sprawling garden bed was full of broken and half-eaten cantaloupes. The other beds all seemed fine. Minnie's rows of spinach, lettuce, and zucchini were still tidy. The tomatoes were carefully staked, and at the back stood a few lines of perfectly grown broccoli and cabbage.

Jim leaned down and inspected the melons, running his finger across the textured beige skin. He saw what had to be teeth marks, but it almost looked as if someone had scraped the outside of the melons with the edge of a serrated knife. In some areas, the knife had cut right through.

"These teeth marks don't actually look like they came from a coyote."

"See? I told you, it's not a coyote. The thing is, well, I didn't quite tell you what I saw."

"What did you see?" Jim looked up at her.

She seemed to be hesitating, then she said, "You'll just think I'm a batty old lady. Even my own daughter, God bless her, just this morning on the phone from Chicago, she told me I was crazy."

"I promise I won't think that," he said, then smiled. "Or, at least I won't say it to your face."

"Oh, well, that's much better. Can you give my daughter some tips?" She laughed. "But you see, Jim, it's just, well, it's clearly bigger than a coyote."

"How much bigger?"

She started playing nervously with the key around her neck. "Now, I know bears can be big, but of course there are no bears on the island, and this was definitely not a bear. It didn't move like a bear, you see."

"Was it a person?" he asked.

Minnie turned and looked at him closely, as though studying him for any sign that he might actually think she was crazy. "It was as big as a man," she said, her voice full of conviction. "But it's definitely not human. It moves strangely. I know I sound bonkers, but I saw what I saw. Ears that hear and eyes that see, the good Lord made them both. And my ears and eyes work perfectly fine, thank you very much."

"But you said it was dark when you saw it, right?"

"Yes, yes. But not so dark as to hide the general size and shape of it."

Jim looked off toward the woods, wondering exactly what she had she seen.

"You've lived here longer than me," he said, turning back to her. "So you know better than I do that it's coyotes that get into people's gardens, especially up at this end of the island, along the End Woods."

"Yes, that's very true."

"But then again, these just don't look like coyote bites."

Minnie sighed. "Well, whatever it is, do you still think coyote rollers will stop it from climbing over?"

He nodded. "It's your best bet."

"I just wish I knew what it was," she said. "I'm telling you, it comes out of the woods. It's big. Like a person. It always comes at dusk, and it moves in a very peculiar way. It looks like Satan."

Jim gave her another smile. "Minnie, I don't think Satan is breaking into your garden to eat your melons."

"Okay, so maybe it's not Satan." She smiled back. "That would be most unfortunate."

He laughed out loud now. "Yes, if Satan is eating your cantaloupes, you're going to need something more powerful than coyote rollers."

She stifled a laugh and started playing with her key again. "But it does move strangely, Jim. It's not right. You might not believe me, but I've been sitting at that dining table every single evening, right next to that sliding glass door, waiting for it. And I see what I see."

Jim looked up to the house and back at the garden. It wasn't far. She would definitely have a clear view.

"Do you believe me?" she asked.

He looked at the woods. Those trees could cast incredibly long shadows in the evening. Minnie was in her mid-eighties. In spite of what she said, it was highly likely that her eyesight was beginning to fail her. "Well, yes, I believe you," he said. "But also, sometimes when the light fades, our eyes can play tricks on us."

"So you do think I'm losing my marbles." She looked away.

"Actually, I think you're as sharp as a tack. But what you're saying just doesn't make sense." He glanced up at the top of the fence. "Listen, I know Bob has a stack of coyote rollers in stock. I saw them just this morning. I'll pick some up and come back to install them for you. That should help."

She nodded. "How much do you think they'll be? It's just. I'm on a fixed income, so I have to be careful."

"Don't worry about it. I'll take care of it."

"Jim, you can't."

"Please allow me."

"No. I won't have it."

"Minnie, my grandmother's gone, and so are both my parents. I'd like to help. Please give me that. Let me help."

She sighed. "You're really too kind to me, Jim Parker. I appreciate it greatly."

It made him happy to be able to help her. He knew she didn't have a lot of money, and in a way he felt like she was a kindred spirit. The chances were that he'd be just like her in another forty years, living alone here at the edge of the End Woods, weak with age, partner dead, daughter moved away. It felt like looking at his own future, and he hoped somebody would be around to help him when he needed it. He immediately started measuring up the length of the fence.

"When can I come back?" he asked, walking along and drawing out his tape measure.

"Let me see. Tomorrow I have bridge and Thursday I've got my quilt guild. But if you come Friday morning, I'll make blueberry muffins to thank you. How's that sound?"

"Who could refuse that? Friday morning it is."

Jim was at the far end of the fence when he saw a single footprint on the ground. He stopped and looked down.

"Minnie, do you garden barefoot?"

"No. Why?"

He pointed at an imprint in the dirt. "It looks like someone was here."

She came over. "Well, I do sometimes run outside barefoot in the morning to get tomatoes for my toast. I do like a fresh tomato on my toast. So it could have been me."

Jim began studying the footprint. He set down the tape measure, bent down, and looked at it more closely. It was definitely from someone barefoot. He looked over at Minnie's feet. They were too small to have made this. Could hooligans have vandalized her cantaloupes for sport? It seemed unlikely. Could a barefoot man really have entered her garden? It might be connected to what he'd seen over at Emmett's.

As he looked more closely, one particular detail began to trouble him even more. There was something odd about this footprint. It looked like it came from a man, but there were other marks. In front of each toe, there was some sort of indentation in the dirt. It reminded him of the points made by the claws on bear tracks. Surely he was reading it wrong.

Sometimes tracks could be misleading. This could be two footprints together, one on top of the other. Or it might even be crafted—someone playing in the dirt with an intention to deceive. He imagined bored local kids playing a trick on an old woman who went to church and wore sweatshirts that said "Blessed." Perhaps they were pretending to be the devil in order to scare her. After all, there wasn't much to do for entertainment on the island.

He reached for his mobile phone to take a picture of the footprint, but it wasn't in his pocket. He must have left it in the car. His hatred of phones extended to his mobile, and he was always leaving it behind and forgetting to put it on the charging pad at night.

"Jim? Are you sure you won't join me for a cup of tea?"

"Sorry," he said, looking back up at her. "I'm afraid not. Thank you. I have to install some video equipment this afternoon. I need to get back."

"Well, of course. Next time. You're such a dear. I do hope those coyote rollers can save my garden. Thank you. You'll come back on Friday, and I'll make blueberry muffins. I do like our chats over a cup of tea."

"Yes, me too. Next time." He took one more look at the footprint. It bothered him. If this was a prank, then how far would they go to scare her? If it wasn't a joke, well, that possibility worried him more. "Listen, Minnie. Until we know exactly what's getting into your garden, you should probably just stay inside at night."

"Oh. Okay."

He didn't want to trouble her, but he felt he had to say it. "And you might just want to make sure you lock your doors at night. Until we know what it is."

"Now you're actually scaring me, Jim."

"No reason to be afraid. Just a precaution."

"Oh, well, if you say so, Jim."

As he drove down her driveway and back to his own house, he had a strange, sinking feeling. Something wasn't right at all.

15

WHEN HER DAD hollered out that he was going to visit the old lady down the road, Ava had mumbled her response from her bed. She'd been hiding in her room with the door shut ever since their fight earlier. She felt bad for losing her temper. If only her mom were still around. Her mom would know how to smooth things over and make everything okay.

There were two things her mom used to say to her all the time, and she remembered them clearly, like small inheritances. The first one was *I'll always be here for you*, which clearly had turned out to be a lie. The second one hadn't been a lie. Quite the opposite; her mom's death had made it even more true.

*You have to be strong, Ava.*

Since coming to Gull Island, Ava had been trying hard to take solace in that phrase. Her mom said it whenever she'd fallen off her bike, or failed a test, or had a bad day, and even that time she broke her arm falling out of a tree and it hurt so much.

*You have to be strong, Avey Bavey. Be strong.*

Ava had always been proud of her mom. Sure, there were plenty of other kids in Ann Arbor who had professors for parents, but her mom was special. She taught courses on social change.

She was making the world a better place. That woman had so much enthusiasm and optimism that it was hard to imagine her ever giving up on anything. The Window Cop, on the other hand, had done exactly that when he decided they should move to this place. He'd given up. He'd turned his back on the world. He'd built himself a wall and was trying hard to shut everything out.

As far as Ava could tell, most days all her dad did was drive around checking his hives. He dealt with farmers only when he absolutely had to. He had no friends. He didn't go out and drink with his buddies, not that he had any to hang out with, that is. He walked alone in the woods. He sat at home in the evenings and read about bees, or he sat at the fire pit and drank beer by himself. It was tragic.

Ava was the opposite. She wanted a lot out of her life—a lot more than this tiny island could ever give her—but she had absolutely no idea how to get it. She felt trapped.

The air in her room was stifling. She glared at the nailed-up window and kicked away the bedsheets. Bailey grumbled.

Could she follow her mom's path? Could she work to make the world better like her mom did? She had no idea, but she knew that what she wanted was big. It was just around the corner, just beyond what she could see right now. She couldn't have a baby. Not now. It would stop her from escaping, from having a big life. She wasn't ready to get married and sit at home and be a mother.

What would her mom have told her to do about Eddie? About the fact that her period was two weeks late? About her future? About everything? There was no way in the world she could talk to the Window Cop about any of that.

With her mom, there had never been the need to hide a thing. Even the first time Ava had kissed a boy, she'd confided in her. She was thirteen. The boy was a couple of years older and had pushed her to do more. Ava refused. Her mom had responded calmly, first asking about the boy, and then quietly talking to her about consent, about how to avoid dangerous situations. While it did feel like bringing up the subject had allowed the floodgates to open, for her mom to surge into her pre-prepared talk about safe sex and birth control, there had been absolutely no judgement at all. Sure, her mom got a little teary and hugged her a lot, but that was it. The Window Cop would have freaked out.

Ava knew, however, that her mom would be disappointed with her today. She sat up in bed and pulled out her journal, trying to figure out how to write about what she'd done, and everything that had happened afterwards with Eddie. It was such a tiny thing, one small mistake, but the consequences were enormous.

She'd agreed to do what Eddie wanted, to have sex without a condom. They'd both been drinking in his car. There were no more condoms in the glove box. At the time, she convinced herself that it would be okay, that Eddie would pull out and it would all be fine. But that wasn't exactly what had happened. Maybe Eddie had pressured her a little. She'd recently moved Eddie up above Bailey in her gratitude list, to the number one slot. Nobody but Bailey had ever been at number one before that. Maybe it had confused her.

Regardless, she knew now that not using a condom had been a dumb move. But here she was. And she had to be strong. She'd told Eddie about it exactly a week ago today, at Potts Bay while they were watching the sunset. That conversation hadn't quite gone the way she expected.

She remembered how good Eddie had looked in the golden light, sitting there beside her in the front seat of his Ford Mustang. His solid football player's build was always a kind of comfort to her, like something you could lean on. The disheveled mess of his sandy brown hair was catching the rays of the sun.

They'd just come back from walking along the dunes. Eddie knew she liked beach pea, which grew there—clusters of purple and magenta pea flowers that sprouted on a long stalk. He'd reached down and picked her some, even though you weren't supposed to touch beach pea since it was endangered. To Ava, the act was both rebellious and caring. She'd loved it.

Back in the car, she held those flowers tightly in one hand. Eddie held her other. Through the windshield, she watched as the sky and water started changing, turning to an intense orange with bursts of red. In that moment, it felt like the world was full of so much beauty that nothing bad could ever happen.

She'd been trying to figure out how to tell him for days. She had no idea how he'd respond, and she wanted to tell him the right way—a way that would make him respond calmly. Sometimes, she knew, he could shut down, and she didn't want him to do that. In the end, however, in spite of her planning, the words burst forward like unexpected vomit.

"I'm pregnant."

He said absolutely nothing. He shifted uncomfortably in the driver's seat.

She waited, nervous, palms sweating. There was a long and terrible silence. Her heart beat wildly in her chest.

Finally he said, "Are you sure?" His voice was clipped and short.

"My period is late. Last night I took a pregnancy test I got from the drug store. Mrs. Carter sold it to me. I hope she keeps her mouth shut." She felt herself rambling. It was as though his silence was somehow causing her to spew up more words.

He just stared out at the water blankly. Then he let go of her hand.

Suddenly she felt like she was sitting there alone. Yes. Here it was. He was shutting down. He was pulling away. The last time this happened it lasted for weeks.

"This sunset is amazing," he said, again with that shortness to his voice. He sounded like a robot.

"Did you hear what I just said to you?"

He nodded.

"I'm going to take care of it," she said. "I am. But I can't tell the Window Cop."

Suddenly he turned in his seat, leaning up against the driver side door, and gave her a somber look. "How will you do it? Go to Canada?"

They both knew it was no longer legal here.

"The border to Canada is too controlled now," she said. "Girls go to jail. I can't go there. Some girls at school say they can get the pills. There's a group of women in the Netherlands who sell them illegally online."

"Is it safe? Will you be okay?" he asked, his voice warming momentarily.

She was happy to hear him ask the question. This was the Eddie she liked, the one who was both strong and kind, the one who picked contraband flowers for her, not the one who pulled away.

"The girls say the pills are safe if you're careful and you do it right." Even as she said this, she pushed stories out of her head, things she'd heard. Stories of girls being thrown in jail for taking them. Stories of rip-off drugs that weren't safe and landed you in the hospital, or worse. "Janet Wong knows a girl over in Au Bois who's a dealer. I can get the pills from her, but they're really expensive. I don't have the money."

"I thought you have college savings."

"I have a savings account, but if I took money out, the Window Cop would know. He checks it. He'd freak."

Eddie was watching her closely, but she couldn't read his expression. She knew he didn't have a lot of money. He'd dropped out of high school and was still living with his parents. His only work was odd jobs he picked up here and there on some of the local farms, but it would be nice if he offered to help even a little.

Instead, he just stared at her with that impenetrable look on his face.

Finally she asked him outright. "Do you have any cash?"

"Me? Why me?"

"You *are* the father."

He looked away and took a deep breath, then looked back. "How am I going to get money?"

"I don't know."

"How much do you need?"

"A thousand dollars."

"A thousand dollars! Seriously? I can't get that kind of money. Your dad's rich. My parents are poor."

She set the beach pea blossoms down on the floor of the car, next to her feet. They were already starting to wilt. "My dad's not rich."

On the other side of the windshield, the sun was turning red and getting lower and closer to the lake. The water reflected this in a long line coming straight towards them, like a rippling red runway. She stared at it. How would she get out of this?

"He's a goddamn Beelord," Eddie said. "Those people are like drug dealers. They buy gold Camaros with stacks of cash."

She looked away from the red runway and back at Eddie. "He's not really a Beelord. He's like the last old-school beekeeper in the entire world."

"I don't have a thousand dollars. I can't help you."

Her heart was sinking into all that red water. "How about help *us*? It's as much your baby as it is mine."

Eddie fell silent again. He put his hands on the steering wheel. She thought he was going to start the car, but he just sat staring out at the sunset.

"Ava," he said. "What if you keep it?"

"Keep it?"

He smiled and reached toward her face gently, tucking a strand of hair behind her ear. "We could settle down."

They'd only been going out six months. She hadn't for a moment considered keeping the baby. While it was true that recently she'd moved Eddie to the very top of her gratitude list, she had no idea what the future held for them. While she liked being with him, she was only seventeen, and he didn't really have a job. He'd grown up on Gull Island, and he wasn't really interested in leaving. It was unclear what would happen when she went away to college, which she was definitely doing. Would they break up? Would they take time away from their relationship? She hadn't worried about any of this because it was a year away. It was like something she'd shoved into the back of a drawer to deal with later.

"You really want me to keep it?"

"Yeah. I mean, don't I get a say? It's as much my baby as it is yours; you said so yourself."

"But it's my body."

He nodded slowly, clearly disappointed in her response. Then he got out of the car and shut the door. She thought he was walking away, but he walked around to her side of the car and opened the passenger door. Without hesitating, he got down on one knee and took her hand. Her stomach dropped.

"Eddie, Eddie, stop," she said, but he had already started to speak.

"Ava Sarafina Parker, will you marry me?"

She felt terrible. This wasn't right. It wasn't real, and it was too soon. She wasn't prepared to deal with this. "Oh, my God, no. Please don't ask me that." Her eyes were starting to well up with tears. They were not tears of joy.

"Too late," Eddie said, still beaming at her. "I already asked. So, will you?"

There he was on his knee at the car door, gazing up, the light from the setting sun still dancing across his hair. He must have seen something in her expression, because slowly his smile began to fade. His brow creased with worry.

"Ava?"

"I don't know, Eddie. I can't say. I'm not ready. It's not what I was expecting."

"You don't want a baby with me." He looked absolutely dejected.

"No, no. It's not that. It's just. I have no choice."

"Of course you have a choice. We always have choices."

The tears began rolling down her face. She adored him for being both sturdy and brave but also thoughtful. Underneath the bulky ruggedness lay a deep sensitivity, and she could imagine being around that heady mix for a very long time. He was a fragile crystal vase in a rough box. She didn't want to break him.

"I'm sorry," she said. "I'm sorry."

His eyes softened, like he was wounded, and he stood. "I understand. You wanted money for an abortion, not a marriage proposal."

She was blindsided. Never in a million years had she thought that he would propose to her. She felt like her response had been cruel and insensitive. For a long time she'd been carefully ignoring the fact that there were two incompatible things she wanted—to be with Eddie and to leave this island. Was she suddenly being forced to make a choice? Had she just made it?

He drove her home without saying another word. She didn't know what to do and found herself filling the silence with random apologies.

When he dropped her off, he didn't even lean over to kiss her like he usually did. He just looked straight ahead silently, waiting for her to go.

She left the flowers in the car.

The next day, when she messaged him, he responded curtly, saying that he was going hunting. She knew this meant he was going to his family's hunting cabin in the End Woods. There was no signal out there, no way to message or call, and she wondered if it was a plan to purposely avoid her.

She hadn't heard a word from him since.

## 16

AS SOON AS Jim returned from Minnie's, he began installing the surveillance cameras near his home hives. It had been a long day, starting with the arson that morning, and he wanted to get the job done before nightfall.

It took a few hours from start to finish. He buried the cabling from the garage to the hives and mounted the two cameras in the trees in the back corner of the property, each about nine feet high off the ground so that they had a discreet view of the hives. The cameras connected to a digital video recorder which he fit under the desk in his bedroom. The video footage could stream to his phone, or he could view it on his laptop.

When he finished, he knocked on Ava's bedroom door, calling out, "Hamburgers for dinner?"

A muffled response came through the door. "Sure."

Something was bothering Ava. She'd been in her room all day. He wished he knew what was going on with her.

A few moments later, as he was throwing the hamburger patties into the cast iron skillet, there was a knock on the front door. It was Deputy Gabby.

"Oh, hi," he said.

She nodded politely from the porch. "Thank you for your call earlier about Emmett," she said. "I've just come from his house."

"Is he back?"

"No. He wasn't there. It does look like an animal got into his garage, though."

Jim looked beyond her, into the trees. "There's been an animal getting into Minnie's garden too."

"It'll be an issue for pest control, then. Listen, do you know where Emmett is?"

"Me?" Jim was surprised by the question. "No. I was just checking because Bob asked me to, when Emmett didn't show up at work this morning. I don't really know Emmett that well."

"I see," she said, watching him closely. "Well, I should tell you that I stopped by Chuck Norman's today. He says you poisoned his hives."

Jim laughed. He wasn't surprised. Chuck had been trying to ruin his reputation with small lies since he arrived here.

"Do you believe that?" he asked Gabby.

She smiled. "No, not that. I've heard from others that you actually offered to help him with his hives. The fact of the matter is that I arrested him. He's in the holding cell right now at the station. I thought you should know."

"Wow, that's good news. Thank you." He felt a wave of relief knowing that the perpetrator had been identified and locked up. Now he wouldn't have to worry about his home hives. Perhaps the surveillance cameras had been a bit of a knee-jerk reaction. He wouldn't need them now. But he also felt angry. He'd offered to help Chuck become a better beekeeper. Instead of trying to improve his own skills, the spiteful, arrogant man had tried to destroy Jim's business. "What's next?" he asked.

"Well, he'll be here a couple of nights while we wait for the Keskkauko County Judge to confirm the arrest. Assuming that goes through, he'll be transferred to Au Bois."

"So you believe me now."

For a moment, Gabby seemed to hesitate, as if there was something else she wanted to say. Jim waited.

"Well," she said, glancing over his shoulder. "I'll let you get back to your dinner." She turned to go but then paused. "Jim, are you absolutely sure you don't know where Emmett is?"

He was confused. Why was she asking this again? "I told you. I don't know Emmett that well. Why would I know where he is?"

"Just checking," she said casually, and then turned, heading back toward her SUV.

Ava finally emerged from her room for dinner and surprised him by agreeing to join him at the picnic table. She nibbled at her hamburger and picked at the salad he'd made.

"Are you sure you're okay?" he asked.

She gave him one of her well-practiced eye rolls and said, "Stop asking me that."

Jim looked at his daughter. Her purple hair was hanging over her eyes. He changed the subject, hoping to bring her out of her shell. "They arrested Chuck Norman for torching my hives."

"Good," she mumbled.

When they finished eating, they cleaned up the kitchen together, mostly in silence, since she continued to greet every statement or question from Jim with short, curt answers. He made a fire in the fire pit, knowing how nice it was to hear the frogs and crickets begin to sing all around, but Ava said she was tired and went to her room. He had no idea how she could be so tired when all she did was sleep.

Bailey stayed outside, curling up at Jim's side. He reached down and pet the dog. He sat there for a long time sipping a glass of whiskey, watching as the woods slowly grew dark. He didn't know what to do about Ava, but he'd just have to keep showing up, keep checking in with her, keep trying to be a parent. He'd decided some time ago that that was all he could do.

He missed Sarah.

For the second time that day, he thought of the moment when

she'd hugged him for the last time, the night she disappeared, how she'd stood behind him in the kitchen and wrapped her arms around him. The world was a terrible place and even the basic, most fundamental parts of your life could change at a moment's notice. People you loved could be taken away from you forever, without warning.

As he stared into the fire, the scotch warmed his throat and made him feel pleasantly numb. He pulled his thoughts away from Sarah and forced himself to think about more immediate things.

He thought of the footprint in Minnie's garden, how he had to have read it wrong. It must have been two footprints that he'd conflated.

A few final streaks of pink ran across the clouds to the west, and then the sun's last efforts faded too. The light in the woods had turned from dusky blue to rich indigo when suddenly Bailey lifted his head and stared into the trees. He began to growl.

Jim looked in the direction Bailey was staring. The End Woods were indeed dark and deep. There could be anything out there—foxes, raccoons, rabbits, deer, coyote.

"It's okay, boy," he said, patting the dog's soft head. He leaned back and took another sip of his whiskey.

Eventually the dog stopped growling, but continued staring, as though on alert. Then he quickly stood up, stepped forward to the edge of the firelight, and began barking wildly.

"Whoa, whoa!" Jim shouted, setting his whiskey down in the dirt and walking over to Bailey. He grabbed his collar and stroked his back. Every muscle in the dog's body was tense. "It's okay, boy. Shhh."

Jim was scanning the woods when he thought he heard a footfall in the brush. Was there somebody out there? He felt a strange shiver run across his skin.

He stayed at Bailey's side, holding the dog back, looking out into the darkness beyond the fire, until he felt the rigidness in the dog's body suddenly ease. Bailey sat down, then leaned over and licked Jim's hand. The moment had passed.

Jim sat back down and stayed there, barely moving, listening for sounds of something in the darkness, until the fire faded into glowing coals and the woods became completely black. The woods were silent, until the soft sound of a great horned owl came down from the trees. Its stuttering song repeated twice, almost as a signal that it was time for him to go to bed.

He threw water on the coals and made his way back inside. On his way to his bedroom, he opened Ava's door a crack to let Bailey in. He felt a deep comfort in the fact that Bailey slept at the foot of his daughter's bed every night.

He continued down the short hallway, thinking of Chuck Norman locked up in the holding cell at the sheriff station. As he climbed into bed, he told himself that Ava and his bees were safe, that everything was fine. And besides, the cameras were set up now. If anything else happened, he'd know about it.

It didn't help, though. He still felt uneasy. His mind raced from one thought to the next—his fight with Ava, Emmett missing, the arson, the strange gray bee, the animal in Minnie's garden, and even Bailey barking into the dark woods. He lay there for quite some time, just looking at the ceiling, staring at the shadows gathered in the corners of the room.

17

THE NEXT MORNING Jim found himself sitting at the kitchen table, waiting for 11 a.m. The best time to inspect a beehive was between 11 a.m. and 4 p.m., when most of the bees would be out foraging, and he was eager to see if he could find that strange, gray bee again.

He'd been up since before first light, and he'd already done everything he could think of to keep himself busy until it was late enough to check the hives.

He'd checked his new video surveillance stream first thing. With Chuck locked up, he wasn't too worried, but he'd wanted to look at the footage all the same. There had been four clear "events" trigged by the motion sensor throughout the night, captured in grainy black and white. Two events were from honey-seeking raccoons circling the hives, one was a coyote walking by, and the last one was a deer stepping out from the woods. His hives were fine.

After reviewing the footage, he'd headed out to get the coyote rollers he promised Minnie. He was at Gull Hardware when Bob unlocked the front doors at 8 a.m. Emmett wasn't there yet, but he wasn't due in until noon. Jim bought enough coyote rollers to cover the top of Minnie's garden fence, and he stacked the long boxes in the back of his truck. He would install them on Friday, as planned. He looked forward to Minnie's blueberry muffins.

When he got home, he'd seen signs in the kitchen that Ava had been up and made toast—the counter was covered in crumbs, and she'd left the honey out—but she was already back in her room.

For the last hour, he'd kept himself busy with invoicing, but he was all caught up on that now. He looked at the clock on the stove. It was 10:30. That was close enough. He just couldn't wait any longer.

He went outside and put on his beekeeping suit. He carried his smoker, hive tool, and hand lens out back, as well as an old glass jar. He'd punched some breathing holes in the metal lid.

The sunlight had been warming his hives for almost an hour and a half. Standing there in front of the hives, he lit the dried grass inside the smoker. When the smoke started coming out in great, white tufts, he opened the top of the hive where he'd seen the gray bee yesterday, and he pointed the tip of the smoker down into the frames of honeycomb to calm the bees. In fact, the smoke masked the alarm pheromone released by guard bees, and it also caused the bees to feed, since they believed their hive and honey stores were about to disappear in a fire. It made the hive easier to handle. He began pulling out the bee-covered frames one by one, prying them loose with the hive tool.

Typically when he did inspections like this, it was quick work. A routine inspection involved a brief feed and pollen inventory, along with a mite check. He knew just what to look for. He didn't necessarily need to see the queen. It was enough to see freshly laid eggs, to find open and covered brood. But this was not a routine inspection. Jim was looking for one of those gray bees he'd seen yesterday. He hoped they weren't all out foraging.

He inspected one side of the flat honeycomb-filled frames and then the other. As always, he was careful to be patient. Whenever he lifted out a frame, he was mindful not to knock it against the sides of the brood box or push it up against the neighboring frames, because that could easily injure or crush the bees.

Although he didn't see any gray bees, he did notice something very peculiar. As he moved from the honey supers and down into the brood chambers, he realized that the hive had absolutely no varroa mites at all.

It made no sense. These days, every hive had *Varroa destructor*. Those little vampires were a large part of the reason bees were dying. They were a bit like ticks—attaching themselves to bees and sucking their amber-colored blood, called hemolymph. They also fed on bee larvae and pupae.

For years, Jim had grown used to seeing the tiny reddish-brown dots in his hives and seeing them attached to the backs of his bees. They looked like little sesame seeds. He knew how to spot indirect signs as well, like sunken and chewed cappings, or larvae slumped in the bottom cells. Varroa also caused deformities in newly emerged bees, with stunted abdomens or misshapen wings.

Because *Apis mellifera* was not the mite's natural host, the honeybees had no natural defenses. The mites had spread worldwide, and the question was no longer how to get rid of them. The question was how to control them in order to minimize the damage.

Jim was exceptionally frustrated by varroa. Since the Global Bee Crisis had been officially declared, it was getting worse, not better. The mites had grown slightly larger over time and developed resistance to many of the treatments he normally used—thymol, formic acid, oxalic acid, beta acids. Over the last few years, he'd become used to seeing more and more varroa in his beehives and watching bee colonies grow weaker as a result.

He checked the frames again. He must be mistaken. But it was true. There were no varroa here. None. He was thrilled, but it was also somewhat unnerving. How in the world had this happened?

The sun was already hot on his back by the time he found

what he had come here for—a grayish bee with two black stripes down both sides of its body. He slowly set the frame against the hive to free his hands. Picking up the old glass jar, he scooped the gray bee into it. Then he screwed down the metal lid.

The bee went berserk, flying up against the lid and the sides, trying to escape. Jim slowly set the jar down in the grass a good distance from the hive. Although smoke blocked alarm pheromones, he didn't want to risk the gray bee's aggression and alarm triggering a defensive response in the others. They were already upset enough.

This bee appeared to be a drone—a male, larger and stouter than a female worker bee, but not as long, thin, or delicately tapered as a queen. He watched the captured drone for a moment. There was something unusual about it that he couldn't quite place —other than the obvious color. Eventually he went back to the hive. The bees had become alarmed, and he was quickly surrounded. It happened sometimes. He remained calm and steady.

He was about to put the frame back inside the hive when he saw a second gray bee. This one had its head in a honey cell, its wing tips sticking out behind. That made it easy to pick up. He took off his glove and used a rolling action with the balls of his thumb and forefinger to pinch and trap the wing tips, just as he'd learned many years ago in his training. The technique required both firmness and a delicacy of touch, along with a good deal of confidence.

This gray bee was smaller than the first, and it kept trying to sting him. It was clearly a female worker bee. Only female bees had stingers. But he was amazed at how long this bee's stinger was. Normally a honeybee stinger was maybe an eighth of an inch at the most. This stinger was probably ten times that. It projected out and reached for his bare fingers, which were fortunately just out of reach. He looked closely. The stinger wasn't barbed, like a bee's. It looked like the smooth stinger of a wasp.

He was surprised. Again, it made no sense. What was this bee?

He walked back over to the glass jar, lifted the lid slightly, and dropped the second bee inside. Holding it up to the sunlight, he looked at the two specimens, and then took his hand lens out of the pocket of his bee suit so he could inspect further.

Sarah had given him this hand lens. It was a beautiful, foldable magnifying glass. The lens was attached to a chrome plated cover, and it swiveled so the lens could slip inside. It was engraved with the words, "My bee nerd." He thought of her every time he used it.

Both bees were still furious inside the jar, but now he could see what was so unusual about them, besides their color. Honeybees were hairy, but these two didn't have much hair at all. Their legs were long and thin, and their waists were narrower and more pinched than usual. He just couldn't fathom how they had been accepted into the hive.

It was true that sometimes guard bees would let in strangers—what the industry called migrant bees—especially when the migrants made an offering at the entrance, regurgitating nectar from their honey stomach. But migrant acceptance only happened with bees of the same species. These appeared to be an entirely different species altogether.

After he put the frame back and shut up that first hive, he saw another gray bee on the landing board of the next hive. This gray bee was another drone, a male. It was making strange movements, so Jim stepped closer to see what it was doing. It slowly dawned on him that the drone was actually *eating* a dead wasp—a yellowjacket.

It looked as though the wasp had tried to raid the hive and had been attacked. Wasps attacked beehives all the time to steal honey, eat the bee eggs and larvae, and kill the bees, and it was not unusual for worker bees to defend its entrance. But Jim had never seen a bee actually *eat* a wasp. Bees were not usually carnivorous. Jim was completely dumbfounded.

He thought of *Trigona hypogea*, the rare South American bee that fed on rotting meat rather than pollen or nectar. It made a kind of "meat honey" from regurgitated carcasses, wasp larvae, and toad eggs. But the gray bee in front of him looked nothing like *Trigona hypogea*, and those South American bees certainly couldn't survive this far north.

Never in his life had he seen anything like this—females that had stingers like wasps, and males that were carnivorous. He went through a mental inventory of species he knew and he came up short. When he checked a few more hives, he found there were at least a few gray bees in every colony—none of which had any varroa mites. They'd infiltrated every one of his home hives.

As an entomologist and biologist, his scientific curiosity had been piqued, and he simply had to figure out what this species was. It seemed unlikely that he'd just found a previously undiscovered member of the genus *Apis* here in his home beehives.

He wondered for a moment if this was a kind of sabotage. Had Chuck Norman released some sort of parasitic species into his home hives? And if he had, why? Was it yet another attempt to destroy his business?

Or was somebody else behind this? Could this, in fact, be a sign of something far, far worse?

# PART 2
# SPECIES UNKNOWN

## 18

IT WAS ONLY a short drive from Jim's property to Hadley Agritech. The grounds for the company were hidden at the eastern end of Reserve Road, just beyond Emmett Jones' place. A rugged, wooden sign at the side of the road read, "Hadley Agritech Research Station: Feeding Our Community."

Jim turned left and headed down a long driveway that snaked between the trees. Although it was close to home, he'd avoided coming down this driveway ever since he moved here.

Now he arrived at a small guard station surrounded by woods. It was a utilitarian structure made of concrete. A man in a dark navy uniform leaned out and asked, "Who are you visiting?" He was serious and unfriendly.

"Lewis Wilson," Jim answered.

"Your name?"

"Jim Parker."

The guard turned and made a phone call. Jim saw a pistol on his belt. The guard nodded and waved Jim on.

He continued to drive through the woods, the glass jar containing the two gray bees at his side. The old wooden hunting lodge that eventually emerged was long and low, with a large green roof. It was nestled peacefully among the trees, with its back to the beach. Brown pine weatherboard made it blend into the trees.

Hadley Agritech had purchased the old lodge and converted it some ten years before, but the rustic appeal of the place did not put Jim at ease. Being a beekeeper had taught him to pay attention. He'd spied several security cameras mounted in the woods on his way in, and now he could see even more cameras mounted discreetly in the eaves. Another armed guard stood at the front doors. This was no charming retreat. This was a research facility for one of the largest global agricultural megacorporations, and they didn't have a good reputation.

He left his truck in the front parking lot and walked up to the building carrying the glass jar in his hand. The two bees inside had calmed down for the most part, although from time to time they threw new tantrums and banged themselves against the glass. The worker occasionally poked her surprisingly long, black stinger through the holes in the lid, so Jim had to be careful to keep his hand clear.

The guard near the door was wearing a wireless radio with an earpiece. His uniform was crisp, and his gun was holstered in his police belt. He watched silently as Jim crossed over the threshold and entered the lobby. Afterwards, he whispered something into his radio.

Inside, pine walls surrounded a large, stone fireplace, and a high-beamed ceiling was hung with an enormous chandelier made of deer antlers. The lodge's old check-in now served as reception, and Jim let the receptionist know he was there, although he supposed that multiple people had already been warned about his arrival.

He sat in one of the large, green leather club chairs. He held the jar awkwardly in his hands and waited.

After nearly twenty minutes, his old colleague entered the lobby. Lewis Wilson was a short, caramel-skinned Black man, and he raised his arm in a friendly gesture as he walked toward Jim across the open lobby. It had been years since they'd seen each other, and Jim was surprised at how much Lewis had aged.

Back when they started their PhDs at Cornell, Jim was twenty-five and Lewis was only seventeen, a bit of a wunderkind. Now Lewis actually looked older than Jim. His hair was thinning, he'd developed a paunch, and he was wearing glasses—round tortoise-shell frames. There were large bags under his eyes. He looked tired and overworked.

Lewis smiled and said, "Who's this summer tourist hanging out in my lobby?"

Jim noticed Lewis' conservative tassel loafers, blue button-down shirt, and khaki pants, and then looked down at his own more casual attire—flip-flops, shorts, and a t-shirt.

"Still prim and proper as always, I see," Jim said, smiling back. "Good to see you."

"And you, Jim." They shook hands.

"Sorry I haven't been in touch until now," Jim said.

"No problem. Beelords are busy people."

When Jim first arrived on Gull Island two years earlier, Lewis had emailed to say he heard Jim had opened up a small pollination business on the island. It was a kind email, carefully worded. Lewis had explained that he was also on Gull Island and doing bee research at Hadley. Jim had emailed back, saying he would get in contact once he was settled in, but he never followed up.

Maintaining contact with people had never been something Jim was good at. Sarah used to push him to contact his friends, and his natural inclination toward solitude had only increased after losing her. In the case of Lewis, Jim's reluctance was exacerbated by the fact that he'd always had significant reservations about anyone who worked for Hadley Agritech.

"I don't really like to be called a Beelord," Jim explained. "I'm a beekeeper."

Lewis raised his eyebrows. "Oh, isn't that quaint. Sounds like some old-fashioned job that no longer exists, like an elevator operator or a milkman."

Jim forced a smile. "I'm old fashioned."

"Careful, it's one small step from being old fashioned to being obsolete." Lewis was smiling, but the look in his eye was direct and a little confrontational.

Jim met his gaze. Lewis had always been both socially awkward and slightly arrogant, and although they got along, there was forever an edge of competition between them.

"I do what works," Jim said now. "Regardless of whether it's long-established or newfangled."

"I heard about the arson," Lewis said suddenly. "I hope they catch whoever did it."

"There's already been an arrest," Jim said.

"Really? Who?"

"Chuck Norman. Deputy Gabby arrested him yesterday."

"Oh, that's a relief." Lewis nodded. "She doesn't waste any time. Is that the sample?" He pointed at the jar in Jim's hand.

"These are the bees." Jim held up the jar. "A drone and a worker. They're not happy in there."

Lewis reached forward and took the jar out of Jim's hand, examining the contents. He pushed his glasses up on his nose and stared at the bees. An intense look passed across his face—a kind of laser-focused academic curiosity. Or was it worry?

"You say they were in your home hives?" Lewis asked, not even pausing to look up at Jim.

"Yes. Clearly it's not *Apis mellifera*."

For just a brief moment, as they stood together staring at the jar, Jim felt like they could have been students at Cornell again, hanging out in the beekeeping club where they first met. Back then they had both been young and idealistic, and in time they had grown to enjoy talking passionately over beers at local bars about the best way to save the bees. Yet during their years at

Cornell, their views on the emerging pollination crisis had begun to diverge.

By the time they finished their PhDs—Jim in Entomology and Lewis in Molecular Biology & Genetics—they had landed on opposite ends of a divided spectrum. Jim wanted to save the natural environment, whereas Lewis wanted to change it. Jim became an academic researcher focused on protecting bee populations with old-school beekeeping, while Lewis began applying his considerable genius at the biotech megacorporations that Jim thought were part of the problem.

Watching his old classmate peering at the bees inside the jar, Jim decided it was really no surprise that Lewis had ended up at a place like Hadley. But Lewis was the only other person on Gull Island who knew bees as well as he did, and Lewis' professional opinion mattered. Jim hoped that they could bridge their differences to identify this species together.

"You didn't, ah, you didn't get stung by them, did you?" Lewis asked.

"No," Jim said. "But I'm baffled. They've been accepted into the hive, and the drones appear to be carnivorous. I found one actually eating a wasp. I couldn't find the species in any reference source."

Lewis glanced around the lobby. "Let's go find someplace to talk."

Jim followed Lewis through a set of locked doors, down a hallway, and into the bowels of the research station. They walked down a long hallway and into a small meeting room with no windows. While the lobby had preserved the rustic charm of the old lodge, the rest of the building had been renovated with bland office finishings—drop ceilings, fluorescent lights, gray walls, and industrial gray carpet.

On the way Lewis asked a tall blond man to bring them coffee.

"Yes, sir," the man said and bounded off.

Lewis closed the meeting room door and gestured for Jim to

sit down. He was extremely careful with the jar as he placed it on the table and sat down across from Jim.

"You say you found these in your home hives?" he asked.

Jim nodded. "Yes."

"Where's your house?"

"On Reserve Road, not far from here."

"How many are there?" Lewis leaned forward. He was looking closely at the bees.

"Each hive seems to have a few at least."

"How many hives?"

"Eight." Jim leaned back and watched Lewis. "You seem to recognize the species. What is it?"

Lewis pulled on the expensive cufflinks he was wearing. "I've never seen it before."

"That's funny," Jim said, confused by the change—from questions to denial. "I thought you looked a bit worried when you first saw it in the lobby. Like maybe you recognized it."

"Oh, you know me, Jim. I get excited when I see bees. It bothers me if I can't identify a species." Lewis laughed, looking back at the glass jar. "Crazy bee people."

Behind Lewis, Jim noticed a whiteboard scribbled with notes. He had begun to read some of the notes when Lewis saw what he was doing. Lewis stood and erased the whiteboard before Jim could make any sense of what was written there.

"What are you doing here at Hadley?" Jim asked.

"I head the Pollinator Team. It's good, but I don't like managing people. Science is easy. People are hard." Lewis smiled awkwardly.

Jim concurred. It was one of the few things that he and Lewis had always agreed on, and it was probably one of the reasons they'd first become friends. "But why Gull Island? Hadley's a big company. You could be anywhere."

"The isolated nature of the island makes it easier to study bees."

"I always thought Hadley focused on seeds."

Like many of the agricultural biotech megacorporations, or AgCorps, Hadley Agritech had built their success on genetically modified seeds, and they were ruthless about protecting their patents. They'd developed a patented herbicide, a weed-killer, along with an array of patented gen-mod seeds that were resistant to that herbicide. It was a common approach for AgCorps. It meant they could spray entire farms with their herbicide, and the only things that would survive were the crops grown from their patented seeds.

Lewis straightened his cuffs again. "Yes, but we also do work with improved bioengineered foods, pesticides, and most recently pollination as well."

"So one day you'll have a patent on the entire food chain. Clever." Jim did not trust the AgCorps. As a traditional beekeeper, he'd always felt like David to their Goliath.

"You know there's a global food shortage, Jim, and the bee crisis is a significant part of that. We would be remiss if we didn't try to help. After all, Hadley hires the best minds in the world." He opened his arms as if presenting himself as an example.

Jim laughed out loud, even though it hadn't been meant as a joke. "So, being such a great mind, if you had to guess, what do you think these bees could be?"

"I really don't know. It may be an unidentified species of wild bee."

"That's unlikely. You know more about bees than anybody I've ever met. Not even a guess?"

"I don't like guessing."

Just then, the tall blond man stepped in carrying two cups of coffee. He looked young and trendy, with his hair buzzed short on the sides and long on top. He was wearing jeans and a t-shirt that said, "Bees are my Bros."

"Here you go." He set the cups on the table.

"Thank you, Brad," Lewis said.

Jim stared at the coffee cup. "Is that real coffee?"

"Absolutely," Lewis answered, smiling again. "Forget that mushroom-based, artificially caffeinated excrement."

Jim's heart leapt at the idea of real coffee. He missed it terribly. Without bees the price of coffee beans had soared, and he no longer drank it at home. It seemed like an extravagance. "Thank you very much."

"It's just one of the perks of working for Hadley," Lewis said. "Have you ever considered it?"

"Considered what? Real coffee?" Jim picked up the cup and took a big sip, relishing the warm, pungent flavor.

"No. Working for us."

The question was so shocking that Jim nearly choked on his coffee. "No, I definitely have not. This is gen-mod coffee, right?"

"Of course," Lewis said. "Grown from Hadley beans. Entirely wind pollinated."

"I have to admit, it's really nice."

Lewis turned to the blond man as he was about to leave. "Stay, Brad. Let me show you what Jim has."

The man closed the door and stood with his back to it, his arms crossed across his chest. Jim realized only then just how imposing he was—he was over six feet tall and solidly built.

"Jim, this is Brad Kelly," Lewis said. "He's my research assistant."

"Research assistant? You look more like a bouncer than a scientist." Jim felt a bit blocked in.

Lewis handed Brad the specimen jar. "Take a look."

Brad exchanged a glance with Lewis, and then turned to Jim. "What are you doing with these?"

"I found them," Jim said. "In my hives at home, on my back acre."

Lewis interrupted. "Jim's a Beelord."

"A beekeeper," Jim corrected.

Lewis smiled. "Right. A beekeeper."

"Where are the hives?" Brad asked.

"At his house over on Reserve Road," Lewis said. "I told him I don't know what this bee is."

Brad squinted at the jar. "Yeah," he said. "I don't recognize it either."

Jim looked back and forth between the two of them. "It infiltrated my hives," he explained, setting down his coffee. "I thought it might be *Andrena cineraria* or *Colletes compactus*. They're both gray, of course. But they don't match this bee's profile. They're both ground nesting, solitary, and of course, they're not carnivorous, which these are. And the morphology doesn't line up. I'm grasping at straws here. Any ideas?"

"Don't know," Brad said.

"It's unclear how it managed to infiltrate my honeybee hives. It didn't seem to be raiding. It seemed to have become a part of the hive. And in fact, one appeared to be defending the hive from a raiding wasp."

Brad shrugged.

"I'm sorry, Jim," Lewis interrupted again. "But we really can't help you."

"You have no ideas at all? What do you think it is? Can't you even take a wild guess?"

Lewis stood up, looking at his watch. "Jim, it's been nice to see you. We have a meeting we have to get to, I'm afraid. Apologies."

Jim stood slowly, feeling somewhat uneasy.

"Can we keep this?" Lewis asked, taking the jar from Brad. "Maybe we can identify it. We'll check our sources."

Jim hesitated and then said, "Thank you."

"I'd keep clear of those hives if I were you." Lewis added, adopting a patronizing tone. "You don't want to get stung by an unidentified species. You don't know how toxic it might be."

"Of course," Jim said. "And if you can help me identify it, so we know how toxic it is, I'd really appreciate it."

Brad opened the door and stepped out into the hallway, waiting for Jim to follow. Lewis gestured Jim on.

Back in the lobby, they both shook Jim's hand, and then he walked out past the armed guard toward his pickup in the parking lot. While Jim knew that Lewis had always lacked social skills, at that moment he couldn't help feeling annoyed. It was as though he'd just been warmly invited into a friend's home but then brusquely asked to leave.

Another guard watched Jim as he started his car and continued watching until Jim finally drove away.

19

THE GULL ISLAND Sheriff Substation was a nondescript, brown building which stood alongside a cluster of trees near the public library. It looked more like a large garage than a sheriff's station. There was a depot for the patrol vehicles, and a hallway led from the depot to the office area, which contained the reception at the front, offices for the deputy and the summer deputy, a break room, and a training room that was rarely used. A single detention cell was tucked away in back, used even less frequently than the training room.

That evening, Deputy Gabby couldn't wait to leave the substation and get home. It had been a frustrating day. She was sitting at her large, slightly worn desk, tapping a pen on the surface. The retrospective approval for Chuck Norman's arrest was supposed to come in from Au Bois today, but it hadn't arrived.

All of a sudden Chuck's raspy voice rang out from the holding cell. "This dinner tastes like crap!"

She ignored him. She couldn't wait to transfer that cantankerous *pendejo* to Au Bois, but she needed the approval before she could do so.

"Crap, I say!" Chuck yelled again.

It was always a hassle to have someone in the holding cell, even when they weren't as bad-tempered as Chuck Norman. Of course detainees needed meals, and you couldn't leave them locked up in the building by themselves all night, in case of an emergency, like a fire. Thank goodness Dorothy Simpson, a local volunteer, was making Chuck's meals. The summer deputy, Eric Crawford, was doing the night shift. Gabby expected him to arrive any minute. Then she could get out of here.

The simple truth was that Gabby preferred being out in the field, not doing paperwork or watching over someone in detention. She liked talking to the locals, directly helping people, and making sure a law enforcement presence was seen. She didn't go to the police academy to sit behind a desk.

Today she'd spent an unfortunate amount of time at her old computer. She'd finished the paperwork for Chuck. She'd also done a bit of research on Jim Parker, investigating his academic credentials, his research, and his personal history. She realized her natural inclination towards distrust had perhaps caused her to be more suspicious of him than she needed to be.

Her research today had taught her that he had a PhD from Cornell, and he'd once been a big-deal academic at University of Michigan. He'd moved to Gull Island a year after losing his wife in horrible circumstances. His history didn't match the profile of someone who would burn his own hives for the insurance money. He had no previous record, not even a speeding ticket. She'd also looked into how much insurance money he would receive from losing his hives. Compared to his hive rental rates, the payout wasn't much at all.

"I say it's crap!" Chuck's voice rang out again.

Gabby shook her head. She was tired. Outside the window, the light was dying. She just needed Chuck to finish eating and Eric to show up for night duty. She decided to look around the depot while she waited. She wanted to check the jerry cans there.

Earlier, she'd stopped by Tom Baker's garage to check out

Chuck's story about his generator. Tom had confirmed that in fact Chuck's generator was in for repair. He also mentioned that he knew Chuck was going through a lot of gasoline lately, because he was having trouble with his solar panels. Gabby had noticed a few red, five-gallon jerry cans in Tom's garage. They were also square and made of plastic.

"They're the only ones that Bob sells," Tom said when she asked about them. "So pretty much all the locals on the island have the same ones."

As she entered the depot now, she looked around for the gas cans she remembered seeing there. She found them in back, and just as Tom had said, they were just like Chuck's, which were just like Tom's, which were just like the one left behind at Bennett Orchards.

This made her evidence against Chuck much thinner. She had probable cause, but little else. She suddenly wondered whether she'd been biased against Chuck because she disliked him. As an officer, she was always examining her own thinking to make sure that biases didn't impact her decision-making. Now she was unsure.

Finally, she heard Eric come in the front door and call out from reception. She had never been so happy to see him.

"Good evening, Deputy Martinez," he said. He was a lanky white kid with big ears and steely gray eyes. Every summer the Gull Island Sheriff Substation was assigned a graduate from Lake Superior College Police Academy in the Upper Peninsula. They were always inexperienced, but Gabby was happy to have a second pair of hands for the tourist season.

"Hi, Eric," she said. "Glad to see you."

She immediately turned her back on him and headed down the hall to the holding cell. She just had to do one more thing and she'd be out of here.

The cell was a bleak place. There was a metal bed frame with a lumpy mattress, sheets, one blanket, a small table, and a toilet in the corner.

Chuck was staring at his empty meal tray. "I see you managed to eat the food you said was crap," she said. "Dorothy Simpson made it, you know."

"Oh, Dorothy," Chuck said. "She's okay."

"And by the way you cleaned that tray, looks like her cooking is too."

Chuck sneered at her. "But you know that Jim Parker is a Satanist."

She held back a smile. She hadn't quite figured out Jim yet, but he was the most unlikely devil worshiper she'd ever met. "A Satanist? Really?"

"Yes, ma'am. He kills animals out in the woods and makes offerings to the devil."

She shook her head. "I need to take your tray, Chuck." She took out her keys, and Chuck stood up at the back of the cell. He already knew the drill. She unlocked the door, took his tray, and slid the door closed with a loud clank before locking it again.

"Good night, Chuck. Eric's here now."

"I didn't do it," Chuck said, as he climbed into bed. "It's my second day in this shithole, and I didn't goddamn do it."

She paused and looked at him, hoping that she hadn't made a mistake in arresting him.

A few minutes later, she was unlocking her SUV out front when a stout figure stepped out from some nearby trees, smoking a cigarette. It was a woman with short, black hair. Her face was in shadow.

"Excuse me, Deputy," the woman said, stepping forward into the glare of the flood light at the front of the substation. "Can we talk?"

It was Kylie Thompson. Everyone knew Kylie. She was the owner of Coyote Kylie's, Gull Island's only bar. She was also a hunter and a trapper, and the three-time champion of the Gull Island Coyote Classic, the annual competition to kill the most coyotes in a weekend. Gabby often saw Kylie laughing and chatting with Chuck at the bar, and she'd heard that they hunted together. While the woman was a bit rough around the edges, she was a law-abiding citizen and people respected her. It was a mystery why she was friends with Chuck.

"Hi, Kylie. Happy to talk. You want to go inside?" Gabby looked back toward the building. It was quiet.

"Nah," Kylie said, shaking her head resolutely. She had one thumb hooked in the belt of her black jeans, and she took a long drag off her cigarette, watching Gabby the entire time. Her jaw jutted out, and the embers glowed in the dusk as they fell to the ground. "I've been waiting for you to come out. If I go in, Chuck will hear me, and he would spit tacks."

"What is it?"

"Well, it's about Chuck." Her gaze was unflinching. She had an open, candid expression.

"Yeah?"

"I know you're just trying to do your job, Deputy, but I know something you don't."

"What's that?"

"Well, I know he was at home Monday night, all night, right up until Tuesday morning. So he couldn't have burnt Jim Parker's hives. He was in his bed."

"How do you know that?" Gabby said, watching Kylie carefully. The woman exhibited none of the trademarks of a liar. Her eyes weren't shifty. She wasn't fidgeting. She seemed calm and purposeful. She could, of course, just be a very good liar.

"Well, this is the part I shouldn't tell you."

"It's okay," Gabby replied. "I need to know the truth."

"Well, you see, I was there in the bed with him."

"Oh. I thought—" Gabby stopped herself. She'd heard Kylie was a lesbian.

"You thought I was a dyke, I know. That's what people say. I don't have much time for that. People can't imagine how a straight woman can beat all the men in the Coyote Classic, so they make up stories to explain it away."

"So you and Chuck are a couple?"

"Chuck doesn't like talking about it. I don't either, frankly. We act like friends. When I stay the night at his place I park my truck out back, in case somebody drives up. This is a small island. People need to mind their own business."

Gabby nodded.

"Besides, Chuck has this thing. He says it would disrespect Elsie's memory."

"I see," Gabby said, pausing for a moment. The story made sense, and it filled in a missing piece. She remembered the two corduroy armchairs at Chuck's place and the empty beer cans on the floor next to each one. For a moment she could see it—Kylie and Chuck sitting there, drinking beers together, laughing and chatting even more comfortably than they did at the bar. "Kylie, do you drink beer?"

Kylie looked surprised by the question. "Doesn't everyone?"

"Were you drinking beer when you were at Chuck's Monday night?"

Kylie nodded. "We always do. I know Chuck might not seem it, but he's a gentle soul under all that huff and puff. He just talks shit sometimes. He got bitter when he lost Elsie. Never been the same."

Gabby smiled. "He, ah, he tells me Jim Parker is a Satanist."

Kylie laughed out loud. "See what I mean? Talking shit. He hates that man with a vengeance. He's angry is all, looking for someone to blame things on. He's wounded." Her voice had gone soft. She was clearly fond of Chuck.

Gabby looked out beyond the light of the flood lamp. The windows of the library next door were dark. She'd had no idea about Chuck and Kylie. In spite of all the rumors and gossip that flew around this island, there were still secrets. The people who settled here tended to be private and guarded. There were countless relationships and goings-on that Gabby didn't know about. "How long have you two, ah, been seeing each other?" she asked.

"Oh, well, we messed around about twenty years ago, but he called it off because of Elsie. Then, we sort of hooked up again after Elsie died."

"Tell me, Kylie. How do you know he didn't leave in the middle of the night to burn Jim's hives? He could have slipped out while you were sleeping. Then slipped back in."

"Well, two things. One, I'm a real light sleeper. Two, we didn't do much sleeping that night, if you know what I mean." Kylie smiled lewdly, giving Gabby a wink.

"Would you be willing to give me an affidavit?" Gabby asked. "About the alibi?"

"What's that?"

"It's a sworn written statement where you explain how you know that Chuck was at home."

"Oh, I don't know. He would not like that at all. Don't know that I would either. Suits me fine people thinking I'm a dyke. Keeps the drunk men away. Assholes."

Gabby understood that. She'd experienced more than a few unwanted advances herself from some of the lonely men on this island. There weren't enough women here. Fortunately, her badge seemed to scare the most desperate men off.

She looked closely at Kylie. "Well, Chuck wouldn't like going to jail for a crime he didn't commit either. We can go in right now, and I can take your statement right away, if you'd like." She gestured back toward the substation. Although she was tired and wanted to get home, Chuck's alibi was more important than her putting up her feet.

Kylie looked at the building. "Well, the thing is, I think he might ditch me for good if I went and told everyone this."

"If you want to help him, I need an affidavit."

Kylie took another deep drag off her cigarette. "Do you think he's going to go to jail?"

"An alibi will help make sure he doesn't. In fact, with an alibi, the case against him is looking very thin. I'd have to let him go."

Kylie threw her cigarette down on the ground and stomped it out. Then she picked it up carefully and put it in the pocket of her flannel shirt. "If I give you this written statement right now, would you let him go tonight?"

Gabby nodded and then opened her mouth to say, "Yes, I would," but Kylie was already walking toward the building.

20



IN THE VERY EARLY hours of the next morning, a strange noise woke Jim from his short and fitful sleep. He didn't know what it was at first. It was a faraway roar, like the sea or a distant train.

As he opened his eyes, he could make out an occasional crackling noise. There was an orange glow coming in his window. He turned to look at the clock next to his bed. It was 4 a.m. It was too early for that glow to be sunrise. He jumped out of bed and looked out toward the back acre.

The light from the fire seemed to fill the entire sky, and the trees made black shapes against an orange blaze. For a moment, in his bleary-eyed state, he thought the woods were on fire. Then, slowly, he realized that the burning was more specific than that. It was coming from beyond the fenced garden, at the back of the property. The trees weren't on fire. His home hives were burning.

He bolted out of his bedroom and ran down the short hallway wearing nothing but the boxer shorts he'd been sleeping in. He pounded on Ava's door, shouting, "Ava, get up! Fire! Come help!"

In the kitchen, he flipped on the back porch light and headed out the back door. He stepped into his work boots, quickly shoved the long laces inside, and ran—in boxers and boots, skin against the cool night air—to the old wooden shed behind the garage.

He opened the door and flipped on the light. A single, bare bulb hung above a rough workbench there, casting dark shadows. He reached under the workbench and grabbed the extinguisher. When he returned to the yard carrying it, Ava was already there, also wearing the clothes she had been sleeping in, shorts and a tank top, plus her favorite black Converse sneakers.

"Dad, be careful!" she yelled at him.

He ran past the garden and over to the hives. The fire was taller than he was. The flames were dangerously close to the pines and maples behind, licking up toward the heavy branches. Thankfully, it was far enough from the house to not be an immediate threat, but he was worried about the fire spreading into the woods. Who knew what could happen if it reached there?

"Ava, get the fire trucks here!" he yelled. "Call 911!"

She darted back into the house, and he turned to face the fire. How had this happened? Chuck Norman was in jail, wasn't he? Who was doing this?

The heat on his face was intense. He pulled the pin on the extinguisher, aimed the nozzle at the base of the fire at the closest hive, and squeezed the trigger. A thick white stream shot out. He swept the nozzle from side to side until the flames died down. The extinguisher had a short discharge time, so as soon as the fire on the first hive was dead, he rushed to the next one. But just as the fire on the second hive began to die down, the extinguisher sputtered to its end. There were still six more hives burning.

He hurried back toward the house, turned on the garden hose, and pulled the end out as close to the hives as it would go. It didn't reach. He ran to the old shed, grabbed two plastic buckets he had there, and ran back to the hose to fill one of them. He stood there in the middle of the backyard, feeling like it was taking forever to fill the bucket. The flames roared.

Ava came running out of the house. "They're on their way!"

As they waited for the fire department to show up, they frantically threw one bucket of water after the next onto the sizzling flames, but with little effect. Each time it seemed to take even longer to fill the buckets from the hose. Jim felt entirely helpless.

When the fire truck arrived, the volunteer firefighters unrolled the long, gray fire hose and began dowsing the flames.

Ava was standing by the old swing set, watching. Jim noticed a few of the firefighters glancing over at her, in those flimsy shorts and tank top.

"Go put something on," he snapped at her.

She glared at him with contempt. "You're in your boxers."

"That's different."

He thought of Sarah, and for a moment he was in a different time entirely. He was in that small room with that scratched white table.

"Jesus," Ava said, disgusted, but she turned and went back into the house. A few moments later she returned in sweatpants and a baggy sweatshirt.

By the time the fire was out, the first of the morning light had begun to infuse the back acre with a faint blue glow. The ground was smoking. The hives were completely gone. In the trees, he could see that the two video surveillance cameras he'd installed were now charred and melted.

Deputy Gabby showed up just as the firefighters were rolling up the hose. Jim and Ava stood looking at the smoking remains.

"Hello," Gabby said, greeting both Ava and Jim.

Jim said nothing. Still only wearing his boxers and his boots, he simply turned to Gabby and nodded. No doubt any minute she'd begin asking him why he burnt his own hives again.

"What time did you discover the fire?" Gabby asked.

"Four a.m.," Jim said flatly. "I heard the burning."

"Did you hear anything before that? Any cars? Anything?"

"No. Nothing." Jim turned to Ava. "Did you?"

"No," Ava answered, then turned to Gabby to elaborate. "My

bedroom is at the front of the house. I didn't hear anyone come up the drive."

Jim added, "I don't like her being in that bedroom."

"Oh, God." Ava rolled her eyes. "Not that old story."

"How do you think they got in?" Gabby said, interrupting their quarrel. "From the road? Or from the woods?"

"Probably from the woods. I would have heard them," Ava said, and then she turned to Jim. "Which just goes to show that the back bedroom is just as dangerous as the front. Bad guys are everywhere, aren't they, Dad?" Her voice was harsh and sarcastic. She turned and walked back into the house.

Around them, the firefighters were packing up the last of their equipment.

Jim turned to Gabby. "Sorry about my daughter."

"She's a teenager," she smiled. "Aren't they, like, aliens or something?"

"Yes. I think so."

"She's fine. You're very protective."

He looked at her closely. "Is that a criticism?"

"An observation. I had a protective father. I empathize with your daughter."

Jim was shocked. Gabby had no right to tell him how to parent. He opened his mouth to object, but the fire truck engine came to life, and he and Gabby had to step out of the way to allow the driver to negotiate its way off the property.

Gabby looked around. "It would be good to know for certain how the arsonist came in."

"I installed wired surveillance cameras," Jim said. "They're gone now." He gestured to the charred remains still mounted to the nearby trees. "But they would have been working up until the fire destroyed them and their wiring. The footage goes directly to a digital video recorder under my desk. We can stand here and guess at which way they came in, but the footage might show for certain."

"Good thinking," Gabby said.

"At least we know it's not Chuck Norman." Jim turned to her. "Is he already in Au Bois? Or still in the holding cell in the station?"

Gabby looked solemn. "I let him go last night. He had an alibi. The evidence didn't stack up."

"You did what?" He couldn't believe his ears. It made no sense. Chuck was the one doing this.

"He's at home," she said, sounding unapologetic. "An alibi goes a long way. And it was a good one. The evidence was just too thin."

"Who's his alibi?"

"Doesn't matter. The alibi is credible. Trust me."

"Trust you? You won't even tell me who it is."

"It's none of your business, Mr. Parker." Her tone had become formal, almost angry.

"None of my business? He's burning my hives. In the middle of a Global Bee Crisis. And you let him go. Or wait. Don't tell me. Now you're going to start accusing me of killing my own bees again, right?"

"I never accused you."

"You implied it."

"I had to consider all the options. I'm sorry." For a brief moment, the look on her face seemed almost kind. "You're no longer a suspect."

Jim was a bit taken aback by the apology. He wasn't expecting that.

She turned away and walked over to the burnt remains to study them. She picked up a stick from nearby and poked at something in the ashes, then pulled whatever it was out and over onto the grass. Turning back to Jim, she said. "Have you noticed anything else out of the ordinary?"

"You mean, besides the fact that I woke up to discover that my hives were on fire and the local deputy is completely useless?"

"Jim, I'm doing everything I can. Why are you so angry at me?"

He was once again taken aback. She was so forthright. "I don't know. I'm just angry. I'm sorry. I've lost so many bees. I want this to stop."

"I understand. I want it to stop too. Please don't fight me."

He nodded, and they fell silent for a moment. The air still smelled of smoke. The sun hadn't yet come up over the horizon, and the light around them was still tinted blue.

"There is something," he said, looking over at the smoldering ashes and remembering the strange gray bees he'd found in those hives.

"What?" she asked.

"Yesterday I found some peculiar bees in some of my hives."

"What do you mean?"

He told her about the gray bees, how they seemed to have infiltrated the hives. Then he told her about his visit to Lewis at Hadley Agritech.

"There was something weird about Lewis' response to the bee," Jim said. "He's a little awkward on the best of days, but this was different. I had a funny feeling."

She smiled. "That doesn't exactly give me a lot to go on, Jim. A funny feeling doesn't give me probable cause."

"I know. But what if it's a gen-mod?"

Just then, Kevin Miller, the volunteer fire chief, walked over to Jim and Gabby, stopping their conversation short. "We'll be on our way now." Kevin had a sharp gray buzzcut, and he carried with him an air of authority that came from a long career as a professional firefighter before coming to Gull Island to retire.

"Thanks," Jim said, shaking his hand. "I really appreciate it."

"Before you go, Kevin," Gabby said. "Let me ask you something." She walked over to the grass near the charred remains and picked something up. It was the thing she'd been poking with the stick. She brought it over to Kevin.

Jim saw that it was a piece of pale green foam, like he'd seen at the other two arson locations. It looked wet from the fire hose.

"What do you think this is?" Gabby asked.

Kevin looked at it closely. He pinched it in his fingers and rubbed it. "Well, can't be entirely sure from just looking at this little bit, but it looks like flexible polyurethane foam."

"What's that?" Gabby asked.

"It's used inside furniture, under carpets, for bedding and packaging, stuff like that. I hate it myself."

"Why?"

"It's not fire retardant. It burns with enough heat."

He handed it back to Gabby.

She nodded and shook his hand. "You and your crew did good work here. Thank you for that."

The three of them walked out to the front of Jim's house together.

When Kevin and the last of the volunteer firefighters climbed into the truck and drove off, Jim and Gabby were left standing by the front porch. Jim was still in his boxers, something he became acutely aware of at this moment.

Thankfully, Gabby was looking at the ground, focused on inspecting the dirt track. "If they came in this way, and if they drove a car in, the fire truck would've most likely destroyed any tracks."

Jim nodded. He hated to think that they'd already destroyed evidence that would help them catch the arsonist.

"Is Ava a sound sleeper?" Gabby asked.

"Why?"

"If a car were to come up the drive, how likely do you think it is she would hear it?"

"Oh, she might not have heard. She's usually dead to the world."

"At least we have the camera footage."

"Yeah, I'll take a look at it."

Gabby paused. "I'd like to review it with you."

"Oh, yeah," he said. "Of course. That makes sense."

She glanced toward the house.

"Now?" he said. "Right now?" He did a quick mental inventory, trying to think if the place was a mess. He felt awkward in his boxers.

She smiled. "No time like the present."

21

"LET ME MAKE SOME COFFEE," Jim said, gesturing Gabby toward the kitchen. He left his work boots on the front porch. "Then we can look at the footage."

Gabby took a seat at the kitchen table, and Jim prepared the coffee maker. It was only then that he looked up and saw Gabby watching him closely. She quickly looked away and smiled. Now it was beyond awkward. He felt like an absolute idiot standing there in his boxers. Outside it had been relatively dark, and there was the emergency of a raging fire. Now, under the harsh glare of the ceiling light, it was all different.

He shifted self-consciously and said, "Ah, while that's brewing I'll just go get dressed."

Gabby was clearly restraining a laugh. She hesitated, as though she was holding back from saying something, then said, "Don't feel like you have to on my account."

Jim smiled, embarrassed. "I'm sorry. I'm basically a hermit. I don't really know how to behave around other human beings."

"You'll get no complaints from me," she said, and finally let go of her laugh.

He grinned at her. "Officer, I don't know if it's appropriate for you to say that to me."

She laughed again. "No, probably not."

He went to his bedroom and threw on a pair of army green cargo shorts and one of his Parker Pollination t-shirts. He grabbed his laptop while he was there. On his way back down the hallway, he saw the light was still on in Ava's bedroom.

He knocked.

"Yeah?" Ava said.

"Can I come in?" he asked.

She gave a long sigh through the door. "Okay."

He cracked the door and peeked his head inside. Ava was on her bed, typing on her laptop. Her fish tank was bubbling pleasantly on the table next to her, the fluorescent fish swimming back and forth. Although he hated those gen-mod fish almost on principle, he had to admit that he did like how calm the tank made her room feel.

"Are you okay?" he asked.

"Yeah." She didn't even look up from her laptop. She continued typing.

"It was a bit scary, the fire."

She shrugged. "It's fine."

Jim walked over and sat on the edge of her bed. "Ava, I was scared. It's okay to be scared."

She rolled her eyes and shut the laptop. "It's not like the house was on fire. It's just your stupid bees."

Jim felt like she'd kicked him. Why was it so hard talking to his daughter? Was she upset he'd mentioned his concerns about her bedroom to Gabby? He stood up and walked back to the door.

"Deputy Gabby is here," he said, without looking back at her. "We're going to review my camera footage."

"Oh, reeeeally?" Ava said, her voice dripping with sarcasm and exaggerated surprise.

Jim turned and saw that she was smiling. It was nice to see, but it did confuse him. "What's so funny?"

"Oh, come on, Dad," Ava said, looking exasperated.

"What?"

"Camera footage?"

"Yes."

She opened up her laptop again and muttered, "I guess running around in your underwear is one way to get a lady's attention."

Jim didn't know what to make of this. It had been three years since Sarah's death, and Ava had never once teased him about a woman. She'd never even asked if he was going to date again. It was as though there had remained an unspoken assumption between them that he would lead the life of a monk for the rest of his life.

"She's a cop," he said, whispering. Gabby was just out in the kitchen, after all, and it was a small house. He felt deeply uncomfortable with the way Ava was pushing boundaries right now. "It's not like that."

She rolled her eyes again. "Sometimes I think you're brain damaged."

"Ava," Jim said in a scolding tone.

"Didn't you see how she's been ogling you all night? She's worse than the firemen."

"Show a little respect. For Deputy Gabby *and* for me."

Ava glared at him. "Well, I guess it's not just teenage girls who should avoid prancing around half naked."

Jim opened his mouth to reprimand her, but he stopped himself. He wasn't going to let her rattle his cage. He turned and walked abruptly out of her bedroom.

There had been a time when Ava's respect for him was something he took for granted. He had authority. As she'd developed into an independent young woman, it was becoming increasingly difficult to maintain any parental authority whatsoever.

He just wanted Ava to do what he said, to be careful, to follow his advice. He didn't want what happened to Sarah to happen to her. But she didn't do anything he said, or if she did it was only after a major argument. She was constantly challenging him. It had gotten to the point where he had to choose his battles carefully.

Sarah would have known how to deal with Ava. He wished she were here.

Back in the kitchen, he saw Gabby standing in front of the small bookshelf, looking at the cookbooks.

"Do you cook?" she asked as he set his laptop down on the kitchen table.

"Yes," Jim said, then stopped himself. "But, well, those cookbooks are my wife's. I mostly just watch YouTube videos." He started pouring the hot coffee into two cups. "The coffee's not real, I'm afraid."

"How long ago did Sarah die?" Gabby asked.

Jim stopped where he stood, holding the coffee pot mid-air, thrown by the question. It was so forthright and direct. He'd never actually told Gabby Sarah's name or that she was dead. He felt vulnerable, like Gabby was touching a wound. Of course news of his past would have spread on the island, and he had no doubt everyone knew what happened. They could have read about it in old news reports if they were that curious. And knowing the people on this island, they would be.

"Three years, one month, and fifteen days," he said. He put the coffee pot back into the coffee maker.

"Wow. Down to the day."

"She died on the first of the month. It makes it easy to count."

"Oh," Gabby said.

Looking across the kitchen at her, Jim noticed that she suddenly looked uneasy. "I'm sorry," he said. "That's morbid."

"No. It's okay. I did ask."

He looked down. Talking about Sarah was still painful. It was like a bee stinger was stuck in his skin. Long after the initial sting, it continued pumping venom into him.

Some nights he still had vengeance dreams where he was beating a man to a bloody pulp. He would wake with his heart racing and anger coursing through his body, like a great torrent of fire and hate. He wondered if it would ever go away, though part of him didn't want it to end. If the pain and anger stopped, would that mean he'd forgotten her, that he didn't care anymore?

"I can access the security footage through my home network," he said, trying to steer the conversation and his thoughts away from this dark place. He pointed to his laptop, then sat down at the table and opened it up.

"I'm sorry," Gabby said. "I've made you uncomfortable."

"No, it's fine," Jim said. "We can watch the footage here."

She sat down next to him and Jim brought up the footage. Their coffees were steaming in front of them, and there was a golden glow in the sky just visible through the kitchen windows.

"The camera has infrared technology," Jim said. "So, it's got a good night vision range."

He started playing the footage at the midnight mark. The grainy video showed the eight hives standing untouched, the trees behind them. Jim skipped forward to the first event: a raccoon passing across the screen, at around 1 a.m., checking out the hives. The next event was at 3 a.m. Jim jumped to it.

Suddenly, they were watching a white shape come out of the woods from behind the hives. In the darkness, the shape was at first unclear.

"Wow," Gabby said.

Jim slowed the video, and they both leaned in. They were very close to each other, focusing on the screen.

The white shape was a person. Judging by the height compared to the hives, it looked to be a tall man. He was wearing some sort of protective suit and was carrying something square in his right hand, down at his side. In his left hand there were strips of something long and thin.

"That's not a bee suit, is it?" Gabby asked.

The image was vague, but then the man came closer into view. The fabric of the suit appeared shiny, almost as if it was made of rubber.

The man turned, and they got a closer look. He was wearing large, rubber boots and thick gloves. The hood was clear in front, and he was wearing some sort of breathing gear.

"That's a hazmat suit," Gabby said. "Why would you wear a hazmat suit?"

"I don't know. It's a bit overkill for bees." He'd seen all kinds of bee suits, including sting-resistant, three-layer ventilated suits, fencing style suits, and even new, high-tech versions that looked almost like space suits. But he'd never seen anyone approach a beehive in a biohazard suit.

"He's tall," Gabby said.

Jim nodded.

The man on the screen turned, and it became clear that the thing in his right hand was a large, square jerry can.

Jim pointed to the screen. "That looks like the gas can you found at Bennett Orchards."

"Yes," Gabby said. "But I've discovered that a lot of people on the island have those."

She was looking back at him and, for a moment, Jim felt staggered. She was so close. At that distance, he could see how beautiful she was. Normally the horrible uniform was all he could see. He forced himself to look back at the screen. It felt like he was being disloyal to Sarah, ignoring the stinger that was embedded in his skin.

"It's Chuck," Jim said. "It's got to be. You let him go."

"We still don't have enough evidence, and he has an alibi."

"You should find out if he has an alibi for 3 o'clock this morning."

Gabby nodded but said nothing.

They watched as the man set down the jerry can and moved toward the first hive. He took one of the long, thin strips he was carrying and bent down. He slid the strip into the hive entrance, just above the landing board.

"He's blocking the entrance," Jim said. "Like I thought. So the bees can't get out."

"That's the foam," Gabby said.

The man repeated this action at each hive with practiced ease. He clearly knew his way around beehives, and it looked like he'd done this before. Then he leaned down and opened the jerry can. He began pouring fuel on each one of the hives. Jim watched, feeling helpless, as though even now he should be able to stop the man.

They watched as he poured a line of fuel between each hive, and then a line from the last hive off across the ground. He stepped into the woods and left the gas can under the trees. Then he stepped back out, and appeared to be struggling with something, using his large, thick gloves. A box of matches. He threw something, a lit match Jim presumed, onto the ground. Fire bolted across the gasoline trail, bursting into flames across the hives in quick succession. The blaze was immediate and intense. Then the man was gone.

"Where did he go?" Jim asked. "Back into the woods?"

"He must have," Gabby said. "The flames blocked the view."

Jim rewound the footage, watching to see which direction the man went, but it was unclear. Then he and Gabby just sat there together, watching the hives burn. Eventually, he brought himself around to fast forward the video until the point when the cameras stopped working. Then he shut the laptop.

Outside the kitchen windows, the sky had turned a brighter shade of blue, and the golden glow from the east was stronger.

Gabby leaned back and took a deep breath. "I'm going to go check out those woods. The sun will be up soon."

"Now's a good time," Jim said. "The morning light casts long shadows over impressions in the ground, making them easier to see."

"You sound like a tracker," Gabby said.

"That's a correct assumption. I'm actually one of those weirdos who gets up in the middle of the night on the first snowfall to track animals through the woods. In those conditions everything leaves a trail. You can follow rabbit tracks, and deer, and coyote. They all tell a story."

"Are you a deer hunter?" Gabby asked.

Jim thought of his father. "Not really. I just like tracking things."

Gabby looked out the window for a moment. "Well, I'm headed outside. I was a city cop before I came here. I might be able to use your help."

He paused and considered this. He definitely liked the idea of helping to figure out who had done this, but he was surprised to find that he also liked the idea of spending some more time with this particular deputy.

"Being a city cop must have been very different to working here," he said.

"I worked on the South and West Side of Chicago, so there was a lot of gang violence, but you name it and I saw it. Homicide, rape, aggravated battery, human trafficking. The occasional robbery we dealt with was practically light relief. It was hard work, to be honest. I got burnt out."

"Is that why you came here?"

She nodded slowly, like she was lost in thought. "To escape. Like a lot of people, I suppose."

"Yeah," Jim said. "I'm one of those."

"I know." She smiled, and there was a gentleness in her eyes he hadn't seen before. He didn't know what to make of it. What, exactly, did she know? It must be that she knew how Sarah died, and he felt suddenly uncomfortable.

He stood up and said, "Let me get my things." In his bedroom he grabbed his watch, compass, and hand lens. He opened up his wallet and looked at his picture of Sarah. It was an old photo, and she was young. It was just after they'd gotten engaged. Her head was tilted slightly, smiling at the camera. She looked happy. He felt confused. What would Sarah want him to do? He slid the picture back in his wallet and left the room.

On the way back down the hall, he stopped at Ava's bedroom door and knocked.

"Whaaat," she called out in annoyance. Her voice was groggy.

"Sorry, Avey. Were you sleeping again?"

From the other side of the door, she grumbled. "It's early. Normal people are asleep."

"Sorry. I thought you were still awake."

"I am now."

"I just wanted you to know I'm headed out into the woods with Deputy Gabby."

"That's romantic."

"Ava, stop that," he said. She seemed obsessed with insinuating there was already something happening between him and Gabby. "We're going to see if we can track the arsonist. That's all."

He locked the front door and then went into the kitchen. He grabbed a couple of granola bars from the cupboard—they might get hungry—and threw them in the pockets of his shorts. Then with Gabby he stepped out the back door, locking it tightly behind him.

The sky to the east was gold and orange against the silhouette of the trees. Morning birdsong had already started, and he could hear the calls of robins, sparrows, and a lone cardinal.

Gabby headed directly to the back corner of the property, where she looked at the trees just behind the scorched remains of the hives. Jim followed.

"The ground is dry," she said. "Except for around here where the fire hose sprayed. Dry ground will make it harder to find any footprints."

Jim pointed into the woods. "There's a lot of undergrowth under the trees here, so that'll help."

They walked up and down the line of trees behind the burn marks, and then Jim stopped.

"Look here," he said, pointing to a spot at the edge of the trees where the undergrowth was pushed down into an unnatural position. "That must be where he left."

"We can go in," Gabby said, "But we need to walk alongside it, not directly on it, to avoid tampering with any evidence."

Jim was impressed. She knew what she was talking about. "I thought city cops didn't know about tracking in the woods."

"I'm not an idiot. I've been here six years."

"You don't really need my help, do you?" he said.

"Sure I do."

Jim nodded as he slowly picked up on the implication. Despite being socially awkward, even he could read between the lines here. When Gabby stepped forward, he followed her, and together they disappeared into the End Woods.

22

AVA COULDN'T BELIEVE that the Window Cop had woke her up again just to tell her that he was going to the End Woods. He was so irritating. She was lying in bed, and the air in her room felt stifling. Her laptop was at her side and Bailey was at her feet. She envied the dog's long, slow breathing and his quick return to sleep.

She'd heard the Window Cop and Deputy Gabby still talking in the kitchen. The walls in this old house were paper thin. She'd heard her dad's footsteps to the front door, and the turn of the lock—he was always locking doors—and then heard them go out the back door. He would have locked that door too, she was sure. Everywhere that man went he was trying to keep things out.

Now she couldn't get back to sleep. Her phone was on the floor next to her bed, and she'd been avoiding it. Last night she'd thrown it face down, and she hadn't looked at it since. As long as she refused to look at it everything would be okay.

Bailey rolled over and put his head on her stomach. It was almost as if he knew she was worried, even in sleep. She loved this darn dog. She stroked his neck and continued to stare at the ceiling. Her skin was hot and sweaty. Someday she was going to throw a brick through that front window, just to open it. Every time she complained to the Window Cop about her room not getting enough fresh air, he told her to just sleep with her bedroom door open. She refused to do that. It would destroy the only privacy she had.

She glanced over at the floor to where her phone was. As long as she didn't turn it over, there was a possibility. There could be a message from Eddie. She imagined the perfect message, the one that would make everything okay.

*So sorry, babe. I've been out of range. I love you. I understand. I support your decision. I'll get us the money.*

It wasn't entirely implausible, was it? She stopped petting Bailey for a moment—he nuzzled her hand to continue—and reached down to pick up her phone. Bailey groaned in protest. She closed her eyes as she brought the phone to her face, making a wish of sorts. Then she opened her eyes, checking for the message from Eddie that was surely there.

But there was nothing. No apology. No declaration of love. Nothing.

As she threw the phone down next to her on the bed, she felt crushed. Suddenly it felt like she could see the entire truth. She saw what she really was—just a foolish, bleary-eyed girl, callously dumped and stupidly pregnant, lying on a messy bed that was covered in dog hair in the corner of a stifling, oppressive room with the window nailed shut.

Bailey jumped down off the bed, turned to look at her, and wagged his tail. She had to get up. He wanted to go out. She walked slowly across the kitchen to the back door and opened it. Yes, the Window Cop had indeed locked it. Bailey bounded outside.

As she stood watching him sniff around, she thought about the possibilities. Maybe, just maybe, Eddie had left a voice message on the landline. She walked over to the phone on the wall, but there were no messages.

She opened the sash windows along the back of the kitchen and looked out toward the back acre and the trees beyond. The morning sun was still low. She was wearing the thin shorts and blue tank top she slept in, and the fresh morning air felt good against her skin. It smelled of fresh pine and dew on the grass. Birdsong came lilting in through the windows. She took a deep breath.

It wasn't unusual for the Window Cop to be gone all day in the End Woods. He often left early in the morning, like today, and she never really knew when he'd be back. He went looking for bee forage. He tracked animals. Even back in Ann Arbor, he was always driving off for time alone in nature. He once told her that the only reason he felt safe leaving her home alone here on the island was because Bailey was with her.

She took her cell phone and went out the back door. Bailey was wandering away, around to the front of the house, sniffing vigorously as though there was a new scent in the grass. She walked out toward the old swing set. While she was able to get messages in the house over wi-fi, she could only get phone reception outside, at the swings. Living here was like living in the Dark Ages.

She stepped barefoot across the dewy grass and hoped that the moment she sat down on the swing, her phone would tell her that she had missed a call. Maybe there was a new voicemail for her. Maybe Eddie had decided to call her phone instead of messaging.

Yes, that was it. Surely Eddie must have called her cell phone. What he had to say was too important for just a message, and too private to leave in a message on the landline, where the Window Cop might hear it.

She felt terrible. She'd assumed Eddie would agree that getting rid of the baby was the best thing. She still couldn't get over the fact that he'd proposed to her. Proposed! And she'd rejected him. Was it the right thing to do? Was she a horrible person? She feared she was. And now he'd left. Disappeared. She thought of the handful of beach pea flowers that he'd picked for her the last time she saw him, and that she'd thoughtlessly left on the floor of his car.

The swing set was a rusty beige thing. The two swings had wooden seats with faded green paint. She sat down on one, facing away from the house. The Window Cop used to talk about getting rid of this swing set, but when she started using it to talk on the phone, he'd stopped.

She checked for reception. The signal showed two bars, but there was no beep from her phone, no notification of a new voice-mail. She called her inbox anyway. "You have no new messages," the calm, nondescript female voice said. It was only then that Ava finally had to accept that Eddie had done nothing at all to contact her. No phone call on landline or mobile. No message. She stared out at the trees.

Over at the burnt beehives in the back corner, she could see an animal sniffing around. She knew that sometimes raccoons hung around her dad's beehives, trying to raid them for honey. This animal was about the size of a raccoon, but it didn't really look anything like a raccoon. It was hairless and gray.

Suddenly it stopped sniffing around. It turned its body toward her and stared. She could make out an unusual noise—a kind of humming with periodic clicking. She'd never heard anything like it. Was it coming from that weird animal?

*Hmmm. Hmmm. Cli-click.*

She looked around the back acre. In the morning light, it was difficult to tell where the noise was coming from. Then the noise stopped. She noticed that everything was surprisingly still. Even the birds had gone silent.

Before she knew what was happening, the animal was running quickly across the grass, right at her. It snarled loudly. It was low to the ground and angry as hell. Dark teeth flashed and snapped. It looked like a little demon.

There was no time to run. She had nothing to defend herself

with. She dropped her phone and pulled herself up, the rusty chains of the swing digging into her fingers and the palms of her hands. Her bare feet touched the wood, and she stood.

The creature was already under the swing set, and it reached up toward the wooden seat with its small, thin hands. It had tiny fingers tipped with sharp claws. Its skin looked moist. Its snout was long and pointed, and its teeth were horrible—fused and jagged and black. It snapped repeatedly at her, biting at the air. It was terrifying.

Ava twisted and tried to knock its face with the wooden seat, but it turned and came at her again from another angle. Her heart was pounding wildly. She moved without even thinking, as if thrown into some kind of shocked reflex. She grabbed the top bar above her and pulled her feet up, feeling exposed and vulnerable in her sleeping shorts and tank top. She began screaming, but it was pointless. There was nobody close enough to hear. Her hands slipped on the bar.

Below her, the snarling creature was pulling back, getting ready to pounce.

23

JIM WAS ALWAYS happy to be in the End Woods. Once, on a research trip to Japan, he'd learned the phrase "shinrin-yoku," which meant forest bathing. The Japanese belief was that being around trees was good for you; it improved your mental and physical wellbeing. He understood this completely. Being in the woods—the fertile scents, the light through the leaves—always made him feel refreshed and alive.

Gabby was walking in front of him, pushing through the undergrowth, and he followed her closely.

"According to your video footage," she said, "it was almost three hours ago that the guy in the hazmat suit left your property. We're unlikely to actually find him."

"True," Jim said. "He's probably back home now, eating whatever arsonists eat for breakfast."

Gabby laughed. "I just want to follow the path he took to your hives. And see if he left anything behind."

"Makes sense."

It was funny because Jim would be doing something like this even if he weren't trying to find an arsonist. He took great pleasure in reading nature's signs, and it wasn't unusual for him to spend entire days wandering the End Woods, exploring the dense trees and swampy bogs. For him, it was about practicing the art of seeing and noticing, of just being present. It was his forest bath.

He'd studied the wetland plants and animals of O'Leary's Marsh. He'd observed the colors of the rocks along the shore of Stone Lake. Multiple times he'd hiked all the way up to the Indian Point Lighthouse and once, when circling back, he'd stumbled across a complex cave just north of Catmull's Thicket. These woods were his playground. He wished he could impart this joy of nature to Ava, but she seemed to barely want to leave her bedroom, let alone come out into the End Woods. When he'd told her about forest bathing, she'd looked at him and rolled her eyes like he was some sort of weirdo.

As he and Gabby walked now, they followed the path of crushed undergrowth that the arsonist had left behind. What Jim loved about tracking was that it required not only a keen awareness of the natural world, but an empathy with the animal —or person—you were following. Tracking didn't just reveal where something had gone, it revealed their state of mind as well. Was it running or walking? Did it move forward in a straight line, with a singular objective, or did it cross sporadically back and forth through the trees? These signals could tell you if it was being chased, if it was panicked, or if it was just meandering.

"I think he went this way," Jim said, pointing to a young sumac bush in the undergrowth. "You see, this sumac's been broken, just recently. The leaves are turned so the lighter underside is facing up. It's likely that our arsonist has been here."

Gabby smiled. "You're good."

Jim looked at his compass. "He's moving northeast, into the old-growth forest."

He pushed forward to the right, and now Gabby began following him. They continued on for a bit. A few rabbits scattered, but otherwise they saw nothing. The sun was coming up, and the morning light was beginning to pass sideways through the trees.

Jim began following a path where the undergrowth had been trodden down. Golden morning light showed spider webs that had been broken recently, where someone or something had walked by. They passed clearings with patches of butterfly weed, with its bright orange flowers and dark green, narrow leaves. Jim was fond of butterfly weed; it was a good source of food for bees, and deer and rabbits didn't like the taste of it.

Soon the thin canopy was behind them. The denser, older forest loomed around them. The trees here allowed less light through, so the undergrowth was thinner. That made it easier to walk but harder to track.

To their right, a large, fallen tree had created an opening in the canopy—revealing blue sky directly above. An enormous, slowly rotting trunk lay on the ground. In old-growth forests such as this, the trees were so ancient that they regularly fell as a result of their own massive weight. They replenished the topsoil as they decayed. This tree had clearly fallen decades ago. Mosses, fungi, seedlings, and ancient ferns were growing up in a microhabitat around the dead tree, creating a rich patch of life on the forest floor.

Jim paused and looked around at the trees. This was one of the few remaining old-growth forests still standing in Michigan, with hardwoods like beech, maple, and oak. Most of the state's forests had been cleared at some time during the original 1800s logging boom, and the remainder had been cleared at a steady pace in the decades that followed. The Gull Island Forest Reserve was like a museum. All of Michigan used to be covered with woods like this.

Not far from the fallen tree, purplish-pink blossoms dotted the ground. "In the canopy openings out here, there's a good amount of Joe Pye Weed," he said, pointing to them.

"Where?" Gabby asked.

"Over there. The purplish-pink blossoms. See it?"

Gabby craned her neck slightly. "Yes. It's a beautiful weed."

"Isn't it?" Jim said. "It blooms late summer through fall. My bees love it. And there's also a lot of native Michigan columbine in the spring out here, where there's enough light. With those plants, plus the local butterfly weed, this place is a veritable bee smorgasbord. Oh, and over that way," he said, gesturing off to the north. "There's an incredible patch of witch hazel."

Her brow furrowed. "What's that?"

"Witch hazel?"

"Yeah." She smiled. "I'm a deputy sheriff, not a botanist."

"It's a large, native shrub that grows bright yellow, spindly blossoms in the fall. They look like yellow spiders covering the branches. It's good for autumn foraging, so the bees can prepare honey for the winter."

Gabby nodded and walked on. Somewhere in the distance Jim heard the rhythmic beats of a woodpecker.

Ava never came out into the woods with him, and he was enjoying sharing this place with someone. He looked at Gabby and suddenly worried that he might be sounding a bit tedious. Not everyone loved nature the way he did.

"Sorry," he said. "I'm rattling on like a big old bore."

"No, not at all," Gabby said. A tender look flashed behind her eyes.

He paused and looked around. They had come to a stand of old-growth white pines. These trees weren't as large in circumference as the Pacific Northwest's redwoods or giant sequoias, but they were nonetheless impressive. Some were over 100 feet tall. Many were more than 300 years old.

"I've lost the trail," he said. He couldn't see which way the arsonist had gone. "Do you see it?"

"No," Gabby answered. "But when in doubt we should proceed in the direction he was headed. He wasn't weaving. He's been following an almost perfectly straight line northeast from your hives. So we should continue that way."

As they continued on, with Gabby leading again, Jim heard a chestnut-sided warbler calling from somewhere. He noted the high-pitched, repetitive chirps, which sounded like it was saying, *Pleased, pleased, pleased to meetcha!* Again the warbler called out, then fell silent. It reminded him of his dad, who had taught him to identify the warbler years ago. It had been a long time since he'd actually laid eyes on one of these birds.

Before long, there was a bright spot in the canopy straight ahead.

"That must be Miller's Track up ahead," Gabby said, referencing the track that provided the only car access into the depths of the End Woods.

Soon Gabby and Jim were stepping out from under the dark canopy and into the light. They had been walking for almost an hour. The sun was up above the horizon, but the morning light was still soft.

Jim looked to the left and the right. Miller's Track made a jagged and curving line heading roughly north from Reserve Road, ending at Stone Lake, about two miles north of where they were standing now. He knew there was a clearing out there, at the edge of the lake, where local deer and coyote hunters often set up base camp.

"Our arsonist must have come in this way, on the track," Gabby said. "He probably drove, and somewhere along here he would have parked and walked over to your place." She looked up and down the track. "Nobody passing by on Reserve Road would have seen his car. And people rarely use Miller's Track at night."

Jim nodded. He liked the way her brain worked.

She began walking north along the tire ruts, and moments later she gestured to a spot on the side of the track where a car had recently been parked. The undergrowth had been flattened by two lines of tires.

"Here," she said. "He would have left his car here."

Jim looked around. "It's about a three-and-a-half-mile walk through the woods from here to my hives."

"It would have been dark for him at that time," Gabby said, looking off into the trees. "He certainly didn't want anyone seeing him."

"True. But it was a clear night last night, so there would have been starshine. And the moon right now is waxing gibbous, so there would have been some moonlight. Even so, he'd probably need a flashlight under the forest canopy. It gets dark under there."

Gabby looked at him. "Waxing gibbous?"

"More than a half moon but not yet full."

Gabby smiled and shook her head. "Waxing gibbous. Witch hazel. The things in your head." She smiled warmly.

"I grew up in Michigan. Downstate. Reed City. My dad trapped and hunted. He took me out with him all the time. He taught me things about the woods."

"Well, I grew up on the Southside of Chicago. We learned different things, like how not to get shot. Now, give me a minute. I'm going to look around to see if our arsonist left anything behind."

Gabby stepped away and Jim looked off into the trees. He heard the warbler again.

*Pleased, pleased, pleased to meetcha!*

The bird was low in the branches to the north. He left Gabby and began walking along the track to see if he could lay eyes on the bird. In the summer, male chestnut-sided warblers were unmistakable. They had dark-streaked gray backs, white faces, black eye stripes, and beautiful, yellow-green crowns. He would love to see a warbler again.

He'd walked nearly a hundred feet or so down the track when he saw some movement off to the east. Looking in the direction through the trees, it was difficult to tell what the movement was. It was certainly no bird. He looked back to see if he could spot

Gabby and signal to her, but the track had made a bend to the right, and she was out of sight. He looked again toward the movement. Something shifted again.

Someone, or something, was out there. It couldn't be the arsonist, could it? He would have left hours ago. Jim squatted down to make himself less visible. The movement was coming from an opening in the canopy, where another large tree had come down. There was a small clearing there, probably sixty feet in front of him, through the trees. He waited, but he saw nothing. Then he heard a rustling. It seemed to be coming from the other side of the downed tree. He looked back along the track again. Gabby was still nowhere to be seen. If he ran back to get her, it might give whoever was there a signal that they were here.

He began moving forward in the direction of the fallen tree. He stepped carefully, trying to avoid any noise. One snapping twig could expose him. His mind raced. Why would the arsonist still be out here when his car was already gone? Something didn't make sense. Could there have been two of them? One driving and one doing the burning? Could the driver have left the arsonist behind?

Jim paused and considered his options. The arsonist could be armed, while he had no weapon on him. It was okay. He needed only to see the man clearly, to identify him before returning to Gabby out on the road. She had a gun in her holster if they needed it.

It was too risky to simply pop up on this side of the downed tree at close range. He changed tack and veered to the left, deeper into the woods. The forest here was full of red maple, along with basswood and some yellow birch. Moving back under the darkened canopy, he became cloaked by shadow. There was less undergrowth to negotiate. It was easier to move silently.

He circled around the northern side of the clearing, keeping his eyes always on the downed tree at its center. Who was moving on the other side of that tree? This wide circle around the clearing was taking longer than he'd planned. Soon Gabby would come looking for him and risk alerting the person to their presence.

Hidden by the gloom cast by the thick canopy, he circled just past the end of the tree. There was that movement again—something rustling. A low hemlock behind the fallen tree blocked his view, but he could see the branches and leaves shifting.

Just then Gabby called out from over near the track. "Jim?" Her voice came through the trees.

The movement behind the hemlock stopped. The only advantage Jim had was that whoever was behind that hemlock didn't know he was here. He didn't answer Gabby. Instead, he began moving more quickly, circling the clearing so that the hemlock was no longer blocking his sight line. He had to see who was there.

"Jim?" Gabby called out again.

A few more steps and finally Jim could see the source of the movement and rustling. It was coyotes. Two of them. He breathed a sigh of disappointment—or maybe it was relief? They were up close to the downed tree, and they seemed to be pulling at something on the ground. It looked like they were feeding. There was blood on their mouths. He couldn't see the source of their meal, but based on their distance from each other, it had to be large. They weren't fighting over it, like a rabbit. It must be a fallen deer.

Gabby called out, "Where are you?" She was closer now.

The coyotes perked up their heads. One stepped away from the tree, ready to run.

"Over here!" he called out, standing.

The coyotes turned and saw him, and they both ran, disappearing into the woods.

"I'm here in this clearing," he yelled, walking forward to see what the coyotes had been feeding on. There was the smell of blood.

"What are you doing out there?"

He couldn't see her yet, but he could hear her as she began moving through the undergrowth toward the clearing.

When Jim reached the spot where the coyotes had been feeding, he was at first confused by what he saw. It made no sense.

It was a human leg. Then the full body came into view.

The coyotes had been feeding on a dead man.

Jim stopped in his tracks. He was hit by the unholy stench of a decomposing body. It was a rank, powerful smell.

He yelled out. "Gabby! There's a body here!"

AVA WAS HANGING onto the top bar of the swing set, trying to pull her feet up. As she looked down, she saw the creature jump. She pulled her entire body up as quickly as she could, heaving with her arms until the bar was at her hips. She felt unsteady as she balanced precariously on top of the swing set.

The creature jumped high, but it missed her legs and crashed back to the ground. It looked up and snarled, snapping its jaws at her, making that horrible clicking sound. It stood still and then it lurched forward, like a spasm.

Her hands were sweaty and slippery, and she was positioned awkwardly. At any moment she might fall head first to the ground. Suddenly, the little demon sprang again. Its jaws were open wide. The black, jagged line of teeth came at her. It jumped higher than before, but fortunately it missed again.

The creature looked up at her, let out that strange hum, and pulled back once more. It was getting ready to pounce again.

Ava didn't know how long she could hang on.

All of a sudden, Bailey darted out from the side of the house and came running. The creature turned to look at the dog and snarled.

"Bailey, no!" she yelled.

Bailey rushed toward it, opened his mouth, and dove, tackling it to the ground. They were turning and rolling across the grass directly below her now, both growling fiercely.

"Bailey!" Ava heaved her belly over the bar. The top of the bar pushed into her stomach.

The creature broke free, turned to face Bailey, and let out a loud snarl. It was half the size of Bailey, but it was unafraid and raging. It arched its back and showed its jagged teeth again.

Ava looked around. If she jumped, she'd land right in the middle of their fight. She didn't know what to do. Bailey was going to get hurt. Already he was lunging at that thing again.

It shifted sideways, opened its mouth, and bit Bailey solidly on the neck. Bailey yelped and swung his head back and forth repeatedly. The creature clung on tightly. Its thick, rat-like tail flicked in the air.

Finally, Bailey managed to fling it off his neck. It landed on the ground with a thud. Even before it had a chance to stand, he ran at it again. It scrambled quickly to the side, but he pounced. This time he managed to grab the entire thing in his mouth. He was directly below Ava, holding onto the thing's back and shaking it furiously. Then he threw it into the air. It almost hit her. She shifted to the right without thinking and nearly fell.

When it landed, Bailey went after it again immediately. Ava was struggling to hang on, and they were still right below her. She turned her body parallel to the rusty bar and brought one leg over, until she was perched on top with a leg dangling down on either side. The metal structure beneath her seemed so small. She felt like she wasn't far enough away from the ground.

The creature twitched and pounced at Bailey again. It rushed at his side and arched its back. Then, in an odd lunge, it seemed to thrust its underside directly at Bailey's body. The dog yelped loudly, stumbled back, and fell. He looked dazed.

Ava screamed, "Bailey!"

The little demon turned to look at her. It ran over to one of the angled poles and began scratching. It was trying to climb up to get at her.

Bailey was struggling on the ground—yelping and convulsing, clearly in severe pain. The creature ignored him. It continued clawing at the swing set, looking for a way up. A strange, amber liquid was oozing like blood from puncture wounds on its back.

Ava held on tightly, balanced on the top bar. Below her, the creature started running from one angled pole to the next. She tried to figure out if she could jump down, away from that thing, and run. There must be something she could fight it with. A stick? A shovel? It was vicious and fast. She couldn't outrun it. She remained frozen in panic.

Bailey was trying to get to his feet. He seemed to be pushing himself forward in spite of his pain. He finally got up and came at the creature again, although more slowly this time. Its back was to him, and he jumped on it. They rolled. Bailey clamped his jaws firmly shut around its stomach and shook it again, even more wildly than before.

The creature let out a horrible scream. As it flailed around, it stretched its small hands and feet toward the dog's face, clawing at him. A red line split open across Bailey's snout, and he threw the thing into the air. It landed on its side, scrambled to its feet straight away, and turned back to face him. It snarled a warning and arched its back. Then it ran at him.

Ava felt herself slipping. She was so precariously balanced. She gripped the bar as tightly as she could.

Below her, Bailey stepped back, clearly weak. At the last minute, as the creature ran at him, he pounced and managed to grab it by the neck. He shook it back and forth ruthlessly. The growls and bellows from Bailey were wild and primal—more like a wolf than a dog. The creature thrashed about in his mouth. Then, with a final and violent shake, it fell in a heap on the ground.

It was still.

Bailey stumbled and collapsed, bleeding in several places. Ava was afraid to come down. Was the creature dead? Bailey needed help. But then the little demon moved. It shifted its front leg slightly. She didn't have much time. It was not dead. It was only stunned.

This was her chance. She jumped down, landing on the grass with a thud. The creature was only a few feet away, trying to lift its head. She stumbled for a moment before pulling herself to her feet.

It was already staring at her, and it was starting to stand.

## 25

JIM FELT sick to his stomach, staring at the body in front of him.

Gabby came around the other side of the fallen tree and stood next to him. "My God," she said. "My God."

The body was in pieces. Parts of it had clearly been eaten. One arm was missing entirely. Both legs had been pulled out of their sockets and discarded nearby. The limbs were mostly just bones. The skin and muscle were gone. On the torso, there were large wounds that looked like teeth marks. The shirt had been thrown back over the face, and the area under the rib cage had been ripped open. Maggots writhed within the wounds.

Jim turned to look at Gabby. She appeared visibly shaken, but then, very quickly, she shook her head and somehow changed. She hardened her face. It was like watching someone put on armor.

"It looks like an animal attack," she said. "Don't move. There might be tracks." Her voice was steady and measured. She looked down at the ground.

Jim saw only leaf litter and low undergrowth. Mosses and fungi covered the area around the downed tree. Some of the fungi had been crushed in what must have been a fight, but there were no visible footprints anywhere.

"I don't see any," he said.

"No, but there was clearly a struggle." She took out her phone and calmly began taking pictures. Then she stepped forward and leaned down slowly to take a closer look at the body.

Jim felt a strange kind of calm overtake him, encouraged by Gabby's impassive demeanor. This was happening. He had to deal with it.

"It's a man," Gabby said. "Older, based on the gray chest hair."

"Do you think it's Emmett?" he said, trying to echo her steady voice.

As though in answer, she took her flashlight off her duty belt and used it to pull the shirt down off of the face.

It was Emmett.

Jim felt horrible. He should have checked the woods on Tuesday. How long had Emmett been out here? Had he still been alive when he was in his house?

A strange kind of vertigo flooded Jim's head. It was one thing to see a dismembered and partially eaten body writhing with maggots. It was another thing entirely to realize, without a doubt, that this body was your neighbor.

He steadied himself, and he forced himself to return back to the facts. "There were coyotes here," he said. "Just now. I saw them. They were scavenging the remains."

"How many?" Gabby asked as she studied the body.

"Two. You don't think they killed him, do you?"

"It's unlikely. They normally shy away from people. Maybe if they were rabid. Of course, they're scavengers and if there's... meat lying around they'll happily eat it."

Jim stepped closer and leaned down next to her. He covered his nose and mouth. The smell was stomach-turning and oddly sweet—an awful combination of rotting meat, stale urine, and some sort of decaying, syrupy fruit. He leaned forward.

Gabby put out her arm. "Don't touch it."

"I won't," Jim said. He was looking at the maggots. He paused to take a deep breath inside the crook of his arm. "The smell is horrible."

"Yes." Her tone implied that she was no stranger to this smell.

He braced himself and concentrated. "I'm not a forensic entomologist. My specialty is bees and wasps, but I do know a bit about blowflies." He was trying to read the signs that nature had placed in front of him.

She nodded calmly. "We studied insect evidence briefly at the academy. What can you tell?"

He felt a kind of comfort as he retreated into his scientific observation. In scientific observation, everything followed an ordered rule. He pushed out the horrifying thoughts of what was in front of him and pointed to the maggots.

"Blowflies will lay eggs on the carcass of an animal within hours of its death," he said. "The same must be true on human corpses. In warm weather, like we've been having, the larvae emerge from their eggs within a day. They go through three stages—the first, second, and third instar. They molt between each stage. You can tell the stage it's in by the size of the larvae and the number of spiracles it has."

"Spiracles?"

"Tiny breathing holes. They're at the posterior end." He took a twig and pointed to one of the larvae. "Fly larvae have the mouth at one end of their body and the breathing holes at the other end. That means they can eat rotting flesh continuously, without having to stop to take a breath."

"Charming," she said.

"I'm just going to turn this one larva over."

He turned it with a twig. Then he took his hand lens from his pocket and held it up to the larvae. It was horrible leaning so close to the body. "Based on what I can see from these, I'd guess that this body has been here for three, maybe four days."

Oddly, this made him feel better. Emmett would have already been dead when he checked his house two days ago. He could not have saved him.

"So," Gabby said, "the body would have already been here before our arsonist arrived around three o'clock this morning."

"Yes, I'd say so." Jim stood and stepped away from the body. It felt like coming up for air.

Gabby followed him, looking off into the trees, toward the track and the spot where the arsonist's car had possibly been parked.

"In fact," she said, "there may be no connection at all between this body and the arson last night. It's entirely possible that the arsonist didn't even know this body was here."

"True," Jim said. Then he smiled faintly. "It only takes an idiot following a chestnut warbler to find a body like this."

"Is that why you wandered off? Jim, you can't do that. What if somebody dangerous was still out here?"

He laughed. "It's been a long time since I've seen a chestnut warbler."

She didn't laugh with him. Instead, she looked at him critically. It was the same way she'd looked at him when they were standing in front of his hives at Bennett Orchards. She was assessing him.

He somehow felt the need to explain. "I told you. I'm basically a hermit. I'm better off left alone in the woods."

As she watched him, he was taken aback once more by how beautiful she was. Even though her stern gaze now held an air of appraisal —as though she were weighing him up, calculating some kind of score—everything around her still seemed to light up when she looked at him. It made no sense. He felt awkward and looked away.

"Emmett walks with his dog Sandy," he said. "Where's Sandy?"

They both looked off into the trees.

"Sandy!" Jim yelled. "Come here, girl!"

There was no sound.

He kept yelling. "Sandy! Sandy!"

Eventually Gabby stopped him. "Jim, the dog's not out here." She let out a long sigh and looked toward Emmett's body. Something like sadness and frustration seemed to fall over her. "I deal with drunk tourists. Sometimes the occasional break-in. I came to Gull Island to get away from things like this."

There was a rustle in the undergrowth nearby. Jim looked up and saw movement in the trees. Bracken fern swayed and moved. Something was coming toward them.

Jim and Gabby instinctively took a step back. Jim saw Gabby put her hand on her gun. The movement came closer.

The ferns parted, and surprisingly, out came Sandy. The poor dog looked sick and tired. Dirt and twigs were embedded in her golden fur. Her head was low, but she bounded over to Jim and Gabby, very happy to see them.

Jim squatted down and greeted her. "Sandy! Good girl! Oh, are you okay?" He looked at her closely to see if she'd been injured, but besides the dirt and evidence of fatigue, she seemed fine. "She must be hungry," he said.

He took out one of the granola bars, opened it up, and gave a piece to her. She wolfed it down.

Jim looked up at Gabby and smiled, but she didn't smile back. She was staring at him again, and she seemed even more concerned.

"You went to Emmett's house to check on him, didn't you?" she asked.

"Yeah." He'd already told her this. He didn't know why she was asking again.

She furrowed her brow, as though she were trying to solve a complicated puzzle in her head. "What day was that?" She crossed her arms and scrutinized him. He felt it. Her gaze had definitely changed.

"Tuesday." He continued petting Sandy. The dog was wagging

her tail and nuzzling his arm. She licked his hand. "I wonder how long this girl's been out here in the woods?"

"I'm going to need you to leave." Gabby's voice had turned harsh.

He stood, confused. "What?"

"I'll take it from here," she said, pulling her radio from her belt. "I need to get backup and secure this scene. Collect evidence. I'll need some officers from Au Bois." She had turned cold and formal. "There are two crimes here. I'll have to block off Miller's Track. For the arsonist, there may be tire tracks at some point we can take impressions of. But more importantly, for the body, I need to make sure evidence is collected and samples are taken. I don't believe there's any immediate danger out here. The body isn't fresh. The arsonist is gone. I'll take the dog to the vet clinic. You can walk back."

"Just like that?"

"Yes," she said abruptly. It didn't feel like the same person he'd been talking to all morning. It felt like she suddenly disliked him, or maybe distrusted him.

He looked at her closely, trying to read her face, but her expression was stony. What had just happened? Had she suddenly become distant because she was uncomfortable with the fact that they'd actually been getting along? Or was it simply due to the gravity of the situation? He was absolutely baffled.

"You sure you don't want more help?" he asked.

"This is law enforcement business. You're already too closely involved."

"But your patrol car is at my house."

"I'll pick it up later." She paused. "Jim, you were the last person known to be at his house. You just left the track and walked straight over here to this random spot in the woods. Did you know Emmett's body was here?"

Jim's jaw dropped. "You think I did this? I told you. I was looking for a chestnut-sided warbler."

She raised her eyebrows. "How tall are you?"

"What?"

"You must be over six foot, right?"

"Six one. Why?"

She nodded. "You need to go. Again, don't leave the island."

He was completely blindsided. It was one thing to be suspected of arson, but now he was he also being suspected of murder?

"You're grasping at straws," he said. "You know that, don't you?"

"We'll talk later."

Anger surged through his body. He turned abruptly and began walking back through the woods toward his house. Sandy started following him.

"Sandy," Gabby called out. "Over here."

The dog paused, turned, and looked at Gabby.

"Go on," Jim said, more harshly than he'd intended. When Sandy remained there staring at him, he walked over to Gabby and handed her the rest of the granola bar. "Here."

He continued on through the woods alone, following the direction they'd come from. He looked back for a moment and watched as Gabby and Sandy stepped out onto Miller's Track. Then he disappeared behind a thick patch of trees.

26

LEWIS WILSON LOOKED up from his computer and out the expansive windows of the research station. The morning sun was streaming in and the blue waters of Lake Michigan sparkled. The sands of Long Bay curved off into the distance on either side.

He was in the middle of writing up a post-mortem report on the recent incident with hive 189, the scale of which he'd largely kept hidden from the ELT, the Executive Leadership Team in Atlanta.

The challenge with this particular post-mortem was that he needed to minimize the perception that he might be responsible for any wrongdoing, but at the same time avoid promulgating any errors of fact. He simply did not want to be caught lying.

The incident with hive 189 had happened two weeks earlier, and it had been a serious setback for Project Defender. There were still some final loose ends to wrap up, and this post-mortem was a particularly important one. He was very much aware that his life's work was at risk.

The high, wooden ceiling had begun to feel oppressive above him. The room was large, and he was alone. Both the ceiling and walls were made of rough-cut pine. He hated that the ELT had chosen a historic lodge for their research facility. It was backward-looking and imprecise. He preferred the cutting-edge labs installed at the south end of the building and the new sub-basement facilities. The rest was just a false veneer.

This morning, as always, Lewis was the first one here. The others all came in closer to 9 a.m. But he was not like the others. He never had been.

He took significant pride in the fact that he was the only one on the island who reported directly to "Crusher Cavanaugh," the Senior Vice President of Animal Biotechnology and one of the most powerful members of the ELT. This very special reporting line meant that he was, quite simply, more important than everyone else on this entire island. He was proud of his long hours, self-discipline, and the powerful combination of respect and trepidation he engendered in the team of scientists below him.

He was also extremely proud to be at Hadley Agritech itself. Although the company had poor taste in architecture, they were nevertheless at the very cutting edge of biotechnology. Last year, Hadley had been the first company to produce a new line of gen-mod dairy cows—expertly engineered with genes from humans to produce milk that was the same as human breast milk. Although controversial, the product had already become a hot commodity to replace infant formula, and it was now making their shareholders wealthier than ever.

What Lewis wanted was to follow that success with another ground-breaking gen-mod. But not for profit. Of course it had to be profitable—that was a given—but his motivation lay elsewhere. He had his own, private reasons. Thoughts of his mother came to him as he looked back at his computer screen. He pulled on his silver cufflinks to keep them even. The cursor blinked.

The incident had been nothing more than a minor breach in protocol during asset transfer. At least that was the official story he was submitting in the post-mortem.

Only Cavanaugh knew the full extent of the situation on the ground here, and that information had only been shared on burner phones with prepaid SIM cards which had been purchased with cash. Both Lewis and Cavanaugh ensured they disposed of their burner phones periodically, to avoid being traced.

Suddenly Brad burst in through the door on the other side of the room. Lewis was instantly annoyed with the rip in the knee of Brad's jeans and his ridiculously casual t-shirt, which read, "If you want me to listen to you, talk about bees."

Brad was a far cry from the professionals Lewis was used to working with. Like so many of the staff on the island, Brad seemed to dress like he was on summer vacation. He was also young and inexperienced, but he was eager and willing to do anything Lewis asked of him. That was why Lewis had invited him to help out with Project Defender. Brad never whined about scientific ethics and code of conduct like some did. And he was discreet.

"Hey, Lewis," Brad said as he walked over. "The job's done."

Lewis glared at him. If this was true, he could complete his post-mortem with confidence. "Completely done?" Lewis said. "You are sure? You've entirely cleaned up the mess you made?"

"I believe so."

Lewis paused, then stood up. "You *believe* so?" At only 5 foot 7 inches, he usually felt dwarfed by Brad, but in this moment his sudden anger made him feel large. "People *believe* in Santa Claus, Brad. They *believe* in the tooth fairy. I need facts, not fantasy. Is the job done, or is it not?"

"Yes, sir. Absolutely. It's done."

"Well, then. I'm glad you fixed your mistake." He sat back down and turned toward the windows. "Now, leave me alone. I have work to do."

Behind him, he heard Brad scurry out of the room.

27

WHEN JIM STEPPED out of the woods, emerging at the back of his property, something didn't seem right. He looked toward the burnt remains of his hives, then scanned across the yard; he could see the fenced vegetable garden, the house, and the small shed behind the garage. The old wooden door to the shed was open, but it was when he looked over at the old swing set that he became deeply concerned. There was some sort of animal in the grass. It wasn't moving. There was a shovel nearby.

"Ava?" he called out.

There was no answer.

He rushed over to the animal. At first he thought it must be a coyote, but it was smaller than that. As he got closer he thought it might a cat. But, as he stood above it, he realized he had absolutely no idea what this thing was at all. It seemed like some sort of mammal, in a way, but it was hairless. The skin was very pale gray and wet with something like slime. Its head had been crushed, and there was an amber liquid seeping from wounds on its body.

"Ava?" he shouted, this time more urgently.

That was when he saw the spill of red blood over by the house. A large area of grass was covered with it. There was a bucket nearby and some old dish towels strewn across the ground. They were wet and spotted with red. Near the porch was a pale purple blanket. He recognized it from Ava's bed. It too was covered with blood.

"Ava!" he yelled as he ran into the house.

In the kitchen, there was also blood on the green linoleum floor, a few bloody footprints making their way to the kitchen counter. The dish towel drawer was open. The kitchen scissors were on the counter nearby, their handles also covered with blood.

"No, no, no," he said out loud. Nothing could happen to Ava. Not after Sarah. It would break him.

He ran to her bedroom. The door was open. He was horrified by what he might find in there. He'd just seen a body half-eaten in the woods.

He paused at the doorway and called out. "Ava?" After no response, he stepped into the room slowly.

The dark purple walls made the room feel close and small. The light from her fish tank was on, and the fluorescent fish moved and darted around. The bed was a mess, the sheets pulled onto the floor. Ava wasn't there. He checked the window. It was still nailed shut. He yelled to the empty room. "Ava!"

He checked the bathroom and his own bedroom too, but she wasn't there either. Checking the front door, he found that it was locked, just as he'd left it earlier that morning. He unlocked it quickly and ran out front, shouting her name repeatedly.

A gentle breeze blew. The dark trees that surrounded the clearing in front of the house seemed to whisper. Gabby's SUV was parked in the driveway. Ava was nowhere to be seen. Then he saw that there were tire tracks across the grass, around Gabby's SUV. His truck was gone. He ran to the kitchen, where he kept his spare keys hanging on a hook just inside the back door. They were gone.

"Bailey? Bailey!" he called. There was no sign of the dog.

He picked up the landline and dialed Ava's mobile number. "Pick up," Jim said as it rang out. "Pick up. Pick up."

It rang a few times, and then went to voicemail. Ava's recorded voice sounded bizarrely casual and out of place as he looked at the blood on the floor in front of him.

*Hi. This is Ava. Don't leave voicemail. I never check voice. Just message me. Thanks.*

"Ava, Ava," he said. "Are you okay? Where are you? There's blood here. Call me. Call me."

As he hung up the phone, the weight of her absence crashed down on him. He realized in that moment that he actually liked it when she was holed up in her bedroom. At least then he knew where she was. His hands were shaking as he took out his mobile phone. There was only 2% charge left. "Damn it!" he yelled. He'd forgotten to put his phone on the charger last night. He quickly messaged her.

*Call me on landline. Blood here. Call me.*

He waited for a quick response. When it didn't come, he slowly fell to the floor, and he began sobbing. Ava was gone.

Suddenly he was back in Ann Arbor again. His heart started racing. His hands were shaking. Every detail of that day came back to him. It was like he was slipping back in time. An enormous wave of panic and fear consumed him.

He felt once more the intense weight of dread and panic he'd felt when Sarah didn't come home from her run. He remembered driving around Ann Arbor that night, looking for her, thinking she might have fallen and twisted an ankle. Maybe she was limping home. Maybe she'd stopped to talk to a friend. But she was nowhere. The streets were empty. He couldn't find her. She was gone.

And now Ava was gone too. It was happening all over again.

28

IT WAS JUST BEFORE 9 a.m. when Ava knocked on the Schusters' door.

Mr. Schuster came to the door, looking as if he was just about to head out to work. He was a funny looking man, with thick glasses and big ears. Ava knew him because he was Marissa Schuster's dad, a friend from school, but he was also the island's only vet.

"Good morning, Ava," he said. "Marissa's still sleeping." Then he looked down and saw the blood splattered across the front of her. "Are you okay?"

"It's Bailey's blood. My dog, he's hurt bad. Please help me. He's in the truck."

Mr. Schuster grabbed his medical kit and rushed outside. He left Bailey where he was in the back of the truck and started taking off the bandages Ava had applied. As he worked, he said something about how nicely she'd wrapped them. Ava was feeling strange and dizzy. She didn't respond. She'd done everything she could to get Bailey here, and now she felt a deep relief, as if she was finished with some horrible exam.

Flashes of that thing kept entering her mind.

The rest of the bandages came off quickly, and Bailey remained passed out. Then Mr. Schuster started work, right there. He anesthetized Bailey and began shaving the fur around his wounds with a small trimmer. As he worked, Ava's mind felt stuck in a loop. She was still thinking about that creature.

When she'd jumped down from the swing set, she'd watched in horror as the gray thing started to stand. It had stared at her, but it was wobbly, clearly still somewhat stunned from its fight with Bailey. She'd wanted to run into the house and shut the door, but at that moment Bailey was still lying injured on the ground. He needed help. She wouldn't leave him.

She ran instead to her dad's garden shed, unsure how long she had before that thing came running after her. She opened the rickety shed door and looked into the shadows there for anything that might help. There was the old shovel. She grabbed it and rushed back.

The creature was stepping towards her but moving slowly, still weak and disoriented. Its hairless, gray legs twitched strangely. Its pale, wet skin glistened. Amber blood flowed from its back where Bailey had punctured it.

She raised the shovel in the air. It looked right at her. It snarled. She swung down as hard as she could, slamming its head with the flat back of the shovel blade. It fell to the ground and shrieked.

She swung at it again. And again. She didn't stop. Her entire body surged with fear and rage. She focused on its head. The blows landed over and over. It stopped making noise, and then eventually it stopped moving. But she didn't quit swinging the shovel. She heard a crack. The skull seemed to break. Something began seeping out of its head. She dropped the shovel at her side. It was dead.

Behind her, Bailey was on the ground. He was trying to get up but he kept falling. It was as if he was drugged. He whimpered, looking up at her in fear and confusion. There were gashes around his face. He was bleeding from multiple, jagged cuts on his neck and legs and from a wound on his side. There was deep red blood all around him on the ground. He yelped and moaned, trying to bark.

She knelt down beside him and stroked the back of his head. "Bailey, Bailey."

Then, slowly, he closed his eyes, as if he was falling asleep. She was losing him. He started convulsing. She held him as his body heaved and jerked back and forth, left and right. He began foaming at the mouth. Then, just as suddenly as it had started, it stopped. His body went entirely limp.

"No! Bailey, no!" She threw her head against his body and buried her face in his black and tan fur. She couldn't lose him. She'd come to rely on him. She wrapped her arms around his neck and cried.

The blood was everywhere, gathering in wet tufts on his fur, puddled on the ground at his side, covering her fingers. His wounds were deep, and they were filled with grass and dirt from the scuffle. He was losing more blood with every second. Placing her hand on his side, she could feel the shallow rise and fall of his breathing. He was not dead. Thank God he was not dead. She had time. She had to stop the bleeding. Nothing else mattered.

She steadied herself for a moment and ran to the back door. Her legs were covered in blood. She didn't care. She had to help Bailey. In the kitchen, she grabbed a handful of dish towels, and stopped to cut one up into strips with a pair of scissors. Her bare feet left blood on the linoleum.

Outside, she filled a bucket with water from the garden hose. The water was clear and cold. It felt like it took forever for the bucket to fill just halfway. It felt like she was fighting another kind of fire.

Bailey's eyes were open as she knelt down beside him. She felt a huge sense of relief. "It's okay, Bailey. It's okay."

She started cleaning the cut on his face, dipping one of the dish towels in the bucket and applying it to his snout. Next she cleaned the cuts on his front legs and side. Then she wrapped the thin strips of fabric around his snout and around a few places on his front legs. She tucked the ends in to keep them tight. The fabric quickly soaked up the blood and turned red.

She noticed a very large swelling on his side. She pushed aside the dark fur to inspect his skin and saw it was red and inflamed. There was a small hole in the middle of the swelling, as if his skin had been punctured. She cleaned that wound too as best she could. At least that one wasn't bleeding.

When she'd finished tending to his wounds, she tried to bundle him up into the back of her dad's pickup. She had to lay him on a blanket from her bed and then drag it over to the back tailgate. Bailey was not a small dog and she didn't want to hurt him. She squatted next to him and slid her arms under his front and rear legs. He was trembling, as though he were cold. She stood and heaved him upwards. His head lolled. One of the bandages came unwrapped. It took several tries, but she was determined, and in the end she managed to get him up into the truck bed.

She threw the blanket on the ground and closed the tailgate. Then she grabbed her phone off the grass, jumped in the driver's seat, and sped off.

"Was it a coyote?" Mr. Schuster asked as he cleaned the wounds with antiseptic.

"What?" Ava said. She'd been somewhere else. Her head felt cloudy.

"Was it a coyote?"

"No," she answered. "It was something else."

"What was it?"

"I don't know."

"It must have been a coyote," Mr. Schuster said emphatically.

She didn't feel the need to argue. It was only Bailey she cared about now. "Will he be okay?"

"To be honest, I don't know." He moved on to suture the wounds.

Her head was a swirling mess of emotions as she watched him work. Bailey had probably saved her life, attacking that thing the way he did.

When Mr. Schuster was done he said, "You should bring him to the vet clinic, for observation."

"And leave him there?"

"Yes, so we can watch him."

"No. No. I'm taking him home, to be with me." There was no way she was leaving Bailey behind, not after he'd stayed at her side and protected her while she was under attack. No way.

Mr. Schuster frowned. "I don't recommend that."

"I'm taking him home." She set her jaw firmly and glared at him.

He paused to think for a moment. "Well, watch him closely, and bring him to me on Monday to check that he's okay. But what about you? Did the coyote bite you?" He looked down at her legs, which were covered in blood. Only then did she realize she was still wearing the thin shorts and blue tank top she slept in. "If it did, you'll need the rabies vaccine," he said.

"No, it didn't. This is Bailey's blood. Thank you, Mr. Schuster."

As she was climbing back into the truck to leave, she saw a message on her phone. It was the Window Cop. She called home immediately.

"Ava, Ava! Are you okay?" Her dad blurted out the words the moment he answered.

"I'm fine, Dad. I'm fine."

29

THE PANIC LEFT Jim the moment he heard Ava's voice. It wasn't happening again. The shaking in his hands stopped. His heart rate returned to normal. The relief was profound as the dread lifted and was replaced by something lighter and brighter—a gratitude that was nearly effervescent. Ava was okay. She was okay. She was on her way home. He would not lose her like he lost Sarah.

Ava had told him about the attack from the creature he'd seen dead in the back acre. As soon as he hung up, he went back outside to inspect it.

Wearing gardening gloves, he turned the animal over to study its anatomy. It was probably ten inches tall at the shoulder, and about two feet long from its head to its hindquarters. Its rat-like tail stretched about a foot long. If he had to guess, he'd say it probably weighed thirty to thirty-five pounds. Its hairless skin was a bleached gray, with a bit of black. But what was most peculiar about the skin was how wet and pliable it was. In places it had traces of a clear mucus.

As he examined the animal closely—studying the forepaws which resembled slender clawed human hands, trying to figure out the skull structure in spite of the obvious damage—he realized something. This animal looked almost like a bald raccoon. The tail, snout, and forepaws were definitely raccoon-like.

The only thing that wasn't consistent with a raccoon anatomy was the teeth. While the skull was crushed, the jaws were still somewhat intact. He lifted the cracked head and pulled the jaws open to look inside.

A hard, chitinous substance formed two black, jagged lines above and below the mouth, where its teeth should have been. He pushed and pulled at them. They almost resembled a pair of insect mandibles. They still moved on a vertical plane, up and down like mammal teeth, whereas insect mandibles moved on a horizontal plane, back and forth, but they definitely had the shape and look of mandibles. What's more, they moved independently of the jawbone. With his gloves on, he pulled at them. They could snap shut while the jaw remained open.

There was no doubt in Jim's mind. This thing had to be a gen-mod. In fact, it looked transgenic. All gen-mods had altered DNA, but transgenic gen-mods had DNA brought into them from another species—like Ava's FluoroFish, which had jellyfish and sea coral genes. This thing in front of him looked like a raccoon with DNA from, well... he didn't know what. He took out his mobile phone to take pictures, but now the damn thing was completely dead. He put it back in his pocket and laid the creature on its belly.

There was a strange fold of skin near the genitals, like a sheath. He pushed on it gently, and a hard, needle-like projection thrusted out. He jumped back, and the thing retracted when he let go.

He pressed gently on the sheath again. When the thing came out, he recognized it immediately. This was not male anatomy. He couldn't believe it, but there it was. It was a stinger. It was made of the same, black, chitinous substance as the mandibles. It curved forward, and it was incredibly long.

This creature had to be what was breaking into Minnie's garden, even if it wasn't as big as Minnie had said. She must not have seen it clearly. The odd scrape marks on her cantaloupes could have easily been made by these strange mandibles. He stood and went quickly inside to call her on the landline. It went to voicemail, and he left a message to reassure her that the thing eating her cantaloupes was dead. He didn't go into detail.

Back in his room, he put his phone on his charging pad. He'd already started mopping up the blood off the kitchen floor when he heard the front door opening.

He rushed out into the living room. The girl standing in the doorway appeared very different from the girl he'd left this morning. There was a strange, disturbed look around her eyes. Her purple hair was a mess. Her cotton shorts and blue tank top were ripped, and she was covered in dried blood. But it was her. It was Ava.

The moment she saw him, she ran to him and hugged him tightly. He couldn't remember the last time that she'd willingly embraced him. She suddenly seemed terribly fragile. Her aloof attitude was gone. She sobbed. He held her.

She mumbled into his chest. "It came after me. Out of the woods. It was horrible."

He stepped back, put his hands on her shoulders and looked her carefully in the eye. "Are you okay?"

She nodded.

"Did it bite you? Are you cut? Is this your blood?" He looked at the dark stains splattered on her shirt, and at the blood across her hands and legs.

"It tried to bite me but didn't. This is Bailey's blood."

"Were you the one who crushed its head?"

"Yes. I hit it with the shovel. Bailey injured it badly. He tried to protect me, but it was still alive."

He was impressed. His daughter was strong, and she was brave. A surge of pride rose up in his chest, but was overtaken by a terrible, heaving sense that he'd let her down, just as he'd let down Sarah. "I'm so glad you're okay."

"What *is* that thing, Dad?"

"I don't really know."

Ava looked over his shoulder to the back door. "I want to go look at it."

"You don't need to see that thing again," he said. He wanted her to go clean herself up. He wanted to make her macaroni and cheese and tuck her into bed.

"Actually, I do." She set her jaw that way that Sarah used to when she was determined.

"No. I'll get rid of it. Don't you worry about it."

She glared at him. "Dad, I killed that thing with a shovel. I think I can handle looking at it. You have got to stop being so overprotective."

The soft moment was gone. She had changed already. Her walls had come back up.

"I'm not overprotective," he said.

She took a deep breath and looked up at him with a clear, open gaze. "Dad, you are." There was no anger in her voice. She spoke evenly, as if she was stating a simple and obvious fact. "You nailed my window shut. You don't want me to go running. And now you're scared that something will happen if I simply look at the thing I just killed with my own two hands. You're always going on about science and the facts. So, how can you stand there and say that you're not overprotective? Just look at the evidence."

It felt like a gut punch. His daughter astounded him. One day she was a moody teenager, and the next she was calmly calling him out on his behavior like an equal. Sarah used to do that too. His head spun. How could she be so much like her mother?

"I just don't want to lose you," he said.

She continued speaking with a kind of steady composure. She was past anger. "If you keep smothering me, you *will* lose me."

He felt himself tearing up, and he tried to push it down. "Ava, please don't pull away from me."

She said nothing, but her stern silence and impassive expression implied something very clear. His behavior would dictate whether or not she was going to pull away. He had a choice.

He wondered, perhaps for the first time, if she was right. Was he overprotective? She was turning into a young woman. She'd just killed a creature that had attacked her. He stepped to the side, opening up a path between her and the back door. "Go ahead. Look at it. Just please wear gloves if you're going to touch it."

"Dad." Her tone carried a gentle scolding.

"Okay, okay. Don't wear gloves. Roll all over the thing. Kiss it if you want. I don't care."

Ava grimaced for a moment, and then she broke into a small, surprised laugh. "Kiss it?"

He smiled. "Okay, well, maybe don't kiss it."

They stood looking at each other. It was clear neither quite knew what to say.

"Bailey is hurt," Ava said eventually. "Help me get him out of the truck. Then I'll go look at it." She turned and walked back outside. Jim followed. He did what she said.

Together they carried Bailey into the house. The poor dog's body was limp and his breathing was heavy. Hank Schuster had put a head cone around his neck to stop him from biting at his wounds. Ava insisted they take him straight into her bedroom.

"I want him next to me," she said. "Will you help me make a dog bed?"

Jim went to the garage and grabbed some thick cardboard from an old box and an old blanket he used as a paint drop cloth. He placed them on the floor underneath the front window, and they laid Bailey there.

There was a very large swelling on the dog's side. Jim pushed aside patches of dark fur to inspect the skin. It looked red and inflamed, almost like a histamine response. He pushed lightly around the swelling, careful not to hurt Bailey, but the dog didn't respond at all.

"He's out completely," Jim said. "Did Mr. Schuster drug him?"

"He told me he used a local anesthetic. He wasn't sure why Bailey was still unconscious, but he said he should wake up soon." Ava knelt down next to Jim and patted Bailey's head. "He's going to be okay, right?"

"What did Mr. Schuster say?"

"He said to watch him closely and bring him to the clinic on Monday."

Jim nodded. "We'll do everything we can for him."

"I want to go look at that thing now," Ava said blankly.

Jim didn't dare say no.

Out in the back acre, Ava wasted no time in getting close to the dead animal. Jim had already hosed down the area to wash away as much blood as he could.

"This thing is disgusting," she said, looking at it intently.

Jim stood behind her. "It didn't, ah, sting you, did it?"

"Sting me?" She looked up at him.

"Yes. It has what looks like a stinger."

"No. It didn't *sting* me. How can it have a stinger?"

"Like a bee, or a wasp, actually."

Jim knelt down next to her, and he pushed on the sheath to expose the creature's long stinger.

"Wow."

"See here? It's smooth, like a wasp stinger. One that stings multiple times." He let go and the stinger retracted.

"What do you mean?" she asked.

"Honeybees have a barbed stinger which gets lodged in the skin of its victim. When the bee tries to pull away, the stinger tears loose from its abdomen and the bee dies. So bees can only sting once. But wasp stingers don't have barbs, which means they can sting multiple times. So, just looking at this animal's anatomy, you can tell that it could probably sting multiple times."

"It moved weird. It sort of jerked and twitched." Ava shuddered in disgust. "Where did it come from? It's a gen-mod, right?"

"It has to be. Do you think it stung Bailey? He has a swelling on his side that looks consistent with a bee or wasp sting, although it's much larger."

Ava seemed to think for a moment. "Well, at one point it did sort of thrust its back end at Bailey, and he fell to the ground. Then he started shaking. He managed to get up again and fight it a bit more, but after that he collapsed."

Jim looked again at the skin. In his agitation earlier, he'd missed something. Only now did he make the connection. The gray and black coloration on the animal was familiar. The black sections made two stripes, which ran lengthwise down either side of its gray body. Could it be?

"I'm going to go take a hot shower and watch Bailey," Ava said, jolting him out of his thoughts.

They stood, and he hugged her. "I'm glad you're okay, Ava. You know I couldn't handle it if anything happened to you. I love you."

She hugged him back. "I love you too, Dad. But think about what I said, please."

He paused, then nodded.

She went back into the house, and Jim turned to look at the creature again. He studied it for a moment, and then he went over to the old red garden shed.

Yesterday, after he left the gray bees he'd collected with Lewis and Brad for identification, he came home and collected more. He'd opened his hives again immediately and took out two more gray workers to study. He'd put them here in the shed in an old fish tank, throwing in some honeycomb and a small container of water. He'd fashioned a lid out of an old window screen and held it in place with a metal grate and a rock.

He looked at them now. The fish tank stood in the middle of his workbench. These two bees wouldn't live long—in summer worker bees lived for only six weeks, and in this tank, away from the hive, their lives would be even shorter—but hopefully they would last long enough for him to get to the bottom of this. Both bees were crawling over the honeycomb. He leaned in and examined their dark-to-light striations.

Yes, there it was. On both, two black stripes ran lengthwise down either side of the body. Anger shot through him.

He needed to talk to Lewis now.

## 30

THIS TIME the armed guard at the entrance to Hadley Agritech stepped in front of Jim and blocked his path. Jim's stomach dropped.

"I need to inspect your bag, sir," the guard said. He was no taller than Jim but much broader. He looked like a former Marine. His voice was low and monotone, and his gaze was full of superiority.

Jim looked down at the black plastic trash bag in his hand. "It's a wild animal. I found it. It's dead. I'm here to see to Lewis Wilson. He knows I'm coming."

The guard shook his head. "I need to see what's inside that bag before you can go anywhere."

Jim opened it up. The guard looked inside and flashed Jim a surprised look.

"Where did you get that?"

"I told you. I found it. It came out of the End Woods."

"I'll need to take it."

"No. I need to show it to Lewis."

The guard took a step back and quickly pulled his handgun from his side, pointing it directly at Jim's chest.

"Set the bag down now and step away."

"Jesus! What the hell!" Jim instinctively put his arms out, still holding the trash bag in one hand. He was shocked to find himself looking down the barrel of a gun. From the corner of his eye, he saw two people in the lobby turn and stare. They stood up from the green leather club chairs and moved to the far end of the room.

"Set the bag down," the guard said firmly.

Jim did as he was told, setting it down in front of him.

"Now step away. Keep your hands in the air."

Jim did so. His heart was racing.

The guard pressed a button on his belt and spoke into his earpiece. "I need Lewis Wilson to the lobby, immediately. We have a Code 9."

Jim stood there—completely stock-still, frightened, his hands in the air—as the guard stepped forward, picked up the bag, and set it to one side. He never took his gun off Jim. It felt like an eternity before Lewis finally walked into the lobby. Jim let out a sigh of relief.

Lewis walked up to the guard and said, very calmly, "Doug, it's okay. He's an old friend. Thank you. Put your gun away."

The guard did as instructed.

Although half the size of the guard, Lewis clearly carried great authority. Lewis turned to Jim and said, "Sorry, Jim."

"He has this, Dr. Wilson," the guard said, pointing to the bag.

Lewis picked it up and looked inside. He appeared as surprised as the guard.

"Says he found it," he said. "Says it came out of the End Woods."

Lewis gave Jim a strange look which Jim couldn't quite make out. It seemed almost suspicious or distrustful. "Come with me," he said.

"Do you need help, sir?" the guard asked.

"No. I've got this. Thank you." Lewis clutched the bag closely and led Jim through the doorway to the inner offices. They began walking down a series of bland gray hallways.

"You need to tell me what's going on here, Lewis." Jim was furious. Something was wrong and he wanted to understand exactly what.

"How long have you had this?" Lewis asked.

"It came into our back acre this morning. It attacked my daughter."

Lewis stopped in his tracks and stared at Jim. He looked frightened. "Is she conscious?"

"Conscious?" Jim said. "Ava? Yes. She's fine. She wasn't seriously hurt, thank goodness."

A visible relief passed across Lewis. His shoulders dropped and he breathed out, then gestured for Jim to continue following him. They walked on in silence until they reached the end of another hallway, where there was a huge set of industrial double doors. Lewis waved the back of his hand at a sensor, and the red light there turned green. He pushed the doors open, and they walked forward.

Inside, the interior changed again. The hallways here looked more like a hospital than an office. The walls were stark white, and the floors were covered in a blue-green, industrial vinyl. The doors were made of stainless steel. One of the doors they passed was labelled "Genomics Facility" and covered with red and yellow warning signs. *Caution. Restricted Entry. Authorized Personnel Only. Biological Hazard.*

"Our lab facilities," Lewis said as he walked up to another door. The sign read, "Microbiology Laboratory. Lab coats must be worn in this area."

He pushed the door open and shouted, "Out! Everyone!"

The room was occupied by several staff members in white lab coats, gazing into microscopes. They all looked up. Although Lewis wasn't wearing a lab coat, and neither was Jim, no one mentioned this—probably because Lewis was the one who made the rules here, and none of the staff here had the seniority to reprimand him.

"I need this room!" Lewis yelled. "Now! Clear out! Someone send in Brad."

Everyone stood quickly, grabbing notebooks and tablets as they scurried out.

Lewis walked over to a metal table in the middle of the room. He put on surgical gloves and pulled out the dead creature from Jim's black plastic trash bag. Its legs and neck flopped onto the table. The amber blood on the gray skin had dried, but the crushed skull was still damp.

"Look at that," Jim said. "It has black stripes down its side, lengthwise, just like those gray bees. What the hell are you doing? Are you making an entire fashion line of gen-mod animals? And branding them with stripes like running shoes?"

"Raccoon," Lewis said, almost to himself. "Damn it." He clearly hadn't been listening to Jim at all.

"Wait," Jim said. "What makes you say it's a raccoon? I mean, yes, for the most part the anatomy's consistent, but it took a while for me to figure that out. Hairless raccoons are barely recognizable. And it's obviously transgenic. Look at the jaws." Jim pointed to the strange teeth. "That's not from raccoon DNA."

Lewis rolled the animal onto its back and inspected its belly and genitals. Then he inspected the wet skin. "It's newly hatched. The cuticle is still soft. I'm surprised it attacked before it had time to harden." He seemed to be thinking out loud, as if he'd forgotten Jim was even there. He inspected the sheath. "It's a female," he said to himself and then suddenly looked up. "Did it sting your daughter?"

"So you know it has a stinger. You made this."

"Answer the question." Lewis' voice was sharp and urgent. He looked back down and pressed at the sheath. The stinger slid out.

"No," Jim said. "It didn't sting her. She's fine. Our dog intervened. He subdued it. Ava finished it off with a shovel. That's why the head is crushed."

"Did it sting your dog?"

"What is this thing?" He was fed up with the subterfuge. He wanted answers.

Lewis snapped. "Answer the goddamn question! Did it sting your dog?"

Jim stepped back. Never in their years at Cornell had he ever seen Lewis like this. The look on his face was no longer fear. It was sheer rage.

"Yes, I think so. There's a histamine response and a puncture wound on Bailey's side."

"Damn it, damn it, damn it. The dog is male?" His voice boomed.

"Yes." For Jim, it seemed as though the walls were shifting, and suddenly he was in a house of mirrors. What had seemed real was only a reflection of something else. He wanted to know what was driving Lewis' fear and rage.

"Thank God." Lewis looked back at the creature. "But even so, it will be hungry. It's unconscious now, right?"

"What?" Jim couldn't follow the line of questioning. Nothing made any sense.

"The dog! It's completely passed out, correct?"

"Yes. Why? How did you know?"

Lewis looked away. "It won't be out for long."

"What are you talking about?"

"Where is it now?" Lewis snapped. "The dog?"

"At home. Hank Schuster already stitched him up."

"Jesus! You took it to the vet?" Lewis glared. His face twisted into a grimace, and his rage filled the room.

"Not me. Ava did." Jim was watching Lewis carefully now, looking for a crack, a way in, an explanation for this tremendous reaction.

"Did Schuster see this?" Lewis gestured quickly toward the creature on the table.

"No. Will you tell me what the hell is going on?" Jim could barely contain the venom in his voice.

Lewis shook his head firmly. "I will not. Hadley Agritech IP is involved here."

"IP?"

"Our intellectual property."

"I know what IP is, Lewis. Are you saying this animal is your IP?"

"It's a… something we've been trying to contain. Can I see your dog?"

Jim suddenly regretted coming here. He should have gone to Gabby. He'd made the decision in anger. He'd wanted an explanation. But he never made good decisions when he was angry.

"Can I see your dog?" Lewis repeated.

Jim stepped back. "I don't know."

Lewis stepped forward and leaned in toward him. "Jim, if this thing stung your dog, then that dog is a danger to both you and Ava."

Jim slowly recognized what was happening. It wasn't fear or rage Lewis was expressing. It was panic.

"Ava is at home with Bailey now," Jim said. "He's sleeping on the floor of her bedroom."

"The dog is Bailey?"

"Yes."

"What time did he get stung?" Lewis asked.

"Earlier this morning. Maybe around 8 a.m."

Lewis was pacing around the lab now, his hand on his forehead as though to help him think. "There's time, but we have to act quickly."

The door swung open and Brad walked in. He was wearing a white lab coat over a tight t-shirt and blue jeans. As he approached, he saw the animal on the table and exclaimed, "What the hell?"

Lewis glared at Brad. "It's newly hatched. It seems that we are *not* clear, after all."

Brad glanced over at Jim and said. "What's he doing here?"

Lewis gestured to the table. "It attacked his daughter."

"I thought we had them all," Brad said.

Lewis turned to Jim. "We need to get to your daughter."

But Jim was already running to the door.

## 31

WHEN JIM GOT BACK HOME, Gabby's SUV was already gone. He threw open the front door and shouted immediately for Ava. She was in the kitchen, and she stepped out into the living room.

"Are you okay?" he asked. "Where's Bailey?"

"I'm fine." She looked confused.

He hugged her tightly. The drive back from Hadley Agritech had been a rush of panic. He hadn't waited for Lewis and Brad, but he knew they weren't far behind him. "I'm so glad you're okay."

"Bailey's really sick. I'm just about to call Mr. Schuster."

At that moment, Lewis and Brad came bursting in.

"What's going on?" Ava asked.

"They're here to help with Bailey," Jim said. "Is he still sleeping?"

"Yeah," Ava said, eying Lewis and Brad suspiciously. "Are you vets?"

"Ava, has anything changed with Bailey since I left?" Jim interrupted.

Ava scrunched up her nose in disgust. "Well, he has these weird scabs forming."

"What do you mean?" he asked.

She shrugged, but it wasn't her normal dismissiveness. She was concerned but perplexed. "It's weird. They're all over, and he's shivering. There's this yellowy liquid coming out of his skin and it's drying. It's getting crusty. I'll show you." She turned to head toward her room.

"Stop!" Brad yelled. He quickly reached behind his back and pulled out a pistol. He must have had a concealed holster inside the waistband of his jeans.

Jim was shocked. "Whoa, Brad. I don't think we need that."

Brad held the gun in front of him. "Yes, we do. I'll go first. Which room?"

"What the hell?" Ava said. "It's just Bailey. He's sick."

Jim was still reeling about the fact that Brad was brandishing a gun in his living room, but he turned to Ava and said, "Brad and Lewis are here to help. They know what's wrong with Bailey." He turned back to Brad, hoping that what he'd just said was true. "It's the second door on the left. After the bathroom."

Ava had a dazed look of bewilderment. "Shouldn't we just call Mr. Schuster?"

Brad ignored her and began walking down the hallway. He eventually called out from her bedroom. "It's safe! He's unconscious!"

Ava looked at Jim, her eyes wide. "What is going on?"

"I'm not completely sure," he said. "But Bailey might be dangerous. Stay here." He turned and followed Lewis, who had already started walking down the hall.

As Jim stepped in the room, he saw Bailey curled up in a ball on the makeshift dog bed, right where they'd left him earlier. Ava had covered him with a spare blanket from the hall closet. Only his head was exposed. There were crusty yellow scabs on his scalp and over his eyes. Brad was standing over him and leering down, pointing his gun at the dog's head.

"No!" Ava suddenly pushed past Jim and into the room. She reached out towards the dog's head.

"Don't touch him!" Jim yelled.

Brad quickly pushed her hand away, still pointing the gun at Bailey.

"Why?" she asked.

Jim wrapped an arm around her shoulder. "Ava, I think Bailey's more dangerous than he seems. Please do what Brad says." While he didn't entirely trust Brad and Lewis, they certainly knew more than he did about what was going on. In that moment, he had no choice but to rely on their judgement.

She stood, looking baffled, but she refused to step away from her dog.

"Your dad's right," Brad said. "He could be infectious." He flashed a worried look at Lewis.

"That's true," Lewis said, pushing his glasses up on his nose. "We have to, ah, take care of your dog before he finishes, ah... Before he gets really sick."

Jim felt conflicted. They weren't just trying to be careful about what they said to Ava to spare her feelings. It was obvious they were hiding things. That feeling of being in a house of mirrors overtook him again, like he was unsure if he was moving closer to the exit or deeper into the maze.

Ava quickly shifted to the side, positioning herself between Brad's gun and Bailey. "Not until someone tells me what's going on."

"Brad, put the gun away," Jim said, wanting to diffuse the situation quickly. Answers could come later. "Ava, come away from Bailey. Now."

Brad lowered the gun but didn't put it away. He held it in his hand, pointed at the floor. Ava didn't move.

Lewis looked at Ava sympathetically and said, "You don't need to worry about anything."

"He's *my* dog," she snapped. "I don't know who you are. I don't trust you."

Jim stood next to Ava, assessing every detail of the situation—the dog, the gun, Ava, Brad, Lewis. It felt like the entire room was on the edge of a precipice. One wrong move—one sudden jerk from the dog, one hasty reaction from Ava, one twitchy finger from Brad—and this all this would go spiraling out of control.

"Brad," he said, spitting out his name in anger. "Put that gun away now, or I will grab it out of your hand and shoot you myself."

Brad put one hand up in the air, as though in a surrender, and said, "Okay, okay." He reached back to return the pistol to its holster, looking at Ava the entire time. "I'm not going to hurt your dog," he said softly. Then, holding both hands out in front of him so she could see what he was doing, he reached down and slowly lifted the blanket off of Bailey. "See how sick he is? He needs help."

Jim was deeply troubled to see the dog's body. It was barely recognizable. Not only were there brownish-yellow scabs forming over his fur, but the scabs on his front legs seemed to be growing, connecting to the scabs on his face. Soon he'd be covered in one giant crust.

"It's getting worse," Ava said.

"He's very sick, Ava," Jim said. He gently placed his arm around her again, and this time she allowed him to lead her away. They walked past Lewis and stood at the door, where she brushed his arm off. She turned back to look at Bailey.

"We need to take your dog back to our lab for treatment," Lewis said, speaking in a condescending manner now, as if he was talking to a little girl. "It'll all be okay."

"Just who the hell are you?" she said.

"Ava," Jim scolded. "Lewis and Brad are from Hadley Agritech. They're scientists. Just look at Bailey. Something is seriously wrong. They can help him."

She turned to Lewis. "When will he be back?"

"As soon as he is better," Lewis said. "Now, if you will leave us for a moment."

"Ava, let's let them take care of this."

In that moment, the only thing Jim cared about was getting that dog out of the house and away from Ava. He gestured toward the hallway.

Ava hesitated, then walked out of the room ahead of him.

Jim lingered around the corner, listening in to the men's conversation.

"Should we tell him?" Brad said quietly.

"We can't," Lewis snapped back.

There was silence, then Brad said, "There's equipment in the truck. I can carry the dog. You stay back."

Jim quickly moved away from the door and walked back down the hallway. He found Ava in the living room near the fireplace. She was looking at one of the pictures on the mantel. It was the photo of her, aged twelve, holding Bailey, who had just been a puppy then. He put his hand on her shoulder.

"I'm sorry," he said.

She shook his hand away.

Brad came down the hallway and through into the living room, empty handed. As he passed by, Ava gave him a look of contempt. He continued on through the front door.

Shortly after, Lewis came into the living room and stood awkwardly. "Brad's getting ready to move the dog."

It was an uncomfortable moment. Ava sat down on the couch and crossed her arms, ignoring everyone.

Several minutes passed, and then Jim heard Brad come back up the front steps. When he threw open the front door and stepped into the living room, Jim was shocked. Brad was wearing a large, white rubber hazmat suit.

32

JIM GLARED AT BRAD. "Why are you wearing that?"

"Just a precaution," Lewis said. His voice was calm and measured. "We have no reason to believe direct contact at this stage carries any risk. But there are some unknowns."

Brad's hazmat suit had a hood with a clear area to see out of, and underneath that he was wearing some sort of breathing apparatus. He wore black gloves and thick, black rubber boots. It was exactly like the suit the arsonist had worn in the video Jim had seen just that morning.

There was no way that this was a coincidence. Jim's anger flared. He wanted to run at Brad and push him back down the steps and out of his house. But he needed Bailey out of here. It took all of his strength to stay where he was, to stand and watch as Brad walked past, through the living room and down the hall to Ava's bedroom.

"Ava, have you been touching Bailey?" Jim said. "Before we got here?" A hazmat suit meant there was risk—either real or imagined—of contagion.

She nodded. "I touched the scabs to see what they were."

"You should wash your hands," Lewis said.

"What?" She looked surprised.

"Go do it," Jim said quickly.

She went into the kitchen, and soon Jim heard the sound of water running.

He wanted to scream at Lewis, but he didn't want to upset Ava any more than she already was. Instead, he kept his voice low. It came out like a growl. "So help me God, if anything happens to Ava I will destroy you."

Lewis whispered, "She'll be fine, but we cannot save the dog."

"What the hell are you doing?" Jim asked, seething. "What is Hadley up to?"

"It's confidential. It's—"

"I know, it's your IP. But I don't care about your goddamn IP. I care about my daughter. Deputy Gabby needs to know you're putting people at risk."

Ava stepped back into the living room at the same time that Brad came back in from the hallway, carrying Bailey in his arms. It looked as if he was holding nothing but a mass of dark brown crust. Lewis opened the front door for him, and Brad went immediately outside.

"You can take care of him?" Ava asked. Her voice cracked slightly, and she followed Brad onto the front porch. "He'll be okay?"

"We'll do what we can," Lewis said, behind her.

Jim stood next to Ava on the porch and watched as Brad carried Bailey toward the white Hadley Agritech pickup truck. There was a commercial cap on the back and the tailgate was down.

Brad was walking slowly, as though afraid to wake the dog. When he was almost at the back of the vehicle, Bailey began to shift in his arms. Brad looked down, and Jim thought he heard a low, soft growl. Brad rushed to the back of the truck and almost threw the dog in.

"Hey!" Ava yelled, running toward him. Jim was right behind her.

Ava reached out to Bailey, who lay in the back of the pickup next to some old bee boxes. Across his body there were strange spots where the scabs had broken off and fallen away, apparently taking with them all trace of dog hair. Patches of wet, grayish skin were revealed underneath. Ava put her hand on one such patch of skin on his side.

Jim quickly yanked her hand away. "Stop touching him!"

"It's not safe," Brad said, his voice muffled through the breathing apparatus.

Ava looked at Brad. "His skin is cold. He's shivering."

"Go wash your hands again," Jim said. Then he saw that Ava was right. Although the dog was still apparently unconscious, he did seem to be shivering.

"We have to cover him up," Ava said. Wait. Just wait." She ran back into the house.

Jim turned to look at Bailey again, while surreptitiously studying the equipment in the back of the truck. At first, it seemed to be a typical collection of beekeeping paraphernalia—a smoker, a mouse guard, and a few spare brood frames. Then, among the mess, he saw two red, plastic jerry cans. He paused. They were just like the one Gabby had showed him at Bennett Orchards, and just like the one carried by the man in the hazmat suit on the video.

It was possible, of course, that Brad could be using those gasoline cans to fight American foulbrood, or to fuel up the truck, but Jim doubted it. He quickly looked into the corners of the truck, knowing exactly what he was looking for. And there it was. His eyes fell on several long, thin strips of green foam. He stared, astounded.

Brad stepped forward and started putting up the tailgate, nudging Jim out of the way and blocking his view.

Jim looked at Brad. He was tall. Just like the man in the video.

At that moment, Ava came bursting out of the house carrying the blanket she'd been using to keep Bailey warm.

"That could be infected," Jim warned.

She ignored him and pushed past him and Brad toward the back of the truck. She carefully laid the blanket over Bailey's shivering body. When she stepped back, Jim could see that tears were running down her cheeks.

Brad quickly closed the cap door, and then he and Lewis climbed in the truck without another word.

Jim put his arm around his daughter, and they watched as the engine started and the truck drove off down the driveway. Then she pulled away.

"Those guys are dicks," she said.

"I'm so sorry, Ava. I'm sorry about Bailey."

"I can't believe you let them take him!" She turned and ran toward the house. The front door slammed behind her.

33

JIM TURNED BACK and looked toward the spot on the driveway where the Hadley Agritech truck had just disappeared behind a cluster of pines. Standing there, he tried desperately to get his head around everything that had happened in the last two days—the burning of his hives, the strange gray bees, Emmett's body in the woods, the gen-mod that had attacked Ava, and now Bailey's bizarre sickness. His head spun.

There was only one possible conclusion he could come to. Brad's hazmat suit, the jerry cans, and the green foam in the back of the Hadley Agritech truck all pointed to one person—or one company, he should say. Hadley was clearly behind the arson. Lewis had probably sent Brad out, like a hitman, to do his dirty work. But the question remained: why would Lewis want to destroy beehives? Jim knew that Lewis, in his own way, loved bees as much as he did. They were precious.

It had to be like foulbrood. You only burned hives when there was something terrible that had to be eradicated. Jim thought of the strange, gray bees. Could it be that? Were they trying to get rid of those gray bees?

He was absolutely certain that Lewis was genetically engineering bees. But now, bizarrely, it seemed that Lewis might also be creating larger gen-mod animals. Lewis had known about that raccoon. He hadn't been surprised by it in the slightest.

Engineering bees was something Jim could understand. No doubt Lewis was trying to solve the Global Bee Crisis. It was every pollination scientist's dream. But what benefit could there be to engineering larger animals as well as bees? It just made no sense. What was he doing? Could it be some kind of additional pollination effort? Was Lewis somehow trying to use larger animals for pollination, as well as these gen-mod bees?

Could it be that one of those raccoons killed Emmett? The raccoon had attacked Ava, and from what Ava said, it had been incredibly aggressive. But how had the sting from that raccoon caused an infection in Bailey? What had Lewis done?

Jim remembered the moment, standing in the lobby of Hadley Agritech, when he first presented Lewis with the glass jar containing two of the strange gray bees. One of the first things Lewis had asked was whether or not Jim had been stung. And then later, he had warned him again.

*You don't want to get stung by an unidentified species. You don't know how toxic it might be.*

Jim had an idea. He was, after all, a scientist. Like any scientist worth his salt, he would run an experiment.

He walked back behind the house, to the garden shed. The rusty hinges creaked as he opened the door. Wan afternoon light seeped in through the small window. He approached the old fish tank on his workbench holding the gray bees. Something was wrong. It looked empty.

His stomach sank as he looked around the shed. He couldn't hear them or see them anywhere. He moved closer to the tank. There was the water. There was the honeycomb he'd placed inside. The screen lid, the grate, and the rock he'd put on top were all still secure. There were no openings. There was no obvious way for the bees to escape.

He put his hands on the outside of the tank, and he began turning it. The two gray bees were behind the honeycomb. He quickly breathed a sigh of relief. He watched their bodies, thinking again of the similarities they shared with that horrible raccoon—the color, the black stripes, the stinger.

If a sting from that freakish raccoon caused a lethal infection, and if the raccoon was somehow related to these bees, what would a sting from the bees do? He leaned down and put his face near the glass.

It would have to be something small—something that would fit in the tank with the bees. He tried to think. A rabbit? Another raccoon? The tank wasn't big enough for that. He looked around the shed, thinking of the countless animal traps his dad used to have—foot-hold traps, body-gripping traps, dog-proof paw traps, and even cable restraints. If only he had some of those here. Jim had never liked trapping.

Then, something caught his eye on the floor. Mouse droppings. There had been mice in the shed last winter. Perfect. He thought he might still have an old live mousetrap, somewhere at the back of one of the dusty shelves in here. After searching, he found it behind a box of slug bait.

He quickly ran into the house, grabbed a spoonful of peanut butter from the kitchen, and back in the shed, he set the trap, placing it on the floor near the droppings. It was just a matter of time. As soon as he caught a mouse, he would give it to the bees.

But right now, he had to get to Gabby. He had to tell her what Lewis was doing.

34

THE PICKUP TRUCK jerked and jolted down Miller's Track as Jim drove towards the spot in the End Woods where he'd found Emmett's body that morning. Gabby must still be there. She hadn't answered her mobile, and Shirley, the receptionist at the station, had said that Gabby was still "out in the field."

He slowed when he came across her patrol SUV, pulled off into the grass at the edge of the track, not far from the clearing where they had found Emmett's remains. Just in front of it was another patrol car, most likely Eric's, the summer deputy. Jim parked nearby and got out.

He could hear voices coming from the clearing.

He felt uneasy being here now. This morning Gabby had asked him to leave this place abruptly. In fact, in the past two days, her attitude toward him had fluctuated so much he was now frankly confused. After initially treating him with suspicion, for a time this morning she'd almost seemed to trust him. They were working together. Then, as soon as he'd found Emmett's body, she'd reverted back to suspicion. He had no idea how she was going to respond to seeing him out here now, but he needed to talk to her.

The yellow police line was visible through the trees as he walked toward the clearing. From a distance he could see Gabby and Eric. There was also another man Jim didn't know, a stocky Black man with a shaved head and a thin goatee. Jim stood far away from the police line and called out to her.

She looked up and saw him. Was that a look of irritation on her face? This wasn't going to be easy.

"Can we talk?" he yelled.

She turned to the others and said something, then walked over. "What are you doing out here again?" she said. "I told you this is law enforcement business."

"I know. I have to talk to you."

"What about?"

"You have to arrest Lewis Wilson and Brad Kelly," Jim said.

She seemed surprised. "Why?"

"A lot's happened since we parted ways this morning."

"Like what?"

He quickly told her about the raccoon attack, the sick dog, the hazmat suit, and the jerry cans and green foam in the back of the Hadley Agritech truck.

She watched him closely as he spoke, but she looked skeptical. When he was done she said, "Let me make sure I have this right. You're telling me that a never-before-seen, genetically modified raccoon attacked your daughter, stung your dog, and gave him a strange illness." She raised her eyebrows.

He paused. "I know it sounds a little crazy..."

"Are you sure it wasn't just a rabid raccoon?"

"It had mandibles and a stinger. It was gray and hairless."

"Wow. Can you show it to me?"

He shook his head. "It's gone. Lewis has it. I left it at Hadley Agritech. I had to rush home to Ava."

"Why did you take it to Lewis? Why didn't you call Animal Services? They deal with rabid animals all the time." She was watching him very closely now. It felt like he was being studied.

"I should have never taken it to Lewis. I was furious, and I wanted an explanation. I wasn't thinking clearly." He shook his head. "But I'm telling you it wasn't rabid. It was a gen-mod. It looked a bit like the bees I found in my hives. Similar markings."

"Do you have pictures of it?"

Jim sighed. "I'm afraid not." His phone was now charged and in his pocket, ready for anything, but that didn't change the fact that there were no pictures of the raccoon on it.

"And what exactly makes you think that this raccoon, ah, *stung* your dog?" Gabby's tone had become patronizing. She clearly didn't believe him.

He took a deep breath and tried to speak as calmly as possible. "There was a mark on Bailey's body and swelling consistent with a sting. It looked like a classic histamine response. And I saw the stinger in the raccoon. It was extremely long and black. It appeared to be made of the same chitinous material as the mandibles."

"But you can't show this extraordinary raccoon to me. Not even a photo."

He became overwhelmed by a growing sense of despair. He didn't think he'd believe himself either. Why had he even bothered coming here to tell her? He was wasting his time.

She leaned forward. "Perhaps you can show me the sting mark on your dog then."

He sighed. "No, I can't. Bailey's gone too. Lewis took him."

"Lewis took your dog." She said it slowly, obviously unconvinced.

"Yes. He said Bailey was infectious. And that he could help."

"And don't tell me. No pictures of that either."

He looked out at the trees. "It was chaos. My phone was in my bedroom on the charging pad."

"So you have absolutely no evidence of any of this. The dead raccoon or the sick dog."

Jim nodded. "They're both at Hadley Agritech." The entire

drive here he'd been beating himself up over this. He'd handed over everything to Lewis. He understood now that two things had clouded his judgement: fear and panic about Ava's safety, and the trust he used to have in his old friend Lewis. From now on he would have to be more careful.

"They're hiding something," he said. "Lewis and Brad. They're both hiding something. I thought I could trust Lewis, but I can't."

"And what are they hiding?"

"I don't know exactly," Jim said.

Gabby looked back towards the clearing. She seemed to be thinking.

Jim watched Eric and the other man. "Who is that with Eric?" he asked.

She answered impassively, continuing to stare out at the clearing. "He's one of the Keskkauko County Deputy Medical Examiners. Dr. Abeo Okafor. He's good. He should be able to figure out what killed Emmett. A Coast Guard chopper brought him over from Au Bois."

For a moment it seemed as though she were speaking to him like an equal again, not a crazy man. He felt a huge relief.

"Where's Emmett's dog?" he asked.

"Eric just dropped him off with Hank Schuster." She turned back to look at him. "I'll talk to Lewis."

Finally, Gabby was taking him seriously. "Thank you. I only saw one gen-mod raccoon, but there might be more."

"Look, Jim. It's likely that what we are dealing with is a serious rabies outbreak."

"But it—"

"Listen to me." Her voice was firm but gentle. "Raccoons are a primary carrier of the rabies virus. I'm sure you know that. Here's what I'm planning to do. I'm going to talk to Doc Lester at the medical clinic and see if there are any other reports of animal bites. I'm also going to call Hank Schuster to see if he's had any pets testing positive for rabies. As far as Emmett's death is concerned, a rabid coyote is the most likely explanation. Dr. Okafor will be able to confirm it soon."

She gestured back to the clearing. The medical examiner was leaning down near the spot where Emmett's body lay.

"This is not rabies," Jim said.

She put her hands on her hips. "Jim, you're a researcher. Have you ever heard of Occam's Razor?"

"Of course I have. Every scientist knows it."

She opened up her arms, gesturing for him to explain.

He cleared his throat. "If you have several hypotheses that could explain a phenomenon, it's best to start by examining the simplest one. The simplest explanation is most often correct. But I'm telling you, rabies does not explain what I saw."

"Regardless, I need to start with the simplest hypothesis, don't I? There are strict regulations around development, control, and release of gen-mods. You don't just find them running around the woods. What you *do* find is rabies. So that's where I'll start."

"What about the other people on this island? This thing could get them. There could be more."

"My job is to protect the citizens and guests of this island, and I take that very seriously. I don't know what you think you saw, but you have to let me do my job. I am the law enforcement here, not you."

"And what about the jerry cans in the back of the truck Brad was driving?"

"I already told you that a lot of people on the island have those. They're the only ones that Bob sells."

"And what about Brad's hazmat suit? And the green foam? It was cut into long strips. Exactly like the guy in the video footage."

She paused and nodded. "Yes. That is suspicious. If true, it could connect Brad and Lewis to the arson."

"If true? I'm telling you it's true. You need to talk to Lewis right away. Find out what's going on for yourself."

"I said I'd talk to him. Is there anything else?"

"Yes. There is." He worried that what he was about to tell her would make her question his account of things all over again. He knew it strained believability.

"What?" she said, sounding a bit tired.

"It doesn't make sense."

She actually laughed. "Oh, but a raccoon with mandibles and a stinger does?"

"I saw a strange footprint at Minnie's house. Something's been eating her cantaloupes. The footprint looked like a person's bare foot. But it was too big to be Minnie's. And there were indentations that confused me."

"How do you mean?"

"It sounds strange. You won't believe me."

"Tell me." She opened her arms, like she was ready to get hit by something.

"In front of each toe, there was a mark, like, well, like claws."

"Claws?"

"Yes. Almost like the claws on bear tracks, but the footprint itself was human. It made no sense."

"A person with claws?" Gabby said. "My, my. Your story gets stranger by the minute. By your account, there are monsters everywhere."

Jim recoiled, remembering Ava's comment yesterday. *A boogeyman lurks around every corner.*

He realized then that perhaps he was wrong about Gabby. She wasn't taking him seriously at all. In fact, she was barely putting up with him. He knew he sounded crazy. How could he make her believe him?

"Look," he said, "maybe I read the footprint wrong, but it was unusual. You should go check it out."

"Do you have pictures of this mysterious footprint?"

Jim shook his head.

Gabby suddenly looked exasperated. "Jim, in case you forgot,

I've got a body lying just over there. I'm not too worried about what's eating the melons in Minnie O'Donnell's garden."

"But—"

"I have work to do. I said I'd talk to Lewis. Now go." With that, she turned her back on him and walked away, into the clearing.

## 35

JIM DROVE IMMEDIATELY to Minnie's. He wanted to look again for that footprint, and this time he wanted to take a picture. He strongly suspected it was related to everything else that was going on somehow, and he was furious that Gabby was disregarding it. He was determined to prove his point to her. He had to give her some kind of evidence. He had to prove he wasn't losing his mind.

Soon he was heading down Minnie's driveway. As he approached her house, the first thing he noticed was the broken glass. The large picture window at the front had been completely smashed. There were shards of sharp glass sticking up around the edges of the window frame. Panic shot through him. He parked the truck and ran up to the house, calling out.

"Minnie! Minnie!?"

He pounded on the door, but there was no answer. It was locked.

Inside the broken window, the curtains were drawn. He scanned around the area quickly for any further signs of disturbance. The bushes seemed trampled on, as though someone or something had climbed over them to get into the broken window, but there was bark mulch in the garden bed, so there were no footprints. There was a rake resting against the porch.

He quickly grabbed the rake, jumped down, and scrambled through the bushes toward the window. He smashed away the remaining shards of glass with the rake, and then climbed in through the window, taking the rake with him.

When he jumped down into the living room, a terrible, pungent scent met him. He'd never smelled this odd smell here before. Was something in here? Every curtain was shut, and every light was on. He held the rake out in front of him, ready to swing at any moment. He was half expecting something to jump at him. But there was no movement. There was no noise. Broken glass lay scattered across the brown carpet.

"Minnie?" he called out. Again there was no answer.

Still holding the rake, he walked through the kitchen and over to the bottom of the wooden stairs that led up to the second floor. "Minnie?"

He listened. Nothing. With all the lights on, and all the curtains closed, he wondered what Minnie was trying to shut out. He began to walk up the stairs. One of the first few steps gave off a loud squeak. He paused.

"Minnie? It's Jim!"

Still nothing. He continued. The smell was getting stronger. It was rank. Something wasn't right.

When he got to the top of the stairs, he looked down a short hallway. There were two doors on either side and one door at the end of the hall. All the doors were open. A long beige rug ran the length of the hallway. It was spotted with blood.

"Minnie!" He ran forward down the hallway.

The blood was thickest in front of the doorway at the end of the hall. He stepped into that room, the rake held up in front of him, ready to swing it down on whatever strange animal was here.

What he saw made him stop immediately. He dropped the rake. He stepped back.

Minnie's body lay on the floor in front of him. There was blood everywhere. The flesh was gone in parts. A leg was missing. He turned away, sick with devastation and disbelief. Something had broken into this sweet old woman's home and slaughtered her. It had hunted her down in her own house. The weight of it hit him like a punch to the face.

Whatever was going on, it was far worse than he'd ever thought.

## 36

GABBY STOOD in Minnie O'Donnell's kitchen, looking out the back window. Blue gingham curtains framed her view of the backyard and the large fence around the vegetable garden. The early evening light outside looked peaceful. Inside, however, the scene just upstairs was like something out of a nightmare.

Jim Parker was waiting out front. Gabby had had to move him outside in order to secure the crime scene.

Dr. Okafor was already examining what was left of Minnie's body. Gabby had left Deputy Eric in the End Woods to transfer Emmett's remains in a body bag to the substation. It was a tough job for a summer deputy, but it needed to be done.

On the way here, she'd radioed Sheriff Turner in Au Bois. Things were getting out of hand. She was going to need more officers. Turner had actually warned her about "overreacting." That didn't give her much confidence that he was going to agree to her request.

But right now she didn't have to worry about that. Right now she had to finish dealing with Jim Parker. She didn't know what to do about that man. She went back out front, making sure to keep the police tape in place at the front door as she went past it. As first responding officer, preservation of the crime scene was her most important job.

Jim was standing with his back to the house, staring into the trees.

She'd spent some time earlier asking him questions about the crime scene. She needed to establish whether he'd made any changes, such as turning lights on or off or opening doors or windows. She'd also asked him about every detail of his last visit here at Minnie's. He was clearly shaken.

"Are you okay?" she asked.

He nodded. "You know, I didn't really know Emmett very well. But I knew Minnie. I helped her. She used to bring over cookies."

"I'm sorry, Jim. I, ah, I have just a few more questions for you," she said, trying not to rush him. "Then you can go."

He nodded slowly, like a man in a trance.

"You mentioned there was an animal that was getting into her garden," she said. "What was it?"

All of a sudden, he snapped at her. "Earlier this evening you told me you didn't *care* about Minnie O'Donnell's garden."

She refused to take the bait. "Please just answer the question. What was it?"

He shook his head. "At the time, it was Tuesday afternoon, I told her it had to be a coyote. She said it wasn't. I didn't believe her. I should have listened." He stared at the ground. "Now I think it must have been that gen-mod raccoon that attacked Ava earlier today. Thank God she killed it. I hope it was the only one."

"I see." Gabby took out her phone and took some notes. "I just talked to Sheriff Turner. He contacted Lewis Wilson earlier, after I told him about the raccoon you saw." She looked up to watch Jim's face carefully before she said her next sentence. "Lewis said the thing you brought to him was a rabid coyote."

"What?" Jim looked genuinely surprised. "Lewis is lying. I told you, Hadley Agritech is hiding something."

Gabby had considered this, but she was struggling. Given

there was no evidence of anything, the version of events Lewis had recounted to the sheriff seemed much more credible. She wanted desperately to believe Jim, but she had to be mindful of her own bias. At this point she was aware that her periodic harshness with Jim was like an instinctual reflex. She was pushing him away so she could remain objective. It would not do her or the investigation any favors if she let her affections cloud her judgment.

According to Lewis, Jim had brought in a coyote carcass as they were old friends and Lewis had access to a lab. Jim wanted to get the carcass tested for rabies. Lewis offered to help with the dog, as it had been bitten and was already showing clinical signs of rabies. Lewis took the dog away since no treatment existed once an animal developed rabies symptoms. Later, he put the dog down. Both the coyote and the dog carcasses had been disposed of in Hadley's incinerator. Lewis saw no reason to keep them. It seemed feasible.

On the other hand, Jim's version of events—a story involving a bizarre raccoon with mandibles and a stinger—was preposterous. Sheriff Turner had asked Gabby if she thought that Jim could be suffering from some kind of post-traumatic stress disorder. Considering the unfortunate circumstances around the loss of his wife, it was entirely possible. She'd seen it before. After a traumatic event, any period of stress could intensify the symptoms of anxiety and trauma, leading to an increased risk of psychosis. Was Jim losing it?

Jim looked back at her and spoke plainly. "Gabby, I know you're having a very hard time believing my story. You want to believe that you're dealing with an outbreak of rabies. And while it's true that the simplest explanation is most often correct, the key part of Occam's Razor is when it says, 'most often.' In other words, it's saying that the simplest explanation is *not always* correct."

She listened to his words carefully. He sounded calm, and he almost seemed rational. Given that he'd just found his neighbor's body in pieces, this was remarkable. "What are you saying, Jim?"

"I'm saying that the rabid coyote hypothesis does not explain everything here. For example, have you ever heard of a rabid coyote jumping through a window to get inside someone's house?"

"No, I haven't." Since taking this rural post, she'd paid attention to a lot of stories about rabies attacks from around the country. Usually a rabid coyote came across someone randomly. Maybe the person was gardening. Maybe they were walking through the woods. The coyote would bite them, but then more often than not it would get scared off and run away.

"You know rabid coyotes don't usually go jumping through windows to rip someone apart in their upstairs bedroom." Jim maintained his composure. There was no anger in his voice or his expression. He came across as friendly and sympathetic, like he was on her side.

She sighed. He was right. Coyotes didn't usually do that.

"I know my story is very strange," he said. "I wish I could prove it to you. But if Lewis won't validate what I'm telling you, then talk to Ava. She saw the gen-mod raccoon too. She killed it." He paused, looking down at the ground for a moment. The evening light gathered in shadows around his eyes. He looked tired. "There's also something else I need to tell you."

Gabby braced herself. The strangest things were coming out of Jim's mouth. She couldn't anticipate what kind of far-fetched story he'd come up with next. "What?"

"Minnie told me that the thing getting into her garden moved strangely."

"What exactly did she mean when she said it moved strangely?"

"She didn't say. But Ava said the same thing about the creature that attacked her today. She said it twitched and jerked. And whatever Minnie saw, it was clear that it was eating her cantaloupes. And it left weird teeth marks."

"Weird how?"

He rubbed the back of his neck, thinking. "It looked like a serrated knife had scraped across the surface. At least, that's what I thought at the time. There might still be some of those half-eaten cantaloupes out there." He gestured behind the house, towards Minnie's garden. "I told her I was going to put coyote rollers on her garden fence, but, well, I was going to do it tomorrow. She was going to make blueberry muffins…" His voice trailed off, and then he added, "You know, the teeth marks on those cantaloupes could have been made by the mandibles on that gen-mod raccoon."

Nothing here was making any sense at all. Gabby's skills as an officer of the law were being pushed to the limit.

"Jim, let's say for a moment that I do believe your story about a grotesque, gen-mod raccoon. You also told me you saw a footprint that looked like a human print, but with claws."

"I did. That's why I came back here. To look at that again."

"How do you explain that footprint if what you saw was a raccoon?"

He shook his head. "I have no idea. Maybe I read the footprint wrong. Or maybe there isn't just one dangerous thing out in the End Woods. Maybe there's two. Maybe the raccoon didn't kill Minnie after all. Maybe something else did. Maybe it's still out there." He looked out at the trees.

"So we're back to the beginning. You have no idea."

He turned to her calmly. "It's not my job to figure this out. You've made that clear. It's your job. But I would like to help." There was no anger in what he said. It felt like an olive branch.

She paused for a moment and studied him. He was indeed handsome in his own quiet, unassuming way. She wished she knew if she could believe him. Was he just a reclusive beekeeper? Or was there something darker beneath his calm exterior? He'd found two bodies in a single day. That was remarkable in itself. It wasn't unheard of for a perpetrator to report a crime, pretending to be a witness. Could Jim be doing that now?

She decided to confront him.

"You know, Jim. What troubled me this morning was that you went directly to Emmett's body. It was as though you knew it was there."

"I told you. I was following a chestnut warbler."

"And you just now found a second body on the very same day. That's quite a coincidence, wouldn't you say? Why are you finding all these bodies?" She held her breath as she watched for his reaction.

"It's not such a coincidence when you consider the fact that I live out here. They're my neighbors." He was keeping a surprisingly cool demeanor—especially compared to how fired up he'd been when she'd accused him earlier. "Something is out there in the woods, killing people. We need to find it. I don't want it coming to my house next. And I don't want *that*"—he pointed up towards Minnie's bedroom—"to happen to Ava."

She saw the pain and fear in his eyes. "Can you show me where you found that footprint?" she asked.

He took a deep breath, nodded and gestured with his head toward the back of the house. It was a casual, almost enticing gesture that invoked a kind of camaraderie. It said that she should follow him, that they should figure this out together.

They walked around the house toward the backyard. Gabby reminded herself to keep her eye on him. This was a crime scene, after all.

Over by the fence that surrounded the garden, Jim looked at the ground. "I don't see it now. It was here two days ago, on Tuesday."

She scanned the ground. It was troubling that there was absolutely no physical evidence to back up his story. "Why don't you show me the teeth marks on the melons?" she said.

He walked to the gate and put his hand on a padlock that locked it.

"Minnie told me she was locking it to keep the animal out," he said. "She kept the key around her neck." He paused. "Maybe it's still…" He shook his head and twisted up his face.

Gabby scrutinized him. Was he cracking?

"We can walk around the outside," she said.

"Okay. The cantaloupes are over there." He pointed to the far corner.

She followed him along the fence to the other side of the garden.

"They're here." Jim pointed down to one of the garden beds. "But all the broken ones are gone. I see no teeth marks here now. Minnie must have cleaned them up."

"So, no footprints today," Gabby said. "And no teeth marks."

He looked at her. "I'm telling you they were here the other day. It was Tuesday afternoon."

"And no dead gen-mod raccoon. And no dead dog. Nothing at all to prove your story." If she set aside her bias, the facts were obvious. Jim's story just didn't add up. She wanted to believe that there was no malice. Something else had to be causing him to spin fantastic stories. It took her a moment to realize that she would actually prefer to believe he was losing his mind than to believe he was intentionally lying. She considered post-traumatic stress disorder again, and she lowered her voice slightly. "Are you okay, Jim?"

"To be honest, I'm trying really hard to hold it together. I just found Minnie's dismembered body. There was so much blood in that room. This morning I found Emmett's body. This afternoon my daughter was attacked by something I've never seen before, and the people I called for help took her dog away. Oh, yeah, and somebody is burning my hives—most likely the people I called for help. And now, to top it all off, the local deputy is treating me like

I'm either crazy or lying. So what do you think? Should I be okay?"

Back in Chicago, she'd responded to as many calls about mental illness as she had about burglaries or stolen cars, and she'd had training on how to deal with people experiencing mental health episodes or PTSD. As she spoke now, she made sure her tone was friendly, clear, and showed both respect and a desire to help. "Jim, have you sought therapy over your wife's death?"

He glared at her. "This has absolutely nothing to do with Sarah."

"Still, it must be hard for you."

"What are you trying to say?" A deeply pained expression passed across his face.

She said nothing, just kept watching him.

"I'm not crazy, Deputy Martinez."

"I'm not saying you're crazy, Jim. But why don't you head home and take it easy for a bit? Take care of yourself."

He looked through the fence at Minnie's garden one last time, and the pained expression on his face slowly fell away.

"I didn't believe Minnie either," he said. "Not when she first told me. I didn't think she was crazy exactly, but I suspected it was her bad eyesight. I actually told her that what she was saying just didn't make any sense. Of course you don't believe me. I wouldn't believe me either."

Gabby took this in slowly. She felt for him. He must be feeling guilty. He was a compassionate man above all else. "I'm sorry. This has to be incredibly hard on you. Go home. Get some rest."

He turned and walked away from her, back toward his truck.

"Oh, and Jim…" She started, but he ignored her and continued walking. She didn't want to say it to him, but she had to. "Jim?" she called out again, following him to the front of the house.

Just as he was about to climb into his truck, he finally turned to look at her.

"Please don't leave the island," she said. "We might have more questions."

His head dropped. He looked both exasperated and incredibly sad. "You suspect me again. You really do."

"I didn't say that. But you and I might need to talk more."

"I'm not going anywhere. Honest people stay."

37

AVA WAS LYING IN BED, watching her fish swim back and forth peacefully inside their tiny tank. Their colors were electric. She envied them for how happy they seemed to be. But were they? Did they want to be free? Did they want a bigger space? Sometimes she wondered.

The makeshift bed they had made for Bailey was still under the window, empty. She took out her journal. She had no idea what she was going to write about. Bailey? Her pregnancy? She certainly couldn't write about her pregnancy. She didn't know what she was going to do about it yet, and she was trying not to think about it. There was still a bit of time. More importantly, she couldn't write about being pregnant. What if the Window Cop read it? Although she hid the journal in her drawer, she couldn't be certain he didn't read it. It seemed like the kind of thing he would do. Ugh.

Instead of writing, she simply looked up at the ceiling and thought about Eddie, about how much she missed him.

There was the sound of something moving out on the front porch, catching her attention. It was a shuffling sound, then silence. She'd shut her curtains earlier, even before the light had started fading. The Window Cop would yell at her when he got home if they were still open. It wasn't worth it.

She got up out of bed and listened. She couldn't hear anything else. She slowly pulled back the fabric of the curtains and peeked out. There was nobody there. But when she pulled the curtain back completely, she could see that something purple was lying on the wooden planks of the porch, just below her window. What was it? She leaned forward.

Flowers. And not just any flowers.

Beach pea.

She ran to the front door, fumbling with the stupid lock in her haste, and stepped outside. The flowers had been laid there carefully, in a loose posy under her window. She picked them up.

"Eddie!" She looked out toward the trees. "Eddie!"

Her heart raced. The shadows were getting long and she couldn't see very far into the tress. Clutching the flowers, she ran down the porch and stood in the middle of the clearing in front of the house.

"Eddie!"

There was no sign of anyone.

38

GABBY WENT BACK into Minnie's house. She walked up the stairs and headed down the hallway, knowing what she would face in Minnie's bedroom. At the door, she paused. The fewer people who entered this room, the better. There was always a risk of inadvertently tampering with evidence.

"How's it going?" she asked from the doorway.

Dr. Abeo Okafor was standing near the body. His shaved head was shining under the bright light overhead. Gabby accepted that he was in charge of this scene now. As he'd been doing with Emmett's case, Abeo was here to determine the cause, time, and manner of death. The remains could not be touched without his approval.

"This was an exceptionally violent death," he said. His light and lilting Nigerian accent belied the horror of his sentence.

She looked at the blood on the floor and the splatters on the wall.

Abeo lifted up a plastic evidence bag, which contained a pair of four-inch long sewing scissors. "It seems she fought back with these. Small, but sharp."

Gabby imagined the sweet old woman fighting for her life. It was because of violence like this that she'd left Chicago. The gang warfare she had faced there had almost made her quit her job in law enforcement altogether. Gull Island was supposed to be a new start. She hadn't expected to see this kind of death here.

Abeo pointed to the far side of the room. "It looks like she was dragged out from under the bed and killed with a cut to the throat. Then her body was dragged here, to the end of the bed, where the right leg was removed. Parts of the body have been consumed—mostly muscle. The quadricep and hamstring on the remaining leg. The bicep, tricep, and brachioradialis on the left arm. There is still no sign of the left leg."

He had the same matter-of-fact tone that Gabby had come to associate with the medical examiners she'd worked with in Chicago.

"When did it happen?" she asked.

"I'll need to complete a full autopsy to narrow the window, but it looks like approximately two or three days ago."

"So," she said, "we're talking Monday or Tuesday."

"Yes, with the most likely scenario being sometime on Tuesday."

"Tuesday. You're sure?"

"Everything is an estimation, of course," Abeo responded. "But I'm relatively sure, based on body temperature and the fact that rigor mortis has already passed. It only occurs during the first thirty-six to forty-eight hours after death."

She nodded. "Jim Parker said he visited Minnie on Tuesday afternoon, around two."

Abeo tilted his head in curiosity. "Is he a suspect?"

"I'm not entirely sure yet." She knew she was still being harsh on Jim, but she had to make sure she was being objective. She couldn't let him get too close.

"Well, if his story is accurate, that would indicate she was alive Tuesday afternoon. That's consistent with the state of the remains."

She was glad to hear at least a partial confirmation of some element of Jim's story, but she needed more than that. "I'm not certain that Jim's narration of events in the past twenty-four hours is believable. There may be some psychosis."

"I see." Abeo raised his eyebrows with a kind of morbid, scientific interest.

"You mentioned a cut to the throat," she asked. "Was that done with a knife? Or maybe with her own scissors?"

"Well, it actually looks like there may have been a serrated knife in use, as there is a somewhat jagged edge to the cut."

"A serrated knife?"

"Yes. But other indicators actually look a bit like teeth marks. Some cuts have an arc to them, like teeth."

She thought of Jim and the strange detail he'd shared about teeth marks that looked like a serrated knife. For a moment, she found herself imagining a raccoon with mandibles, and suddenly she understood what she wanted above all else. Her bias was plain and strong. Her desire was grim but clear.

The version of reality Gabby preferred—the one she really wanted to be true—was the version where Jim Parker was neither lying nor suffering from psychosis. If that version of reality also meant that there actually did exist a mutant raccoon on the island that was out here killing people, well, then that was just something she'd have to deal with.

"Can I ask a crazy question?" she said.

"Certainly."

"If there were a medium to large animal that had, let's say, mandibles for teeth, like an insect, would that explain the nature of the cuts?"

Abeo looked at the body, a surprised look on his face. "Actually, yes. But of course such an animal is unlikely."

"Yes, of course."

"Although..." Abeo's voice trailed off.

"Yes?"

"There were similar cuts and marks on the body of Emmett Jones. And these were also not entirely consistent with a coyote attack."

"Do you think it's an animal?" Gabby asked.

"I don't think so."

"Why?" She knew Abeo was a rational man. He would have a logical reason for his conclusion. In fact, she was relying on his rationality to make sure she didn't go down a bewildering rabbit hole.

"A footprint."

Gabby looked at him intently. "What kind? A raccoon?"

"No, not a raccoon. It's over here." Abeo pointed to the far side of the bed. "It's human, but it's odd."

"Odd how?" She remembered another of Jim's strange details —he'd shared so many of them—about the footprint in Minnie's garden that looked like it had been made by a person with claws on their feet.

"Come look." Abeo gestured for her to enter the room, and then he led her around the body and toward the nightstand. "Here," he said, pointing at the floor.

There was a bloody, barefoot print.

"This is good," Abeo said, "because barefoot prints are as unique as fingerprints. By this print, I can already estimate that the killer was around five foot ten."

Gabby thought of Jim. He was six foot one. This wasn't Jim's footprint. Thank God. "So what's odd about it?" she asked.

"See these marks here, in front of the toe pads?"

"Yes."

"They almost look like claws."

Just like Jim had said. She remembered his exact words.

*Maybe the raccoon didn't kill Minnie after all. Maybe something else did. Maybe it's still out there.*

The realization swept through Gabby like a cold chill. The entire time, Jim Parker had been telling her the truth.

39

Sunset was less than an hour away, but when Jim finally got back home from Minnie's house, it seemed to be getting dark faster than usual. Night would soon settle into the woods.

As he pulled up in front of his house, he saw the purplish glow of Ava's fish tank in the gap between her drawn curtains. He figured she was probably lying in bed, messaging her friends or scrawling through social media. That was all she seemed to do. He'd messaged her while he was waiting outside Minnie's house, telling her that he was held up and would be home as soon as he could. He didn't tell her that Minnie was dead. He didn't know how.

He parked his truck in the garage and walked to the back door. The gentle sound of crickets rose up out of the woods. He should have done more. It was his fault that Minnie was dead. She'd asked him for help, and he'd failed to protect her. The weight of this pushed down on him.

For a moment he paused and stared out into the back acre and over toward the swing set, thinking of Ava there, defending herself. There were still patches of dried blood on the ground. This green patch of land, once a precious space that felt protected by the trees all around, had somehow turned into a combat zone. He shuddered at the thought that what happened to Minnie could have happened to Ava.

He looked over toward the burnt patch of ground in the far back corner. He'd spent so much time back there in the last two years—harvesting honey in the autumn, supplementing feed with sugar syrup in the winter as the bees huddled for warmth, and watching the bees come alive again in the spring. Now that back corner was nothing but a barren void. Everything was falling apart. His neighbors were dead. The small paradise he'd made for Ava and himself had absolutely disintegrated.

On the back porch, he slipped off his boots and reached for the door. It was unlocked. A wave of anger and frustration ran through him. He knew he'd locked both the front and back doors when he left. As usual, Ava must have gone outside and forgotten to lock it when she came back in. He'd told her countless times that she needed to keep all the doors locked when she was home alone. It was more important now than ever.

He stepped inside.

"Ava, I'm home!"

She didn't answer.

The kitchen light was on, and there was a pot on the stove with some leftover macaroni and cheese—Ava's go-to meal whenever he wasn't home.

The pot and the pasta inside were cold, the bright orange cheese clumping the macaroni noodles together like a thick glue. An empty mac and cheese box lay on the counter, next to an empty packet of instant cheese mix. A sprinkling of orange powder was scattered across the countertop. Frustration ran through him again. It was as though Ava believed she was the only person in the house.

He opened his mouth to yell out, but he stopped himself. She'd just been attacked. Her dog had been taken away. He should cut her some slack. At her bedroom door, he knocked quietly.

"Leave me alone," she said from the other side.

"Just wanted to make sure you're home safe," he said.

Back in the kitchen, he took a beer out of the fridge, popped it open, and took a long swig. Then he took out a fork and carried the pot of cold mac and cheese over to the kitchen table, where he ate it directly from the pot.

The landline rang, startling him. He answered it reluctantly. It was Gabby.

"Jim," she said. "You know the footprint you described, like a human print with claws?"

"I don't want to have this conversation again." He was tired of her not believing him.

"There was a footprint like that in Minnie's bedroom, in blood."

His stomach dropped, and he felt a flash of anger. He was right all along, and this was finally proof. "I told you."

"I know, Jim. And you know what this means as well as I do. Something, or someone, is still out there. And it's not a gen-mod raccoon. It's bigger. It's probably worse. I wanted you to know. You need to be careful tonight."

He felt emotionally ripped in two different directions— immense relief at not being treated like a crazy person, and indignation that it took this long.

"Jim?" Gabby said.

"Yeah?" He could barely think. He was worried about Ava.

"I believe you. I'm sorry."

He tried to let go of his anger and indignation. She was, he told himself, only doing her job. "Thank you."

"I'll talk to you tomorrow," she said. "I'll need both you and Ava to come to the station to deliver a statement."

He hung up the phone and looked toward the kitchen windows, which revealed the darkening End Woods outside. He stepped onto the back porch and stood there for a moment, watching the trees and the fading light. What, he wondered, was out there?

The evening chorus was strong now, sparrows hidden in the trees, chirping wildly. Off to the left he heard a robin singing its evening song: *cheer up, cheer up, cheery me.* Toads and crickets trilled from the shadows—a steady, rolling tune.

Then the noise stopped. First the crickets hushed. Next, the toads went quiet. The birds stopped chirping. One after another, they simply turned off—like flipping a series of switches—until the cacophonous evening chorus became an absolute, deathly stillness. He peered out into the gloom. His blood ran cold.

Suddenly, a clanking sound shot out from over by the garden shed. He froze. It sounded like a rake or a shovel falling over, knocking into something else. For a brief moment he considered yelling out to scare it away, as he would if it were a coyote. But he stopped himself. It might not be a coyote. He should be careful. Instead, he listened.

He heard a shuffling noise, like something moving through grass, but the light was too low to see much now.

Turning quietly, he went back inside to grab a flashlight. While there, he stopped at Ava's door and knocked again. "Ava, there's something outside. Stay in your room, okay?"

The door opened. She stood there in purple sweatpants and an oversized black hoodie. The black light from her fish tank glowed behind her.

"What do you mean?" she asked.

Jim tried not to look too worried, although the strange, gradual silence from the woods had deeply unsettled him. "I heard something moving," he said. "It's probably nothing. Please just stay in your room while I check it out."

"What if it's one of those things? A gen-mod?"

He didn't want to scare her. "Nah. Some garden tools fell over by the shed. It's probably a deer. You just stay in your room. And keep the door shut."

"Why don't you call Deputy Gabby instead?"

"What? And tell her that some garden tools fell over?" Jim forced a smile. "I think she's busy."

"I should help you," she said.

He paused and looked at her. The purplish glow surrounded her like an aura. She was fearless. He was proud of her. She'd killed that animal today. But what was out there now could be much worse than a gen-mod raccoon. He couldn't risk losing her. He would not fail again, not with Ava.

"It's fine," he said. "Just promise me you'll stay in your room."

She crossed her arms, looking a little angry. "Whatever."

He walked away, hearing her bedroom door shut behind him.

On the back porch, there was still total silence from the woods. He shone the flashlight over toward the shed. There was no movement and no noise coming from that direction. He scanned the back acre—the garage and the shed, the garden, the swing set, the scorched bit of earth in the far corner where his hives had once stood, and the picnic table in front of him. The small flashlight barely cut through the growing dark.

The shadows were quickly getting blacker along the edge of the woods, as though gaining momentum against the dying light. Perhaps whatever had made the noise had moved on. He turned the flashlight off and waited, thinking that it might be afraid of the light.

The night seemed to come rushing in as his eyes struggled to adjust. There were no stars out. Behind him, the light from the kitchen came through the windows. He could hear nothing but his own heart, which was beating fast. Was the thing out there gone? Did it go around to the front of the house? Was it by Ava's bedroom window?

A twig snapped from near the garage. It was a large sound, made by something heavy. He looked through the gloom over at the garage. There was something on the ground—a shovel. That was supposed to be in the garden shed. Why was it there? It wasn't there a moment ago. Was it? He felt his breathing quicken. There was a rustling, and his ears pricked up. A slow breeze had started and was moving the leaves in the trees.

Ava had said the gen-mod had run at her fast. He had to be ready for something to run at him. He felt his chest tighten.

But nothing came. Still, he sensed something odd. Like a presence. Something that he couldn't quite name. It felt like he was being watched.

Then he heard it. A low hum, along with a strange, sporadic clicking. He listened. There was something vaguely familiar in that clicking sound, but he couldn't figure out what. It didn't sound entirely mammalian, nor reptilian, nor avian. It was almost insectoid.

*Hmmm. Hmmm. Cli-click.*

He quickly flicked the flashlight back on. Something moved at the edge of the soft beam—a gray blur darting to the left. It was not small. It was not close to the ground. It was certainly not raccoon-sized. When he tried to follow it with the light, it was already gone. It must have shot behind the garage. He went back inside, slamming the door shut behind him.

Ava was standing in the doorway to the kitchen, staring in from the living room.

"What was it?" she said.

"I told you to stay in your room. It's nothing. A coyote."

She studied him. "You're lying."

"Go back to your room." He set the flashlight on the table.

"You need help."

"No, I don't!" he shouted with everything he had in him. He heard his voice booming through the house as though it were coming from someone else. Even to his own ears, it sounded like the roaring of a madman.

Ava looked at him and recoiled.

He held up his hand in the air to apologize. He just wanted her to do what he said. "It's out there now, Ava. Go to your room."

"Was it a gen-mod? Like the other one?"

He paused, then nodded, changing tack. The best way to keep her safe was to make sure she knew the danger. He looked at her. "It's bigger."

Her mouth fell open in astonishment. "What do you mean?"

"It's bigger than the gen-mod raccoon that attacked you today. I didn't see it clearly, but it's definitely larger than a raccoon. Please, just go to your room."

Her face changed from bewilderment to something calculating, like she was trying to figure out how to solve a problem they shared. "But I can help you."

He felt on the edge of screaming again, but he stopped himself. "I will take care of this myself." His voice was tight and firm.

"How?" she asked.

He pointed to her room. After staring him down, she stomped off and slammed her door loudly.

He went into his own room. Getting down onto his knees, he reached under the bed. There was a black case he wanted that was behind a few pairs of old boots. When his fingers reached it, he pulled the case out.

It was oblong and made of industrial aluminum. It had silver clasps and a combination lock. He entered the four-digit combination on the rotary dials. His dad had set the number years ago. The lock gave way, he opened the silver clasps, and flipped the lid back.

Inside, was his old Winchester Model 70, cradled by dark foam. It had a rifle scope and a 24-inch barrel. It was walnut clad, with a satin finish and blued steel. The surfaces were burnished from use. Yes, he thought to himself. He would take care of this himself.

40

AS JIM LIFTED the old Winchester out of the case and set it on his bed, he listened for any noise outside. There was none.

He looked down at the gun.

*A rifle for life.*

It had been a gift from his dad on his tenth birthday—the only present his father had ever chosen for him—and he'd kept it all these years. Jim had never enjoyed hunting and trapping, two things his dad loved. But on his birthday that year his father had given him a gun just the same, a present which obligated him to join his dad deer hunting. Even back then, Jim was more interested in collecting bugs.

He could still hear his dad's gruff voice as he'd opened the box that day.

"That's a Winchester Model 70. The rifleman's rifle," his dad had explained. "This one's a .270 caliber. But the Winchester doesn't kick so bad as some. Got a fast bullet, travels flat. Easier to get on target than a lot of rifles."

His older sister and his mother watched closely, both clearly surprised by the size of the gun.

"Wyatt, don't you think it's a bit big for Jimmy?" his mother had said.

His dad just shook his head. "Nah. It'll be fine. Besides, I'll help him, and he'll grow into it. This is a rifle for life. It's registered in my name for now, course. But I'll transfer it to him when he's eighteen."

His father spent a long time teaching Jim about that gun. He wanted Jim to be safe, so he obsessively taught him everything—how to safely shoot it, how to care for it and store it, even how to disarm a man who was pointing it at him at close range. Jim supposed that, in his own way, his father had been as worried about safety as he was.

Since coming to Gull Island, Jim had begun to take care of this old gift again. Just three months earlier he'd cleaned it and sighted the scope. Although he hadn't realized it at first, he'd slowly begun to understand that his caring for this gun was a way of remembering his father. It was like laying flowers at a graveside.

Over the past year, he'd begun to see his days hunting with his father in a new light. Although he didn't much enjoy it at the time, he understood now that hunting was the only way his dad knew how to relate to him. It had never been about killing, not really. At least, that wasn't the most important thing. For his dad, hunting had been a way of spending time with him, something men were allowed to do together. The same was true of all the gun safety lessons. It was time together. So in many ways this gift of an expensive rifle—too big really for a boy of ten—had been his dad's expression of love for his son, and of hope for lifelong friendship.

Jim wished he'd understood that simple fact while his dad was still alive. He wished he'd continued hunting with the old man. This made him think of how he wished that Ava would help him care for his hives. She had no interest. She'd outgrown the bee suit he'd bought her when she was younger, and she had never wanted another. He wished he could find something to do with her, the way his father had taken him hunting.

*BAM!*

A loud noise rang out from behind the garage. It sounded as though one of the long wooden planks stacked there had come crashing down. Whatever was out there, Jim did not want it near their house. He thought of the broken front window at Minnie's. He pictured her body in the bedroom. His stomach turned. That was not going to happen here.

He stepped over to his wooden dresser and opened one of the drawers. Toward the back, behind a jumble of socks, there were two boxes of .270 caliber ammunition.

Muscle memory kicked in. It felt like being back with his dad. He lifted the gun off the bed, slid the bolt handle back, and loaded the cartridges, clicking them down into the magazine with his thumb one at a time. Then he slid the bolt handle forward and rotated it downward. Finally, moving the safety into the middle position, he walked out of the room. One more click and it was ready to fire.

Ava was in the kitchen, her face to the glass of the back windows, peering into the quickly growing darkness.

"Get in your room," Jim said.

"You need my help."

"I don't need your help!"

Ava flashed him an angry look and left the kitchen.

The flashlight was still on the table. He knew he couldn't aim the rifle and hold the flashlight at the same time, so he left it there. He'd have to rely on the back porch light.

Opening the back door, he stepped outside. He switched the safety on the rifle fully forward. It was now ready to fire.

The porch light had an old, solid metal shade, which meant that its yellow light spread out across the grass for only fifteen feet or so, then stopped abruptly. The edge of the picnic table was illuminated, along with the patch of grass around the porch, but beyond that, dusk wrapped like a thick noose around the hard-edged circle of light.

He tried to look out into the space just beyond, scanning the area near the garage. There was no sign of anything. The air was still. Tension held his shoulders in a tight grip.

He took a long, slow breath—something his father had taught him.

The old man used to say, "Check yourself," when they were hunting. He was talking about slowing down, taking a mindful breath, being aware of the body, relaxing the muscles in the shooting arm before taking the shot. His father knew how to hunt, and he knew that presence of mind was critical.

Jim assessed his situation now. He could either stay close to the house or step forward into the yard. It was better to have his back to the house, to stop anything coming at him from behind.

Some shrubbery stirred and leaves rustled off to the left. What was it? He couldn't tell. Something shifted just beyond the edge of the porch light, across the grass. Was it just a trick of the light? No. Something was out there. It was coming closer.

A gray figure slowly formed out of the shadows, and as Jim began to see the outline of the thing, it was not what he expected. The thing was tall. It was clearly no raccoon, nor a coyote. He couldn't make it out exactly. It was standing on the grass just beyond the edge of the light and seemed to be shifting oddly. In the dim light, it would remain completely still, then jerk forward, then pause again. Its movements were unpredictable.

Was it a person? Perhaps it was a hermit, someone living in the woods. Someone sick or crazy. He thought of Minnie and Emmett. He was angry. He thought of Ava. He was scared. Why was this person here? What had this person done? Who was it? Or *what* was it?

He pointed his scope at the spot in the darkness where the figure's chest must be, his finger poised on the trigger. Could it be just a man, standing in the shadows? Was his fear getting the best of him? He couldn't be sure.

Jim yelled, his voice full of hostility. "What do you want?"

There was no answer. He felt a growing sense of dread. What-ever it was, it was watching him. He didn't know whether it might come running at him.

He knew the laws. His father had taught him at a young age. In Michigan, it was legal to use deadly force against someone who was *inside* your home or in the process of actually breaking *into* your home, but the law was murkier if you shot someone outside. Just the summer before, there had been a case in Traverse City where a man had been charged with manslaughter for shooting someone who had wandered drunk onto his property.

As Jim stood waiting, finger on the trigger, the noise came again.

*Hmmm. Hmmm. Cli-click.*

It was an inhuman noise, and it seemed to be coming from the shape in front of him. What was it he recognized about that noise? His biologist's brain reeled.

"Get out of here!" he yelled.

It had to be a drunk old man. It had to be.

But the sound grew louder and more forbidding, like a threat.

He pointed the rifle into the air and fired a warning shot. The bullet cracked the darkness.

The figure didn't run. It continued to jerk and twitch randomly, but apparently not in response to the gunshot. For just a brief moment, the eerie hum and clicking sounds stopped completely.

Jim quickly pulled the rifle bolt handle up and back, expelling the spent cartridge. Then he pushed it forward and down again, locking it into place, ready for the next shot.

As though nothing had happened, the figure took another step toward him. It came to the point on the grass where the soft yellow porch light met the growing darkness, just fifteen feet away from where Jim stood.

There, at the edge of the light, Jim saw two bare feet. *Human feet.* Only they were gray. There were two discolored ankles. It was a person, clearly. Was he dirty? Those were definitely a man's feet, weren't they?

But even in the gloom, Jim could make out that something was not quite right. The skin of the feet seemed thick. And at the end of its toes, which he could barely make out in the grass, there appeared to be long, dark toenails. They were more like claws actually.

A chill ran up his spine. He remembered what Minnie had said.

*It comes out of the woods. It's big. Like a person. It always comes at dusk, and it moves in a very peculiar way. It looks like Satan.*

He stared deep into the darkness, breathing heavily. His heart was racing.

The gray creature took another step forward, moving farther into the circle of light. Its body shifted erratically. Jim could now see its strange, ashy legs from the knees down.

Then it began walking directly at him.

He fired a second time, aiming for the thigh. There was no time to take a breath. The gunshot boomed.

The noise that came back from the gray shape was strange and terrifying. He'd clearly hit it. It made a sharp screech. It sounded like two noises at once—a grown man yelling, combined with something akin to sharp metal grinding on stone. The creature stopped and stepped back out of the light, then it went quiet. Jim didn't know how it was still standing. He'd hit it squarely in the thigh. He was sure.

It began walking toward him once more. It wasn't even limping. It screamed again, but this time it was a strange, broken howl. Again, it was terrifying, as though it had come straight out of the depths of hell. This was no drunk old man.

Just then, Jim heard one of the kitchen windows opening. He glanced back and was shocked to see his daughter there, pushing the wooden sash up. She was slightly higher up. She could see it better. She was trying to help him, but he was afraid for her safety.

"Get back in your room!" he yelled.

He quickly turned again to the creature. It was still approaching. He raised the rifle and shot at it again, aiming directly for its chest. It jerked back sharply in the shadows, then righted itself. It made that horrible shriek again.

Behind him, Ava began screaming. "Go away! Go back!"

Her words made no sense to him. He was out here fighting for their lives. He wasn't about to go away. He yelled, "I said in your room!"

She ignored him, and continued screaming, "Go away!"

The creature stopped its approach, and just stood outside the circle of light. Jim raised his rifle once more.

"Run!" Ava yelled.

She was not yelling at him, Jim realized. She was yelling at the creature.

Suddenly the gray shape turned around and ran. It darted between the shed and the fenced garden and headed straight into the woods.

Jim watched it go, rifle raised. He waited. Several minutes passed. Slowly, one by one, the toads and crickets started singing again. It was gone.

He turned and looked at Ava. He was furious. "What are you doing?" he yelled.

She looked at him and slowly closed the window.

## 41

JIM WENT BACK INSIDE and found Ava in the kitchen in the dark.

"What the hell are you doing?" he shouted.

She was standing by the windows, looking out into the darkness. He locked the door tightly behind him.

"What was that?" she asked.

"I don't know. Why did you leave your room?"

"I heard it."

He looked at her as she stood there by the window in her large black hoodie. She seemed small inside it. Her purple hair was a mess from lying in bed. A lock was falling down over one eye.

"Why did you tell it to run away? It's dangerous, Ava."

"It was yelling. It sounded like it was hurt."

He sighed. She was so naive. She had no idea what she was doing. "Don't be silly," he told her. "That thing would kill you in a heartbeat if it had the chance."

He lifted his rifle, switched the safety back on, and set it on the kitchen table. Then he went over to the windows, stepping around his daughter, and pulled the thin curtains shut.

"I don't want it to be able to see in," he said. "Are the curtains in your bedroom closed?"

She sighed in annoyance. "You lose your shit if I don't close those curtains every night. Of course they're closed."

He didn't bother scolding her for her language. It wasn't worth the fight right now. He went over to the living room and pulled the curtains closed in the front window.

She followed and stood at the edge of the room. "I don't think closing the curtains is going to help."

"This thing was on two legs," he said. "It was different than what came for you earlier. It's gray, but darker."

"The little gray thing I killed came in the morning." She paused for a moment, contemplating something, and then she sat down on the couch. "It wasn't nocturnal."

He looked at her closely, surprised that she was commenting on something like this.

"This thing just now," she continued. "It seemed nocturnal. They're different."

Jim nodded. She was trying to figure it out. He'd never thought that Ava had inherited his scientific brain. Perhaps he'd been wrong. He wished for more moments like these—where his daughter was a collaborator, a supporter—and fewer of the ones where they were fighting.

"But it was early, wasn't it?" he asked, sitting down next to her.

"Huh?" She tilted her head quizzically and turned toward him.

"When that gen-mod raccoon came out of the woods this morning and attacked you," Jim said. "It was early, right?"

She nodded. "I couldn't get back to sleep. Somebody woke me up. Several times." She rolled her eyes. "It wasn't totally light when I went outside."

"They both could be crepuscular." Jim looked over towards the drawn curtains.

"Crep-what?"

"Crepuscular. It rhymes with muscular."

"What's it mean?" Ava asked.

"Some animals are nocturnal, or active at night, and some are diurnal, which means they're active during the day. But others are neither. They're what's called crepuscular—primarily active at dusk and dawn."

"Like what? Which animals?"

"Fireflies are crepuscular, and bats, wombats, hyenas. A bunch of others. Coyotes can often be too, but not always. If these two things we've seen are related—the thing that came out of the woods just now, and the thing that attacked you this morning—well, that might be the answer."

She paused and played with the ties on her hoodie for a moment. "So you think these things might come out at both dawn and dusk?"

"Possibly. They might hunt then."

"So if you wanted to avoid them, you'd just go out in broad daylight, or in the middle of the night. You'd avoid going out at dawn and dusk."

"Theoretically, yes."

She nodded slowly, then yawned.

"Go to bed," he said. "I'll stay up and watch for it." He wanted to give her a hug, but she was so funny about them. It was never clear when it was okay. He stayed where he was.

"But if it's crep... ah..." Ava waved her hand as though she were too tired to bother saying the word. "If it's a dawn-and-dusky, then it won't come in the dark, right?"

"It's less likely, but sometimes crepuscular animals are active if the moon's bright. They don't do well in total darkness, or in full daylight." He pulled the curtain back and looked outside. "The moon hasn't risen yet, and there's cloud cover, so it's getting really dark now. Maybe it'll stay away."

She paused, clearly thinking about this for a moment, and then she stood abruptly, as though she'd made some sort of decision. "Okay, well, good night." She turned and started walking down the hallway.

"Ava?" Jim called out behind her.

She paused and looked over her shoulder. "Yeah?"

"I love you."

She nodded slowly. "Love you too, Dad." Then she went to her bedroom and closed the door.

Jim sat there for a moment, thinking about her being in that bedroom with the window that looked out onto the porch. Of course closed curtains were not enough. He got up and went out to the front porch, flashlight in hand, and he stood looking at Ava's window. Dusk had passed, and it was dark. The crickets and toads were still singing. When he shined the flashlight out into the trees around the house, the beam faded into nothingness.

The longer he stood there looking into the night, the more uneasy he became. It was out there still, somewhere. It would come back, eventually. Maybe later tonight. Maybe just before dawn. Maybe not until tomorrow night at dusk. Or the next night. Thoughts of Minnie's front window raced through his head. He looked back at Ava's window. Glass was so easy to break. He simply could not risk losing her, not after Sarah.

With that, it was as though a switch had been flipped in his head, and he was pulled into thoughts of what happened in Ann Arbor. Memories swarmed his head, and he almost felt dizzy. He pushed the thoughts away, but they kept coming at him. He put a hand out on the house for balance. Closing his eyes, he was shocked to see Sarah coming down the stairs in her running clothes. He was fully back there again. The past was smashing into the present. He sat clumsily on the porch step, his head in his hands. Scenes played out in front of him that he couldn't stop.

The morning after he'd gone driving around the streets of Ann Arbor, looking desperately for Sarah, a woman had called. She said she was the investigator. He remembered her voice perfectly. It was both quiet and authoritative. She wanted him to come to the police station. He asked if he could bring Ava, but the woman said it was best if he came alone.

Suddenly, Jim was no longer sitting on the front porch of a

small house on Gull Island. He was in the Ann Arbor Police Department building on Huron Street, sitting at that scratched, white table in a small room. The investigator was looking at him with a somber face. She was introducing him to a man who was sitting next to her. A grief counselor, she said. The man had gray hair and kind eyes. For a moment Jim wasn't quite sure why he needed a grief counselor. Surely they were going to find Sarah. She was going to be okay. Everything was going to go back to normal.

Then the penny finally dropped, and he realized what was happening. He was going to need help with grief. He stared at the scratches on the table. They were long and frantic, as though made in some hysterical frenzy from within, as though someone were trapped inside the table, trying to get out.

The investigator spoke calmly. She told him that earlier that morning a local resident had been walking along the Gallup Park pathway, near the Dixboro Dam, and noticed something in the water. They took a closer look and found it was a body. The police later confirmed that it matched Sarah's description and clothes.

"There are signs of assault," the investigator said.

The counselor tilted his head. "Are you able to look at a picture of the body to determine whether or not it's your wife?"

Jim went blank. Everything turned off. He stared at the man.

"Are you okay?" the man asked.

"I can do it," Jim said. Inside his head he repeated words over and over. Please let it not be her. Please let it not be her.

"I'll present the photograph face down," the grief counselor said. "It will be a picture of a person's face. The face will be surrounded by a blue sheet similar to those found in doctors' offices. You can turn it over when you're ready. You have all the time in the world."

Jim nodded. It was all he could do. The man put the photo on the scratched, white table, face down as promised. Jim stared at the back of the photo. Please let it not be her. He reached forward. His hand was shaking. He turned the photo over.

She looked like she was sleeping, except for the fact that her hair was wet. Her face looked a little bit swollen. But it was Sarah.

It was definitely Sarah.

## 42

SITTING THERE ON THE PORCH, Jim shook his head and touched the house again, as though it would anchor him. He felt the rough wood siding. He threw off the memories of Ann Arbor. He locked them away again. They were horrible.

He had failed to protect Sarah. There was no way around that. He had failed to be there when she needed him. He would *not* fail to protect Ava. He would not lose her. He would not turn over another photograph to see Ava's face. He would not find her body in pieces, dismembered like their neighbors. He would do everything in his power to stop that from happening. He did not care at all how crazy he might seem. Anyone who thought he was crazy for what he was about to do could go to hell.

There was a stash of old plywood in the shed. He could use that. He stood and quickly made his way around the house to the shed. When he opened the door, he heard the gray bees in their tank buzzing. He reached in and turned on the light. They were still there, the two of them, their sleek gray bodies looking menacing.

The plywood was leaning against the wall. He grabbed several sheets of it, a hammer and some nails, and carried it all back to the front porch. Then he began hammering the plywood in place, boarding up Ava's bedroom window.

On hearing the noise, Ava pulled back her curtain, and saw what he was doing. As expected, she screamed at him. He ignored her, so she came out and stood on the porch.

"What are you doing?" she yelled. Her face was twisted with anger.

He stopped hammering. "I'm keeping you safe."

"Safe! Safe! You're insane!"

"Ava, Minnie is dead too." He spoke calmly, trying to counter her anger. "It came through her front window. It broke through the glass."

She stepped back, clearly shocked.

He took a deep breath. He should have told her earlier. He stood there holding the hammer at his side, his other hand keeping the plywood in place. "I found her body in her bedroom. I'm making sure that doesn't happen to you."

"You think what we saw out back is what killed her?" She spoke quietly.

"Yes. That thing you just told to run away. I'm certain of it." He turned abruptly and went back to hammering, finishing the top two corners.

Ava stood watching him. "So, closing my curtains and then nailing my window shut really wasn't enough. You need to board it up too." There was a certain objective flatness to her voice, as though she were commenting on dry facts, but underneath that detachment there seemed to be something gathering steam.

"I'm not just boarding up *your* window. I'm boarding up all of them. Mine too. The back and the front. Everywhere."

"Are you serious?" Anger was beginning to creep back into her tone. "You don't think maybe you're being just a little bit paranoid? If that thing wanted to kill us, we'd already be dead."

"Today I found the bodies of two of our neighbors. Two of them. Both were killed violently. Parts of them were eaten. I don't care if you or anybody else thinks I'm paranoid. I'm keeping us both safe. It's my job."

"Great," she snapped. "So, now I have to sit in my room with the window boarded up? It's not enough that I can't even open it. Now I don't get any light either?"

Jim snapped back. "Well, why not live a little and leave your room for once? How's that?!"

"Why don't you just lock me in a cell somewhere?" she shouted at the top of her lungs. "Put bars all around me and slide my food under the door! It'll have the same impact!"

The force of her voice surprised him. She stormed into the house, slamming the door behind her. He went back to hammering the last of the nails in the plywood. As he worked, he kept looking over his shoulder to monitor the darkness. He didn't want to be taken by surprise.

By the time every single window was boarded up, he had to admit that the little house looked derelict in the beam of his flashlight. It was okay, he told himself. The boards would come down soon, when they got rid of whatever was out there in the woods.

Only then did he remember that he'd left the shed door open. He didn't want something getting in there and hiding. He made his way towards the back of the house again. As he approached the shed, he heard the sound of something scuffling inside. It wasn't the sound of the bees. The single bulb over the workbench was still lit, and light spilled out onto the grass at his feet.

He paused. The sound was sporadic. It seemed to be coming from the floor. He stepped forward and peeked inside. There it was. Something was caught in the live trap he'd set. He moved closer.

A mouse. Just what he needed. It was a deer mouse, with white feet and belly and a brown back and head. He reached down and grabbed the little guy, and carefully maneuvered him into the fish tank, removing the metal grate cautiously so the gray bees couldn't escape.

Even before he put the metal grate and rock back in place, the bees had descended on the poor mouse, stinging it repeatedly. He watched horrified. The mouse jerked and jumped, but eventually it slowed and stopped moving. Being a lover of animals, he felt bad. Even so, he needed to know what would happen. He'd check on it tomorrow.

Finally, he shut up the shed and went back to the house. He got his rifle and circled the house several times, staring out into the darkness. He sat on the porch and kept watch for a while near Ava's bedroom window. His head kept bobbing as he tried to stop himself from falling asleep. The day had been long and difficult, and he was exhausted. At around midnight, he went back inside and locked the doors. The windows were boarded up, he told himself.

They were safe.

43

THERE WAS a crick in Jim's neck when he woke the next morning. He was lying in the hallway outside Ava's door, clutching his Winchester. It was late, almost 10 a.m. He scolded himself for sleeping through the sunrise, when it was likely that the creature would have been active—assuming his theory about it being active at dawn and dusk was right.

He'd spent all night wishing that Bailey were still sleeping in Ava's bedroom with her. His own sleep had been light and fitful. He'd gone back out and walked around the house several more times during the night, always listening for the sounds of crickets, frogs, and the owls. If they were making noise, he believed the creature wasn't nearby. He'd eventually grabbed a pillow off the couch and settled here in the hallway.

He stood up now, rubbed the crick out of his neck, and immediately knocked on Ava's door.

"Ava? You okay?" he asked.

The answer was muffled and sounded annoyed. "Sleeping."

He went to his room and picked up his phone, which he'd very intentionally left on the charging pad last night. He slipped it in his pocket, picked up his rifle, and went out the back door.

The late summer air was clean and crisp. He walked around the house once more to make sure everything was in order. If the creature was crepuscular, it would be most active at dawn and dusk, so it wouldn't be back until this evening. Nevertheless, he wanted to be sure it wasn't around.

Next he went to the garden shed to check on the mouse. The poor thing had become completely inert. Brown scabs had formed all across its skin, just like Bailey, but these scabs had fused and now covered the mouse completely. It appeared dead.

He wondered if it had been a long and painful way to die, or if, after the initial sting, the mouse had been completely unconscious, like Bailey had been. He looked at the bees—they were still alive—and he checked the rock on the lid to make sure it was secure. He took pictures of everything with his phone, the mouse, the bees, the tank. Then he shut the shed door.

As he walked across the back acre, his phone beeped. It was a message from Bob. "Have you seen the news?"

Jim went immediately into his bedroom and sat at his desk. Even though it was mid-morning, with the boarded-up windows the entire house was dark. He opened up his laptop and looked at his local newsfeed.

There was a video from the Keskkauko County Sheriff, Ray Turner, that seemed to be getting a lot of views. The briefing had been filmed in front of the Gull Island Sheriff Substation and posted earlier that morning. Sheriff Turner hardly ever came to the island. Crime was so low here that there was rarely a need. Jim felt instantly reassured to know that the sheriff had come now. He played the video.

"We want the residents of Gull Island to be aware of a situation we're currently dealing with," the sheriff said. He was wearing his brown uniform, with epaulets and two front pleated patch pockets on his shirt. The gold, five-pointed sheriff's badge shone against the brown fabric. He had gray hair with a severe buzzcut and a large, bushy mustache. He was staring out at people off-camera.

"But before I begin this briefing," he continued, "I'd like to stress that the situation has been contained and the threat is over. I repeat, there is no immediate threat to the residents of Gull Island."

Jim was surprised. Why would the sheriff say that? Had they killed the gray thing he'd seen last night?

Sheriff Turner looked down and began reading from a prepared statement. He seemed somewhat nervous and fidgety.

"In the early hours of yesterday morning, August 16th, a local deputy discovered a body in the Gull Island Forest Reserve, known by locals as the End Woods. Yesterday evening, we received a report of another death, a local resident whose body was found in her home at the edge of the same stretch of woods. Our medical examiner has estimated these two deaths to have occurred on Sunday August 12th and Tuesday August 14th respectively. The deaths are consistent with an animal attack.

"In addition, yesterday afternoon, a young woman was attacked by an extremely aggressive rabid coyote at a private residence not far from where the two deaths occurred. The young woman survived that attack uninjured, and the coyote has been captured and destroyed." The sheriff's voice cracked slightly. "Therefore, the threat is, uh, over."

Jim couldn't believe what he was hearing.

The Sheriff looked up from his statement and spoke to the people who were present. "I'd like to thank Deputy Sheriff Gabby Martinez and Deputy Medical Examiner Abeo Okafor for all of their extremely hard work. Their diligence on this case is greatly appreciated by the people of Keskkauko County and Gull Island in particular. We will not at this point identify the two deceased persons, as next of kin have not yet been notified." His eyes darted around and he shuffled his feet. "Until such time, I ask for your patience. But the critical message is this: the danger has passed."

Jim felt his pulse rising. It was not a rabid coyote that had attacked Ava. It was a deadly gen-mod. Gabby said she believed him. Had she not told the sheriff? Was the sheriff in denial? He wanted to talk to Gabby and find out what was going on. He had to tell her about the thing that came to their house last night. There was no reason to believe the threat was over. No reason at all.

He realized suddenly that he had to get Ava off the island. He clicked over to the website for the Gull Island Boat Company. There were only four ferry departures daily, and they often got booked up in advance. The morning ferry had already left. The midday and the afternoon ferries were completely booked. However, he did manage to secure two tickets for the last ferry out that evening at 9 p.m., as well as a spot for his pickup. Then he flicked off an email to his sister in Detroit, saying that he and Ava needed a place to stay that night.

Was he being overprotective? He didn't think so. He leaned back in his chair. What would Sarah say? If he was honest with himself, he supposed there were times in the past when he'd been overprotective, but not now. Not now.

When they'd first moved in, maybe his fears about Ava's window had been a bit irrational. Possibly his response—nailing the window frame shut—had been excessive. It was painful to admit, but he supposed that he had been reacting to what had happened to Sarah. He took a deep breath. He recognized that his refusal to let Ava go running was also born from the same base fear.

Now, as he looked up at the light coming in from the edges of his own boarded-up window, Ava's words came back to him. *If you keep smothering me, you will lose me.*

But surely what he was doing now was different. Boarding up the house last night, buying tickets to get Ava off the island—all of this made perfect sense given the current situation. He wasn't being paranoid. There was something in the woods behind their house. Two of their neighbors were already dead. His behavior was perfectly justified. Wasn't it?

He wished he could ask Sarah.

He went to Ava's bedroom door. "Ava?"

This time his daughter's response was short and sharp. "What?"

"We need to talk."

"I don't want to." She sounded resentful and irritated.

He leaned his forehead on the door. "Are you just going to sit in your room all day? It's dark in there now."

There was a pause and suddenly the door flung open. He pulled back.

"No kidding," Ava said. "I wonder why it's dark in here. Look at it."

Her bedroom was indeed bleak and gloomy.

"You never should have painted your walls such a dark purple," he said.

"Oh, yeah. It's the walls. Definitely. The window's nailed shut and covered with plywood, but that has absolutely nothing to do with it."

"I'm sorry, Ava. It's for your own safety. Listen, we really do need to talk."

She sighed. "What now?"

"We're leaving."

"What?"

"I've got two tickets for the last ferry out today, at nine tonight. I'm taking you to Aunt Terri's."

"You're kidding me."

"I'll come back to prep my hives for winter, and I'll see if I can help Gabby find whatever's out there, but right now I need to get you off the island."

Her mouth hung agape. "No way. I don't know where Eddie is. He and I haven't talked in over a week. And those guys from Hadley Agritech still have Bailey. I'm not leaving."

"People are dead, Ava. More might die. You saw that thing come out of the woods last night. You can call Eddie from Aunt Terri's. She's got that futon in the basement. We're driving through to Detroit tonight."

"What about Bailey?"

"We'll get him later."

"You are totally crazy."

He bit his tongue. "Before we go, you and I have to give a statement to Deputy Gabby. We need to tell her in detail everything we saw yesterday—the gen-mod raccoon and that thing last night too. Did you take pictures of the gen-mod raccoon?"

She rolled her eyes. "Of course I did."

He was relieved. Even though Gabby now believed him about the gen-mod, those pictures would help prove what was going on. He asked Ava to send him her pictures that minute, and she did.

"Good. I'm headed down into Saint Peter right now," he said. "Let's go talk to Gabby now."

Ava paused for a moment, growing still and quiet. Then she looked up at him. "I don't want to."

"What? You have to tell her what you saw. I can send her your pictures of the raccoon, but you need to tell her your story."

Ava twisted a lock of her purple hair. "If you want me to leave, I need to pack some things. I need to get ready. I'll talk to Deputy Gabby later."

"She needs help figuring out what's going on."

"Either I pack now, or I talk to Deputy Gabby. If you want me to leave the island, I need some time, don't I?"

Ever since she was little, Ava had been a master negotiator, and Jim wondered if he was being out-negotiated now. Nevertheless, her argument made some sense. He looked into her room and saw that it was a mess. "How much time do you need?"

"More than you." She stood there staring at him, looking cool and self-possessed. For some reason Jim couldn't specify, this made him slightly uneasy.

"Okay," he said. He was tired of fighting her every step of the way. Every small decision was a battle with Ava. "You can talk to Deputy Gabby later, when we go down to catch the ferry. I'll be gone an hour or so. Keep the doors locked at all times."

"The doors are always locked in a goddamn prison."

"Hey. Language."

She let out an exaggerated sigh and shut the door in his face.

Before he went to his truck, he stepped out into the back acre and walked over to where the creature had stood last night. He looked there for more footprints. It was a grassy area, and there were no traces of anything. When the creature ran away, the path it took had been between the fenced garden and the shed, then off into the dark. Assuming it continued directly north into the End Woods, it would have crossed the ashen remains of his beehives.

He walked up to the edge of the ashy ground at the far back corner of his property. It was astonishing that just recently this spot had been alive with his healthy queen-rearing hives. Now it was like a wasteland. There were some planks of half-burnt wood remaining, but for the most part, the fire had created a layer of fine ash. The trees at the edge of the woods were scorched.

He studied the ground. And there it was, directly across the ashes—a clear track of footprints that looked, at first, entirely human. Based on the distance between the prints, he could tell it had been running. He looked closely. On each footprint, in front of each toe, there was the perfect indentation of a long, sharp claw. He took out his phone again and took picture after picture after picture.

This thing was what had stood in Minnie's garden. This was what had found her in her bedroom. This was what had killed her, and probably Emmett too. And last night it had come to his house.

He was firmly resolved. He would not let Ava stay on this island one more night.

## 44

JIM PARKED his truck outside the Gull Island Sheriff Substation. The bland, brown building had several patrol cars parked outside. As he walked up to the front door, Sheriff Ray Turner came out.

"Jim Parker?" the sheriff said, the moment he laid eyes on him. Jim was surprised the sheriff knew him on sight.

"Yes, Sheriff. I—"

"You listen to me." The sheriff glanced around, as though checking to see if anyone was in earshot. Then he brought his face right up to Jim's and lowered his voice. "You best pull your head in. You understand?"

Jim could smell cigarette smoke and cheap aftershave. He took a step back. "What are you talking about?"

"You just be careful." Then he walked away and climbed into his patrol car nearby.

Jim felt like the ground had just shifted beneath him. What was going on? Why was the sheriff threatening him?

He immediately went into the substation, looking for Gabby. Shirley was sitting behind the desk in the small front reception area. She was a heavyset white woman with a huge mop of large, loose curls.

"Shirley, is Gabby around?"

"She's busy," Shirley said.

Jim saw two uniformed deputies drinking coffee in the training room to the left. They looked up at Jim, and they watched him. They were probably the additional officers from Au Bois Gabby had said she needed. This was clearly getting bigger.

Suddenly, Gabby popped her head out of her office, which was just behind the reception desk. "It's okay, Shirley. Come in, Jim." Her voice was serious and businesslike. She turned back to Shirley. "I need to take a witness statement. Give us some time."

"If you say so."

Gabby gestured for Jim to enter and closed the door behind him. He sat down and told her quietly what had just happened outside with Sheriff Turner. He found it disconcerting that she didn't seem surprised. Instead she leaned forward and spoke in a furtive whisper.

"Something is happening." She glanced toward the door. "Sheriff Turner has requisitioned all of Dr. Okafor's notes, photographs, and files regarding both Emmett's death and Minnie's. He said he needs to do his own assessment. He's brought in some of his cronies from the mainland. It's an old boys' club. Those two deputies out there, Mark and Scott, they're his fishing buddies. On top of all that, he's actually replacing Dr. Okafor with another medical examiner, who's on his way from Au Bois now."

Jim was taken aback. "Why? And why did he say there was no threat at his briefing this morning?"

"That message was against my advice," she said, clearly frustrated. "I'm worried, Jim. I have to tell you that I think you might be in danger."

"How?" He was starting to feel slightly paranoid. At first Gabby had treated him with a good deal of suspicion, and now that she was finally on his side, there were others who were against him. "What kind of danger?"

"I don't know, but the sheriff has tried multiple times to convince me that you're suffering from psychosis. You know I thought that myself. If I hadn't seen that bizarre bloody footprint for myself last night at Minnie's, I still might."

Jim looked at her closely. "I saw more of those footprints," he said. "Something came to my house last night."

Her eyes grew wide. "What?"

He told her about what he and Ava had seen behind the house. "It left footprints in the ash. This time I took pictures."

"Thank God," she said, smiling. "We'll make a detective out of you yet."

He showed her the pictures of the footprints, as well as of the lifeless, encrusted mouse and the gray bees. "I also have these." He then brought up Ava's pictures of the gen-mod raccoon.

Gabby sat silently, taking it all in. Then she looked up at him. "Jesus, Jim. What's going on?"

"I don't know."

At her request, he sent all the pictures to her private email address. The implication of the email address was clear to Jim. She was keeping all of this away from the sheriff's eyes. She was going outside of the law in order to help him. He was simultaneously overwhelmed with gratitude and fear.

"Where did the sheriff go just now?" he asked her.

"To Hadley Agritech to take official statements from Lewis and Brad. He's insisted on doing it himself. He's also going to search their vehicles to confirm your story about the foam and the hazmat suit."

Jim was deeply uncomfortable that a man who had just given him a veiled threat was responsible for gathering information from Hadley. "Is he in Hadley's back pocket?" he asked.

"I don't know. But let me tell you what I do know." She explained to him that Dr. Okafor had confirmed that the wounds on Emmett's and Minnie's bodies were similar, and that the cuts, gashes, and scrapes looked as though they'd been made with something like a serrated knife. "Jim, neither body had bites that were consistent with a coyote attack."

Jim had to stop himself from saying, "I told you so." Right now he was just grateful that Gabby was sharing so much information with him. She was finally treating him like an ally. "A serrated knife," he said. "That makes it sound as though their wounds are from the mandibles on that gen-mod raccoon."

Gabby nodded.

"But that can't be right," he said. "It can't have been the raccoon that killed Minnie. The footprint was from a human-like figure with claws. She even told me she'd seen it. She said it was as big as a person. I dismissed it."

"I've been thinking about this," Gabby said. "If we're dealing with gen-mods, who's to say that the thing with the human footprint doesn't also have mandibles? Right? Almost anything is possible."

Jim considered this. He hadn't seen the creature's face last night. It could have had mandibles. He watched as Gabby turned and looked out the window.

"There's something else I need to tell you," she said, turning back. "Two more people are missing."

"What? Who?"

"Two local kids. Mike Smith and Ash Patel. They went into the End Woods last night. They haven't come back."

Jim knew those boys. They went to school with Ava. They were both about to be seniors. His heart sank. "Wait a minute. Why didn't the sheriff mention that in his briefing this morning?"

"He's decided not to release that information yet. He says he doesn't want to alarm people unnecessarily. Those boys could be out there hunting or fishing. But between you and me, I think he's trying to keep it quiet. He's got people searching for them now."

"You've got to stop people from going into the End Woods."

Gabby nodded. "I know."

At that point Gabby began the formal interview process,

placing a tape recorder in the middle of the desk. There were a lot of questions, and Jim went over everything in detail—the gen-mod raccoon, the episode with Bailey, the creature coming out of the woods last night. His recounting of events prompted him to tell Gabby more about the mouse in his garden shed. "It's dead, but it's still in my shed."

"I'd like to see the mouse."

"Come back to my place. I'll show it to you. Then you can interview Ava as well."

Gabby agreed, and as they both went outside to their cars, Jim noticed Chuck Norman's red pickup truck parked across the street. What was unsettling was that Chuck himself was sitting there in the driver's seat, just watching Jim. Chuck's gaze never left him.

Jim was close enough to see that there was a mean, vengeful look in his eyes.

## 45

AVA WAS LYING IN BED, trying to figure out what to do. Still no messages from Eddie. She threw her phone down and curled up under her covers, peeking out toward the fish tank, where the little danios turned and darted like luminous, striped purple bullets. A faint line of light was slipping in around the edges of the plywood that now covered her bedroom window.

She missed Bailey. She missed Eddie.

In that moment, she absolutely hated the Window Cop. She felt like she was slowly being sealed inside a tomb. And now she was going to be dragged away to go sleep in Aunt Terri's basement.

She wanted Eddie lying alongside her now. She wanted him to wrap his arms around her and say, "Hey, babe, I love you," like he used to. He was still number one on the gratitude list. His place there was secure, but it had been nine days since she'd last talked to him, the day she told him she was pregnant.

He'd never been silent for this long before, and her mind whirled with anxiety. Why had he not stopped to talk to her when he brought the flowers yesterday? She was so afraid that she'd completely destroyed his heart. Those flowers had given her hope.

There were a few possibilities, some of them more pleasant than others. Eddie was probably still living what he called "the simple hunter's life" at his family's cabin in the End Woods. He wouldn't have mobile reception to know about the latest developments. He would have no idea what was going on, no idea of what was lurking nearby. If these things were active just at dawn and dusk, as her dad had said, then he might be in danger.

Eddie had told her about his routine there. Unaware of the danger, he would be getting up before dawn every day and heading out alone into the woods to hunt. At dusk he'd be sitting unguarded in front of the cabin, drinking bourbon and Coke and watching the fireflies come out.

There were other possibilities, but they were too horrible to think of. She closed off those parts of herself, those suspicions that made her terrified. They were too unthinkable to allow in, so she locked them away. Still, she feared they might be true.

She got out of bed and went to the living room. At the closet by the front door, where they kept the coats, she bent down and pushed everything aside, looking for her old backpack. Her mom had bought it for her years ago for a school camping trip. It was ridiculous—bright purple with a cartoon unicorn eating a rainbow-colored ice cream cone. In spite of the fact that she'd completely outgrown it, she still had a fondness for that backpack. It was purple, after all, but more importantly it reminded her of a time when everything was okay, when her mother was still alive.

Back in her bedroom, she threw in some clothes, a hoodie, and some toiletries. Then she put on her most comfortable jeans, an old plaid shirt of Eddie's, and her hiking boots. It was going to be a long walk.

She went out to the kitchen and grabbed a stash of instant macaroni and cheese, some fruit, and a water bottle. Who knew how long she'd be gone? She took some granola bars as well. One thing was clear. She had to get to Eddie, and she wasn't leaving this island until she did.

The most important thing was to tell him about the danger. Then she could talk to him about her pregnancy. She didn't know what it meant for the future. She was still afraid of being trapped, but she didn't want to break his heart. The flowers must be a sign that he was coming around. She was lucky to have him. He loved her.

What if he abandoned her because she didn't want to have this baby? She couldn't change that. But they had to talk. If he was too hurt by her decision and if he shut her out, then at least she would know the score. She would be on her own. She would take care of it herself. She would get the money out of her account and make up some excuse to hide it from the Window Cop.

*You have to be strong, Avey Bavey. Be strong.*

It was noon now. She had to leave before her dad got back. She felt bad, but this was the man who had nailed and boarded her window shut, who constantly stifled her with his own fear. What if he came after her? He could follow a trail like nobody she knew. A head start was the only advantage she had.

She went to the kitchen and left a note on the chalkboard, telling him she was going to her friend Claire's house. That would buy her time. There was no way she was telling him where she was really headed. She simply had to get to Eddie, and she didn't want the Window Cop stopping her.

The timing of her departure was perfect. It would be safe out there during the middle of the day—assuming her dad was right. But what if he was wrong? What if whatever was out there was active during the day?

She went to her dad's bedroom, looking for the rifle she knew he kept under his bed. She pulled the case out, but it was locked. She didn't know the combination. She didn't know where the bullets were. She didn't even know how to load it. Her dad had always refused to teach her how to shoot. She slid the case back under the bed and went out to the garage.

An old wooden softball bat was leaning in the corner there. It was one her dad had bought when they'd first came to Gull Island, when he wanted her to join the softball team to make friends. She'd refused. But now this bat might come in handy.

At the picnic table, close enough to the house so her phone could get the wi-fi connection, she opened her maps app. Most of Gull Island came up as a large green block with few features identified, but she could see Stone Lake, and she could see Indian Point. Eddie had told her that his family cabin was in Catmull's Thicket. She'd never been there, but she knew it was between Stone Lake and Indian Point.

She saved the screenshots of the maps to her photos. There was no reception where she was going. Her best guess was that it would take less than two hours to get to Eddie's cabin. Daylight would last until almost 8:45 p.m. There was plenty of time.

Her backpack felt solid on her back as she stepped out into the middle of the grass and looked at the trees surrounding the property. Even now, with the sun almost directly above, the darkness of the End Woods loomed like a massive, ominous wall.

"It's the middle of the day," she said to herself. "It'll be fine."

She gripped the softball bat tightly in her right hand, and she stepped forward into the shadows of the trees.

## 46

JIM WATCHED as Gabby got out of her SUV in front of his house. She looked at the boarded-up windows and smirked. "You meant business."

"I did." He looked at the house and hoped Ava was nearly done packing. "Let me show you that mouse."

They went behind the house and into the back acre. It was just after midday, and the woods bordering the property were dark with shade under the thick canopy. As he and Gabby approached the garden shed, he heard a strange banging sound from inside. He paused at the old wooden door. It was a violent, sporadic thud.

"What is that?" Gabby said.

"I don't know." He pulled the rusty handle and swung the door open.

His eyes adjusted to the relative gloom inside the shed. The thudding noise continued, again and again. It was coming from the workbench, from the fish tank that sat there. He turned on the light. What he saw surprised him. The screen lid was shaking. The metal grate and the rock which held down the screen were thumping and shifting. The mouse was jumping up and smashing its head on the underside of the lid, as though trying to get out. It saw him approach, stopped jumping, and stared at him.

It was clearly the brown field mouse, but it was also no longer a brown field mouse. Just like the raccoon, it was gray and completely hairless. Two black stripes ran lengthwise down its side, and it no longer had the short claws of a field mouse; they were now longer and thicker, and black. But its mouth was the most surprising. Where its teeth had been, tiny black mandibles snapped shut repeatedly as its jaw stayed open.

The brown, scab-like covering that had previously encased the mouse was now lying to the side. The crust looked like it had served as a pupal casing, from which the mouse had emerged, changed. It was a gen-mod.

It started making a strange noise.

*Hmmm. Hmmm. Cli-click.*

It was the same sound he'd heard last night, coming from the creature he'd shot behind the house. The only difference was that this noise was smaller, like it was coming from a more diminutive source, which it clearly was.

The mouse, if he could still call it that, began pacing back and forth. It was watching them both now. It was trying to figure out some way out of the tank, almost making a plan of attack.

"What the hell is that thing?" Gabby said.

"I don't know." He looked for the two gray bees inside the aquarium. They were on the honeycomb, still living, but ignoring the mouse. He looked at their gray bodies, the two black stripes on their sides.

He turned to Gabby. "It's the bees," he said. "It starts with the bees."

"You think the bees did this to that mouse?"

"There's no other explanation. That mouse was normal when I put it in there with them. Now it looks like them. It's transgenic."

He remembered when he'd checked the first pieces of footage from his surveillance cameras on Wednesday morning. There had been two events where the cameras had recorded raccoons circling the hives, seeking honey.

"The gen-mod raccoon that attacked Ava wasn't created by Hadley," he said, thinking it through. "It was probably just a raccoon that got stung. It's some kind of infection. It's contagious."

He reached out toward the lid in order to make sure the rock holding it down was stable. The hairless mouse jumped up at his hand and hit the glass. He quickly pulled back.

Standing at a respectful distance, he watched the creature as it continued to hum and click and pace. Its eyes were strangely black and iridescent.

Several times he'd handled those gray bees himself, transferring them into jars, putting them in this aquarium. He felt sick. If a sting from one of these bees could do this to a mouse, *and* to a raccoon, what would have happened if one had stung him?

He thought of the aggressiveness of these creatures, but that aggression combined with a human's capacity to think... The thought made his blood run cold. Was that what he'd seen behind his house last night? It was a nightmare.

"It must be actively viral," he said.

"What do you mean?" Gabby asked.

"These bees are a gen-mod. One way you make a gen-mod is to transfer genes using what's called a viral vector."

"What's that?" When she looked at him now, there was nothing critical in her eyes. No suspicion. She was fully on board.

"It's a technique molecular biologists use all the time. You have to start with an actual virus, but you modify it to make it less dangerous. Then you use the natural infection qualities to deliver genes into target cells. It's effective, but you have to be meticulous. If you're not careful, you can accidentally create a contagious virus."

"You're saying that's how these bees became infectious," Gabby said.

"I can't think of any other way." He looked at the bees and the mouse. "I have to destroy them."

"They're evidence," Gabby said. "They can help demonstrate what Hadley is up to."

"But not alive. They're too dangerous. They can still be evidence if they're dead."

She nodded. "Absolutely."

They both took pictures of the mouse and the bees with their phones. The mouse was watching them, still pacing and humming and clicking. Jim wondered if it was a female mouse or a male. Could it sting? Only female bees had stingers, but what about these gen-mods?

Under the workbench he had a small, white bucket containing rodent bait. It was a block bait with an anti-coagulant poison. A mouse could receive a lethal dose after just one feed, but there was a time lag between ingesting the poison and the death.

He took out a block. It was blue and had the consistency of a hard cookie. He put on a pair of beekeeping gloves.

"Stand back," he said.

Gabby took a step back, closer to the door.

"Actually," he said. "You should go outside. I have to open the lid."

"I'm fine here," she said.

Holding the bait in his left hand, he moved the stone and the grate on top of the screen, and quickly shifted the screen lid just enough to drop in the bait.

The mouse jumped up and snapped at his fingers but missed. When Jim quickly put the lid back, it began running in circles—clicking and snapping and jumping and hitting its head on the underside of the lid. It was furious. Jim and Gabby both backed up and watched.

Eventually the mouse sniffed at the bait, but didn't eat it, instead stepping away. It looked back up at Jim and Gabby. There was a strange, ravenous hunger behind its black eyes.

"It doesn't want that bait," Gabby said. "It's more interested in us."

Jim agreed. "Perhaps it prefers live prey."

Gabby visibly shuddered. "Well, it's clearly not afraid of the fact that we're much bigger than it is."

"We need to kill the bees too," Jim said, taking some insect spray off a nearby shelf. One of the dangers of broad use insecticides was that they killed bees, so it should work. He sprayed it into the tank and watched as the mouse hissed and clicked in irritation. The bees buzzed loudly and started flying around, but then they settled down. They didn't seem affected at all.

The mouse continued to stare.

"They're not dying," Gabby said, looking around. "We could burn them, but the shed is too close to your garage and house, and anyway that would destroy the evidence. Lewis will know how to kill them."

"There's no way I'm going to Hadley again, but I can ask Lewis to come here. I'll just need your help to make sure he doesn't leave with the evidence."

Gabby smiled. "I'll make sure of that."

Jim grabbed another rock from behind the shed and put it on the lid next to the first one, just to be safe. Then he went inside to call Lewis on the landline. He expected to find Ava packing, but she wasn't even home. There was a note on the kitchen chalkboard.

*Claire's picking me up. Going to go to her house to say goodbye.*

He took a deep breath. He supposed it should come as no surprise that she'd left without telling him in advance. She never listened to him. Why would she start now? Her room was still a mess, and it didn't look like she'd packed anything at all.

He quickly called Ava's mobile, but she didn't answer.

As he was standing in the kitchen trying to figure out what to do next, Gabby walked in the back door. "Did you call him yet?"

"No," he said. "Ava's gone."

He looked again at the note on the chalkboard. Ava was a teenager. Of course she wanted to say goodbye to her best friend. The note had been scribbled quickly. She was trying to do everything before they caught the ferry. At least she'd agreed to leave the island. He knew he needed to give her some space. It was just so hard to do.

In the meantime, he had to deal with the mouse and bees in the shed. What would happen if they got out? He had to figure out how to kill them. Ava would be back soon, and together they'd leave the island this evening.

He called Lewis. It was a receptionist who answered. When he finally got ahold of Lewis and explained what he had in his garden shed, Lewis said, "I'm on my way."

JIM STOOD with Gabby in front of his house as they waited for Lewis to arrive. Soon Brad pulled up in the same white Hadley pickup truck he'd been driving the day before, with Lewis in the passenger seat. Seeing that vehicle, Jim's anger flared again. He thought of Brad's hazmat suit and the equipment he'd seen in the back—the red jerry cans and the strips of green foam. He remembered how Brad had carried Bailey away.

He felt conflicted. Sure, Lewis was a friend from way back, but he was also responsible for this entire mess. Jim tried to hold his anger in check. What he needed to do right now was to kill what was in that shed. Then, maybe he and Gabby would get some answers. By tonight, he and Ava would be gone.

Lewis stepped out of the truck first and said, "Where is it?" He looked scared.

"Brad had a gun yesterday," Jim warned Gabby.

She quickly stepped back, drew her gun, and aimed it at Brad as he stepped out of the driver's side. "Frisk him, Jim."

After a quick pat down, Jim found Brad's pistol in the concealed holster in his waistband.

"Leave that in your truck," Gabby said.

Brad followed her orders, while Jim frisked Lewis—he wasn't carrying a gun.

Lewis and Brad looked up at the house with its boarded-up windows, and they looked shocked.

"Some creature came to my house last night," Jim said. "Ava told me I was being paranoid."

Lewis looked at Jim closely and lowered his voice to a whisper. "You are not being paranoid."

Jim felt the hair on the back of his neck stand up. He shook his head. "The mouse is in my shed."

Brad immediately began walking toward the back of the house, as though he knew exactly where the shed was. How long had Brad spent walking around this property that night he burnt the hives?

Jim rushed past him and stood in front of the shed door, putting an arm out to block Brad and Lewis from going in. "You're not taking it with you this time."

Gabby stepped up. She still had her gun trained on them. "That's right," she said.

"Okay, okay," Lewis said. "Just show it to us. Are they contained?"

"Yes, they are." Jim opened the shed door, and Brad and Lewis both stepped inside as Jim flicked on the light. The thudding noise began again as the mouse started jumping up to push the lid loose. The two rocks didn't budge.

Lewis turned to look at Jim, his face full of fear and anger. "What the hell are you doing, Jim? You're playing with fire. You can't keep them in a fish tank, like pets."

Jim felt his body tensing. "You wouldn't tell me what was going on. So I had to figure it out myself. I've been studying them."

"Did you intentionally give these bees a mouse to sting?" Brad asked, clearly shocked.

"Yes. How do we kill them? The mouse won't eat the mouse bait. The bees aren't hurt by household insecticide."

Without another word, Brad turned around and began walking back to his truck. Gabby trailed him closely, her gun on him. Jim and Lewis followed behind. At the back of the Hadley pickup truck, Brad reached out to open the cap door. When he saw Gabby's gun, he paused. "Let me get my weapon. I can kill it."

"I'm not trusting you with a gun," she said.

"It's not a gun. Not with bullets anyway. You can't kill them with bullets." Brad began opening the cab door.

Gabby raised her pistol. "Wait. Freeze!"

Brad stopped, holding his hands in the air. "I just need to open this and pick up my weapon."

"What is it?" Gabby said. "Tell me first. Your weapon. What is it?"

Jim was taken aback by the absolute authority in her voice. There was force and power within Gabby. He could picture her on the streets of Chicago, dealing with violent gang members and drug addicts.

"It's an impulse gun," Brad said.

Gabby's body visibly stiffened. "You said it's not a gun."

"It isn't, really. It'll help us. It won't hurt you. Let me show you."

Brad began moving slowly. This time Gabby didn't stop him. He reached into the back of the truck and pulled something out. When he turned toward them, he was holding a long, chrome tube. It was roughly three feet long. Brad held it out for them to see.

It resembled a rocket launcher or a small silver cannon. There was a large pistol grip in the middle of the tube and a vertical foregrip at the front, like on an assault rifle. Two black hoses came off it—one in the back and one in the middle—which led to two cylindrical chrome tanks, which Brad was now slowly slinging onto his back.

Then Brad began walking back to the shed. The others walked behind, Gabby with her gun still on him. Brad stopped about six feet from the open door of the shed.

"Stand back," he said, lifting the silver weapon.

Jim saw him pull back on a black valve at the top of the barrel. "What are you doing?" he asked.

"I'm filling the reservoir." The gun hissed until a V-shaped stream of liquid trickled out the front. When Brad let go of the valve, the trickle stopped. "You need to stand back," he said, and then he lifted the gun, aiming it directly into the shed. Everyone else stepped back, and he pulled the trigger.

An intense boom rang out against the silence of the surrounding woods. A burst of mist shot forward violently and through the doorway of the shed. The pressure hit the walls with a rough shake. There was the sound of glass shattering and things falling off shelves.

With nowhere else to go, the mist rolled back out of the shed and back toward them. A wet fog was everywhere. They all stepped back farther, coughing and choking.

"Get away!" Brad shouted. "Get away!"

They ran across the back acre and stood on the other side of the old picnic table. Jim watched the strange mist rolling. They waited there until it had mostly dissipated. Then they went back over to the shed. They pulled parts of their clothing to their faces to cover their mouths.

Jim went into the shed first. Boxes of slug killer and jars of liquid fertilizer had fallen to the floor from the impact. Shovels and spades had been knocked over, and on his workbench, the glass fish tank was shattered. He looked through the broken bits of glass. Under several thick shards, he found the two gray bees and the bizarre mouse, all dead.

"Now," Gabby said, turning suddenly to Brad and Lewis. "You two need to tell us what you know." She pointed her pistol at them and gestured to the picnic table. "Have a seat."

BRAD AND LEWIS walked over to the old picnic table, hands in the air, and sat down. Brad slipped the chrome tanks off his back and set the impulse gun on the ground.

Jim watched with respect and more than a little awe as Gabby took total control of the situation. The sun was bright in the canopy of the End Woods all around them. It was mid-afternoon, and there was plenty of time till dusk.

"Jim," Gabby said, "there are evidence bags in my glove box." She threw him the key fob to her patrol car. "Collect the two dead bees and mouse into bags and lock them in the vehicle."

Lewis grizzled and said, "Those are Hadley Agritech IP."

Gabby raised her pistol. "You're in no position to make demands."

Jim followed her instructions while she kept the gun trained on Lewis and Brad. After the evidence was locked in her car, he came back and stood at her side.

"Thank you, Jim," Gabby said. Then she moved her gun back and forth between Lewis and Brad. "You need to tell us what the hell is going on. Two people are dead. Jim and I now have pictures, lots of them—the gray bees, the mutant raccoon you swore was a rabid coyote, that mutant mouse you just killed, *and* some strange footprints we haven't yet identified. You may also be interested to know that two more people are currently missing. Teenagers. Locals who went out to drink in the End Woods yesterday at dusk. They didn't come home."

Lewis looked horrified and shook his head. "Sheriff Turner didn't tell me about the missing kids."

Gabby nodded. "We haven't released the information yet. Besides, I suspect Turner tells you what you want to hear. Now, you two have a simple choice to make. Either you can tell us what's going on with a gun pointed at your heads, or without one. Which will it be?"

Jim watched Lewis carefully for a response. He knew Lewis, or at least he had known him once. Lewis was both awkward and arrogant, yes, but he wasn't heartless. Surely he wouldn't hold back while people were dying. Yet he was just sitting there, staring down at the table in silence with his arms crossed. Perhaps he was too far gone.

Brad turned to him. "Lewis, they've already seen it. Jim just ran an experiment and saw an entire metamorphosis in his garden shed, for Christ's sake. It's too late. It's out. We should just tell them."

When Lewis refused to even look up, Gabby spoke up again. "Maybe you just want to wait for more people to die."

"Lewis," Jim said. "How long have we known each other? Tell me what's going on. Tell an old friend."

Lewis paused, took a deep breath, and uncrossed his arms. He pushed up his glasses and looked at Gabby. "Okay. Put the goddamn gun away."

Gabby holstered her gun, and she and Jim sat across from Lewis and Brad at the table. Jim felt deeply guarded. He reminded himself not to let his friendship with Lewis cloud his judgement. The atmosphere was tense.

Then Lewis began to speak. "Five years ago, when I first joined

Hadley Agritech, the Executive Leadership Team had wanted nothing more than a simple, pesticide-resistant variation of *Apis mellifera*, the western honeybee. The company's goal was to develop a patented pesticide and a corresponding, patented gen-mod bee that was resistant to that pesticide. They wanted to market the two products together. That paired approach has been extremely effective for our herbicide-resistant seeds, and they wanted to replicate that success for honeybees. Well, I saw a larger opportunity, so I proposed something more ambitious."

"You've always been ambitious," Jim said.

"As have you," Lewis responded. "Each in our own way. Of course, bees currently have multiple threats, both chemical and natural. I wanted my gen-mod bee to be strong. My proposal was to create a bee that was resistant to common pesticides, except for one."

"Necarichlor," Brad said, reaching down and tapping the silver impulse gun on the ground at his feet.

"At least that part worked," Lewis said, and he gave Brad a rueful smile.

Jim thought Lewis seemed strangely driven to talk. It was like watching floodgates opening. But then again, even as a student he always liked to talk about his accomplishments.

"Nobody could accuse us of trying to run a monopoly if our gen-mod bees could be used with any common pesticide. And they'd be strong. Nothing would hurt them. But I also wanted a very significant behavioral change. My bees needed a new defensive ability against natural enemies. A healthy bee should be able to fight off predatory wasps and, more importantly, destroy varroa mites."

"You've been wishing honeybees could defend themselves better ever since our beekeeping club days," Jim said. "Remember that time we lost our hives to a wasp attack?"

Lewis nodded. "Remember? How could I forget? It was carnage." He turned to Brad and Gabby. "It lasted for days. The wasps came for the honey, and they killed most of the bees for food. We lost five hives. Anyway, I proposed to Hadley that I engineer a pesticide-resistant, mite-free, wasp-proof superbee. After a lot of discussion, I finally got the Executive Leadership Team to agree."

"He called it Project Defender," Brad said, giving a thumbs-up. "Genius."

"The first thing I did was hire Brad here," Lewis said. "Don't be fooled. He's no slouch himself. He had the two areas of expertise I needed: honeybees and microbiology. He'd just come from doing postdoc research on how the honeybee gut microbiome is altered by in-hive pesticide exposures. Perhaps more importantly, he has a certain willingness to do whatever it takes to save the bees. He's become my right-hand man."

Brad smiled.

Lewis shifted in his seat. "I knew that, in creating my superbee, the hard part would not be the simple act of gene editing using Crispr."

"What's Crispr?" Gabby asked. "I'm a cop, not a scientist."

Jim cut in and turned to Gabby. "It's a technique that lets you choose specific DNA segments, cut them out, and replace them with others. It's pretty widely used and relatively straightforward now, although it does have its risks. The hard part is determining exactly which genes to cut and replace."

"That's right," Lewis said. "Of the two fundamental changes I've been after—resistance to common pesticides and an ability to defend itself—the pesticide resistance was the most straightforward. I started out by studying previous research, which revealed a natural variation in pesticide resistance among honeybee populations."

"Wait a minute," Jim said, leaning forward. "Are you talking about the connection between pesticide resistance and higher levels of certain enzymes?"

Lewis gave Jim a warm, enthusiastic smile. "Exactly. The

mixed function oxidase and glutathione transferase enzymes, in particular. Jim, it would be so good to have you on my team."

"That's not going to happen," Jim said, and he leaned back. He wished that Lewis would just drop that idea. "So, you engineered a honeybee that had higher levels of those enzymes?"

"Yes. The trick was collaborating with Hadley's pesticide scientists to design a bee that was susceptible to only one pesticide, offered by Hadley. Just one. Necarichlor. I wanted a kind of insurance." He let out a quiet, dejected sigh.

"What about the second change?" Gabby asked. "The bee's ability to defend itself."

Lewis shook his head and his jaw visibly tightened. "That's where things started to go wrong. Their ability to defend themselves led to problems, but there is another problem as well, one that we never expected. It's the biggest problem, and it's the one that terrifies me the most."

49

AVA KNEW that something wasn't right. She'd been walking almost two hours, and she still wasn't there. Admittedly, she'd stopped a few times to figure out where she was. There wasn't always a clear path. The trees and underbrush were thick in many places. She felt uncomfortable out here, like a foreigner in a strange country.

At least her compass app worked, despite the fact that there was no mobile reception. She figured it relied on satellite GPS signals, not cellular towers.

The maps she'd saved to her photos told her that she'd have to pass by an area called O'Leary's Marsh and then eventually she'd reach Stone Lake. If she could go straight through the marsh, and if the woods weren't too dense, she might arrive at her destination in about an hour and a half—or longer if she had to go around the marsh or if the walk was difficult. She put away the phone and pressed on.

The trees crowded her, and she pushed branches out of the way. Eventually, after some time squeezing through the narrow paths, the ground in front of her rose slightly, which she hadn't expected. She thought Gull Island was pretty much flat. The underbrush opened up, and she came across an odd path that looked like some sort of animal trail. She followed it for as long as she could, until it led off to the west, when she had to look back at the compass app. She continued north again, breaking away from the trail and through the underbrush.

Eventually the land sloped down, the trees thinned somewhat, and the woods gave way to a wetland. This had to be O'Leary's Marsh. There were swampy grasses everywhere. The air opened up in a way that made her feel less claustrophobic, and the still water reflected the blue sky perfectly. She stepped forward but it was obvious the marsh was deep. She would have to go around it.

She headed to the west. The sun felt hot. At one point she stepped on what looked like solid ground, but she found herself stepping into the marsh, causing a few startled ducks to take off in flight in front of her. Her hiking boots became drenched. She backed up and continued around. She hated the outdoors.

It was almost 3 p.m. when the open space of the wetlands finally retreated behind her. She felt uneasy entering into the woods again. Her feet were wet, and her boots were heavy.

The trees quickly became even thicker than usual. The canopy above was such a dense, dark green that it completely shut out the bright sky. It felt like twilight here. She didn't like it. She wanted to stay in the sun. She looked around. Would dawn-and-dusky animals wander through woods in the middle of the day if the thick shade made everything feel like twilight?

Just then something stirred in front of her, and she stopped dead in her tracks. There was a cluster of bushes straight ahead, which were shifting and moving in the shadows. Something was in there. Her heart raced. She lifted up the softball bat and held it in front of her with both hands, ready to swing.

She remained silent, hoping that whatever it was had been sleeping and would settle back down again. But the bushes kept moving, and her heart kept racing. She started to back up slowly, trying not to make any noise. In spite of the cool air in the shade, her brow began to sweat.

As she stepped back with her left foot, a twig snapped. She froze.

The bush in front of her shook. Something jumped out. For an instant, all that she saw was a flash of grayish-brown. The thing was heading directly at her. But as she gripped the bat tightly, preparing for an attack, it quickly shot off to the left.

A doe. In the time it took to recognize what it was, the animal was gone.

She took a couple of deep breaths, still holding the bat at the ready.

"Just a deer," she said out loud, as though to the woods. "It's the middle of the afternoon. There are no monsters here."

Lowering the bat, she looked around. She wanted desperately to get where she was headed. There was plenty of time before dusk. As long as she arrived before dusk, everything would be fine. Everything would be fine.

Still, the cluster of bushes in front of her seemed to hold a lot more darkness. Was there anything else in there? She cut to the right, into the trees, to avoid disturbing those bushes again. The wet socks in her boots were rubbing now, and she could already feel a blister forming on her right heel. She was feeling tired, and she wanted to sit down, but she was too afraid of losing time.

50

"HOW DID things start to go wrong?" Jim asked. He felt like he was prompting Lewis down a trail, from one breadcrumb to the next, trying to keep him talking.

Sitting there on the other side of the old picnic table, Lewis had a pained expression. Jim understood that this conversation had to be difficult for him. On the one hand, Lewis' ego made him happy to talk about his accomplishments, but on the other, his pride made it difficult for him to admit any failures.

"Tell us about the biggest problem," Gabby said.

"I'll get to that," Lewis said, and then he swallowed hard. "Creating the new defensive ability was extremely challenging, though the idea itself is rather simple. I wanted the hive to make better use of the drones, the male bees. From this basic premise the complications spun out wildly. I've been working on it in parallel to the pesticide resistance ever since arriving on the island. It isn't easy to change the elaborate social arrangements of a beehive. I wanted to take genetically determined behaviors from a few donor species and insert those behaviors into the target species, *Apis mellifera*."

Jim cleared his throat. "The problem with that approach, of

course, is that animal behavior is often dictated by a combination of genetic and environmental factors."

"You're absolutely right," Lewis said. "I went through a long series of trial and error experiments, modifying genes and seeing which behaviors changed. But I got there. Once I determined the target genes, then came the relatively straightforward editing task. My team did that." He looked at Brad.

Brad gave Jim and Gabby a strange, sad smile, and he continued the story. "Yes. At that point it was just execution. We cut out the honeybee genes Lewis no longer wanted and replaced them with the new ones from the donors. To perform the gene transfer we used a viral vector."

"I knew it," Jim said under his breath.

Brad took a deep breath. "Unfortunately, the usual viral vectors weren't effective on honeybees. We experimented with engineered adenovirus and lentivirus vehicles, but with no success. In the end, Lewis had another genius idea."

"Not so genius, considering the outcome," Gabby said sharply.

"It was just practical," Lewis responded. "I thought we could use one of the pathogens that's actually killing the honeybee in order to save it. I developed a honeybee RNA viral vector based on the genome of the Deformed Wing Virus. It delivered genetic material into honeybee cells surprisingly well."

Jim said, "But what behaviors did you change, exactly?"

Lewis looked at Gabby. "You probably already know this, but there are three types of bees in a hive. The queen, the workers, and the drones. The queen and workers are female, and the drones are male. The queen, in normal circumstances, is the only one who lays eggs. The workers perform a wide range of jobs— foraging for pollen and nectar, making honey, and defending against intruders."

"Typical," Gabby said. "The women do all the work."

Lewis smiled. "Yes, this is true. The drones, on the other hand, have only one job. They impregnate the queen. Once a year they fly out of the hive, gather around a virgin queen who is on her mating flight, and they mate with her in the air. Upon doing so, their penis is ripped from their body and they die."

"But what a way to go," Brad said, laughing and throwing his hands in the air.

"Other than that," Lewis continued, "the drones are basically useless. In fact, they're so useless that any still alive at the end of summer are physically dragged out of the hive by worker bees and left to die outside on their own."

Gabby laughed. "In my work as a Chicago cop I saw more than a few deadbeat husbands who should have been given the same treatment."

Jim laughed with her. He liked this Gabby.

Lewis continued on in his flat, scientific manner. "If there's a design flaw in the social arrangements of a beehive, it's the fact that drones are rather underutilized. Since they don't forage or contribute to making honey, I figured that they could be turned into carnivores—hungry for the proteins provided by the bodies of varroa mites and invading wasps."

"Ah," Gabby said. "I see."

Jim was equally impressed by Lewis' foresight and horrified at the thought. He sat forward. "You turned honeybees into carnivores?"

"Not the entire hive," Lewis said, pushing up his glasses. "Just the drones."

"But how did you get around the pheromones?" Jim said, and then he turned to Gabby. "Varroa mites have evolved a trick to mask their presence. They mimic bee pheromones in order to hide in plain sight. To the bees, varroa mites smell like other honeybees, so the bees don't recognize them as pests or invaders. It's a very clever camouflage."

"What exactly are these pheromones?" Gabby asked.

Jim realized only then that he was feeling the need to impress her with his knowledge. He knew it was juvenile, but he couldn't help himself. He really did like her. He wanted to complete the journey from someone she suspected to someone she respected. "Pheromones are like a chemical communication system that's critical for a hive to function. The bees secrete them though special glands and use them to communicate all sorts of things—from brood recognition and egg marking to social behaviors and alarm signals."

Gabby turned to Lewis. "Were these pheromones the biggest problem you mentioned?"

"Oh no," Lewis said. "The pheromone signature was a challenge, but it was by no means the biggest problem. Eventually the way forward became clear to me. One by one, I determined the species from which I needed to borrow genes. From *Vespula vulgaris*, the common wasp, I took a different pheromone signature as well as the carnivorous habit I needed. From *Megalopta genalis*, the Central American sweat bee, I took a genetically determined behavior that causes the species to be crepuscular."

Jim interrupted. "That means the foraging happens at dawn and dusk, so during the day there would be more bees in the hive to protect against wasp attack."

"Precisely," Lewis said. "The gene transfers we made resulted in honeybee drones that not only hunt and kill varroa mites, but invading wasps as well. They're hungry. They're propelled by the pleasure of eating their enemies. A bit like wasps."

Gabby sat forward now. "Did you never stop to think about the danger of creating these things?"

"Of course I did," Lewis said, waving a hand dismissively in the air. "We had safeguards."

"And how have those safeguards worked for you?" Gabby said, her voice dripping with sarcasm.

"It would have been fine if it weren't for one rather significant mistake." Lewis shot a glance at Brad before continuing. "Because I wanted my gen-mod bees to be visually distinctive, I took from *Pompilus cinereus*, the leaden spider wasp, genes for the gray coloration. I then manipulated the exoskeleton to make it stronger. I also added two black stripes down the length of the body."

"Like running shoes," Jim quipped. He didn't like how much Lewis was playing with the natural order of things.

"The stripes are indulgent, I know," Lewis said. "Some may accuse me of showing off. Every single one of my gen-mod bees, both male and female, has this striking presentation. It took a great deal of trial and error, but I must admit I'm extremely proud of it."

"And it's good for branding," Jim said contemptuously. This was why he would never join an operation like Hadley. They were only interested in marketing products and making money.

Lewis looked at Jim and smiled. "My friend, you have always been a skeptic."

"Me?" Jim said. "A skeptic about playing God for marketing purposes? Guilty as charged. What's the business model, Lewis? How is this gen-mod bee supposed to make Hadley money? Aside from encouraging people to use pesticides with impunity, that is."

"Well," Lewis said, "I had to make sure the colony wouldn't produce a new queen on its own. Of course, as you know, queens are created when worker bees feed royal jelly to larvae. After a long series of experiments, Brad and I identified the genes which cause workers to do this—to feed larvae with royal jelly instead of the usual worker jelly. Then we edited those genes out. Snip. My new bees simply don't make queens."

"But you need queens for new hives," Gabby said.

Lewis nodded. "The 'business model,' as Jim has so crudely put it, relies on Beelords purchasing new queens directly from Hadley Agritech. We produce them in the lab. The average lifespan of a typical honeybee queen is three to four years. Our queens live only one year."

"Of course, in order to ensure frequent sales," Jim said, fighting the urge to roll his eyes like Ava would. "And with increasing pesticide use across the board, other pollinators would be dying quickly. You'd have the one pollinator that could survive. So much for pretending you don't want a monopoly."

"The skeptic speaks," Lewis said. "The final result was Variation 324b. When the first of its kind emerged from its wax cell, I was thrilled. What followed was three months of careful lab observations, during which my team demonstrated the success of the variation. There was one more stage of trials left, but I was eager. So I finally gave 324b a name. I called it *Apis tiffiana*. You know how it is with entomologists."

"How what is?" Gabby said. "I don't normally hang out with entomologists."

Brad spoke up. "If an entomologist loves or respects someone, he'll name a bug after them. It's the ultimate compliment."

"Charming," Gabby said.

Jim turned to her. "There's a renowned Swedish entomologist, René Malaise, who famously named a sawfly in Burma *Ebba soederhalli*, after his second wife, Ebba Söderhell."

"Entomologists are weird," Gabby said, shaking her head and smiling.

There was that light, Jim thought. Every time she smiled. She seemed like a mighty goddess who'd just descended into a room of nerdy, bug-loving men. He turned back to Lewis. "So who did you name *Apis tiffiana* after?"

Lewis looked down, suddenly going quiet.

Brad jumped in. "His mother. Tiffany Wilson."

"Yes," Lewis said. "But my excitement was premature. That was before Brad's mistake."

JIM WATCHED as Lewis glared at Brad, stood up from the table, and took several steps away. Gabby tensed and put her hand near her holster. She was tracking Lewis carefully. On the other side of the table, Brad suddenly sat up straighter and pushed his shoulders back. He looked defiant.

"Tell them what you did, Brad." Lewis said. His voice was strained.

Jim wanted to hear what Brad had to say, but he was also starting to really worry about Ava. He kept listening for Claire's car pulling up in front, dropping her off. But no car ever came.

Brad seemed more than happy to pick up the story from Lewis. "We had a large, enclosed glasshouse where we ran the stock."

"By stock, you mean the bees, right?" Gabby asked.

"Yeah. The glasshouse had a double sealed airtight entry, with a closed-loop ventilation system. NASA prototype technology. We didn't want the bees getting out until we finished the trials. Then we'd do a controlled release, once we knew everything was safe."

Brad's swaggering, cocky manner came through with every word he spoke. His voice was loud and full of bluster. "The trials were going really well. I was running all of them. But three hives in particular were outperforming the others. They had stronger grooming habits. The drones were hungry for mites. They did so well at grooming other bees and devouring varroa that they cleared out the parasites entirely. When the next generation of varroa emerged, the drones ate them too, even before the little mites had a chance to reproduce. So that meant the drones completely eradicated varroa from the colony. It was amazing. We'd done it. There was just one issue."

"And what was that?" Jim asked. He wanted desperately to understand what had led them all to this point.

"The bees started dying," Lewis said, remaining off to the side. "That was where things started to go wrong."

"Entire colonies were left abandoned," Brad continued. "We didn't know why. It was almost like Colony Collapse Disorder. I checked to make sure they weren't escaping the closed-loop ventilation system somehow, or the double sealed, airlocked entry. But they weren't. I looked all over that glasshouse for dead bees, and that's when I found something disturbing. I didn't find dead bees. I found pieces of dead bees."

"What was killing them?" Gabby asked.

"Well, those bees were the only insects in that enclosed environment. Other than the varroa, there was no other protein for the drones to eat. *Apis tiffiana* females, the worker bees, have a diet that's essentially the same as the western honeybee. Pollen, nectar, honey. We thought the drones would go back to eating honey once the mites were gone, but that's not the way it turned out."

Brad leaned back and watched everyone, pushing out his chest. "I don't mind saying that I was the one who figured it out." He looked at Lewis. "Am I right?"

"Yes, you're right." Lewis closed his eyes and nodded.

Brad beamed. "I just took a frame out of a hive one day, and I sat down in the glasshouse and I watched it for hours. The workers were going up to the young drones to feed them, just like you'd expect, and that was fine. But the older drones wanted nothing to do with the honey supply. Instead I found they were leaving the hive."

"Normally drones don't leave the hive much at all," Jim said. "Except to mate with queens."

"You got it." Brad pointed at Jim like he'd just won a prize. "Turns out, the drones were hunting down other bees, from the other hives. First they hunted the foragers, when the foragers were alone. They attacked from behind, like wasps do, to avoid the sting, cutting them in half, eating them, carrying bits away for later. Once they cleared a hive of workers, they went for the remaining drones."

"Carrying bits away for later," Jim said, turning to Gabby. "Of course. Just like the thing in the End Woods."

Gabby nodded and explained to Lewis and Brad. "The victims we've found have been dismembered. Limbs have been missing."

Brad and Lewis looked at each other, alarmed.

Then Lewis said to Brad, "You haven't yet explained how we discovered the biggest problem. Tell them what happened next."

"The plan was to expand to a second glasshouse," Brad said. "It was going to be the last trial. Lewis wanted to test different predator species by filling the second glasshouse with wasps. We hoped that the drones would defend the hives well, but also that after the drones finished clearing their hive of varroa mites, they'd start going after the wasps rather than their own kind. So I stocked the second glasshouse with predators, as directed. *Vespula pensylvanica* and *Dolichovespula aculate.*" He turned to Gabby. "Yellowjackets and bald-faced hornets."

Gabby nodded. "The ones that ruin picnics."

"Bingo," Brad said, pointing again like another prize had been won. "We wanted to transfer the three best-performing hives from the first glasshouse into the new environment. Lewis put me in charge of the stock transfer. I did very well within the constraints that were set for me."

Brad shot Lewis a quick glance, and then he turned back to Jim and Gabby. "You see, the second glasshouse was only about fifty yards away from the first. That's all. But a lot can happen in fifty yards."

"Tell them what happened," Lewis said.

Suddenly Brad's shoulders slumped and his chest deflated. He put his hand through his blond hair as he looked down. His cockiness evaporated.

"Things didn't go as planned."

## 52

"WHAT DO YOU MEAN?" Jim asked. "Exactly how did things not go as planned?"

Brad continued, but his voice was softer now. "Everything went really well at first. My preparation was meticulous, I have to say. I sealed the three hives we wanted to move. I smoked them, to pacify the bees, and then I wrapped them in layers of plastic, with mesh openings so they could breathe, of course, but I made damn sure those bees wouldn't get out."

"So they couldn't escape between glasshouses," Gabby said. "And get out into the environment."

Brad nodded.

"Did you do this alone?" Jim asked.

"No. I worked with Sato, another research assistant."

Lewis seemed to prickle at the mention of this. He huffed and shook his head.

Brad looked at Jim and Gabby, and the expression in his eyes was almost sheepish. "We don't really talk about Sato anymore."

Suddenly Brad leaned back, as though trying to regain his earlier confidence. He threw his shoulders back again. "In addition to wrapping those three hives, I also put them inside heavy duty, ventilated plastic containers that clipped up along the sides. It was a kind of double protection. I was being very careful.

"We had a flatbed truck to move the hives, and a forklift to load them. The problem was this. We couldn't get the forklift inside the glasshouse, because the airlock was too small. So we had to carry the hives out by hand. From there we used the forklift to load them onto the back of the truck, and then we drove the fifty yards to the second glasshouse."

Lewis cut in. "And what happened at the second glasshouse? Tell them." He was still standing away from the table, as though trying to create distance between himself and Brad.

"Well," Brad answered, "we unloaded the hives off the truck with the forklift, and then we stacked them near the airlock. Of course, we had to carry them over the threshold and into the glasshouse by hand, because again the airlock was too small for the forklift to go in. It was just me and Sato doing the heavy lifting. Lewis was supervising. He didn't want anyone else there." Brad looked over at Lewis. "I said we needed another pair of hands."

Lewis turned his back to the table and looked out at the woods.

Brad continued. "We carried the first hive in without a hitch, although it was heavy. And we were in bee suits. And those suits are hot. Then we lifted the second hive and carried that one through the airlock as well. It was stressful. Sato was working hard. He was tenacious, that guy. I was sweating a lot inside my suit. Lewis was pointing and yelling orders."

"It wasn't my fault," Lewis said.

"The third hive was the smallest. But by the time we got to it, I was exhausted. So was Sato. I hadn't really slept for two nights because, you know, the boss gave me responsibility for the stock transfer and I didn't want to screw it up. I'd been up all night preparing, trying to figure out how to do it with just two people. I was really tired. I think that's why it happened."

"What happened?" Gabby said.

"I fumbled. You know, it happens. I felt like the star quarter-back fumbling at a key point in the big game. We should have had two other people, one on either side of that hive to catch it. But there were no other people. Just Sato and me.

"I was backing into the airlock. I didn't really have the weight stable, and my foot hit the threshold. Stupid. Clumsy. An accident. I should have had the strength. The coordination. It makes no sense. I pride myself on strength. Just dumb luck. Sato was on the other side. He tried to compensate, but when I went back I, ah… I pushed up. I pushed the hive up. I didn't want those bees to come crashing down on me. I pushed them onto Sato."

Brad looked down and started rubbing his hands. "It knocked Sato off balance. The hive tilted toward him and, well, it fell right down on top of him."

Gabby let out a small gasp.

"Sato had his bee suit on of course, but one of the clips on the container had come undone as it tipped. Or before. I don't know. But it must have snagged his suit, because he had a rip. The container came crashing down, and the side came right off. The force of the fall made the hive boxes break through the plastic wrap. Out came the bees. Into the wild. Just like that. They were everywhere. They swarmed on Sato. Got inside his suit. He was on the ground screaming. I smelled bananas."

Brad looked over at Jim. "You know how a bee's alarm pheromone comes out when they sting? How it attracts other bees to the sting location? You know it smells like bananas."

Jim nodded. He'd smelled that alarm pheromone many times. He thought of it every time he ate a banana.

"Well, *Apis tiffiana* must have a very active alarm pheromone because they swarmed on Sato so fast. And they sting repeatedly. Like wasps. I jumped into the swarm and dragged him away. At least I did that. I thought about running but I didn't. I wanted to run."

"Where was Lewis this whole time?" Gabby asked, looking over at him.

He didn't answer.

"Lewis was gone," Brad said quietly.

"I went to get necarichlor," Lewis said, sounding defensive. "The pesticide to kill them. I didn't run."

"He didn't have a bee suit on," Brad said. "At that point there was nothing he could have done, to be fair. It was already too late."

"What happened to Sato?" Jim asked.

Brad looked tentatively at Lewis, as though seeking permission to continue. Lewis quickly shook his head: no.

"It's just like the one that's out there now," Brad said to Lewis, gesturing to the End Woods. "They need to know."

"He turned, didn't he?" Jim said. "He became transgenic. Like the mouse. Like the raccoon."

Lewis gave a large sigh of resignation, and then spoke slowly, with a tremor in his voice. "And so we have come to the biggest problem. Yes, Jim. As your little experiment with the mouse demonstrated, the venom is a biohazard."

Brad shook his head. "What happened to Sato was horrible."

## 53

"I KNEW IT," Jim said. "You accidentally created a contagious virus, didn't you? It transfers aggressive DNA from another species into the host organism. That's what changed Sato."

Lewis answered with a small nod. His shoulders slumped, and then he spoke. "The viral vector we used to edit the bee genome was faulty. Either the virus wasn't totally disabled, or there was some mutation and it became active again. The unintentional result is a new virus that's both replication-competent and pathogenic."

"What does that mean?" Gabby said.

Lewis turned to her. "It's both infectious, and it causes disease —in this case by inserting a combination of wasp and honeybee DNA into the host, causing the host to become transgenic.

Brad spoke up. "We think it only takes one sting, but Sato had hundreds. He went completely unconscious after around thirty minutes. Then the scabs started. Like on the dog. You saw it. It's a pupal casing. We suspect that the speed of the metamorphosis varies based on the amount of venom received. Sato emerged completely transformed after only eight hours. We watched the stages back at Hadley. There's a sealed observation area in the basement."

Lewis looked up at them. "It was incredibly fast when you consider the cellular regeneration required." He shook his head and looked up at the trees. "Sato was the first vespling."

"Vespling?" Gabby asked.

Lewis continued staring at the branches above them, so Brad answered. "That's what we call a viral hybrid. When they're human we just call them a vespling. But obviously there are raccoon vesplings, and mouse vesplings. Dogs too. Whatever gets stung."

"And what happened to Sato?" Jim asked. "Is he the one out in the woods now?"

"No," Lewis said. "That's not Sato. I don't know who that is. We took care of Sato. There's no cure."

Gabby said, "You killed him."

Lewis glared at her, visibly upset now. "Let's just say, he's no longer a danger to anyone."

Jim shook his head. He couldn't imagine how horrible it would be to see someone transform that way. He tried to get his head around it. "So, the bee venom contains a contagious virus, and it's delivered through a subcutaneous injection—the bee sting. It's the perfect transmission route."

"I'm afraid so," Lewis said. His voice was clipped, as though he were trying to shake off his emotions. "Only one hive escaped that day. One hive. That's all. I immediately put Brad on clean-up duty. He had to clean up his own mess."

Gabby shook her head. "Did you tell any state or local authorities about this? That you had an accidental release of a genetically modified organism?"

Brad stifled a laugh. "Sheriff Turner is practically on the Hadley payroll."

"That's not true," Lewis snapped. "Anyway, I had good reason to believe we could contain it ourselves. And I needed absolute discretion. I had no idea one small hive would spread so fast."

Brad looked over at Jim. "I checked the area closest to the release site first. I destroyed wild hives. It was only, what, four days ago that I discovered *Apis tiffiana* had infiltrated your hives at that blueberry farm and that apple orchard. I hope you understand why I had to do what I did."

Jim did understand, but it didn't make him any less angry. "Why didn't you use this pesticide to kill them?" Jim gestured toward the impulse gun at Brad's feet.

"I had to destroy any trace of them, for obvious reasons," Brad said. "And of course they're not fire resistant. They're still bees."

Lewis walked back over to the table now, and he sat down next to Brad. "Chuck Norman had nothing to do with the hive arson. Brad did it alone, under my direction."

"You let Chuck get arrested," Gabby said. "And you never came forward."

Lewis looked down. "I know."

Jim was absolutely horrified as he thought about the possibilities. "If there are more of those bees out there, it could be disastrous. We could have more of those things, those vesplings, as you call them. More people could turn."

"All the bees are gone," Brad said. "I'm sure of it. I've combed every inch of this island."

Lewis pushed up his glasses. "I wanted the situation contained before I formally briefed Hadley headquarters in Atlanta. I didn't want anyone else to know about the accidental release until Brad had it cleaned up."

"Wait," Gabby said. "You haven't told Hadley headquarters about this yet?"

Lewis looked at Gabby with some disdain. "I'm not an idiot. I've been keeping my supervisor abreast of the situation the entire time, albeit discreetly."

Brad smirked. "Lewis reports directly to someone they call 'Crusher Cavanaugh.'"

Lewis shot him an angry look, then turned back to Gabby. "Cavanaugh's been briefing others on the executive leadership team on a need-to-know basis."

Gabby looked shocked. "So, do the big wigs at Hadley know there's something out in the End Woods here killing people? Or not?"

"It's complicated," Lewis said. "I'd say that communication with the Executive Leadership Team is, well, fraught. Cavanaugh knows. I received strict orders to bring the situation under control. Brad has already begun combing the woods with an impulse gun, trying to find the vespling and kill it. And more help is coming."

"But it's a person," Jim said. "Or used to be. There's no way to reverse the transformation process?"

"Reverse it?" Brad gave him a mocking grin. "We barely understand it."

"But it's a virus, right?" Gabby said. "There are ways to treat viruses."

"I tried everything to save Sato," Lewis said. "Believe me. Nothing worked."

"Could Sato, ah, sting?" Jim asked.

Lewis shook his head. "Like bees and wasps, only the females sting. But even the males are horribly dangerous. That raccoon that attacked Ava, it was female. That's why it had a stinger."

"So you admit it wasn't a rabid coyote," Jim said.

"Of course it wasn't," Lewis said.

Jim shuddered. If Ava had been stung by that raccoon, he didn't know what he would have done. Likewise, if he'd been stung while handling the gray bees, it would have put Ava in terrible danger.

"How did they spread so fast if they can't produce queens?" Gabby asked.

"Something changed," Lewis said. "Somehow they began producing queens. I suspect the genome is extremely unstable. There was a mutation."

"If they're breeding new queens then we're in serious trouble," Jim said.

Lewis looked at Jim with some disdain. "I'm aware of that, Jim."

"We've got them all now," Brad said. "But we think they were behaving like Africanized bees."

Gabby nodded. "You mean killer bees. How?"

"By attacking," Brad said. "From what I've seen, it seems they would attack an existing hive, kill the queen and replace her with their own. Every time I thought I'd burned the last hive, I found another. Jim, that day you brought in those two *Apis tiffiana* specimens in your glass jar, I thought they were all gone. But at least they're gone now."

"I told you that thing came here last night," Jim said. "One of those things you call a vespling. It came after Ava and me."

"You were very smart to board up your house," Lewis said. "It seems as though you might be living in its hunting ground. I understand that it already killed your neighbors, Emmett Jones and Minnie O'Donnell." Suddenly, Lewis looked very tired.

"How do you know the names of the deceased?" Gabby asked. "That's not public knowledge yet. Did Sheriff Turner tell you?"

Lewis shrugged. "It's a small island. People talk."

Jim looked over at Brad. As angry as he was about the situation, he felt for this young man, trying to fix everything on his own. "It's not all your fault, you know."

"Yes, it is," Brad said. "I fumbled. I pushed the hive on Sato. If I didn't do that, none of this would be happening."

"No," Jim said. "Lewis engineered those bees. He was in charge of the project. They were dangerous. The entire thing is his fault. The viral vector he developed was faulty. It's his negligence."

"There were unintended mutations, Jim," Lewis spoke sharply. "I had no way of knowing."

Jim stood. "Lewis, it was your job to know. Look, I think you both need to go now." He'd had absolutely enough of this conversation, and was growing increasingly worried about Ava. He wanted nothing more at this point than to get his daughter off this island. This place was a nightmare.

Lewis stood quickly. He looked like he was about to explode at Jim.

Gabby stood and put her hand on her holster.

Then Lewis turned to Brad. "We're done here. Let's go." He walked away abruptly and headed toward their truck at the front of the house.

Brad stood too, but then paused and looked at Jim. "The vespling will probably come back here, Jim." He lifted the chrome impulse gun and set it on the table. "Keep this. We've got two others."

Jim hesitated. He had no need for that weapon. He and Ava were leaving on the 9 p.m. ferry. He explained as much to Brad.

"Crepuscular animals can come before then," Brad said. "Let me explain how this works."

He showed Jim how the gun worked and how to fill the reservoir from the tanks so the gun was ready to fire.

"It almost seems like a fire extinguisher," Jim said.

"Actually, it *is* a fire extinguisher," Brad said. "I had to improvise. They're what we use at the research station. It uses small amounts of water in high velocity bursts to put out fires. Shoots fifty feet. I took out the extinguishing agent and replaced it with necarichlor, which acts like a neurotoxin. It affects the central and peripheral nervous systems, and it causes tremors, paralysis and then death. Suffocation is what kills them, because they can't breathe."

"How toxic is it to humans?" Jim asked.

"Only mildly."

"Earlier you said you can't kill these things with bullets. Are you sure?" Jim said.

Brad gave him a troubled look. "I'm sure."

"Then why did you bring your pistol into my house when you were dealing with Bailey, after he was stung?"

"Your dog hadn't turned yet," Brad said. "Before they turn, you can shoot them. And even after they turn, when they first come out of the pupal stage and their skin is wet, you could probably shoot them then too. But very soon after they emerge, their skin hardens. Just like insects. Then a bullet won't penetrate. Sure, if you could get a good shot at it, you'd bruise it, push it back a bit, but you wouldn't kill it. Its skin is a mixture of flesh and exoskeleton, with multiple cuticle layers. It seems to disperse the kinetic energy from high impact assaults."

"That's impossible," Jim said.

"It's not," Gabby said. "Kevlar vests do it."

"The skin on these things does it too," Brad said. "That raccoon vespling your daughter killed, its skin hadn't yet hardened. Otherwise the shovel probably wouldn't have killed it."

Gabby said, "Tell me again. Why didn't you use necarichlor on the hives?"

Brad nodded. "Fire kills the bees. They're not fire resistant. And like I said, we didn't want to leave any trace of them. But we've never tried to kill a vespling with fire. You'd probably need a big fire. And anyway, for a full vespling, the necarichlor in this impulse gun covers a wide range."

"How do you know all this?" Gabby asked.

"We ah, we studied Sato, before he, ah..." Brad's voice trailed off. There was an awkward silence.

Suddenly, Lewis called out from the front of the house. "Brad! Now!"

"Do you think there's more than one out there?" Jim asked, ignoring Lewis.

"It's hard to say," Brad said.

"I suspect we'd have more bodies on our hands if there were more than one," Gabby said. "But who knows?"

Jim looked out at the woods, then back at the chrome impulse gun on the table. If the vespling came back tonight before he managed to leave with Ava, at least he'd be ready.

## 54

AS SOON AS BRAD, Lewis, and Gabby drove away, Jim went into the house. He couldn't believe Ava wasn't home yet. Where was she? He pushed away a small sense of panic, took a deep breath, and messaged her.

*Where are you? You okay?*

He began packing his own things, just to distract himself, but when several minutes had passed without an answer, his worry began to grow. He told himself that Ava had probably just got caught up with Claire. She was having fun. She was saying goodbye. He tried to ignore his other, darker thoughts. It was daylight. The vespling was not out yet.

Was she still angry because he was making them leave the island? Because he'd boarded up the house? Was she punishing him because they'd been arguing? He had no idea. She was most likely just being thoughtless. He paced. He checked his phone.

It was 6 p.m. when he decided to go out to find her. She'd been gone all afternoon. It had been long enough. He wanted her home.

He didn't have a phone number for her friend Claire, but he knew where the family lived. They had one of the big houses on the eastern shore, looking out over Jason's Bluff, only a short drive away.

By the time he pulled up at the end of their driveway, he had worked himself into a fury. It was incredibly disrespectful of Ava not to respond to his calls and messages, when she knew they were leaving that night.

Claire's mother came to the door and looked surprised to see him. They didn't really know each other, but they knew who each other was. She had a pale pink sweater and perfectly coiffed hair. Jim asked if Ava was there.

"She's not, I'm afraid."

"Ava told me that Claire picked her up today. Do you know where they might have gone?"

"Oh, that's impossible. Claire's been gone for two weeks. She's visiting family in Chicago. Back next week."

Jim's heart sank. "I'm sorry to bother you. My mistake."

Driving back down that driveway, his panic took over. Why had Ava lied? Where the hell was she? Next, he drove to Eddie's house, which was inland. Once again the memories of driving around Ann Arbor, looking for Sarah, plagued his mind, and he felt a horrible kind of déjà vu.

When he pulled up in front of Eddie's modest home, he saw Eddie's mother sitting out front. Her name was Doris. She had messy gray hair and a smoker's voice.

"Ava ain't here," Doris said.

"Is Eddie here?" Jim asked.

"Nope. He went hunting over a week or so ago. Hasn't come back. Like his father. Doesn't want to work. Only wants to hunt. Useless piece of crap boy."

"If Ava shows up here, could you have her call home, please?"

She nodded. "I'll tell her. She's a nice girl. Too good for Eddie, I'd say."

When he got back home, he called out for Ava again. She wasn't there. He messaged her once more.

*Please let me know you're okay.*

She didn't answer. It was almost 7:30 now. He was thinking about Sarah, about the night she didn't come home, the night he drove around Ann Arbor looking for her. The same terrible, churning mass was now growing in the pit of his stomach. He thought about that small room with the scratched white table. He was terrified.

He went into Ava's room and sat down on the edge of her bed, trying to figure out what to do. The dark, purple walls closed in on him. The lights were off, and the curtains were open. Pale evening light from outside leaked in around the edges of the plywood on the other side of the glass.

The air in this room, he had to admit, was stagnant. The space felt hot and small. Ava had been so incredibly upset at him for boarding up her window. He wished she'd understood he was just trying to protect her.

He looked around the room at her scattered things as though they could tell him where she was. The closet door was still open, and he glanced down at the pile of shoes scattered there. So many shoes, and all she ever wore were those black Converse sneakers...

Wait. They were still there. Her black Converse sneakers were lying haphazardly on top of the pile. What was she wearing right now? The only time Ava didn't wear those shoes was when she was dressed up, or when she went into the woods, which was almost never.

He turned on the overhead light, got down on his knees in front of her closet, and started rifling through her many pairs of shoes. He had no idea how many pairs of shoes she had, but he knew exactly what he was looking for: her hiking boots. He looked in the back of her closet, tossing shoes out into the middle of the room.

The hiking boots were missing.

He ran to the front entry closet. If her old backpack was also gone, it would confirm his suspicions. He knew that it should be there, at the back of the closet. It was a child-like, bright purple backpack with a unicorn on it. Surprisingly, Ava still used it from time to time. He shifted aside the vacuum and a broom. The backpack was gone too.

It hit him. It finally hit him. He was such a fool. He'd never considered the idea that she would go looking for Eddie, that she'd head off into the woods. She'd mentioned that she hadn't heard from him, and that he had gone to his family's hunting cabin.

*My God*, he thought. His daughter was in the woods.

And now it was twilight.

And something was out there.

He went to the shed and grabbed his good flashlight. The shed was still a mess and there was broken glass on the floor. There was a terrible chemical smell from the pesticide Brad had sprayed.

He walked along the northern boundary of the property. With the powerful beam from the flashlight, he scanned the edges of the trees and tried to find a place where Ava might have passed earlier that day. There was one spot where the grass looked crushed. He stood in front of it and squatted down. He held the flashlight low to the ground. Tracks always shadowed better by flashlight than by sunlight.

There. A footprint, with a lug sole. About Ava's size. That was it. He was right. She had gone into the woods. Her trail was relatively fresh, but without knowing her exact destination it could take a long time.

He ran into the house and called Eddie's mother immediately. Her raspy voice came down the line, and he explained the situation.

"Well," Doris replied slowly. "We don't much like to talk about where our cabin is."

"What? Why?"

"We don't like people poking around our place. The Benson

family cabin is hidden, and it's good hunting around there. Secret."

Jim took a deep breath. He gripped the cordless handset tightly and walked over to the kitchen table. He looked out the windows at the woods. It was getting dark. Ava was out there. "Please, Doris. It's important. My daughter is gone. I need to find her. She needs my help."

Doris broke into a cough. When she caught her breath, she spoke. "I don't know if your daughter needs your help. She's a very smart, independent young woman."

Looking out at the fading light, he thought about how protective he'd become of Ava. He wondered for just a brief moment if Doris was right. Perhaps he should leave Ava alone? Perhaps he shouldn't go after her?

No. Of course not. There was something out there, something dangerous, a vespling, and Ava was out there now with it. He had to find her.

"You know that something is out in the woods killing people, right?" he said.

"Yes. Rabid coyote, Sheriff says."

"It's worse than a rabid coyote. Much worse. Two people are dead and two more people are missing. Ava and Eddie may both be in danger."

Doris paused, then said, "There's some dense woods between Stone Lake and the Indian Point Lighthouse, at the northern tip of the End Woods."

"Catmull's Thicket?" Jim asked.

"Yes. You know it?"

"Not well." Even with all the time he'd spent in the End Woods, he hadn't spent much time in that area. It was in a large, round basin, and the woods there were dense and often impassible. The air always held a chill from lack of sun. He always went around that place. It was unfriendly and seemed to push him away.

"The cabin is there, in the middle of Catmull's Thicket. Eddie's great-grandpa built it. We have a small patch of private land in the middle of the reserve. Historic rights. It's due south of Indian Point Lighthouse, about halfway between the lighthouse and the lake. Now don't you tell anyone."

"Thank you. I won't."

As soon as he hung up, he called Gabby. On Gull Island, he'd always ignored the basic survival tip to tell someone where he was going before he ventured into the wilderness. He knew the End Woods well enough, and certainly Ava understood that if he wasn't around he was probably in the woods. But things were different now. Not only were the End Woods suddenly more dangerous, but he felt a connection to Gabby. He wanted her to know where he was going, just in case.

When she answered, he told her what happened, and where he thought Ava had gone. "I'm going to Catmull's Thicket to find her. I'm taking Brad's impulse gun, and I'm taking my rifle. I'm going to get Ava and bring her back home again."

There was silence on the other end of the phone.

"Gabby?" he said, wondering if she was going to try to stop him. Maybe he shouldn't have called her. She was a cop, after all.

"Wait," she said. "Just wait."

"Why?"

"I'll be right there. I'm going with you."

55

AT THE OTHER end of the island, down in the town of Saint Peter, Chuck Norman had been drinking at Coyote Kylie's for about an hour and a half. He hadn't moved once from his favorite stool, the one farthest from the door. He'd ordered some spicy chicken wings and fried potato wedges, which he ate at the bar so he could be close to Kylie. In their usual style, she'd been chatting with him all evening in between serving customers.

He liked to think of her as his buddy, nothing more, nothing less. A buddy with benefits. And those benefits weren't just physical. She was a good time in a variety of ways. He enjoyed going to bed with her, but she'd also taught him a lot. He'd never learned as much from anyone about how to hunt as he had from her.

"I'm telling you, you got to see this," she insisted. She was excited and trying to show him something on her phone. "It's the thing."

All evening long, there had been a weird tension in the bar. People were nervous about the dead folks, even though Sheriff Turner had said it was all over. Folks knew about the two boys who were missing. Word had spread. Some said the boys were just hunting.

Chuck didn't exactly know what was going on, but he knew one thing. Jim Parker was up to something. He'd seen that arrogant prick talking to Deputy Gabby, seen him looking like a man on a mission. Chuck was still angry as hell about losing two nights in jail to that man's bullshit. He'd like to get back at him.

He hadn't yet told Kylie what he'd done, that he'd gone over to Jim's property. He'd watched from the woods, and he saw Jim talking to Gabby and those two men from Hadley Agritech, the Black guy and the blond frat boy. They were planning something. He'd seen the strange silver gun the blond guy had given Jim. They were going hunting. He knew it. But for what?

Kylie was standing on the other side of the bar and leaning over toward him. She had that excited glint in her eye she sometimes had, like when she saw a coyote coming out from a tangle of willows, or when she wanted to step outside and look at the stars.

She pushed her phone at him again, and he smiled. The simple truth was that he came here not for the booze but for Kylie. He'd forgiven her for blabbing about their friendship the minute he realized she did it to get him out.

"Alright, alright." He made a big show of being annoyed, set down his beer, and took her phone. "What am I looking at?"

"It's from the hotel webcam, yesterday at dusk." She pointed at the screen.

He knew the webcam well. It was mounted on top of the Harbor View Hotel on Main Street and looked across the street to Hadley Park, and Saint Peter Harbor just beyond. It was useful. He sometimes checked it from home before he took his boat out, just to see what the water was doing.

"Bob Morris just sent it to me," she continued. "Just now. Can't believe it."

Chuck stroked his long beard.

"He told me not to tell anyone he sent it to me, and not to share it. So don't say anything. This clip is just the bit where you can see it."

"See what?"

"Watch it."

"I would if you'd quit talking to me about it." He pushed play.

On the small screen, the timestamp in the corner indicated that the footage was from two nights ago, Wednesday at 8:29 p.m. The video showed a view of the flagpole, the park benches, the start of the path that led down to the public beach, and the water in the distance. The American flag flapped lazily in a slight breeze, but otherwise there was nothing moving.

"Nothing's happening," he said.

"Keep watching," Kylie said. "It comes from the right."

He saw it then. There was something moving at the edge of the screen, a figure coming up from the beach. It was silhouetted against the water, which was reflecting the last of the day's light. The figure looked like a person, except for how strangely it moved. It twitched and paused and then jerked forward.

"What the hell is that?" he asked.

Kylie didn't answer.

The figure crept up to the park and squatted down near the benches, as though it were hiding. It was bald and naked and muscular. Something wasn't quite right about its jerky movements. Then suddenly it shot up and bolted across the screen to the left, running in a low crouch and disappearing from view.

He felt a chill, as if he'd seen something other-worldly or ghostly. His brain couldn't make sense of it. He looked at Kylie, whose face had a similar concerned expression to his. That unsettled him even more. The air seemed to shift and warp around them, separating them from everyone else in the bar. Nobody else here had seen what they'd just seen.

"Did Bob mess with this footage?" he asked. "Seems jerky, like he sped it up in parts. Made it strange."

She shook her head. "I asked the same thing. Watch it again and look at that flag. It keeps moving gently, real slow, the whole time that thing moves all weird like the video was sped up. But it's not the video. That's how it moves."

Chuck watched the clip again. Kylie was right, as usual. The woman appeared to be rough as guts, but she was someone who paid attention to the little things and understood how to use them. He'd once seen her make a squeak with her mouth on the back of her hand, pretending to be a mouse to draw in a thirty-pound coyote for the kill. It was impressive.

He handed the phone back to her and downed the rest of his beer. "Well, I'll be damned," he said.

"Damned is right."

"Can I get another?" he asked, nodding at the empty glass.

"No fights tonight," she said and winked at him.

"No fights," he said and smiled. He never smiled as much as when he was with her. Even when he tried to be grumpy, she always broke through. She made him feel like his tattoo was true. He was lucky.

Kylie left her phone in front of him as she walked over to the beer taps. She waited on two tourists before coming back with his beer.

"What do you think that thing was?" he asked.

She started unloading glasses from the dishwasher. "I can tell you what it's not. It's no goddamn rabid coyote. I trust Sheriff Turner about as far as I can throw him."

"They say he used to be a lawyer."

Kylie smiled. "I rest my case."

"Must be what's killing folks," Chuck said. Then he thought of something. "Let's get it. We'll be heroes."

"Last time I went hunting with you, you nearly shot my foot off. You shoot at anything moving."

"That was a mistake. I said sorry and all that."

"Deputy Gabby will get it," Kylie said, but she seemed interested. Chuck could tell.

When he gave the creature some more thought, he suddenly

understood. This was why Parker had come rushing out of the substation with Deputy Gabby earlier that day. This was why he was talking with those men from Hadley Agritech. This was why they gave Jim the silver gun. They were working together. He knew it.

"I've seen some things that make me think Jim Parker's involved. He's all high and mighty. Let's get that thing before he does."

"I'm not getting in any competition with Jim Parker, thank you."

"But I am. Because of him I spent two damn nights locked up in that shithole they call a jail cell." He took a heavy swig of his beer and wiped his chin. "You share that video on your newsfeed?"

"I told you Bob asked me not to. He's afraid of causing a panic."

"People need to know, what with those kids missing and those other folks dead. I think you ought to share it. Let folks know what's out there. It's responsible."

She picked up her phone, wiped the screen on her jeans, and put it back in the pocket of her denim shirt.

Chuck asked, "You think I got cooties?"

She leaned in. "If you do, then I guess I got 'em up inside me too."

He laughed and took a sip of his beer. He really did like her. She wasn't uptight or worried about being proper. He'd never slept with a woman who felt so much like a pal.

"I suppose people do need to know," she eventually said. "And I suppose it would be good to take it out. Make sure nobody else gets hurt."

She stepped away to serve that microbrewery crap to some guys in fancy jeans. Kalamazoo Tangerine Stout. Ann Arbor Bacon Maple Ale. Who called that beer? All the locals knew she kept those weird craft beers on tap for the tourists.

He truly believed that he could catch that thing himself. But if he couldn't, he knew Kylie could. And he just wanted to take the glory from that Jim Parker. Maybe he and Kylie would end up on the front page of the *Gull Gazette*. He liked that thought.

When Kylie came back, he said, "So, are you with me?"

She smiled. "Might be. I'm always up for a hunt. But you gotta be careful."

"Of course. Look, I can head out now. But when can you get out of this dump?"

She gestured broadly. "The advantage of owning this fine establishment is that I can leave whenever the hell I want, as long as I put someone else in charge. I'll get Tony to take over." She pointed to the other end of the bar, where Tony was mixing a drink.

"Great," Chuck said. "But you should post that video on your newsfeed first. So folks know. Nobody deserves to die. Not even these stupid tourists that crowd up your bar and drink that sugarpiss beer you serve them."

Kylie laughed. "It's the tourists who pay my bills. You be good to them." She took out her phone and tapped around for a moment. Then she looked up at him and said, "Done."

"Done what?"

"Just shared that video to my newsfeed. Now down that beer, and let's get out of here."

Chuck raised his beer in a toast, and he smiled.

## 56

JIM KNELT DOWN in his bedroom, pulled his gun case out from under the bed, and took out his Winchester. He attached the sling —a long, brown carry strap—to the front and rear of the rifle, on the underside of the stock. He knew Brad had said the rifle would be no use against the vespling, but he just wouldn't feel safe out there without it.

From the back of his sock drawer, he took out the two boxes of ammunition. In total, he had about thirty rounds. It should be enough. He wished he had a weapon-mounted hunting light, or a night vision scope, but it was too late for that now.

He had a waist pack that he could wear in front, and he grabbed it from his closet. He shoved the ammunition, a compass, and his map of Gull Island inside the pack, and then added in his good flashlight, two small headlamps, and a small water bottle too. The night air would be cool so he grabbed his black Parker Pollination fleece.

It was almost 8 p.m. and he hadn't eaten dinner, but he had no time for that now. He threw a bag of trail mix in for good measure.

He turned off all the lights in the house except for the floor lamp in the family room and the front porch light—just in case Ava came home. He left the back door unlocked—she might not have her key—and wrote a note on the chalkboard telling her to stay home.

Outside the light was beginning to turn a deep, velvety blue. The long summer evening was dying bit by bit.

He walked over to the picnic table and looked at Brad's impulse gun. Could anyone really be safe with a gun that just shot mist? It was counterintuitive. He picked up the twin tanks that powered it, and he slid his arm through the shoulder straps until the tanks were nestled on his back.

He held the impulse gun to get used to it, right hand on the pistol grip, left on the foregrip. It was as long as a rifle, but there was no sling. He would have to carry it in front of him. He was hoping that Brad was right, that this thing would kill the vespling. He had certainly seen it kill the mouse and the bees, but the vespling was much bigger.

He went over Brad's instructions on how to use it in his head. Pull back the black valve to fill the reservoir. Grip the gun tight since it has significant recoil. The digital indicator on the back showed there was enough necarichlor in the tanks for eight shots.

Just then, he heard Gabby's SUV on the dirt driveway. He walked around to greet her.

When she stepped out, she pulled out two Kevlar vests. She offered him one, which he put on under his gear. He offered her one of the headlamps in return.

"I'm good," she said, gesturing to the flashlight next to the police radio on her belt. "You sure you need your rifle as well as that impulse gun?" she asked, looking at the sling he had over his right shoulder.

He was carrying the rifle muzzle up, butt down, just as his father had taught him when carrying it over the shoulder. "I just feel like I can't go out there without it."

"I understand. I've got mine." She pulled a Glock 40 out of its holster and showed it to him. "If we have to, we can bruise the thing with bullets, to keep it back, and then finish it off with the impulse gun."

Jim nodded. "Have you talked to Sheriff Turner?"

"Let's just say I still have a job. Barely," she said, holstering her gun. "He said I was sticking my nose where it doesn't belong. He said he has it under control."

"Do you believe him?"

"Well, two people are dead and two more are missing. So no, I don't think he has it under control."

"What about the evidence? Did you give him the bees and the gen-mod mouse?"

"No. I can't trust him. I wouldn't want the evidence to disappear. I put them in my refrigerator at home. At least for now. It's not protocol, but it's the best I could do."

"Makes sense," Jim said, then paused. He didn't know how to phrase what he wanted to say. His heart thumped a bit. Seeing her standing there next to him, carrying the authority and training of her uniform, her confidence and her power, he felt, well, he felt safe. "I, ah... I just want to say, thanks."

"Thanks? For what?"

"For believing me. For coming here and helping me. It's nice to not be doing this alone."

She smiled at him. There it was again, Jim thought—that smile, the way she lit everything up.

"Let's go get your daughter," she said. "And while we're at it, let's kill that damn monster."

He laughed. "Yes, let's." Then he paused. A wind picked up through the trees. "How human do you think it still is? Do you think it knows what it is?"

Gabby looked at the ground and shook her head. "I hope not. That would be terrible."

They walked together to the edge of the woods. Jim checked his watch. It was 8:30 p.m. The sun would be going down soon.

The shadows were dark, but in patches the light hitting the sides of the trees was gold. It was beautiful, and quiet, and still. The vespling was probably out there now, somewhere, and so was Ava.

He took the flashlight out of his bag and found the spot where Ava had stepped out of the back acre and into the woods.

"There," he said. "She left there."

Gabby gestured him forward. "You go first. You're the tracker."

He nodded. With the house at his back, north was dead ahead. He pushed aside a thin branch, and he entered the woods. Gabby followed behind.

He looked into the shadows. He had to find Ava before the vespling did.

PART 3
THE END WOODS

57

A PROFOUND STILLNESS enveloped Jim and Gabby as they moved deeper into the trees. They fell into silence and listened to the woods. The crickets and frogs and birds sang mournful evening songs. The canopy above them appeared like thick, black lace against the fading light of the sky. Jim turned off the flashlight and let his eyes adjust.

As he walked, he reprimanded himself for not figuring out earlier where Ava had gone. If she'd left around noon, which was likely, she was a good eight-and-a-half hours ahead of him. If he'd left when he first started worrying about her, he would have already found her by now. They'd already be back home.

There was, he thought, a small chance that he was wrong, but he doubted it. She never wore those hiking boots. Eddie was missing. This is something she would do. She would put on those boots and head into the woods. She was stubborn and determined and brave, after all. Like her mother.

His only consolation was that Ava had travelled during the day. The vespling was active at dusk and dawn, so she'd chosen a smart time to set off. Right now, when he and Gabby were in the woods, was the worst possible time. But it couldn't wait. He had to find her and get her off this island. There was no other alternative he was willing to consider.

They continued on, and he paid close attention for flattened grass and broken twigs. He listened to the woods for any hint that the vespling might be nearby.

A lavender light was now beginning to fill the space between the trees. The weight of the rifle sling on his shoulder felt reassuring. The tanks on his back grounded him with their heft.

He imagined Ava already settled into the Benson family cabin with Eddie for the night. Eddie was a hunter. Although Jim didn't much like him, he knew the boy would know how to keep Ava safe.

At least the trail wasn't yet cold. There had been no rain. There were still signs of someone passing here. He was almost certain it was Ava. He knew her habits, her weight, and even what shoes she had on. It helped him track her.

The grass cleared in front of him, the path turning into a sandy brown dirt underfoot. He paused and shone the flashlight low across the ground. At first there was nothing, but then—there, slightly further on, casting shadows against the bright white glare —he saw a footprint.

"Lug soles," he said to Gabby, showing her the print. "Those are Ava's shoes."

He held his hand next to the print, checking for scale. Yes. It was the right size for Ava, and it wasn't too deep. If it was deeper, it would have likely been made by someone heavier than her. Next, he looked at how level the print was. A prominent toe depression would indicate running. A heel depression with a slide mark would indicate fatigue. This print looked flat and steady.

"She was walking, not running," he said. "And not yet tired. There's no slide mark. She was okay, at least when she passed by here."

Gabby shook her head. "I could use you on a crime scene or two, Jim Parker."

"I've been with you on crime scenes. Two, in fact."

She laughed. "Yes. That's true." She reached out and touched his arm. "Let's not do that again, okay?"

"Deal."

A bit further on, the ground rose and a deer trail cut diagonally across the track they were following. He checked along it, looking for signs, and found another of Ava's footprints under his flashlight.

They followed the trail until it suddenly veered off to the west. At that point he spotted an opening that headed off the trail and into the brush. There was a twig that had been bent from someone passing by. Ava was headed north, toward Stone Lake.

"She must be using a compass," Gabby said. "She's staying north."

He felt a small rush of pride for Ava as he and Gabby followed the opening into the brush. Soon the woods sloped down. When they reemerged from the trees, they were looking out at still water, sedge grasses, and sphagnum mats—a kind of floating moss mat.

"O'Leary's Marsh," Gabby said.

"Beautiful. Isn't it?" Jim turned off the flashlight for a moment. "One of the best ways to notice what's happening in the woods is to do nothing, to just watch. Signals reveal themselves."

The wetland was surrounded by a wide meadow which was in turn ringed by a mature forest of beech and maple. The water was perfectly still. The sun was just below the horizon, and the western sky was gold and red, catching on the edges of a few scattered clouds. The warm colors spilled out into lilacs and greens further up. All this was reflected perfectly in the mirrored surface of the water.

Standing next to Gabby, he almost had to fight the urge to put his arm around her. This was not the time or the place for that. It could get awkward fast. What would Sarah say? He pushed the feelings away.

The sunset colors would die quickly, he knew. The fall equinox was a month away, and the fastest sunsets always happened around the equinoxes. But in that moment, right then, it was beautiful and almost peaceful, standing there with Gabby, even though they were both aware of the danger.

Evening birdsong rose up all around. Swallows flew over the marsh, darting and diving to catch the evening insects. A pair of cormorants perched in a dead tree nearby, silhouetted against the multicolored sky. In the distance, on the other side of the water, a gentle breeze moved through the trees.

Eventually the woods gave off a signal—a bird plow. In the beech and maples on the other side of the marsh, first one bird and then another flew off in the same direction. The birds that were perched highest in the trees took flight first, followed by the ones lower down.

"See that?" Jim said. "A bird plow."

"A bird plow?"

"The path of the birds makes the shape of an old-fashioned plow in the sky. They all flew to the east. That means something must be coming from the west, something they see as a threat."

He looked at his watch again. They'd been walking for nearly forty minutes, and they'd only come a mile. Tracking someone typically took longer than walking, as you had to pay attention to details and move slowly to avoid missing anything.

"There," Gabby said. "Flattened grass."

They stepped forward into the meadow that surrounded the marsh and followed the trail. It was clear even in the dusky light, and Jim left the flashlight off. He didn't like the thought of announcing themselves in that open space. He stopped and put it back in his waist pack.

The trail led them to the edge of the wet ground and dark water. There it abruptly stopped, and the boggy grasses and sedges began.

"It just stops," he said.

For a moment, he was consumed by a terrible thought. What if Ava had drowned? What if she'd tried to go directly though the marsh and got tripped up by the sedges? He quickly reminded himself that Ava was no imbecile—reckless, perhaps, headstrong, yes—but she was smart enough to realize she couldn't go through it.

"She would go around," Gabby said.

"Yes, you're right. She would."

They both looked to the west, which looked like the shortest way.

"If we go west, it might put us in the path of whatever was scaring the birds," he said.

Gabby looked to the east. "That would take us too far out of the way."

"West it is," he said.

As they began rounding the wetlands, they stayed far enough from the water to avoid getting their boots wet. The grass was low now, and there was no discernible track to follow. They moved quickly. Jim just wanted to get to the other side of the marsh. Neither of them said it, but it was clear they both felt exposed.

Suddenly a noise came from the trees directly up ahead. Branches were rustling and breaking. They both immediately stopped and listened.

Something was up there.

58

JIM HEARD ANOTHER BRANCH BREAK. It was a thick branch, by the sound of it. Whatever was up there, it was large, and it was close. He gestured to Gabby to squat down beside him. They were upwind of whatever it was, and he was afraid that it might smell them.

There was a sound of running feet. Something was moving toward the trees. The noise continued and then there was a thud, like something falling to the ground. The running stopped.

Gabby bent down very low and gestured away from the water, toward the trees to their left. She was suggesting that they withdraw. Jim nodded. Whatever was directly up ahead, he certainly didn't want to be upwind of it. They moved together into the woods.

It was darker under the canopy. The reds and golds in the sky were already fading, and only a very small amount of light was filtering through. He heard rustling sounds from the edge of the meadow.

He and Gabby each stood behind a wide trunk. Gabby had her weapon in her hands, pointing skyward, ready to turn and shoot.

He took a slow breath. Pulling the sling off his shoulder, he quietly set the rifle down. Then he lifted the strange, silver impulse gun.

Gabby walked forward, circling around to where they'd heard the noise, and he followed behind. They were approaching it from under the trees now, so they were no longer upwind. The meadow beyond the woods was deep blue with afterlight, and there was definitely something moving out there.

He could make out a shape, seeing it from the side. He stepped forward slowly, letting his eyes adjust to the soft glow and deep darkness around him, feeling confident that the trunks of nearby trees were hiding him.

From behind another tree, Gabby pointed towards it.

He nodded back.

It was difficult to see from here, in the fading light, but it seemed like a person, squatting down in front of something on the ground. But that wasn't exactly right. It wasn't a person. Not exactly. It moved strangely. The dome of its head appeared bald and covered in cadaverous gray skin. He thought of the raccoon.

As he stared into the blue shadows now, he could hear the revolting sounds of chewing and flesh being torn. The creature was eating. There was no struggle. Its meal was clearly already dead. He tried to get a better look at what it was devouring, but the long grass and shadows hid too much. Even so, that strange creature was definitely what he'd seen in his back acre last night. He was certain. It had to be what killed Emmett, and then Minnie, and possibly those missing kids in the woods. It was feeding on people. It was hunting. What was it eating now? Was it a person? Was it Ava? God no, don't let it be Ava. He shut the thought out.

He had to stop it. He had to kill it. He had to keep Ava safe.

He shifted down into a prone position and crawled forward. Gabby stayed back. The undergrowth rustled beneath him. He paused, hoping that the creature's loud chewing and tearing noises would mask the quiet rustling he was making, and then he moved forward again, even further away from Gabby. She was still back there, behind him somewhere. He no longer knew exactly where.

He was now within thirty feet of it, hidden by the trees, but his view was still impeded by the long grass and shadows. He thought he saw some kind of spiny growth coming off its forearm, but he couldn't be sure. Could it just be a branch?

Even in those shadows, however, it was clear that the creature moved erratically. It twitched and jerked to the left and to the right as it shoved its head down into whatever it was eating on the ground. It tore at it.

When it was chewing, it lifted its head, looking around. Even as it scanned the surroundings, it continued to shift unpredictably. Jim couldn't quite make out the details, but it was holding something limp in its hand, like raw meat. After it finished chewing, it shoved more towards its hungry face. And always there was that strange, erratic twitching throughout its body. For such a relatively human shape, the movement was deeply disturbing.

He looked down at the silver gun, and he shifted his body to prepare to shoot. A twinge of panic rose in his chest. He recognized the twinge as the thing his father always taught him to fight against. He hesitated, but then reached toward the black valve of the impulse gun and pulled it. The hiss started as the reservoir began to fill. The vespling looked his way. It had heard him. He panicked, let go of the valve, and froze.

A gentle breeze picked up through the trees behind him. He felt it on the back of his head and neck. The vespling sniffed the air. It had caught his scent.

It got up and ran to the right, out of his sight entirely. He tried to follow it with his eyes, but he couldn't find it. He looked frantically back and forth, but it was nowhere in the meadow.

He looked around. Had it come closer to him? Was it behind

him? It seemed to have made absolutely no noise. He rolled slightly on his side and looked back into the trees, where it was darker. Could it be hiding back there? Where was Gabby? He watched the woods for a moment, but he saw nothing. Then he turned back toward the spot where it had been eating. It was as though it had vanished.

Out over the marsh, the swallows were no longer darting through the sky to hunt insects. They must have nested down for the night. Then he slowly realized that absolutely everything had gone silent. The evening birdsong had entirely stopped. The tree where the cormorants had been perched was now empty. The evening had become eerie and still and deadly quiet.

He sat up and rested his back against a nearby tree. He looked to the left and to the right and turned occasionally to peer behind. He still couldn't see Gabby.

The light was fading fast. His flashlight would help him to see, but he knew that the light would also announce his location. The creature could be anywhere.

Then he heard it. It was the same noise he'd heard before—the steady hum and occasional clicks. The sound had a strange quality that meant he couldn't exactly tell where it was coming from. It seemed to bounce off the trees and come at him from every direction.

*Hmmm. Hmmm. Cli-click.*

Something moved in the darkness, in the trees to his right, about twenty yards away. There was a rustling sound, and some branches moved. He looked in that direction, trying to spot it, holding up the impulse gun, prepared to fire.

The noise stopped. His eyes remained trained on the area. A shadow shifted.

He lifted the impulse gun again. There were a few bushes over that way in the undergrowth, and he watched them for movement. His throat was suddenly dry. His heart hammered loudly in his chest.

One of the bushes moved. It was over there. There was no time to wait for a direct line of sight. He stood and slid the valve back to fill the reservoir, as Brad had showed him. The gun hissed loudly.

"Don't waste a shot!" Gabby yelled. "It's just me!"

59

"GABBY," Jim said. "I lost you for a moment."

He looked around for the vespling. He stood slowly, still eyeing the darkness for any other movement nearby.

She came forward out of the shadows, her handgun posed in front of her.

Jim heard the ghostly hoot of a great horned owl come up out of the woods. The stuttering song repeated twice. *Hoo-h'HOO-hoo-hoo.*

There was no sign of the vespling.

"What happened?" Gabby asked, lowering her weapon. "Why didn't you shoot it? I didn't hear the impulse gun go off."

"It ran away before I had a chance to fire. I wasn't fast enough. It heard me and caught my scent." He hated that he missed his chance, and he hated telling Gabby that he'd done so. "Then it made that noise it makes, that humming and clicking. It made it last night too, behind my house."

"The mouse made that noise as well," she said. "Even from that little thing it was menacing."

Only then did Jim finally realize what was familiar about that noise.

"It reminds me of something I heard once, years ago," he said. "I was in Japan on a research trip. One day I ended up with Japanese giant hornets on my mesh veil, right by my face. They're the thing people call 'murder hornets.' They were snapping their mandibles. It's an acoustic threat."

"So that noise means it's hunting," she said.

"It seems so."

Now Jim heard the call of an Eastern whip-poor-will rise up from around the marsh. *Whip-poor-will! Whip-poor-will!* The eerie song of that bird, which was also a crepuscular species, always reminded him of late summer evenings growing up.

He walked back to where he'd set down his rifle and slung it over his shoulder again.

They began moving forward with caution, Jim holding the impulse gun in front of him, and Gabby her handgun. As they stepped out into the meadow, the blue afterlight was vanishing, replaced by a million shades of gray and black. Tall grasses filled the space in front of them. The spot where the creature had been eating was cloaked in shadow.

Gabby took her flashlight from her belt and held it tightly alongside her handgun, so that the beam was illuminating the potential path of her bullet. "Let's keep going," she said.

Jim took out his headlamp. Their two white beams of light crisscrossed in front of them.

"It was eating over there," he said.

Soon he saw something lying dead in the grass. His stomach dropped. What was it? An animal? A person? A large area of grass had been flattened down. There was a lot of blood.

Gabby stepped forward. There were entrails stretched out across the ground at her feet. Behind her, Jim couldn't quite make sense of what he was seeing.

"It's a deer," she said.

Thank God, Jim thought.

Large parts of the carcass had already been consumed. It was a doe. The left rear leg had been torn off and was missing. Chunks of fur were scattered nearby.

He heard the whip-poor-will call out again. "It's definitely no longer around," he said. "The birds stop singing when it's nearby."

"How do you know that?" Gabby lowered her gun and turned her flashlight in his direction. The chrome impulse gun in his hand shone brightly in the light.

"I might not be that quick with a gun, but I know nature," he said. "Observing it is my job. I've seen this vespling twice now. The birds went quiet both times."

She pointed at the remains on the ground. "It's got a voracious appetite. And it definitely takes parts for eating later."

"We need to kill it," he said.

She nodded. "Let's get around this marsh and back into the trees on the other side. I don't like being in the open."

They walked on, Jim in front now and Gabby following. He paused. They were still in the open meadow.

"You should take this," he said. "You're faster with a weapon than me. I can use my rifle. I know it better. The impulse gun is what matters."

She looked around and then nodded, holstering her gun and putting her flashlight back on her belt. She took the impulse gun from Jim, slipped the chrome tanks onto her back, and held the gun in front of her with two hands.

Her eyes went to the digital indicator on the back of the gun. "We still have eight rounds," she said, and then she appeared to be feeling the weight of it. "The reservoir's not full. You didn't have it prepped. That's why you missed your chance."

She pulled the black valve to finish filling the reservoir. The gun hissed, and then the V-shaped stream of liquid trickled out of the front. She let go of the valve.

"I'll take that headlamp you offered earlier," she said, and Jim gave it to her.

They continued walking, falling into an easy pace side by side. The muddy smell of the stagnant marsh filled the night air.

Jim held his old rifle in his right hand. He was still scanning the ground, looking for a sign of Ava having passed this way, but he saw nothing. He'd lost her trail. He didn't see any signs of the vespling either.

"I don't know what I'll do if something happens to Ava," Jim said.

"She's going to be okay, Jim," Gabby said. "We'll find her." She paused and they continued walking. "You know, just because something happened to Sarah, that doesn't mean something is going to happen to Ava."

Jim stopped and looked at her. He felt instantly angry, but he didn't know why. Gabby was just trying to help. "I know," he said and started walking again.

A moment later, Gabby said, "What do you think made Ava go into the woods?"

It felt like she was picking at a wound. He didn't like these type of questions. Still, he answered. "She really thought I was overreacting when I boarded up all our windows," he said. "But I think what pushed her over the edge was when I told her I was taking her off the island. She didn't like that at all."

"Can I tell you something?" Gabby said. Her voice had gone soft. What was coming next was going to be something he wouldn't want to hear.

"That depends," he said with a sad chuckle.

"Do you want to know what they call you?"

"Who?"

"The local boys. They call you 'Guard Dad'. They tease Eddie because he's dating Guard Dad's daughter."

Jim was taken aback. "Really?"

"Everyone knows you nailed Ava's bedroom window shut when you moved here."

"What? How?" He was shocked that something so domestic, just between himself and Ava, could be island gossip.

"Oh, kids talk. Ava probably complained to one of her girl-friends." She paused. "Jim, as a daughter who had an overprotective father, at least when he was sober, can I tell you something? There's a time Ava needs to feel looked after, but there's a time when she needs to have you step away. Your challenge is figuring out which is which. She won't always be able to tell you."

Jim had no response to this. He didn't know what to say.

"Sorry if I'm butting my nose in," Gabby said. "Honestly, I feel for her, and I just thought someone had to tell you what we can all see."

"We?"

"People on the island."

"Nice to know that my parenting is a topic of local conversation."

"It's a small island." She laughed lightly. "There's not much to talk about."

They walked on for a minute or two, then Jim said, "Thank you. I know you're probably right. It's been hard since Sarah... well, it's been hard. I'm afraid I don't make a very good single dad."

"I wouldn't say that. You clearly love her."

Jim nodded. "That much I suppose I'm doing right." He laughed. "Not sure about everything else."

He took a deep breath, feeling grateful that Gabby had told him this. She was looking out for him in more ways than one. He felt something slowly opening up. He glanced over at her as they walked.

"Gabby, there are moments when I know I'm being overprotective, and I know it's because of what happened to Sarah." He looked off into the trees. "But now that something is in these woods killing people, how can I *not* be overprotective? If I didn't do everything in my power to keep my daughter safe, wouldn't *that* make me a bad father? If anything happened to her I'd never forgive myself."

Gabby offered him a calm, luminous, lovely smile. "I suppose it's hard to get it right."

"Yes, it is. But I promise you this. When all of this is over, when I have Ava out of danger and off this island, I will work hard not to be overprotective. I don't want to lose her because I'm smothering her."

Gabby nodded. "I'm glad to hear you say that."

All of a sudden, two clear shots rang out. Gunfire to the north. Jim and Gabby both stopped in their tracks and looked toward the sound.

"What's that?" Jim said.

"Too early for deer hunting," Gabby said. "Season doesn't start for another month."

"Whatever it is, there's something over there."

Gabby nodded. "And that's right where we're headed."

60

THEY CONTINUED NORTH, and soon entered the beech and maple trees just north of the marsh. They fell into single file, with Jim in front again. Although they weren't as exposed here, they also didn't have the same range of vision. Looking around with the headlamp was futile, as it revealed only a small patch of tree trunks and leaves. Jim fought the idea that there was something hiding behind every branch, and he tried to stay focused on just moving forward, heading north.

Earlier, when they'd been standing on the south side of the marsh, the bird plow had come up out of these very trees. That meant that not too long ago the vespling had passed through here. The thought made him uneasy.

They moved as quickly as they could, but it was slow going in the dark. Gabby fell behind him slightly. He could hear a low murmur from her police radio.

Eventually they emerged at Stone Lake. It was a decent-sized lake for a small island—about a mile and a half across and rumored to be deep. Jim knew it was cold because earlier that summer he'd gone swimming in it on one of his walks. Those days seemed so far away now. He'd had no fear of this place back then.

"We have to go around the lake," he said to Gabby. "Over there is Catmull's Thicket." He pointed across the lake. "That's where Ava is."

"Jim," Gabby said. "I should tell you."

"Tell me what?"

"It just came through on my radio. They just found the bodies of those two local boys, Mike and Ash, just east of the lake." She gestured to the other side of the water.

His heart sank. "Damn it."

"They were dismembered," she said. "Just like Emmett and Minnie."

They both stood in silence for a moment.

He looked toward the east. There seemed to be some light over in that direction. "Are the cops there now?"

"Yes. A couple of the officers from Au Bois."

"Do you need to go help?"

"I'm technically off duty. Besides, I'm here helping you."

He nodded. "Thank you."

"Also, it sounds like there's a bit of commotion in town," Gabby said.

"What do you mean?"

"Apparently, there's a video circulating of the vespling, caught on a webcam in Saint Peter."

"It's going into populated areas now?"

"It seems so. The video footage is from two nights ago."

"Then it's only a matter of time before it starts killing people in town." He looked off toward the east. "If we keep to the western side of the lake we'll avoid them," he said, and he grinned. "You know, cops always ask too many questions. They'll want to know why we're out in the woods tonight."

"Are you trying to make me go rogue, Jim Parker?"

He let out a sad laugh. "I think you already are."

They fell into formation side by side again, walking around the rocky shore of the lake. Jim wished the shoreline were sandy, because then he would have been able to find traces of Ava. He was going on faith now. He hadn't seen anything of her trail since O'Leary's Marsh.

A gentle breeze rippled on the water, and the stars shimmered across the sky. At one point, Jim thought he saw a light flash across the water, coming from the east, but then it was gone. It was possibly headlights from a patrol car.

It took around thirty minutes to round the lake. Jim knew that the northernmost point of Stone Lake had a small inlet, a little bay where a creek came out of the trees and emptied into the cold, deep lake water. He headed towards it. When they approached, the creek made small bubbling sounds. He and Gabby stood there, the open stretch of Stone Lake at their backs.

That was when he saw it. Tracks, in the mud at the edge of the creek. He shone his headlamp in that direction, then went forward. Footprints. A barefoot human. In front of each toe, the indentation of a claw.

"It was here," Gabby said.

"It probably came here to drink."

He stood and looked to the north. Not much further away they would find the dense trees of Catmull's Thicket. It was the oldest, most untouched stretch of forest on Gull Island, and it formed a damp basin that started just north of where they were, running all the way to the Indian Point Lighthouse at the top of the island. The land in that basin was thick with mighty trees and was full of rotting and precarious trunks that jutted out at strange angles.

The cabin was supposed to be due south of the Indian Point Lighthouse, about halfway between the lighthouse and Stone Lake. He pulled out his map from the waist pack. Gabby peered over his shoulder.

It looked like the lighthouse was due north from this inlet. The creek went north into the woods but quickly headed off to the northeast. If they went directly north from this spot, and if the cabin truly was halfway between here and the lighthouse, then they should come across it in less than a mile. It was hard to know how long that travel would take, given the dense, tangled nature of Catmull's Thicket, but they were in the last stage of the journey now.

When the first bullet hit the mud near Jim's foot, he didn't know what it was. For an instant, his mind struggled to make sense of the tiny impact. Then he jumped to the side and dropped to the ground, letting his instincts take over. Next to him, he could see that Gabby had done the same. Loud cracks rang out from somewhere along the edge of the lake, and more bullets hit the ground with wet thuds. Debris flew into the air.

They both crawled forward frantically up the slope into the trees.

Gabby shouted, making a strange guttural noise. She'd been hit.

And the bullets kept coming.

## 61

JIM CROUCHED low under some shrubs, with Gabby huddled next to him, as the bullets fell around them. She was holding her leg tightly with both hands and wincing in pain. He quickly reached over and turned her headlamp off to hide them. Eventually, the bullets stopped.

"Who the hell is shooting at us?" he said under his breath.

She said nothing, still holding her leg.

"Let me see," he whispered. He couldn't make out much in the darkness, so he made a small tent from his head to her leg, using his black fleece. He turned on his headlamp. There was a tear in her beige pants near her calf. The area was soaked with blood.

He pushed up her pant leg so he could inspect the wound. She made a sharp intake of breath, but she didn't flinch. While there was a lot of blood, it didn't look like the bullet had entered the flesh.

"It grazed you," he said, turning off his headlamp again. "Anywhere else?"

"No."

Another bullet shot out and hit the ground nearby. They both ducked down instinctively when they heard it hit.

"We have to get away from the gunfire," Gabby said. "They know where we are."

"Can you walk on it?" He slung his rifle over her shoulder, stood next to her, and helped her up. "Put your hand on my shoulder. Put your weight on your good leg."

She wrapped her arm around him, and they stood up together. He was taken aback by how slight she felt next to him. Her frame was so small.

"Wait," she said. "The impulse gun." She gestured to the chrome gun that was trailing on the ground. Her foot had become tangled in the two black hoses.

He picked it up and untangled her foot. "Now, let's go."

She transferred her weight over to him, and he took it, along with the weight of the tanks on her back. They moved forward as quickly as the darkness and their awkward bearing would allow. They moved together, like one slow and cumbersome animal, deeper into the trees. Behind them, from the edge of the lake, a few more shots rang out.

They continued awkwardly for a few minutes, until they came to a large, downed tree surrounded by brush. It was covered with moss and fungi. They were out of immediate danger. Gabby sat down on the ground and leaned her back against the tree.

"Hold this up to block the light," he said, handing her his black fleece.

He grabbed the first aid kit that he always kept stashed at the bottom of the waist pack, and turned on his headlamp to look again at her leg. The bleeding had already begun to slow. He washed the wound with water from his water bottle, added some antibacterial ointment, and wrapped it up tightly with rolled gauze.

They could hear voices on the other side of the tree, approaching them. It was a man and a woman.

"For Christ's sake, you cannot shoot like that," the woman said.

Jim quickly reached up and turned off his headlamp. He leaned in close to Gabby, so close that he could smell her strawberry shampoo.

"I just get excited," the man answered. "And I just get going. Something happens."

Jim recognized the gruff, gravelly voice. It was Chuck Norman. Which meant the other person must be the woman everyone called Coyote Kylie.

"How many times do I have to tell you," Kylie said. "Identify your goddamn target or it could be your drinking buddy you shoot next."

"You're my only drinking buddy, and you were right next to me."

"Yeah, well, keep acting like a dipshit and you won't have me to drink with neither."

Gabby leaned forward, as though to get up, but then she hesitated. Jim gave her an imploring look, shaking his head, and put a finger over his lips. She nodded and leaned back.

"You hear something?" Kylie said.

Jim and Gabby froze.

"Nah. Nothing. Come on. We got to find this thing and kill it before Jim Parker does."

The two continued squabbling as they walked on.

Jim and Gabby sat in silence for several minutes, then Jim spoke quietly.

"What the hell?"

"I could have arrested him for reckless use of a firearm. But I'd have to take him in now. And then Sheriff Turner would know I'm out here."

"You're definitely a rogue cop now." He smiled.

"The vespling is more dangerous than Chuck. It's not far, and we're best prepared to kill it." She gestured toward the impulse gun. "Besides, I need to help you find Ava."

Jim was relieved. He didn't want Chuck to know that they

were out there. What if Chuck decided to follow them? The man was a liability. Wherever he went, there was trouble.

"With that video of the vespling circulating," Gabby said, "people will be nervous. Nerves make people like Chuck trigger happy."

"I think Chuck is always trigger happy."

Jim finished wrapping Gabby's leg with the last of his bandages and checked his compass to reorient himself to north. Then he turned off his headlamp and put everything away in the dark.

"From their voices," Jim said, "it sounded as if they were headed northeast, probably following the creek. If I'm right, the Benson cabin is due north of here. We shouldn't come across them again."

They both fell quiet for a moment, listening to the woods. Jim heard nothing, not even nocturnal birdcalls, which made him uneasy. His eyes were slowly adjusting to the darkness.

"Try standing," he said, putting his arm out to help her up. "We need to move. No headlamps. Can you walk in the dark?"

"I think so." Gabby stood, holding the impulse gun. She grunted when she put weight on her leg, but then she took a step forward. "I can manage."

"Why don't we get rid of those heavy tanks on your back? Let me take the impulse gun."

"No," Gabby said. "I can shoot faster. If we don't shoot this thing quickly when we come across it, we're dead."

They headed north again, Jim leading the way with his rifle poised to shoot and clearing debris out of their path to make it easier for Gabby, who was limping now. She had trouble stepping over the roots of trees which were forming small trip hazards along the way. Jim warned her of each obstacle as it came up.

Gunshots came periodically from the northeast.

"God only knows what they're shooting at now," Jim said.

His watch told him it was just after midnight. They'd been out in the End Woods for over three-and-a-half hours now. It was all taking far too long, and he felt increasingly anxious to get to the Benson cabin. He reassured himself that Ava would already be there, sleeping comfortably, with Eddie to protect her from the vespling.

"It sounds like they're getting further away," Gabby said. "Further to the east."

"You think so?" Jim said. "I hope you're right."

The ground began to slope upwards, and they found themselves walking along a ridge which dropped away sharply to the right. A layer of undergrowth with rotting leaves and loose stone made the path slippery. In the darkness it was hard to see the edge of the ridge, and Gabby was struggling.

Jim was frustrated that she wouldn't let him take the heavy impulse gun, but he supposed she was right.

"Do you need my help?" he asked, turning back to look at her.

"No. I'm fine," she said sharply. "But I need my headlamp."

He watched her for a moment. With her injured leg, she seemed unstable. Her advice about Ava came back to him.

*There's a time when she needs to have you step away.*

In the end, they both turned their headlamps back on, even though doing so made them easy targets, and they continued walking. At least now they could see the ground in front of them.

As he walked, Jim looked down into the considerable gully that dropped away from the ridge to the east. He realized that he was looking into the heart of Catmull's Thicket. It was dense with trees and nearly impassable.

"Catmull's Thicket," he said, gesturing into the dark basin.

"Terrible spot for a cabin."

He wanted to get a bit further along the ridge before they headed down. It was a maze down there. Once they entered, they would be slowed even more.

Then, out of the darkness behind him, he heard Gabby shout. There was the sound of something sliding. As he turned, he saw the brightness of her headlamp descending into the deep basin. She was tumbling down, her arms and legs flailing, her body sliding and rolling, breaking branches on the way.

"Gabby!" Jim yelled. Panic and guilt surged through him as he strained to see her in the dark. He swung his rifle round and started scrabbling down the ridge toward her. It was steep.

He heard a loud thud from her direction and then brief silence, before she began yelling out again, screaming at the top of her lungs. "Back! Stay back!"

"What? Why?"

"Bees!"

62

A STRANGE NOISE began to rise out of the darkness—a deep vibration, a terrible buzz. This was the sound of bees under threat. They were angry. Jim pointed his headlamp into the trees, but he couldn't see Gabby. The murmur of the bees grew louder and louder.

His rifle and waist pack were slowing him down, and halfway down the slope he dropped them. He grabbed his flashlight, which threw out a long beam. He could find her at a distance with this. He had to get Gabby away from those bees. A swarm of angry bees could kill.

He watched every step down the steep slope, careful not to lose his footing, going as quickly as the precarious terrain would allow. His boots slid in patches of loose gravel and dirt.

Somewhere up ahead, Gabby was shuffling in the undergrowth. Leaves rustled. The light of her headlamp shone through the branches. And then, suddenly, there was a deep boom.

Gabby's voice rose up. "Stay away! Stay away!"

He still continued moving forward.

Gabby screamed, "They're gray! Don't come any closer!" There was a hissing sound, followed by another boom.

Then her headlamp went dark.

"Where are you?"

There was no answer.

"Gabby?"

"Stay where you are," Gabby said. "Stay there."

Jim's flashlight cut through the darkness around him. He couldn't find Gabby in the tangle of trees. There was a mist in the air. The beam illuminated the tree trunks, flooded the low saplings and shrubs of the understory, and shot up into the canopy. There were small things catching light like sparks in the darkness, a kind of movement twenty feet above. Bees were flying high in the trees, above where the hive had to be. They were furious and ready to attack. He wished he had his bee suit.

Brad had said he'd combed every inch of this island. Obviously he'd missed this hive buried here in Catmull's Thicket. If there was one hive of gray bees out here, could there be more? More people could turn. There could be more vesplings.

Gabby coughed and then called out. "The hive is in an old trunk here. They're dying. Give it some time." She coughed again.

"Are you okay?" Jim yelled. He wished he could see her face.

"I'm okay. I'm okay. Just don't come over here. You cannot get stung, Jim. You cannot get stung."

"Are you?" Jim asked.

There was no answer.

"Have you been stung?" he asked again, more urgently.

"Wait till they clear."

Jim's body went cold with dread. He told himself that there was still a chance she was perfectly fine. Anything else was unthinkable. His anxious mind began spinning, twisting logic and reason until he could easily imagine a scenario where Gabby could fall into a beehive in the dark and not get stung. He turned off his flashlight and his headlamp, and he sat down on the ground some distance from where she and the hive must be located. The terrifying buzzing started to slow down.

"Clear?" he asked into the blackness.

"Not yet," Gabby said. Her voice sounded weaker. "It seems like a strong poison, but it'll be a while before they're all dead. There are a lot of them." She was coughing periodically between her words.

He pulled his t-shirt up over his mouth and breathed through the fabric. His lungs were becoming irritated as the poisonous mist slowly spread. Pockets of starlight peeked through the gaps in the canopy above him. Gabby had gone silent.

"You okay?" he called out.

She coughed. "Still here."

He got up slowly and moved as quietly as he could back up the slope to the spot where he'd left his rifle and waist pack. In the darkness he felt for his things, and took everything back down the slope towards Gabby. He was careful to stay far enough away to be out of reach of the bees.

"Keep talking to me," he said, raising his voice to reach her.

There was nothing but silence.

"Gabby?" Jim said. He looked into a cluster of shadows, where he'd heard her voice. Where was she? The trees stood like angry giants between them.

Finally she answered. "Stay away. They're not all dead yet."

Jim felt inside his pack and took out his first aid kit.

"I need to ask you a favor," Gabby said. "I need something." Her voice had taken on a calm, matter-of-fact tone.

"What?" he said, squinting into the trees and listening carefully. Gabby had to be okay. He needed her to be okay. Small noises came, like she was shifting on the ground. There was a crinkling and crunching as she moved.

"What do you need?" he said. "Just tell me. Anything."

"I need you to kill me."

63

IT WAS NEARLY 1 a.m. and Lewis was still eavesdropping on the police radio, drinking gin and tonic. He'd been doing this for hours now, listening as things unraveled. Earlier he'd heard one of the deputies report that he'd found the bodies of those two local kids.

"No more," he said out loud to the empty room now. "Please. No more deaths."

With every new development, he was finding it harder and harder to recover from Brad's stupid mistake. While he could plant rumors that the video of the vespling was a hoax, it was going to be very difficult to convince people that something as simple as a rabid coyote was to blame for four deaths over the course of just two days.

The night air greeted him as he stepped back out onto the balcony and looked at the dark expanse of Lake Michigan. The moon was nearly full, and it sparkled on the vast blackness of the water. The sky was patchy with gigantic, unfurling clouds. For the first time in a very long time, he felt lost and small.

He thought of his mother, of how much he'd wanted her to be proud of him, of her chipped front tooth when she smiled at him.

There was a scene he played out many times in his head, where he imagined telling her about all of his accomplishments. She would be seated in one of the vinyl green armchairs in the dementia ward back in upstate New York, staring absentmindedly out the window as she so often did, and he'd walk up to her and kiss her on the forehead and say, "Hello, Mama."

She'd turn to him and smile and maybe that day she'd recognize him, maybe not. He'd tell her who he was, and she'd nod and say, "Of course, I know you." But he would never know if she was telling the truth or not.

It didn't matter. He'd simply say, "Mama, I need to tell you something."

"Yes, child," she'd respond, smiling.

There would be her chipped tooth again, something she'd had since she was a girl, aged fourteen, when she'd fallen on a log while crossing a stream in Tennessee. When Lewis had secured his first good job, years ago now, he'd offered to pay to fix that tooth, but she always told him, "The good Lord made these teeth for eatin', not for lookin' pretty. Don't bother me none. Spend that money on someone who needs it."

On this particular day, in the scene in his imagination, he'd tell her what he'd done. He'd tell her about how he'd managed to solve the Global Bee Crisis. He'd tell her about how he'd fixed the world, making pollination abundant again. That soon there'd be all the old foods back in the grocery stores, all at the old prices. Soon everything would be back to the way it was supposed to be. People like them, people who struggled to feed their family, they would soon be able to afford to eat fresh fruits and vegetables again. All because of what he'd done.

She would smile back at him. She would know him now, clear as a bell, and her eyes would brighten. Her fog would lift, and she would lean forward to him and say, "Well, now, little Lew, I don't understand how you did all that, but you know I sure am proud of you, my sweet son. So very proud. I always knew you'd do a great, good thing. You've always had a mighty brain in that head of yours. Lord knows where you got it from."

Lewis would grab her hand and say, "From you, Mama. I got it from you."

She'd laugh then, as if it were some very funny joke. But he knew it was true. Lewis knew the difference between lack of intelligence and lack of education. And this woman, his mother, was as sharp as a tack. He could never pull anything over on her. She figured out everything quickly, knew what he was up to even before he did. She'd never had more than a fifth-grade education, but her mind was a firecracker—at least it had been, before the fog came.

Now, standing on the balcony, Lewis feared he would never have that conversation with his mother, would never be able to tell her of his achievements.

He made himself another drink. Was it his fourth? His fifth? He went back up to the spare room where the police radio was and sat at the desk. His eyelids grew heavy, and his head began to nod.

64

JIM'S STOMACH DROPPED. "What are you talking about?"

Gabby's voice came back to him out of the darkness. "They stung me. You need to shoot me."

For a moment, he said nothing, his brain going into its scientific version of autopilot, as it always did. He worked through the other possibilities. Could he carry her out? Could he get her help? Take her to Lewis? There must be some other option.

"I'm not going to shoot you," he finally called back. She was still hidden there, somewhere in the obscurity of the nighttime trees.

She let out a weary laugh, and it rose from the gloom. "Maybe I should make a lot more noise," she yelled. "That way Chuck will come back and finish me off."

"Don't say that."

They fell silent.

"Are they dead now?" Jim said, raising his voice just enough to reach her. "The bees?"

"Some are dead," she said, sounding tired. "Not all I don't think. Stay where you are."

"How many stings do you have?"

"Who knows. Lots." Her voice was becoming softer by the minute.

He got up and started walking toward the sound of her voice. Brad had said it took only one sting. He wanted to help her. He had to help her.

"Are you coming over here?" she asked.

"Yes." He was determined.

"Not yet. Stay where you are. It's not safe yet."

"You need help," he said, not willing to wait any longer. There were antihistamines in his first aid kit. He would help her however he could. He had to do something. Anything.

"No. You can't. It's dangerous."

"Are they dead?"

"I think so, but there might still be some alive."

He turned his headlamp on and walked forward. She was lying alongside a large, dead tree, covered in dirt and leaves. The tree was wet with spray. An opening in the side of it was clearly home to the beehive.

As he knelt down next to her, the light of his headlamp made her squint and look away. He was horrified by what he saw. Her face and hands were covered with hundreds of raised red welts, each with a small white mark in the center, where a stinger had punctured her skin. The chrome impulse gun and the twin tanks lay on the ground at her side.

There were dead bees all around her and at the base of the tree. They were gray, with the two stripes down their sides, just like on those he had found in his home hives.

"I guess Brad missed this one," she said, smiling slightly, tilting back her head strangely. "Silly boy."

Jim reached for her face, but she brushed his hand away.

"Don't touch me," she said. "We don't know how contagious it is. The venom's a biohazard, remember? Back up. You can't risk getting infected. We don't need another one."

He took out four tablets from the first aid kit, and set them on a rock near her, along with his water bottle. "Antihistamines," he said. "Take them."

He stepped away and sat down on a downed tree branch, having checked it first to make sure there were no bees on it. There was always a possibility of being stung by a recently dead bee. He turned the headlamp off, just in case Chuck and Kylie came back. He didn't want them to find him. Darkness flooded in. The moonlight filtered down and threw crisscrossed shadows through the trees.

"It doesn't matter," Gabby said. He could just about make out her face in a patch of moonlight. "Antihistamines can't save me. We've seen what happens. It's horrible. You need to do it. Shoot me… please."

"It's not going to happen that way."

"It has to," Gabby said. "Please. It's too late."

"It can't be."

She laughed. "Bees. Who knew it would be bees? I've been caught in gang crossfire on the streets of Chicago. I once had an angry drug dealer come at me with a nine-inch knife. I come here to escape all that. And what gets me in the end? A bunch of goddamn bees."

"This isn't the end for you. Not yet."

She shifted her body backwards, until she was able to lean back against the tree. "True. They said that guy, Sato, had thirty minutes before he went completely unconscious. So, hey, I've got plenty of time."

"Stop it," Jim said. He was not going to lose her. He could not lose her. Never since he'd lost Sarah was there a woman he could imagine being with again.

"Stop what, Jim? Speaking the truth? God, you're stubborn."

"I'm stubborn?" Jim said. "You wouldn't let me take the impulse gun. Even when you were struggling."

He'd been thinking about how the injury had destabilized her, and suddenly he became furious at Chuck. He cursed that man. If

Chuck hadn't shot Gabby in the leg, she never would have fallen, and she never would have hit this hive. She never would have been stung. This was Chuck's fault. Chuck was an irresponsible, thoughtless man, and he had no idea how much damage his carelessness had caused.

"It's a good thing I didn't give the impulse gun to you," Gabby said. "Otherwise you would've run right down here to spray these bees and got stung too. Then we'd both be out of commission. At least now you can continue on. Someone needs to kill that vespling."

"Gabby, no. There's got to be another way."

She went quiet for a moment. A gentle breeze moved though the dark and twisted around the trees all around them. Then she said, "You're right, Jim. I shouldn't have asked you to shoot me. I'm sorry."

He felt a huge wave of relief. He could have never shot her. He didn't know how they were going to move forward from here, but he would figure it out.

"I have my handgun," she said. "I can do it myself."

"What?"

"It's better this way. When they find my body, they'll see I did it myself. It won't implicate you."

"No, no, no." He was trying frantically to analyze his way out of this, to evaluate the available information and come to a different conclusion. This was not an acceptable outcome. There must be another way.

"Look, Jim. I saw glimpses of that vespling back by the marsh. I saw what that thing did to Emmett, and to Minnie. I will not become one of them. Do you understand? Here is what you are going to do. You will take this impulse gun from me—you need it —and you will walk away from me. You will leave me here. You will find your daughter. You will kill that vespling. I will take care of myself."

There it was again, her authority and command. How was it

that even when she was lying on the ground, covered in toxic bee stings, with an injured leg, she still held so much power?

His head spun, thinking about that mouse that had gone from such a gentle little field mouse to such an angry monster, about the gen-mod raccoon that had attacked Ava, and about the destroyed bodies of Emmett and Minnie.

"Lewis said there's no cure," Gabby continued. "It's clear this is how it has to be. You have to do what I say. If you don't, you'll have two vesplings on your hands. That would put you, your daughter, and everyone else on this island in double the danger."

They sat in silence for a moment.

"Jim?" Gabby said. "You still there?"

"Yes. I'm here."

"I can feel it moving through me." Her voice sounded tired. "It feels, I don't know… cold. You better go. I don't know how long I'll have the strength to… to take care of myself."

It was like foulbrood, he thought suddenly. The infected bees had to die in order to save others in the vicinity. Sometimes drastic measures were the only way to stop a terrible thing from spreading. It was the right thing, he told himself. The facts all pointed in this direction, and she herself had requested it.

He stood and slowly walked over to her. When he reached her, he knelt down.

"Don't touch me," she said. "Don't."

"Okay. I won't." He looked at her. Her hair was pulled back in that practical ponytail she favored. She wore no makeup, as always. Even covered in bee stings, her olive skin and her dark eyes were as striking as ever. She was amazing. He took it in, all her beauty and her power.

"You know, Jim," she said. "If things had been different, when this was over, I was planning on asking you out on a date."

She laughed, and he laughed with her.

"You know what?" he said. "If you had done that, I definitely would have said yes."

She nodded. "That's good to know. Maybe in another world, but not this one. You take care, Jim Parker. I see great things for you."

"Goodbye, Gabby Martinez."

He stood. The monstrous trees seemed to lean in. The patches of moonlight glowed like silver wildflowers scattered across the ground around her. He picked up the impulse gun, slung the tanks on his back, and walked away.

As he was climbing the slope back up to the ridge, he could hear her talking quietly to herself. Was it a prayer? An attempt to gather courage? He would never know. By the time he was back at the top of the ridge, her voice had faded behind him. He paused for a moment, and suddenly he heard the gun discharge. It was a horrible, irrevocable crack, exploding up out of the darkness and echoing all around.

He paused and whispered. "God bless you, Gabby."

## 65

LEWIS WAS startled awake by Deputy Gabby's voice coming in over the police radio. It sounded urgent. He'd fallen asleep at his desk with his half-finished gin and tonic nearby. Now he sat up and listened.

"Deputy Gabby Martinez here," she said. "I am in Catmull's Thicket. I've just fallen into a hive of gen-mod bees, and I've been stung."

His attention sparked. Even though he'd just been drifting towards sleep, he was now fully alert. Not another hive. Anything, but not another hive.

"These bees are toxic," Deputy Gabby continued, speaking directly to central dispatch. "They cause a full body metamorphosis. I've destroyed this hive, and I will sort out my immediate situation, but something must be done."

Thank God, Lewis thought. She already destroyed the hive. He waited for her next words, but she paused. He could hear her breathing. She must be in significant pain. Sato had said it was agonizing—much worse than the usual sharp, burning pain at the sting sites. Before Sato had fallen unconscious, he had said it felt like there were razor blades in his veins.

"There is at least this one beehive in Catmull's Thicket," Deputy Gabby said now. "And that likely means there are more. You have to evacuate the island immediately, for the safety of all concerned. These hives must be eradicated, and the gen-mod creature that's currently out here must be killed. Jim Parker knows how to do it. He's hunting it now. Hadley Agritech has a poison that will kill it, and a kind of spray gun. They know everything. Talk to Brad Kelly and Lewis Wilson."

The sound of his own name coming across the police radio felt like a gut punch.

He heard Gabby take a long, slow breath, and then she said, "Tell my mother and father I love them."

The radio went silent.

Lewis threw his glass across the room, where it shattered against the wall. Brad had failed. Not only had he made the mistake that triggered all of this, but he'd failed to clean it up. How could he have ever trusted him? How could he have missed any of the *Apis tiffiana* out there? If Gabby had been stung, if there were more hives, she was right. The risk was huge. How had those bees spread so quickly? How?

Suddenly everything became very clear. He knew what he had to do. He should have done it a long time ago.

He was going to have to call Cavanaugh.

66

JIM CONTINUED along the ridgeline that encircled Catmull's Thicket. The land was flat to his left and sloped down to his right. The ridgeline was clear, and he was able to move here more quickly.

He walked as quietly as possible. He came across no one. The rifle felt awkward over his shoulder, and it kept sliding down his arm. The tanks from the impulse gun were heavy. Why had Gabby insisted she carry these tanks with her injured leg? He kept thinking of that gunshot, of her in the darkness below him. He pressed on for a few minutes, but then he stopped, overcome by emotion.

He sat down on the ground and held his head in his hands. Gabby was gone. That strong, incredible, kind woman was gone. The world was overwhelmingly dangerous. Even quiet places like Gull Island were full of an underlying terror. There was no safety anywhere. People he loved, even people he decided he might be able to love, they all disappeared. His mind kept going back to Ava. Where was she? He forced himself to stand, and he began walking along the ridgeline once again. He took long, deep breaths. He moved forward. He had to.

When he thought he must be about midway between Stone Lake and Indian Point, he turned and descended down the slope. His feet slipped on the steeply angled forest floor. Rotting wood and organic litter slid out from underneath him and threatened to send him tumbling down. In this way he moved in a half-walk and half-slide down into the tangled blackness at the center of Catmull's Thicket.

Although the moon was shining, it was occasionally hidden by cloud, and the canopy here was especially thick. It was so dark along the flat land at the bottom of the basin that he could barely see a foot in front of his face. The light from the headlamp seemed to be absorbed by the night. He tripped on roots and decomposing branches.

The trees loomed all around him—tall, concentrated, and dense. This basin had never been cleared during Michigan's logging boom of the late 1800s—probably due to the difficult access. As a result, it was like going back in time, seeing what Michigan would have looked like before the woods were cleared. Some of these trees were more than 400 years old. It was a place of memory, a place of the past.

Here the beech and maple trees of Stone Lake were joined by conifers—white pine, red pine, and hemlock. Lofty branches formed a cooling canopy above him, causing the air to feel strangely chilled. Dead trees remained amongst the living, some still standing, while others had fallen and were at various stages of decomposition. Rough, woody debris was scattered everywhere, along with a fine blanket of pine needles. Broken tree trunks stood like grave markers. Some appeared twisted and hunched, like creatures in the shadows.

Catmull's Thicket was different to every other patch of old-growth forest Jim had seen in Michigan—although admittedly, old-growth forests in the region were few and far between. Usually, their thick canopies stopped seedling growth, and over time that led to an empty understory that was easily passable.

Here, however, the compact nature of the trees and the large number of downed trunks and branches meant that the entire place had become a complex maze, with one obstruction after another.

Although these woods were fascinating in their own strange way, he found them cold and dark, dank and foreboding. A shiver ran across his back. There was a reason he'd always avoided this place. But Ava was here, somewhere. At least he hoped she was here, so he continued forward. It was still deeply troubling that he'd lost her trail back at the marsh. Had she turned off and headed somewhere else? As he walked, he made a small prayer that he hadn't come all this way for nothing.

He realized then he didn't actually care about killing the vespling. He just wanted to find Ava and take her away from this island.

He passed by more fallen trees, more rotting branches on the ground. After moving through one particularly tight, dark space, he saw a contorted shape in his peripheral vision. Was it a body? His stomach dropped. He turned and shone his headlamp directly onto it. It was gray and bent. His eyes adjusted and his thinking cleared. It was just another rotting branch.

The shadows and the chill were playing with his imagination. He took a deep breath and tried to concentrate. He was here to find a cabin, but it was difficult and exhausting to move through this thicket with a dual tank system strapped to his back—not to mention carrying an impulse gun and keeping the rifle shouldered. Gabby was right. He should have left the rifle at home. In every direction more trees and more downed trunks blocked the way, knotted and chaotic. It was like walking through a strange, tangled labyrinth.

If only a wide gap would open up, exposing the cabin. But that never came. This place was frustrating and confusing. He tried to move in a straight line, but the force of the disordered woods turned his path in directions he hadn't planned for.

After what felt like a very long time, he saw something between two trees—a number of wooden trunks stacked vertically, about thirty feet away. It seemed too orderly to be by chance.

As he got closer, it became clear that what he was looking at was the wall of the cabin. He was approaching it from the side. The dense woods grew right up to the edge of the cabin, as though the trees themselves were trying to crowd the structure out and push it away. When he finally stepped out of the tangled forest, he was close enough to touch that rough log wall. The wood was strangely cool. Ava would be inside sleeping safely. He was counting on it.

The cabin itself was squat and long, and it appeared barely tall enough for a fully grown man to be able to stand up inside. The old trunks that made up the wall seemed as though they might come tumbling down any minute. At the corners, the logs hadn't been cut cleanly; the ends were angled and uneven just past the saddle notches that held them together. This building was not made by someone who cared about order and precision.

There was no window on this side, so he walked toward what he thought was the front. He passed a path to an outhouse and then came to a very small clearing around the entrance to the cabin. A cold fire pit lay in the center of the open space, with a few logs for benches.

The door was made of broad, weathered planks of wood. A carved wooden sign to the left of the door read, "Benson Cabin Keep Out."

He took his hand off the foregrip of the impulse gun and knocked. The door sounded thick. There was no response from inside. A small window was positioned to the left of the door, but the curtains were pulled. He called out, "Ava? Are you in there?" Again, no response.

There was a padlock latch on the door, but the padlock itself was lying on the ground. The cabin was unlocked. He reached for the door handle.

That was when he saw the beehive, just to the right of the door. He froze. It was an external hive, nestled above him in the eave, directly under the shallow pitch of the gabled roof. Curving forms of exposed honeycomb hung down in orderly, parallel rows. Some of the comb was broken, as though something had been pushed against it. Thousands of bees moved slowly across the surface. He held his breath.

In the light of his headlamp he could see them clearly. These bees were gray. *Apis tiffiana.* The bright light had begun to unsettle them, and they were quickly becoming active. He reached up to his headlamp and hit the switch which turned the light from white to red. Bees couldn't see red light. They didn't have a photoreceptor for it.

He watched the gray bees crawling across the surface of the hive for a moment, studying them. In so many ways, it behaved like a normal hive. Then he slowly and calmly stepped back from the porch and turned away from the hive to breathe out. He looked to see what was around him.

He would need an escape route if he was going to destroy this hive.

67

IN THE RED glow from the headlamp, the thick, tangled trees appeared like a scene from hell. Jim spotted a gap behind him, which led to a path that went straight into the woods heading south. There. That was how he would escape.

He was going to have to run quickly, so he had to unburden himself. He slid the shoulder strap of his Winchester down his arm and set the rifle on the ground at the edge of the clearing. He unclipped the waist pack and set that down too. Then he backed up along the narrow path as far as he could, still carrying the impulse gun, keeping a direct line of sight to the exposed beehive.

What had Brad said? It shoots fifty feet. He backed up farther, wanting as much distance as possible. He couldn't risk getting stung. The red light didn't travel very far, and the beehive quickly became obscured by shadow in the overhang of the roof.

He had to remain calm. His father's voice came to him, that old expression. *Check yourself.* He took a breath, relaxed the muscles in his arm, and pulled back the black valve. It hissed. The now familiar V-shaped stream of liquid trickled out the front of the gun as the front reservoir filled. He held the grips tightly. When it was ready, he raised the gun to aim, and he pulled the trigger.

An intense boom burst out into the silence of the dark night, and a powerful recoil drove the butt of the gun deep into his shoulder. A burst of necarichlor, spreading nearly six feet wide, shot forward in a violent and misty explosion, catching the red glow of his headlamp as though it were smoke born of fire. His senses became heightened. Everything seemed to slow. The strange cloud churned as it hurtled through the air, moving toward the dark cabin with the force of inevitability until it hit the beehive. There was a thump and rattle and the sound of shattering glass.

In the aftermath, a trail of mist hung in the air before him, catching the light and making a line that seemed to connect him to the cabin like a long, red umbilical cord. His shoulder throbbed from the recoil. Even as he pulled the top valve back a second time to reload the reservoir, he could hear the bees buzzing in anger. He aimed again and shot. Another great cloud hurtled forward, making another clean hit. The gray mass of bees rose and swarmed, looking for the source of the attack.

The bees were coming for him. He had to get out of here, and he knew he wouldn't make it with these tanks on his back. He remembered Gabby falling, hindered by the burden. He bent down, clumsily threw off the tanks, and dropped the impulse gun at the side of the path. In his haste, he kicked the gun as he ran away from the cabin.

The light of his headlamp bobbed as he rushed forward down the path. Tree trunks flashed by, bathed in red. The trail tapered quickly and soon disappeared in the tangled woods, but he kept going. He jumped over fallen branches. He moved around trees. He could hear the swarm behind him.

Finally he found a low space under a large, fallen trunk, and he crawled in. The sounds of violent buzzing filled the woods. Breathing through his t-shirt, he huddled in the glowing red darkness. The force of the two clouds he'd just shot had surprised him. There was so much power in that impulse gun.

After a while, the buzzing began to fade, and then finally it died completely. He waited longer, just to make sure they were all dead. The fact that he'd just come across a second *Apis tiffiana* hive in Catmull's Thicket terrified him. Had Brad not come down into the thicket? Had he assumed the space was too dark and cold for bees? Or had he just failed to find them in this obscure and twisted maze? Jim's worst fear seemed entirely possible. There could be even more of these hives out here.

When he finally crawled out from under the tree, the night had changed. The mist had cleared. Everything was quiet again, except for something in the distance. The sound of slow steps—the ground crunching, leaves whispering. Was that Chuck and Kylie again? He was angry and frustrated. He wanted Chuck gone.

Then he heard something else.

*Hmmm. Hmmm. Cli-click.*

It wasn't Chuck. It was the vespling. But which direction was it coming from? The entire thicket was engulfed by that horrible acoustic threat. He just wanted to find his daughter, but now he was in imminent danger.

The impulse gun. He needed it. He dashed as quickly as he could back to where the path had tapered out, back towards the cabin, but when he bent down to pick up the weapon, he couldn't find it. He remembered kicking it when he'd run past. It must have slid it into the undergrowth. He reached into a tangle of branches just off the path.

The hum and the click were getting louder.

His fingers touched the gun. There it was. But as he went to lift it, something held it back. It was tangled somehow. He got down on his hands and knees and stuck his head into the under-growth to look closer. He tugged. The black hoses that connected the twin tanks to the gun itself were caught on something.

He glanced around quickly, trying to figure out where the vespling was coming from, but the sound was reverberating off the trees. It seemed to be coming at him from everywhere.

Although his hand remained on the gun, he couldn't pull it out. The urge to yank it free was almost overwhelming, but he was afraid of breaking the hoses. If he broke this weapon he'd have no defense. He'd die before he found Ava.

He got down on his belly, and he reached deep into the twisted branches. Where was the gun caught? Panic filled his chest, and his breathing became shallow and quick. He tried to focus, tried not to think of the approaching vespling. He followed the line of the first hose with his fingers from the gun to the tank, trying to feel for where it was snagged.

There were two footsteps to his left. He slowly turned and looked up.

Standing less than ten feet away, in full view in the center of the narrow path, was the vespling. The red glow of his headlamp illuminated it completely. It was tilting its head back, raising its nose, and scanning the woods with jerky movements.

The face, oddly, seemed human. But there was no hair at all. It was broad-shouldered and muscular. Black stripes moved down its sides. Three long, thick, spiky growths sprouted along the underside of its forearms—they looked like the spiny structures on the legs of some insects. Its hands appeared human, but its fingers were tipped with long, black claws. From his close proximity on the ground, he could see that the three long, spiny growths that sprouted along the underside of its forearms also ran down the back of its calves. He saw the human feet, with claws.

The creature glanced down. Its eyes were shaped like a human's, but there were no whites, no irises, no pupil. They were entirely black and yet somehow also iridescent, strangely catching the red light. It held its lower jaw open wide. A pair of black mandibles glistened inside an otherwise human mouth—snapping violently while the jaw stayed open, still sounding out that acoustic threat. The clicking noise resonated inside the creature's mouth, mixing with the deep-throated hum that sounded like a determined, angry growl.

It was thoroughly disturbing to see something that was so human and yet so profoundly not human at all. This horrible creature somehow imperfectly resembled an actual human being. So much so, in fact, that looking at it gave him a strangely familiar feeling of recognition, and at the same time it filled him with a deep and overwhelming sense of revulsion and horror.

Jim realized then that it wasn't looking at him at all. It was looking around, almost as though it could smell him but not see him. It was dark here. Was it the red light? Not only bees but wasps were unable to see red light. The vespling was crepuscular. It preferred dusk and dawn. That meant it needed low levels of light but didn't do well in complete darkness. If it couldn't detect the red light at all, then it must be struggling to see. This was Jim's only advantage. But he needed the impulse gun.

He tugged on the gun, and a branch snapped. The vespling jerked its head and looked in his direction. He tugged again, but the gun still wasn't free. Then, the creature pounced.

Jim let go of the gun and rolled away, but a clawed hand grabbed his leg and pulled, digging into his ankle. A sharp, piercing pain shot up his leg. He pulled his other foot back, aiming to land a solid kick at the creature's face, but its reaction was lightning quick. As his foot shot out, the vespling grabbed it and stopped his kick cold. While it hadn't been able to see him ten feet away in the darkness, it seemed able to track every movement directly in front of its face.

It held on to both of his feet and began pulling him toward it effortlessly, as if it was dragging a rag doll.

68

AS SOON AS it had tugged Jim close enough, the vespling pounced on top of him again. Its mouthparts snapped eagerly and came directly at him. He twisted to the side. Pain careened through his body.

The repulsive mandibles were deep in his side. Its arms were wrapped around his waist. He reeled in pain and shock. One of the long spines on the creature's forearms pierced his thigh. He swung his right arm forward and then thrust back with his elbow, ramming it into the vespling's forehead. The mandibles sank deeper into his skin. It was incredibly strong.

Panicked now, he swung his arm forward a second time, thrusting it as hard as he possibly could, drawing from a well of strength deep inside him in spite of his overwhelming pain and fear. This time his elbow connected with the creature's eye.

The mandibles unclasped, freeing him, and he kicked and clambered across the ground. A terrible agony exploded inside him as he struggled to stand. He was cut badly. His headlamp had fallen off. The impulse gun still lay tangled on the ground somewhere near the writhing vespling, but he could no longer see where. The only thing he could do was to escape, to run.

Patches of moonlight lit the path as he sprinted away, pain flaring with every step. The vespling wasn't far behind him, and it was fast. Jim darted across the small clearing, crunching dead bees under his boots. The hive above the cabin door was silent and dead. When he pushed on the door, it protested on rusty hinges, but a dark maw opened in front of him. The vespling was already coming across the clearing. Jim scuttled inside and slammed the door behind him.

There was no lock on the door handle, but in the gloom he saw a door bolt. He frantically slid it across to secure the door. The room was dark behind him. A forceful bang sounded out from the other side of the door, and the entire cabin seemed to shake. The vespling was out there, pounding noisily, and this bolt wouldn't hold for long.

He saw the shadow of something in the darkness nearby. It was an old wooden trunk on the floor. He ran over and he heaved it, large and heavy, across the rough floor planks to block the door. He stepped back. The bolt strained and the trunk jostled as the pounding on the door continued. A dreadful, low growl rumbled from outside.

On top of the trunk someone had left a small, battery-powered camping lantern, and he scrambled to turn it on. White light cast shadows around a messy room. He put his hand on his side. It was warm with blood, and a piercing pain started to grow. His ankle was burning and bloody too. He pushed the pain away, like he did everything else.

Outside, the vespling expelled air with a hacking sound. Was it aggravated by residual necarichlor on the hive?

The pounding stopped. There was total silence for a moment, followed by the sound of more bees crunching underfoot. It seemed to be walking away. Or was it going around the cabin to another entrance?

Jim looked around the room for another way in. The space behind him was such a dark mess that at first it was hard to make sense of anything. Broken equipment was strewn about everywhere—busted pieces of a gas camping stove, half of a fishing pole, a cracked cast iron pot. He held up the small lantern. The light wasn't strong, and it barely managed to illuminate the room. Shadows hid in the corners.

The cabin seemed to consist of one large, rectangular space. There were two bunk beds at the back, pushed against the side walls and piled with clothes. A round table stood in the middle of the room. There were only two small windows—one in the front, above a short kitchen counter, and one on the back wall between the bunk beds. There was no other entrance.

And there was no sign of Ava. Even in the midst of his fear and pain, this sudden realization broke his heart. Where was she? Where was his daughter? He felt lightheaded and unsteady. How had everything disintegrated so much since he woke that morning —just four days ago now—and learned that someone had torched his hives at Connor Davies' blueberry farm? Now Ava was not here. Was she safe? Where would he look for her next? He couldn't lose her. He simply could not lose her.

Outside, the footsteps continued to crunch slowly, and he suddenly realized there was broken glass across the countertop under the front window. The small front window was broken. Was that the noise he heard when he shot the impulse gun? The footsteps came closer, moving in an almost calculated way, and then they stopped outside that broken window. It was going to try to come in that way.

He stepped back, set the lantern on the table, and looked around for something to fight with, when a hideous gray claw shot through the open window and ripped out the curtain. The bald, gray head of the vespling jerked forward, and it looked inside. Jim could see its dazzling, dark eyes scanning the room.

Then it opened its mouth and to his surprise and horror, it spoke.

"Leave us," it said. "Alone."

Jim's stomach dropped. How was it speaking? What was it, exactly? Deep inside that hideous creature, just how much humanity was left? He stepped back, and his foot slid across the floor.

The vespling turned, and it looked directly at him. "Leave us. Alone," it repeated, this time seething with rage.

The voice was similar to the shriek Jim had heard behind his house—two noises at once, a human voice infused with metal on stone. This time, however, instead of a wild shriek the voice held a man's seething baritone. The words themselves came out chopped and halted, like someone speaking with a tracheotomy, breathlessly.

There was a wooden bat lying on the floor next to the round table, and Jim limped over to grab it. A sharp stab of pain rose from his right ankle, where the creature had grabbed him. He held the bat in front of him as he stepped to the window. Gritting his teeth from the pain in his side, he swung the bat and smashed the vespling as hard as he possibly could, hitting it right in the face.

It screeched loudly and jerked back out of the window, bringing its claws up to its strangely human nose. The thing was angry now, and it rushed again toward the small opening. It was crawling up and getting ready to come inside. Its head poked fully through the window, and its shoulders looked like they were going to fit through.

Jim turned and squared his body toward the creature, ready to beat it back a second time. The dark mandibles were opening wide and snapping.

Just as he was about to swing the bat, a gunshot cracked outside in the darkness. There was yelling. He could hear a voice. It sounded like Kylie.

"It's here, Chuck! Over here!" she yelled.

The gun went off again, and the vespling let out an ear-splitting howl, as though it had been hit in the back. It jerked away from the window and turned around to face the other way.

Kylie's panicked voice came from outside. "Oh, shit."

There was the sound of footsteps running, and the vespling seemed to follow in pursuit. It was gone.

Jim thought first of Kylie. She had no idea that conventional guns were useless against that monster. He had to help her. He had to get back to the impulse gun. But could he go out there without getting shot himself? He thought of what had happened to Gabby. Chuck was out there; Kylie had called out to him. That idiot was prone to shooting indiscriminately.

It didn't matter. He had to risk it. He stepped toward the door, ready to do whatever he could to fight off the vespling.

Just as he reached down to move the trunk, a hellish, muffled scream rose—not from outside, but from inside. It came from the very back of the cabin.

Something was in here with him.

## 69

JIM TURNED AROUND. The light from the small lantern on the table was just not bright enough, and he squinted into the gloom. He looked for movement. Had something climbed in the back?

The glass on the back window was intact, and the window was shut. He could see no movement. Nothing had come in that way. He could still hear the vespling outside—that terrible hum and click. It sounded like it was moving away from the cabin, away from him. It was hunting Kylie and Chuck.

The scream rose again from the back of the cabin. It was still muffled somehow, but it carried such jarring tones that his head spun from the dual reverberations—metal grinding on stone and the primal shriek of a dangerous beast. He squinted in the dark. All thought of what was happening outside left his mind as he became consumed by this new, more immediate threat.

Staring intently toward the back of the cabin, he continued to grip the bat. He was absolutely terrified. He couldn't see well, and there was something here. His rifle was out in the clearing, and the impulse gun was tangled at the edge of the path. This pathetic bat was all he had. He grabbed the small lantern and carried it with him—the bat in one hand, the lantern in the other. Then he stepped around the table, trying to see what was hiding here. On the left side of the room, rabbit and beaver pelts hung from the ceiling. On his right, a wood burner stood against the wall. He could see nothing moving, nothing that looked like a threat.

He began to approach the bunks at the back of the cabin. Was it under a bed? Where the hell was it? The lower mattresses were piled high with blankets, jackets, and other bits of clothing. At the very back of the room, against the far wall, he could see a crudely built wooden nightstand cluttered with hunting paraphernalia: fishing lures, a deer call, and a hunting knife. But there was no creature. Was it not in here? Had the scream actually come from outside the back window?

He started moving toward the nightstand to grab the knife, but before he got there something jolted wildly on the bottom bunk to his immediate right. He turned. Another quick shake caused the pile of clothes on the bed to fall to the floor, revealing a strange, yellowish-brown shape. It was bumpy, vaguely oblong, and almost the length of the bed. The surface looked like a massive, crusty scab. It was already splitting down the center, and two gray hands were poking through. They were covered in a viscous liquid, like a clear mucus. The digits unfurled, revealing black claws at the fingertips.

Jim became instantly transfixed. He was watching the birth of a vespling. He'd never seen anything like it, at least not on this scale. Of course, he'd seen first-hand as countless bees had chewed their way out of their cells, watching patiently, and he'd seen monarch butterflies break free from cocoons, but never before had he witnessed the emergence of anything this substantial, this portentous. It was truly miraculous.

He thought of the pupal stage of honeybees, of how pupa chewed through their brood cell cap and emerged as callow bees —newly hatched with a soft cuticle that took time to harden.

They didn't leave the cell for a few hours, and in that state they were vulnerable.

He could kill this creature easily, soon, but he hesitated. Not now. Not yet. He was rapt. It felt like a discovery. He dropped the bat, set the lantern on the nightstand, and started taking pictures with his phone.

The creature's arms pushed out and reached up toward its head, pulling at a large piece of brownish crust on its face. The mouth looked human until it opened, exposing its black mandibles. It took a hungry bite of the casing in its hand. As it chewed and swallowed, it writhed. The casing around its midsection cracked in places and fell away. Suddenly it let out another horrible, discordant shriek. This time it wasn't muffled, and Jim leaned away from the deafening, mind-boggling noise. It was the cry of a nightmarish newborn.

The entire top half of the vespling had emerged now, but its legs were still encased. It folded its arms across its chest, as though it were cold. It was bald and naked. Hair and fabric appeared to be stuck to the inside of the pieces of pupal casing, which were now scattered across the bed.

Jim leaned forward. Its eyes were closed. It seemed to be sleeping or tired or confused. Its skin was moist and glistening, and it was a much paler gray than the vespling he'd just seen outside. But it had the same two black lines moving down its sides, the same claws on its hands, the same spines down the backs of its forearms. It opened its mouth again, and its mandibles closed—not quickly in aggression, but slowly, like it was stretching. Its hands opened and the claws gleamed.

He remembered the feel of the other vespling's claw on his ankle, and he looked down at the blood around his foot. Those claws and those mandibles were shockingly sharp. The thought shook him out of his scientific trance. He reached toward the hunting knife on the nightstand and picked it up.

This creature was amazing, but he had to kill it. It was dangerous. He quickly lunged forward with the knife, aiming for the chest. As he did, he felt the pain from his earlier wounds flash through his side and his ankle.

Suddenly the creature opened its eyes and rolled away from the wall, toward him. The knife connected with its left arm instead of its chest. The blade cut easily, slicing through pliable skin. On impact, the vespling emitted another horrible, dual-toned scream. It shoved his arm as it screamed, and his forward momentum caused him to fall onto its mucus-covered body. Already its legs had broken free of the casing, and it rammed one of its bony knees directly into his groin, sending him reeling and tumbling to the floor.

For a moment, Jim was incapacitated and entirely unable to move out of a defenseless fetal position. Doubled over and writhing in pain, he felt like he was going to vomit. Everything hurt. His chest was wet with slime. He scurried across the floor, backing away from the bed. He managed to get up on his hands and knees to look at the creature.

It was not in an attack position. It lay on the bed, breathing heavily, its arm secreting an amber blood. He looked around for the knife but couldn't see it. There wasn't much time. He jumped onto the bed, wrapping his arms around the creature's throat, and he squeezed. It reached up and grabbed his hands. It tried to kick him, but he avoided its knees and feet, lying on top of it and pinning it down. It was still weak. Horrible, wet choking sounds came from its throat as it gasped for air.

In that moment, everything seemed very far away, as though Jim weren't actually there in that room, as though he were watching out of someone else's eyes. His entire being was focused on crushing this throat, strangling this thing. He couldn't let this monster do what the other one had already done. He couldn't let more people die.

So when the words came out, he was shocked and confused. Its voice was gasping and barely audible. But then the words came again, perfectly clear.

"No, please. Papa."

## 70

JIM JUMPED BACK. It wasn't possible. He looked at the hairless creature in front of him—the inhumanly gray body, the black claws on its hands and feet, the mouth opening and closing, exposing those mandible-like teeth and the pink, human tongue just beyond.

Only then did he see the beaded bracelet wrapped improbably around the callow vespling's ashen wrist. He looked closely. The creature was watching him. He could see clearly the black letters on square, silver beads. *CIAO LIAR.*

His stomach churned, and he was both confused and horrified. He took several steps backwards, shaking his head, trying desperately to retreat from this stark reality. Inside him things shifted. It felt as though suddenly there was a dam forming deep within him —a massive wall rising in order to hold back some horrible, unthinkable thing.

"No, no, no," he said.

On the bed, on either side of the gray body, he could see fragments of fabric attached to the insides of the broken pupal casing. It seemed as if bits of clothing had disintegrated and become stuck to it, as if broken down by a kind of acid. He now recognized the leg of her favorite jeans and a piece of that old plaid shirt she wore. When he saw what was now clearly her purple hair, loose and stuck to the casing, he recoiled. Only the thick, black wire of the bracelet and the metal of those lettered beads remained on her body. Only those solid things had withstood what must have been a brutal environment inside that cocoon.

No. He refused it again. This was not her. It could not be her. Even as he spoke his next words he refused to believe them.

"Ava?" he cried. "Is that you?"

It didn't respond. He stepped back even more, as though by further moving away from it, he could change things, could undo whatever had happened. That was when he saw the bright purple backpack on the floor next to the bed, not far from those terrible clawed feet. He saw the cartoon unicorn holding an ice-cream cone. And there were the hiking boots—*her* hiking boots— arranged neatly on the floor, as though someone had taken them off and placed them carefully at the side of the bed.

His scientific brain reeled, trying desperately to ignore the evidence in front of him, grasping for some other explanation. It could not be true. The dam inside him grew higher and thicker as he shut out the obvious. He was not letting these thoughts in.

The creature opened its horrible mouth then, its eyes closed as though talking in a half sleep. "You cut. Me. Why did. You cut. Me?"

It wasn't quite her voice, but at the same time, it was. Slightly more metallic. With a halting, breathless cadence. But he could tell. He knew her voice.

"I'm sorry," he said, crying now, that terrible dam cracking slightly, the force and power of everything he feared looming tall on the other side, threatening to drown him. He stared at the thing that was lying before him, this thing that he loved. There was mucus on his hands from when he'd tried to choke her. It smelled foul. Small pieces of that dam were breaking away, crumbling. This was his daughter. He loved her, and he was afraid of her. He wanted to run from her, and he wanted to protect her. He was so deeply disoriented. Everything he felt seemed to cancel out every other thing he felt, and he was left immobilized.

"Ava, Ava," he said. He was an empty shell speaking. There were no other words to be said. He repeated her name again and again. "Ava."

Its arms were shifting erratically from side to side, almost twitching, moving much more quickly than his daughter ever would. Perhaps it was not her. But that was her face. Above all, he recognized her face, so much like her mother's, even now, with all those revolting changes. There was no doubt. There was the strong line of her jaw. There were her intense cheekbones.

Even the shape of the body looked like hers—in spite of the spines that ran down her forearms and calves, in spite of the black stripes down her sides and the dark claws on her hands and feet. Those were his daughter's slender shoulders. These were her thin legs.

"Where," she said, and she took another breath. "Where is. Eddie?"

He didn't know how he had the presence of mind to answer the question. He felt like an automaton. "He's not here," he said.

She moaned. "He has. Changed," she whispered. "He is." She looked down at her hands, turning her wrists and gazing at her claws. Her head fell back on the bed. "He is. Like me."

Inside Jim, thin cracks split and grew. He thought about the hive above the door. Eddie had come to the cabin. Of course he'd been stung. Of course Eddie was the vespling. How had he not seen that before? Had Ava always known? Had she suspected? He remembered how she'd called out to the creature in the backyard. *Go away! Go back!*

The realization hit him now like a quiet thud. A small, smooth stone thrown at that colossal dam. It suddenly made sense. Of course the vespling had come to their back acre. Eddie had been looking for Ava.

As he stared at her, he ran through the events in his head, trying to understand how this had happened to her, how she had changed. Eddie wouldn't have been able to sting her.

Tears trickled down his cheeks as he made the connection.

"You were stung by the hive above the door, weren't you?"

For the first time since emerging from the pupal casing, she looked directly at him. Those were not Ava's eyes. Even in the murkiness of this room, he could see that they were black and shimmering, like the other vespling's eyes. They were rainbowed oil slicks on dark water.

Then he noticed three shiny black spots on her forehead. They formed an upside-down triangle, and they had the same iridescent sheen as her eyes. He recognized these spots as ocelli, the light-sensitive organs found on the head of many insects. A shudder ran up his spine. So much of her was Ava, but so much of her was not.

"Eddie," she said, haltingly. "He did it."

"Eddie did what? He stung you?" This made no sense. Lewis himself had said that only the female vesplings could sting, just as with bees and wasps.

"No," Ava said. "He held me. Against the bees. He pushed me. Into the hive. He wanted me to change. He said he wanted. To be with me."

Jim froze for a brief moment, stunned, and then the shock morphed and grew. Eddie had done this. Eddie had done this to Ava. Eddie had *willingly* done this. The cracks across the dam inside of him became thicker until the trickle turned into a heaving, angry churn. He knew this feeling. He'd felt this before, this rising and vicious rage. It was the same, uncontrollable fury he'd felt at the unknown man who'd hurt Sarah.

Close behind that surge of anger, as before, came a horrible wave of guilt. He'd failed Ava, just as he'd failed Sarah. He'd failed to protect his daughter as he'd failed to protect his wife. It had happened a second time. Different, of course, horribly different.

But still, somehow, the same. What good was he if he could not protect the ones he loved? What good was his knowledge, his intellect, his entire being, if everyone he loved experienced unimaginable horrors he was helpless to prevent?

The dam inside him broke then. As he stood there looking at Ava—it was Ava, it was truly Ava—everything suddenly gushed forward in a massive torrent. He began to scream. There were no words coming out, only primal shrieks and wails that were caught up together with tears and cries of sadness and loss. His daughter, poor Ava. Poor, sweet Ava.

He ran to the table, yelling unconsolably, and he grabbed the wooden edge and flipped it into the air, along with everything that was on it. Maps and compasses and spoons and bowls spun and tumbled to the ground, shattering and clanging. The table landed on its side and rolled. He looked around fitfully. He felt closed in, trapped, and completely impotent.

"I will find him," he shouted, turning to Ava.

She was leaning up on her elbows in the bed, trying to prop herself up, clearly startled by his fury and rage.

"I will kill him," he said.

If he'd ever wanted to kill the vespling, that feeling was nothing compared to what he felt now. In fact, it wasn't the vespling he wanted to kill at all. It was *Eddie*, the monster who had done this to his daughter.

He wanted all of this to be over, as before, but his driving motivation had fundamentally changed. It was no longer about protecting Ava. It was too late for that. Now what he wanted was vengeance.

"No," Ava said firmly. "You. Will not." She took a deep breath and stood, looking at him with a gaze so firm that it seemed to demand submission. Her black eyes shimmered powerfully in the light. This was not his daughter. There was a new fierceness in her. She had never looked at him like this.

"He did this to you!"

"I said no," she answered, firmly, but then wobbled, as if the effort of standing had been too much, and she sat back down on the bed, exhausted.

Jim thought of the damp, white, tousled look of newly emerged bees, before their exoskeleton and wings hardened. Ava was so vulnerable right now.

"Are you okay?" he said softly.

She laid back and held her arm across her stomach. "I am. So hungry." She reached for the pupal casing, broke off a piece, and began to eat it.

He cringed, completely revolted at the sight of her eating that crusty scab-like thing. "Is Eddie the only vespling?" he asked, looking away for just a moment. "Are there others?"

She shook her gruesome head slowly and she swallowed. "He said. He was. The only one."

"So he killed Minnie and Emmett, and those kids in the woods."

"Yes. He didn't want to. He said he was. Hungry."

A terrible banging started then, and Jim jumped. It was coming from the cabin door. The vespling was back. Eddie was back. Urgent fists were pounding on the wood. But something sounded different this time. It was not as loud, not as strong.

Then the pounding was followed by a voice—a fully human voice. It was a man screaming urgently.

"Lemme in! I heard you, Jim! Let me in!"

It was Chuck Norman, and he was on the other side of that door.

71

JIM LOOKED OVER AT AVA, lying there on the bed, exposed, weak and unprotected. Chuck was yelling repeatedly outside. That noise was going to draw the vespling back, draw Eddie back.

Jim picked up the bat, walked over to the door and yelled, "Get out of here!"

"That thing's out here!" Chuck shouted, clearly panicked and afraid, pounding again. "Let me in!" The door bolt rattled.

Jim would have been angry with anyone who appeared in front of him right then. His anger was a blind animal, looking to pounce at anything that moved. The fact that it was Chuck Norman who appeared in this moment only made it worse.

He realized then that he'd never hated a man more than the way he hated Chuck. He loathed his pathetic combination of dishonesty, carelessness, and arrogance, and he was furious to have him getting in the way yet again. He thought of all the petty, ridiculous lies Chuck had spread about him since he'd arrived on the island. He thought of the irresponsible bullets Chuck had shot, injuring Gabby, later causing her to fall into a hive of deadly gen-mods, and ultimately leading to her death. And he thought again of Ava at the back of the room—vulnerable, grotesque Ava. He didn't know what to do about her. She was a monster. She was his daughter.

He knew only one thing. There was no way he was going to let Chuck Norman inside this cabin. He would sooner listen to the man get eaten alive on the other side of the door.

He yelled, "Go away!"

It went quiet outside for a moment, and there was the sound of footsteps and more bees crunching underfoot. Then suddenly the barrel of a shotgun jutted through the broken window, pointing directly at Jim.

Chuck growled, "Open that door, or I'll blow your head off."

"Well," Jim said, completely furious, "just climb right in." He clenched his fists around the bat, ready to swing at Chuck's head.

Chuck's face came closer to the window. "What? So you can take my gun as I'm squirming through this tiny opening? No way. Open the goddamn door."

The barrel was pointing directly at Jim, and even in his anger and rage Jim knew this wouldn't work. He had to get that gun away from Chuck and use it against him. He stepped to the door, slid the door bolt back, and pulled the wooden trunk back only slightly—just enough to create a small gap.

Chuck was already there. Jim could see his lopsided nose and long, red beard on the other side. He was wearing a denim shirt with the sleeves cut off, the "Lucky" tattoo on his right bicep exposed. He was gripping the shotgun tightly, and he was shaking.

"Lemme in now!" Chuck yelled, glancing over his shoulder at the clearing behind him. Beads of sweat on his brow glistened.

"Where's Kylie?" Jim asked through the gap.

"Out there." Chuck looked to the woods and creased his brow. "It went after her. Lemme in!"

"You *left* her?"

Chuck gave a small gesture of resignation.

Jim hadn't thought his opinion of Chuck could get any worse, but now cowardice and betrayal seemed to join Chuck's other character defects.

"But she's your friend," Jim said. "Your girlfriend, I hear." He wondered how a man could so easily walk away from someone he cared about when they were in desperate need.

"Just let me in!" Chuck's voice now took on a higher pitch. He was clearly panicked. Suddenly he shifted, and the end of his shotgun jutted through the opening, pointing directly at Jim's face. "Now!"

Jim stepped back, and Chuck heaved his shoulder against the door. The trunk slid a few more inches.

"Wait," Jim said. "There's something blocking the door. Let me move it. I'll let you in. Back up."

Chuck reluctantly did so. Jim shut the door and bolted it.

"Hey!" Chuck yelled.

"Just wait!" Jim yelled back, bending down and dragging the trunk away from the door. He felt its weight.

When he was young, he'd always thought his father was crazy, obsessively teaching him gun safety—everything from cleaning a gun to disarming someone who was threatening you with one. He'd been a reluctant pupil. Now, in this moment, he hoped he remembered how to do it. It required the other person to be careless and forget about safe distance. Fortunately, he already knew Chuck was careless.

He unbolted the door, but before Chuck had the chance to enter, Jim stepped forward quickly, blocking the way. Chuck looked confused and pointed the shotgun at him again, this time almost touching his chest with the barrel. Perfect.

Jim knew that he had to move fast. Chuck was frightened and impulsive and would shoot quickly. Jim swung his arm around, shoving the barrel of the gun away and grabbing the very end of it. Then, before Chuck knew what was happening, Jim reached out with his other hand to grab the body of the gun. With both hands, he quickly pushed up and rolled the gun at Chuck's face. The stock of the weapon slammed directly into his head.

Seconds later, Jim was holding the shotgun and aiming it at Chuck. He'd quickly stepped back to where Chuck couldn't grab it, and Chuck was a bit dazed.

"Don't shoot me," he said. His tone had changed. His power was gone. He was pleading.

For a moment Jim actually considered pulling the trigger. It would be so easy. His anger was pushing him to do it. He paused and took a deep breath. He checked himself. No. Shooting Chuck in cold blood would make him no better than the vespling, no better than Eddie.

"Get out of here," Jim said, his voice full of disgust. "Let's just see how lucky you really are."

"What the hell are you doing?" Chuck held his hands out in front of him, palms out as though they would stop the gunfire. He stepped forward.

"Back up or I'll kill you right here!"

Chuck took several steps back. "Please, just let me in. It's out there."

"Then you better run," Jim said. His resolve was hardened by his grief and his rage.

Chuck's eyes grew wide as he realized, with absolute horror, what Jim was doing. "You can't," he said. "You're a good man."

Jim laughed at how rich that was, coming from Chuck. He looked him in the eye and said, "And you're an asshole."

Chuck shook his head in disbelief. "I need my gun."

"This gun won't help you. Go." Then, losing patience, Jim pointed the gun into the air and fired off a warning shot while yelling at the top of his lungs. "Ruuun!"

Chuck flinched and turned, and then he took off, running into the dark and twisted woods.

72

AFTER STEPPING BACK into the cabin, Jim bolted the door and set Chuck's shotgun against the wall. He didn't need it. He needed the impulse gun.

He wanted desperately to kill the vespling. His head was spinning. He looked at his side. He was still losing a lot of blood.

Ava pushed herself up and asked in a weary voice, "Where is. Eddie?"

"I don't know," he said, abruptly, still trying to figure out if he was talking to his daughter or to something else. What was she now, really? How dangerous was she? He knew only one thing in this moment. He was going to find Eddie, and he was going to kill him.

He lifted his shirt. There were jagged lines from the vespling's mandibles. His ribs were the only thing that had stopped the bite from going deeper. He hoped the viral DNA wasn't infectious through bites.

"I'm going to find Eddie," he said to Ava.

"Bring him back," she said.

He didn't answer. He opened the door and walked out.

The clearing in front of the cabin was completely flooded with brilliant moonlight. The clouds had parted and the moon was bright. The trees at the edge of the clearing were monstrous and distorted, like gray shapes that were leering at him. Each one was an arm, or a leg, a torso. The night was quiet. There were no gunshots, no hum and click. Nothing. Eddie could be anywhere.

His mind was blind with rage. He crossed the clearing as quickly as he could, and then started down the path at the other side. He needed the impulse gun. The near-total blackness of the woods consumed him. He didn't care.

At the spot where he'd dropped the gun, he got down on his belly and sank both of his hands deep into the undergrowth. His anger focused him like a laser. He touched the gun, then felt the tanks. He found where the hoses came out and followed them with his fingers until he located the spot where they were caught on a gnarled branch. He quickly unhooked them. The weapon was free. He scrambled to slip the tanks on his back, gripped the gun firmly, and looked back toward the cabin.

He needed the advantage of surprise. He turned and went the other way, off the path, deeper into the woods. He climbed over several branches. A large, broken trunk rose in front of him, with a deep shadow in the center. He reached forward blindly. The trunk was entirely hollow. He nestled in the small space, tucking his arms and legs in tightly, the impulse tanks pushed up against his back and the gun against his chest. Eddie was bound to come back for Ava. He waited.

It didn't take long for that sound to rise out of the woods again. *Hmmm. Hmmm. Cli-click.*

At first, it seemed to be coming from somewhere behind him, but then it seemed to be coming from the right. The noise echoed all around. His head felt muddled from pain and the loss of blood, and he reached down to touch his wound.

Would Eddie smell his blood? Wasps had an incredible sense of smell. If vesplings did indeed share wasp genetics, then it was likely Eddie would be able to smell him from a great distance. Jim suddenly realized then that he couldn't simply stay here, hiding in this trunk. Eddie would find him. Then he would be trapped. The only way out of this was to surprise him and proactively attack.

Just then the humming and clicking sounds stopped. The night went quiet again. But there were no night birds calling—no owls, no whip-poor-wills, nothing. Eddie was still nearby.

Jim moved quietly, crawling away from the small area of shelter he'd found. He loosened his belt and tucked the impulse gun inside it. He needed both hands. He looked up into the trees.

The conifers here had tall and straight trunks with very few low boughs. They would be difficult to climb. But he saw a tall tree stump, next to a thick tree with high, solid branches. He stepped up onto it, using it like a kind of footstool so he could climb into the high branches of the thick tree. He reached out— the pain in his side piercing now—and pulled himself up.

He began scrambling upwards. A gnarled, dead branch under his left foot split in two, almost causing him to fall, but he quickly grabbed another branch and shifted his weight. One particularly large bough loomed above. It was roughly twenty-five or thirty feet above the ground, and it looked like it might hold him. Several smaller, thinner branches were the only way to get there. If he grabbed them close to the trunk, where they were thickest, they could take his weight.

He moved up one branch at a time, the pain in his side intensifying with every reach, grab, and pull. The heavy tanks on his back threatened to throw him off balance. By the time he made it to the large bough he was sweating heavily, partly out of exertion and partly out of pain. Then he straddled the branch, with his legs dangled down either side.

From here the woods looked peaceful. The moonlight caught the tops of the trees. Spots of silver hung in the branches. Looking down, everything became darker as less light made it through the thick canopy to reach the ground. He took several deep breaths and sat, balancing himself carefully. The rough bark of the tree pressed into his legs and backside. He touched his ribs and his hand came away a strange, blackish red in the moonlight. He was still bleeding badly. His head spun, and it took all of his focus to hang on.

*Hmmm. Hmmm. Cli-click.*

From below him in the woods, that terrible noise was rising again. He shifted his weight on the branch. Off to the left, he could just see the small clearing in front of the cabin. Ava was over there, what was left of her anyway. His head swam, and things became a blur.

They never found the man who attacked Sarah, and even now in this tree he still felt an overwhelming anger just knowing that the man had not yet been punished. He did, however, know who did this to Ava, who had held her against her will and changed her. He could not wait to kill him.

Clutching the impulse gun, he pulled back the black valve, and the V-shape stream trickled out as before. He cringed when it hissed, for Eddie might hear him. When the reservoir was filled, he clasped the valve in place, and he waited. His eyelids felt heavy. It was now after 3 a.m.

When he saw something gray cross the clearing, he knew he had him. Eddie was crouching down, then moving along the path, coming closer to where Jim was hidden. A gap through the branches revealed him pausing not far from where Jim was, looking around and smelling the air like an animal. Then he stepped off the path and walked through the maze of the woods, heading in Jim's direction. He came directly to the base of the tree, and he looked up.

Jim thought he was safe. That creature, Eddie, would never figure out how to get up here. The lower branches were too high. But it looked up again, simply reached out, grabbed onto the tree, and started to climb. It didn't need branches. Its claws dug into the bark.

The pain in Jim's side was so severe now that he could barely hold the gun and aim, but he knew he had no choice. Something in him overrode it—a deep awareness that this was his chance for revenge. As he balanced precariously on the branch, he leaned over to get a clear shot. He held the gun firmly—one hand on each grip, his right index finger on the trigger, the wide chrome barrel pointing down at the terrible gray thing that was climbing up toward him. His anger roiled and seethed. He took a deep breath, aimed, and pulled the trigger.

Once more, a great, churning cloud shot out, catching the moonlight this time. It shimmered down through the trees toward the target, churning like a small but powerful thunderstorm, appearing silver and gray against the deep blackness below. The recoil pushed him off balance, pivoting his entire body and throwing him to the left.

Before he knew what was happening, he was tumbling headlong through branches toward the ground.

## 73

ONE BRANCH after another smashed into Jim as he fell through the old hemlock. A particularly thick limb smacked against the wound in his side, causing bright white points of pain to spark in his vision. His arms flailed, and he grabbed for anything, trying to stop his fall. Every branch slowed him. When he finally hit the ground it was with a loud and painful thud. He was lying on a bed of pine needles.

A nightmarish and pain-filled shriek was rising up in the darkness alongside him, piercing his ears. He'd heard something like this noise before, back when he'd shot the vespling in his back acre with his rifle. But this time, the sound was more intense, more protracted. It was a guttural blood-curdling scream.

Jim's vision was blurred. Blood flowed from the many cuts on his hands and face. He was coughing. The air was full of stinging mist. He moved his arms and legs cautiously, but nothing seemed to be broken. He tried to roll away, but the tanks were still strapped to his back. He crawled on his belly, the impulse gun trailing behind him, dragged by the hoses connected to the tanks. When he was far enough, he turned back and looked toward the creature.

Eddie—it was Eddie, he could now see—was still shrieking. He was flailing on the ground, scraping his clawed fingers against his wet, gray body, and then rubbing his eyes frantically with the palms of his hands. He was clearly in pain, trying to get the thin layer of liquid off his skin.

Jim picked up the impulse gun, and he got up on his knees. The pistol grip was still in one piece. The hoses were intact. The black valve still worked. He pulled it to fill the reservoir, then clasped it back in place, aimed, and fired directly at Eddie a second time.

A powerful cloud of mist burst out, hitting Eddie in the chest, and vaporized everywhere. The boughs of the trees seemed to hold the spray down, immediately filling the air of the understory with a low-hanging vapor. Eddie's shrieks doubled in volume, and he thrashed even more violently than before.

Jim was coughing harder now. He pulled his t-shirt up against his mouth again and walked over to where Eddie was writhing violently. He took some pleasure in it, remembering what this monster had done to Ava, to Minnie, and Emmett, and to those kids in the woods.

Eddie looked up at him. His strange, iridescent eyes flashed yellow and orange in the shadows. He looked furious. He reached out his muscular arm, his gray hand, the five black claws unfurling, but Jim was far enough away to be out of reach.

He was not afraid of Eddie now. He did not step back. Instead, he actually stepped closer. As he did, a new pain shot through his left knee, most likely from the fall. It didn't matter. Eddie was weak and dying. That was the only thing Jim cared about right now. His anger consumed him, and he wanted nothing more than to finish Eddie directly, at close range. He wanted to watch him die.

He dropped the impulse gun, slipped off the heavy tanks, and jumped on top of that horrible gray body. As rage filled his veins like a feral drug, he began to punch. He beat Eddie down, pummeling him into the dirt. Sharp claws struck out and slashed back at Jim's arms and chest and face, but he just kept punching. Even as he felt the cuts burst open across his skin, he battered that grotesque thing. He hit it over and over and over. The gray skin was flexible but strangely dense, and pain shot through Jim's knuckles with every thrust. That didn't matter either. There was a strange kind of pleasure in it. He became nothing but fists and vengeance. All other parts of him were gone.

He was driven entirely by a desire for retribution, by what this repulsive man had done to his daughter. Eddie had harmed Ava horribly, changed her possibly forever. Jim's love for her was vast and overwhelming, and in that moment it became equaled only by the rage felt for Eddie—rage for doing something so reprehensible, rage for committing an act so selfish and thoughtless and with no consideration for the lasting impact. What kind of monster was he?

Slowly, the image of Eddie on the ground changed to something else. He morphed into the stranger who killed Sarah. He became another kind of monster. But exactly what kind of monster was that man—the one who had attacked Sarah, who did the unthinkable to her and then threw her body in the river like a broken twig? Jim had spent the years since her death feeling fearful, trapped, silenced, lonely, and powerless. Today it was the same thing all over again. Only now, here—punching the thick gray skin of this beast beneath him—did he finally feel fearless, empowered, liberated, and ultimately, avenged. He was killing two men at once.

Eddie had started wheezing. His chest heaved, and his movements slowed. Jim took one last, deeply satisfying punch. Then Eddie's head dropped to the ground and slowly, quietly, his chin fell to the side. In that subtle movement Jim saw something from Eddie, a kind of resignation, an admission that it was nearly over. This was the brink of death.

Eddie's face was illuminated by moonlight, and now that he lay prone, his expression seemed remarkably human—in spite of those horrible mandibles, dark eyes, and the three ocelli in the middle of his forehead. Something familiar had appeared in the crease of Eddie's brow and the bridge of his battered nose, something that made Jim think of the self-assured young man who had first come to the door to ask for Ava, who had shaken his hand and called him "sir." The iridescent eyes began to fade, releasing pale purples and blues and greens, like two slowly sinking oil spills.

At that moment Jim saw what he thought might actually be a teardrop. He couldn't be sure. It might have been the necarichlor rolling down Eddie's face. Those strange, shimmering black eyes could have been simply irritated by poison, stinging terribly, streaming water. But it didn't seem like it. Eddie's nearly human face appeared full of a deep and overwhelming sorrow. Was this terrible monster in front of him crying?

But it was gone as soon as it came. Eddie became enraged. He shook off whatever sadness he might have had, took a laborious breath, and opened his mouth—all of a sudden seeming far less human as the black and chitinous mandibles inside spread wide. He screamed a monstrous, excruciating scream, which shot upwards with a fire and fury. Jim held Eddie down as he seemed to rage against his own death. He was screaming at Jim, but he was too weak to push him off.

Then Eddie's head fell back with a thud onto the ground, his arms gave way, and he slowly collapsed. He lay there beneath Jim, and he became perfectly still.

Jim stayed on top of him, pinning him for a moment longer, and he watched until he was certain that Eddie was finally gone. Then, as the moon cascaded down through the trees, Jim began to cry. He fell to the ground and heaved. He curled into a ball and held his stomach and howled. He released all the anguish he felt at what had happened, at how the two people he loved most in the world had been hurt and broken and taken from him. He sobbed and wailed, and he finally grieved.

74

WHEN HIS TEARS EVENTUALLY STOPPED, Jim stood and gave Eddie's grotesque body one last, angry kick. He dried his eyes. A calm came over him at that point. Something lifted. He was empty. He thought of Ava in the cabin, of her terrible transformation. She was like Eddie. He knew what he had to do now. He didn't know how he would do it. It was as unthinkable as everything that had already happened. But he knew what had to be done.

He looked down at that strange gray thing on the ground and wondered what could be left of someone after such a terrible change. In spite of every non-human thing about that creature now, the face was still recognizable, and the basic shape of the body still spoke of Eddie. It was a monster with the build of a high school football player.

How much of Eddie was left inside, and how much of him was missing? How much of that young man's heart and spirit—his soul—had been subsumed by viral DNA? Before his transformation, Eddie had been a normal teenage boy—a bit smug, yes, and of course not nearly good enough for Ava, but generally respectful and hard-working. After his transformation, Eddie had terrorized the entire island.

What was Ava capable of now that she too had changed? Since finding her, since learning who had done this to her, Jim had been so driven by the desire to kill Eddie, to seek vengeance, that he had never stopped to consider what lay next. Ava posed the same terrible risk to the people on this island. She would do what Eddie had done. More people would die.

He picked up the impulse gun and looked at the counter. There were two shots left. It had taken two shots to kill Eddie. He slipped the silver tanks on his back, gripped the weapon, and began walking back to the path.

The tangled thicket moved past him, forcing him to lean down under low branches, to climb up over fallen trunks. The trees seemed to bend him to their will. He pushed away all thought of what he was about to do, what he *had* to do. If he thought too much, he would never be able to do it.

When he arrived back on the path, he did not pause. He pressed forward. One small hesitation would stop him. One thought of the act he was about to commit would destroy him. The path took him back through the woods to the small clearing in front of the cabin. He saw his Winchester where he'd left it near the edge of the trees, and did not move to pick it up. It would not help him. He walked over to the weathered planks of the old cabin door.

As he reached for the handle, he wondered how quickly Ava would regain her strength. How soon until she was as strong as Eddie? Could she have already reached that point? He'd been gone maybe an hour, at least he thought it was that much. Time now felt like a dream.

He stepped back, lifted the impulse gun, and pulled the valve to fill the reservoir. The weapon hissed and then released its trickle of liquid. There. Now it was primed and ready to shoot.

He wondered how his daughter would greet him when he

entered the cabin. How much of Ava would still be Ava? He pushed open the door.

The pale, white glow of the small camping lantern still lit the room. Ava was standing at the back window, looking out. She turned to him. It was difficult to tell in the low light, but her skin looked drier now—yet perhaps not completely hardened. Even so, she looked stronger already. He barely recognized her.

He brought his mind back to the two shots left in the gun. He held it high, and he stepped forward.

She spoke then, in that strange and breathless way of the vesplings.

"I need to. Tell you." She took a step toward him, holding her stomach, looking confident, almost formidable, apparently unafraid of the gun.

"Tell me what?" he asked angrily, his finger on the trigger, ready to shoot. This was not Ava, he told himself. She was already gone. His daughter was already dead.

She looked at him square in the face with those strange, luminous eyes.

"I am pregnant." She paused, glancing behind him, as if looking for someone. Slowly her face changed. Some realization seemed to be washing over her. "Where is. Eddie?"

Jim's mind reeled. He gripped the gun tightly. "Pregnant?"

She nodded in an unusual, jerky manner.

He tried to make sense of it all. How long? When? What did her transformation mean for a pregnancy? He shook his head in disbelief. "How?"

Ava looked at him, and she rolled her eyes.

Jim saw it clearly, and in that moment it felt like his heart nearly stopped. *She had rolled her eyes.* It was not quite as fluid as before—there was that jolting movement—but he knew then that this was still his daughter. Ava was not dead. She was here, standing in front of him. She had once again dismissed him in her familiar, contemptuous, teenage way.

Then she said, "I think. You know. How."

Although breathless, it sounded like something Ava would say, and he felt an odd, conflicting relief. Inside that altered body, underneath that horrible gray skin, beyond those dreadful claws, this was Ava. He could not kill her. Others would want to slaughter or study her. He had to protect her. He also had to protect others *from her.*

He lowered the impulse gun and took a deep breath. Every effort he'd ever made to keep his daughter safe had somehow brought him to this moment. He looked at her closely and spoke, his voice strained and full of grief.

"I know a place where you can hide."

LEWIS WILSON STOOD in his sleek, gray kitchen still feeling a bit drunk but now also highly caffeinated. After smashing his drink against the wall, he'd made a large pot of coffee in an effort to sober up. A sandwich helped soak up the gin in his stomach. But in spite of his efforts, his balance was still slightly unsteady, and his head was still cloudy. He was feeling incredibly nervous about the phone call he was about to make.

The clock over the stove told him it was nearly 4 a.m. There was no time difference between Gull Island and Atlanta, and Cavanaugh didn't like being woken up in the middle the night. But he couldn't wait any longer. He needed to tell Cavanaugh about the recent events before it hit the morning news.

His biggest concern was not the two bodies found just hours ago. That was horrible, of course—more innocent people were dead—but they were already gone. There was nothing he could do about that now. At this point, he was most worried about the beehive Deputy Gabby had reported out in the End Woods. Where there was one, there were most likely more. This was far from over.

He picked up his burner phone off the counter. It was cheap, simple, but it did the trick. He dialed the only number he ever called on this phone. It rang three times. There were some fumbling sounds followed by Cavanaugh's groggy voice.

"Hello?" she said.

He pictured her in that grand home she owned in one of Atlanta's most affluent neighborhoods. He'd been there only once. French doors everywhere had opened out onto sweeping views of lush, southern gardens. Staff in black bow ties had served Wagyu steaks and platters of expensive, pollination-dependent vegetables. That night it felt like he'd finally made it.

Now, however, he knew that he'd been wrong. He had not made it at all. He'd merely been living on borrowed time. Everything he worked for was now in tatters, and he was about to be cast out.

"Hello?" Cavanaugh said again.

"There's been another development," he said, his heart pounding fiercely.

"What is it?" Her voice was sharp and already irritated.

He tried to answer as calmly as he could. He told her about the bodies of the two local kids. He told her about the additional hive, about Deputy Martinez getting stung, and about how the deputy had referred to Hadley Agritech—and to himself and Brad in particular—on police radio.

Cavanaugh went silent.

He looked down at the luxurious black granite countertop in front of him. This house was rented. He would probably lose it soon. He would probably lose his job, his research, his purpose. Solving the Global Bee Crisis was the only thing he had ever wanted to do. It was, he believed, his calling.

After what felt like a very long time, Cavanaugh finally spoke again. "Is it still out there?"

He knew she was talking about the vespling. "I believe so," he said. "I understand Jim Parker is hunting it. He's the beekeeper I told you about."

Lewis wondered what Jim was doing out there now.

"Why not the local sheriff?" Cavanaugh asked. "I thought you had him in your back pocket. Why isn't he out there hunting it?"

"He is, or rather, his men are. I gave him two of our modified impulse guns. He promised to send some men out last night, but I haven't heard anything yet. If they're out there, they're staying off police radio."

After another long pause, Cavanaugh said, "I just can't believe you've let things get so completely out of control."

Lewis didn't know how to respond. It was true. He had failed. He said nothing.

She shot out another question. "Are you sure your gen-mod bees can't get off that island?"

This question annoyed him. He had walked her through this several times already. She knew as well as he did that Hadley had chosen Gull Island due to the island's closed ecosystem. Perhaps she just needed reassurance.

"While *Apis tiffiana* is stronger than most honeybees," he said, "it's highly unlikely to make it across that much open water."

"Do you understand what'll happen if those bees make it to the mainland?"

His annoyance suddenly flashed into anger. "Of course I understand the implications. In fact, if you'll recall, I was the one who originally briefed you on the risks."

"Don't cross me, Lewis. You won't like what will happen."

He held his tongue. She had a staggering amount of power over him and his life. He resented her for this. He was truly under her thumb.

She continued speaking. "I'm taking over control of this mess you've made. I should have done it a while ago. I kept hoping you'd clean things up quietly, but obviously you're not capable. I need to call some people, strike up a deal if I can, and brief the CEO. I'll get back to you with next steps."

"Who are we involving?" he asked. He didn't want an outside

party coming in. "I don't want to lose control of my research."

Cavanaugh snapped back at him. "Do you really think this has ever been *your* research? How pathetic. And you've already lost any semblance of control you might have had. Project Defender belongs entirely to Hadley Agritech, and so far it's been nothing but a liability. We'll do with it what we want."

Lewis felt like the rug was being pulled out from underneath him. He was well aware of the fact that the intellectual property belonged to Hadley, but this was his life's work. How could Cavanaugh be so dismissive? He'd shaped the direction from the very beginning.

"However," she continued, "I do believe I can turn this ship around. When I've finalized plans, I'll let you know."

She hung up before he had a chance to say another word.

He stood in silence for a moment, not moving. He looked again at the countertop. He stared down at the polished concrete floor. What exactly was she planning? And who was she going to contact to "strike up a deal" as she'd said? He had his suspicions, but he hoped he was wrong.

Eventually he poured himself another cup of coffee and sat down at the table. The vastness of the lake suddenly seemed over-whelming and ominous outside the windows in front of him. The sunrise was hours away. He decided to sit here and wait for it to come. There would be no sleep tonight. He felt like he was turning a puzzle in his head, trying to figure out what was going to happen next, and how he should respond.

He took a mouthful of coffee and stared out at the water. He had a horrible, sick feeling in his stomach about what was yet to come.

*Get updates about Vespling Book 2 and a map of Gull Island when you join the mailing list at www.jaredgulian.com.*

# GET EXCLUSIVE CONTENT

Connecting directly with readers is one of the things I love about writing. If you join my mailing list at www.jaredgulian.com, you'll get bonus content plus exclusive updates on new books and upcoming deals.

All mailing list members receive a free "Jared Gulian Starter Kit," which includes:

- a map of Gull Island (drawn by hand)
- a behind-the-scenes short story about my misadventures as an American city boy in rural New Zealand. (Called "hilarious" and "delightful" by reviewers on Amazon.)

Visit www.jaredgulian.com to join.

# GRATEFUL FOR A REVIEW

**Enjoy this book? You can make a big difference.**

Reader reviews are one of the most powerful marketing tools an author has—especially for indie authors like me.

If you have enjoyed this book, I would be very grateful if you could spend a few minutes to leave a short review on Amazon.

Just go to the book's Amazon page and click the "Write a review" button.

Thanks heaps,
Jared

# ACKNOWLEDGMENTS

If it takes an entire village to raise a child, then it takes a secret cabal to write a book. I owe deep thanks to the following, in semi-chronological order.

The community of writers and teachers I found at Mark Dawson's Self Publishing Formula for teaching me about writing, publishing and marketing.

The helpful, smart people in the r/genetics forum on Reddit for answering my preliminary research questions. (Everyone thought I was a mad scientist.)

My sisters, Alecia Jones and Rebecca Weliver, for joining me on that pre-COVID road trip to Beaver Island—the inspiration for my fictional Gull Island.

Writer friends Anne Coombs, Jan Farr, Susan Varga, and Caren Wilton for offering encouraging feedback.

Entomologists Phil Lester and Matan Shelomi for responding to those random emails about bees and wasps.

My team of ace editors: Emily Yau for developmental and line editing, Caren Wilton for copy editing, and Donald Weise for proofreading.

An entire gaggle of beta readers for their extremely helpful responses: Rhonda Harris, Jeff Lehman, Mary Ann Miller, Karen Monks, Diane Pape, John Saunders, Brendan Schoone-Jongen, and Holly Selden.

My launch team of nearly 50 generous people for getting the word out.

All of the supportive readers who followed me on an unexpected journey—from an olive farming memoir with chickens to a science fiction thriller with monsters. (I bet you didn't see that one coming.)

And above all to my partner, CJ, for his adventurous, swashbuckling heart, for giving me fantastic and meaningful feedback even when I didn't want to hear it, and for being at my side for over 27 years now.

Thank you.

# SOURCES AND INSPIRATION

In writing this book, I was inspired by these sources.

Anthes, Emily. *Frankenstein's Cat: Cuddling Up to Biotech's Brave New Beasts.* Oneworld, 2013.

Benjamin, Allison and Brian McCallum. *A World Without Bees.* Pegasus Books, 2009.

Carey, Nessa. *Hacking the Code of Life: How Gene Editing Will Rewrite our Futures.* Icon, 2019.

Chadwick, Fergus, et al. *The Bee Book.* Dorling Kindersley Limited, 2016.

Gooley, Tristan. *The Lost Art of Reading Nature's Signs.* The Experiment, 2015.

Jukes, Helen. *A Honeybee Heart Has Five Openings.* Scribner UK, 2019.

King, Madonna. *Fathers and Daughters.* Hachette Australia, *2018.*

Lester, Phil. *The Vulgar Wasp.* Victoria University Press, 2018.

Meeker, Meg. *Strong Fathers, Strong Daughters.* Regnery Publishing, 2006.

Schmidt, Justin O. *The Sting of the Wild.* Johns Hopkins University Press, 2016.

Sjöberg, Frederik. *The Fly Trap*. Pantheon, 2014.

Tautz, Jürgen and Diedrich Steen. *The Honey Factory: Inside the Ingenious World of Bees*. Black Inc., 2018.

Warner, Bernhard. "'Invasion of the 'frankenbees': the danger of building a better bee." *The Guardian*, October 16th 2018, theguardian.com.

# ABOUT THE AUTHOR

My name is Jared Gulian (pronounced GHOUL-eee-in), and I'm still not sure how I ended up living in paradise.

I was born in Pontiac, Michigan and grew up in the suburbs of Detroit. Michigan is still near and dear to my heart.

After spending four years in enchanting Japan, I now live in rural New Zealand with my partner, two beautiful horses, a gang of cunning chickens, and one dopey but lovable pet pig named Dougal.

You can follow me on social media or read blog posts on my website.

www.jaredgulian.com
jared@jaredgulian.com

facebook.com/jaredgulian
instagram.com/jaredgulian
goodreads.com/jaredgulian
twitter.com/jaredgulian
youtube.com/jaredgulian

# ALSO BY JARED GULIAN

If you enjoyed *The Last Beekeeper,* discover the hilarious and heart-warming "behind the scenes" memoir.

**An Olive Grove at the Edge of the World:**
How two American city boys built a
new life in rural New Zealand

For Jared Gulian, leaving the United States and coming to tiny Wellington, New Zealand, was a big enough switch from the bright lights of big cities. So when his partner CJ decided they just *had* to buy a rundown olive grove in the Wairarapa Valley, it was almost too much to cope with.

First they'd have to drive over the dangerous Remutaka ranges to get there, and Jared was terrified of heights. Then they'd have to figure out what on earth you do with 500 olive trees that hadn't been pruned for years, a geriatric rooster, warring hens, an obese kunekune pig, cast sheep, marauding cattle, and understanding your neighbors when they said "yiece" but meant "yes".

In this delightful memoir, Jared Gulian describes the first four years of their new life in the country, its disasters and small triumphs, its surprises and pleasures. But most of all he describes the warmth of the local community that welcomed them, saved them from certain peril, taught them how to cook, how to care for animals, and how to understand and love the land.

If you love Peter Mayle, David Sedaris, Frances Mayes, or James Herriot, this charming adventure is for you.

Buy now for a story that will feed your heart and make you smile.

~

Reviews for *An Olive Grove at the Edge of the World*:

"One of the most delightful books I have read for some time. As I turn the final page, I feel like I am close friends with the author... Wonderfully written."

NEW ZEALAND LIFESTYLE BLOCK MAGAZINE

"A heart-warming tale with many laughs and a few tears... written with wit and warmth."

MANAWATU STANDARD

"Very funny and endearing... A comedy of small disasters and small triumphs, but also really beautifully written."

TILLY LLOYD, UNITY BOOKS

"Hugely entertaining and whimsical, a great yarn about following one's dream and changing one's life for the better!"

-GOODREADS REVIEWER, 5 STARS

*The Last Beekeeper: Vespling Book 1*

Copyright 2021 by Jared Gulian

ISBN 978-0-473-57092-7 (paperback)

ISBN 978-0-473-57093-4 (ebook)

Publisher: WaysOut Press

Cover design: Books Covered

Word count: 117,000

Version: 1.4IS



www.jaredgulian.com

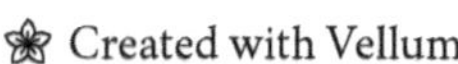 Created with Vellum